Forgetting What I Couldn't Remember

The Rewind Duology Book 1

Dear Gwendolyn,
    Thank you so much
for reviewing my book!
I hope you love it :)
♡ Love,
    - Angelina Singer :)

Angelina Singer

I want to dedicate this book to the real friends that I have been so blessed to finally find. Every single one of you was absolutely worth the wait - you know who you are. Also, a special shout out goes to my author friends Joel, Syreeta, and Ife for all your feedback and encouragement while I wrote this story. You have made me a better writer, so here's to you!

Cover art by Gracie Knight

One: Toxic Barrier

"What do you mean that you know best?" The girl sitting next to me shifted her gaze from her book to stare back at me through slightly puffy eyes, recently moistened by tears.

"I just mean - I'm older, I have more life experience than you do."

"Yeah? How old are you anyway, lady?"

I smirked, and shook my head nearly imperceptibly. I could easily pull the respect card and tell her how rude that was, but I remembered when I was just like her and how much that would have totally pissed me off. "Old enough to know that what you do in your life now, will matter. None of what you see around you seems important, but I promise you that it is."

She sighed, and then returned to her book, one that I vaguely recalled reading from my own childhood, a story about orphaned children finding a magical world through a coat closet. I could spoil the ending for her to get her attention, but somehow, I felt that would be crueler than necessary.

"I hear ya, but I'm still trying to read, and you're still a stranger." She curled a dirty-blonde ringlet around her index finger in a sort of nervous defiance, and then chewed on the end of it.

"You're right, I have no real right to be bothering you, and I guess I should apologize for that." Satisfied with what I admitted, her face seemed to ease into a relaxed smile, and then she lowered the book momentarily to meet my gaze. "But I'm not going to, because I mean well and you know that." She rolled her eyes even though I couldn't understand why. I really wanted to help her, and yet, this is how she was treating me. Just fantastic.

"Whatever. Just let me read. I didn't ask *you* to come over here and bug me."

"You didn't have to."

"Huh?"

I sighed, looking around at the park-goers enjoying the pleasant spring climate in this suburban neighborhood bordering

Los Angeles. There were a few toddlers climbing the wooden steps up to the curly purple plastic slide, while a couple teenagers appeared to be quietly chatting while swinging in the warm breeze. Yoga-pant clad moms of younger children drank an afternoon cup of coffee while tapping mindlessly on their oddly small and chunky smartphones. *Is this really how life was supposed to be?* I scoffed at the meaningful moments and memories snuffed out by monotony and routine.

"Just tell me what you want from me so I can get on with my life. My *gosh* you're weird."

The caustic bite of her words filled me with an indescribable distaste for any and all children under the age of fifteen. At twenty-two years old, I found myself practically unable to recall the details of what childhood was like. The world, with all its heartbreak and disparities, had hardened me beyond what I could see through. My depressive mood and discomfort in my own life had rapidly formed a toxic barrier between me and the world I wished I lived in. And my past was a whole separate issue I wish I could forget.

I looked over at the younger girl next to me, who had seemed happy to go back to her reading in the absence of an answer from me. I wasn't ignoring her - I just got lost in my own thoughts, I guess. *What else is new?*

"Sorry, didn't mean to ignore you." I was greeted by silence as she wordlessly continued reading. I watched her eyes hungrily flit back and forth on the page. "I'm not doing this very well, I guess."

"I'll say." Her focus remained on her book, but her sarcastic tone provided the rest of the inflection needed to understand her context.

"What if I told you I could fix this?"

She paused reading, and slowly turned her body toward me from where she sat on the bench a couple feet away from me. "Fix what? How weird and annoying you are?"

I bit my tongue to avoid cussing her out like the angsty punk bands I used to be into. *Who am I kidding, I still loved them - I just hesitate to publicly admit that.* "No, but perhaps you might want to put down that book and socialize a little?"

"Nah, I'm good. Thanks though." Her head remained stuck in her book, until I managed to coax her out of it by slyly grabbing it out of her hands. "Hey! Give it back!"

Placing it just out of her reach on the rock wall behind me, I did my best to get her attention. "You can have it back *after* you hear me out."

Clearly tired of struggling, the younger girl begrudgingly relented and plopped back on her side of the bench in a disgruntled heap. "You have like ten minutes before I start screaming 'stranger danger'."

I wanted to believe she was bluffing, but given how precocious she was, I doubted it. "Fair enough." I paused for dramatic effect, but then realized I was wasting precious time. "It seems that you're isolating yourself, and I just don't want to see you do that."

A puff of air from her puckered lips dislodged a couple stray pieces of hair from her clammy forehead. "What do you care? I'm just a bookworm, always have been. Books are better company than most seventh-graders, I swear."

I sighed. "Surely you don't mean that."

"Why wouldn't I? They just don't understand me, and I realized they're not worth the trouble. Besides, when I used to try to hang with them, they'd ignore me. There's only so much of that a person can take!" The venom in her frustrated voice assaulted my ears with a newfound hatred. Middle-school-aged kids often had far too much freedom to accomplish anything meaningful.

"Hey I get it, middle school is a weird time. Heck, the hormones alone are killer even without the teenage angst, I mean your body's changing and -"

A curt hand gesture stopped me in my tracks. "I'm all clear on that, thanks. Besides, you're still a stranger, so I wouldn't be asking you questions about that awkward stuff anyway."

I opened my mouth to respond to her problematic claim, until I remember how I felt about all that when I was younger, and calmly changed the subject.

"You have about seven minutes left, by the way."

"I'm going to need more time than that."

"That's not my problem."

I sighed, for what felt like the millionth time today. "Take it from me - when you're older, you'll regret not trying harder to make friends. It's an important part of life! I know it's hard - I had a hard time too. It's difficult for us introverts, isn't it?" I smiled sweetly, trying to lighten the mood. She wasn't the least bit amused.

"They're idiots, all of them. I don't want to be friends with Summer and her hoard of jerk wads."

I nodded. "That may be true. But isn't there anyone else you can talk to?"

The girl shrugged. "Not really."

We both sat in silence until she asked me something I realized I had no real answer for.

Two: Congealed Cheese

As I arrived home from yet another lecture, I found myself daydreaming about a month or two from now when I'll have graduated from college. I've never been the academic type, but I figured that school was probably a good idea, especially since my dream was always to do something with media. Communications was the direction I took, and I don't regret it. But somehow, school never scratched the creative itch the way I expected it to. Now, it's just a countdown until freedom, holding me back from reaching my goals.

Turning off the ignition on my black Volkswagen bug, I rolled my eyes at no one in particular. *What goals do you have besides graduating in one piece? None, you idiot. Step it up or regret it forever.* I mumbled a couple choice words to lessen the sting of defeat I felt from my bitter internal voice. Then I grabbed my book bag from the passenger seat and fished my house keys out of the depths of my purse.

Mom greeted me with a tired but polite smile from where she sat at the kitchen table with her afternoon tea, poring over the latest issue of some sort of home renovation magazine. "How was your day?"

I shrugged. "Fine, I guess. I'm just ready to be done."

"Really? I thought you liked school?"

"The school itself is fine. I'm just not a fan of all the bookwork. It's not like I can just wake up and suddenly be a screenwriter or a famous talk show host."

"The right job will find you at the right time, Vera. Believe that."

I looked out past my mom toward our pleasant backyard, decorated in the vibrant colors of springtime. The almost neon green of the trees danced happily in the breeze amidst a blue raspberry late-afternoon sky.

"I want to believe that, I really do. But I just... don't." I picked up my book bag and purse, and then headed toward my bedroom-turned sanctuary. As of late, it's been the only place I've been able to practically shut out the entire world. I don't identify with those overly dramatic emo chicks on mid-2000s MySpace who hated everything and sported gaudy, overdone makeup and fringed haircuts, but I can relate to how they felt. Sometimes, my loneliness haunts me at the very same time that solitude comforts me.

"Vera, dinner will be ready in about an hour. Plus, Grandma and Grandpa are coming over to see us. Isn't that nice?"

I shrugged again. *Sure, it's not like I have piles of coursework to do. Oh wait...* "I have a ton of homework, so I won't be able to visit long. Besides, it's a Thursday night - what's the occasion?"

Mom pursed her lips in frustration. "Does there have to be an occasion to see your family?"

"Well, no, but -"

"Marvelous. Wash up and be ready to eat in an hour." Mom breezed out my bedroom door without a care in the world, which was incredibly ironic since our family situation was actually pretty tense.

My dad has been missing since I was thirteen years old. My mom told me any time I asked that he just... left. But I have a feeling there was more to the story than she let on. Since then, Mom was lucky enough to nab an editing gig for a pretty popular magazine, which has allowed us to live comfortably even in Dad's absence. Her demanding job kept her busy enough that there wasn't a lot of time to grieve - for better or worse. My older brother, Jet, took it the hardest though - he was sixteen years old at the time, so he had more vivid memories to be haunted by. I remember how aggressive he got, sometimes getting into trouble at school for fighting and talking back to his teachers. Luckily, he's since mellowed out, working full time as a video game developer for a tech company - but he wasn't always that way.

Whereas for me, my subconscious brought images of my dad only in shadowy reflections of days gone by. I was old enough when he left to remember things, but I think a lot of that stuff ended up being repressed. As for Mom, she coped the best she could, sometimes crying in the bathroom late at night when she thought no one could hear her.

Jet trudged through the hallway outside my room, punctuated by the slamming of his own bedroom door. We've never been super close, but I know that he'd have my back if I ever needed him.

"Kids! Come on out and say hello!" My mom's voice bellowed up the stairs from the foyer, notifying us of the spontaneous visitors joining us. I hesitated to put down my textbook, but ultimately relented, lest I upset my mom and make everything more frustrating than it really had to be. I did that plenty of times throughout my teen years, and it was never worth it. Jet, although older than me, appeared to have yet to learn that lesson. As I walked down the hallway toward the stairs, I still saw the luminescent glow of his laptop in his dark room poking out at the doorjamb.

"Vera! How are you, my dear? You must fill us in on all the happenings at school. Any job offers yet?"

I smiled politely as my grandmother hugged me, and my grandfather patted me warmly on the back.

"Now Milly, there's no need to pester the girl! Let's just go eat, shall we?" Grandfather did his best to relax the situation - he's always been good at anticipating my emotions, sometimes even better than I could.

"Seb, I'm just asking her about her life! Is that too much to ask?" A hand on her hip challenged my grandfather's assertion with an extra dose of sass. Mom tried and failed to hide the giggles that fought their way out of her throat.

He shook his head in defeat with a smile plastered across his face and led her into the kitchen with a gentle hand on her lower back. Always the romantics, my grandparents' love language seemed to be their bickering.

"Where's Jefferson?" Grandfather looked around to take in the various disarray of our living space. There was still some laundry laid out on the couch, and some shopping bags I didn't get to put away yet from my latest dose of retail therapy.

"Probably with his headset and laptop testing out a new program. I'll go see what's keeping him." Mom briskly marched up the stairs and to his door, and then some muffled scuffling and voices carried down to the kitchen in the relative silence surrounding us.

"Mom, I told you I'm too old for you to grab my ear like this... oh, hey Grandpa! Grandma. Uh... how are things?" Jet rubbed his earlobe gingerly, while Mom casually walked to the oven to check on what I assumed was lasagna, based on the heavenly scent filling the room.

"Better now that you're here, my boy!" Grandpa patted him on the shoulder, while Grandma reached up to deposit some of her pink lipstick onto Jet's pale, clean-shaven cheek. He rubbed it off immediately.

"Ugh, right. Okay. Well, as nice as this is, I gotta finish testing some new software before the meeting tomorrow, so..."

"Yeah, and I gotta study for an exam..." We both tried to back toward our rooms but Mom popped the lasagna out of the oven and our watering mouths persuaded us to procrastinate a bit longer.

"Both of you sit, and offer your grandparents something to drink! I raised you better than that, geez." Mom rolled her eyes and started plating up the lasagna as I volunteered to fill some glasses with ice water for everyone.

"Jefferson, how is the video game playing business treating you?" Grandpa smiled at my brother as he set down the salad bowl on the table between my mom's garish porcelain sunflower centerpiece and the wooden paper napkin holder.

"I'm actually a *software developer and programmer* for a video game company, but yeah, it's been good, I guess." Jet plopped a pile of lasagna on his plate, and then hungrily dug into it without waiting for anyone else - much to our mom's distaste.

"Same difference. And how are you doing, Vera? Almost graduated, correct?" Grandma smiled at me from across the table as the cloud of her very potent perfume filled my nostrils, and I silently griped that the taste of mom's award-winning lasagna was being tainted.

"Yep, just a little over a month to go."

"That must be so exciting! This is when your life is going to start, young lady." Grandpa lifted his glass a foot off the table as if to salute my assumed accomplishments, and then took a swig of the ice-cold water.

"Well, yeah, theoretically. I have no idea what I'll be doing yet though."

Grandpa nodded and smiled. "Well you have time - don't rush the process, Vera. You are far too talented to be concerned. Do you have any ideas about what you might like to do?"

I shrugged. "I dunno, does Ellen Degeneres have any job openings?"

My grandparents exchanged some amused glances with my mom, who shrugged. "What can I say, the girl likes to talk, might as well make a career out of it."

I laughed politely even though I didn't find any of their comments even remotely funny. "Well I just mean, I'm studying communications because I'd like to work in media somehow - if not my own talk show, it could be fun to work on one." I tossed my hair for dramatic effect, and then stared down at my plate, poking at a clump of congealed cheese.

We ate in silence for a bit, until Jet asked what I've been wondering all evening.

"So why the visit on a random Thursday?" He wiped some tomato sauce from his mouth and then zoned in on our grandparents' blank stares. They exchanged an unspoken conversation and then my grandfather cleared his throat.

"Well, I guess now's a good enough time as any to tell you - Edgar's in town."

Three: Starving Hyena

"Why are you even here bugging me right now?"

Her question, though pretty standard in its diction and tone for a frustrated middle-schooler, had nuanced undercurrents threatening to undo everything I came here to accomplish.

"Let's just say, I have a unique vantage point that you couldn't possibly relate to. I'm trying to prevent... something I know you wouldn't like."

She huffed, clearly dissatisfied with my admittedly lame explanation. "So, you're going to try to fix something, that you can't tell me about. Okay, yeah that clears it up for me. Great."

I shifted my gaze back to the otherwise pleasant late-spring day. And then a solution came to me.

"Okay fine! I'm an old acquaintance of... your mom's, and I thought I'd come by to hang out with you a bit?"

Her eyes locked with mine. "Well *that* doesn't sound dangerous at all..."

I shrugged - I was completely out of options. I know it was pretty unsettling and weird, but this was something I had to do, and I couldn't think of a better way to accomplish it. "Well, okay, let me prove it then. Ask me something only your mom would know."

The girl nervously tugged on a rogue piece of her sandy blonde hair that managed to escape from the garish ponytail it was imprisoned in. "Okay, fine. Tell me the name of Mom's boyfriend from high school that she never shuts up about."

I smirk, trying not to be too relieved that I knew this one. "Blaine Thomas, right? Wasn't he a guitarist in some lame cover band?"

Her face turned a bit white at the ease of which I recalled the name. "How did you know that? You're way younger than my mom, you wouldn't have gone to high school with her."

I shrugged. "Well, my mom knew your mom... they went to high school together." *Good save, Vera.*

The girl next to me seemed to relax a bit about the details I gave, until she prodded a little more excessively than I had answers for.

"Okay, so what's your mom's name?"

I pause. *Focus, you can think of something to cover this.* "Sarah, but they weren't super close. Your mom might not have mentioned her to you."

Satisfied with that, the girl visibly released the visible tension in her shoulders. "Oh, um, okay I guess. I still don't really know you though, so I'm gonna bring someone with me for extra backup..."

I rolled my eyes dramatically. "I'm harmless, I swear!" I raised my hands in mock submission police-cruiser style, but the girl remained stoic and on guard. Who could blame her? I'd do the same thing in her shoes.

Sighing again, she got up off the bench and walked over to a boy sitting alone on a swing by himself. A quick conversation seemed to get him to follow her back over to me. "So this is Alex, he's in my class and I'm bringing him with me in case you try anything funny." The boy appeared about her age, with his hands shoved in the pockets of his baggy jeans paired with a backwards baseball cap and 90s-style basketball sneakers.

I tried not to audibly chuckle at her pathetic attempt at security, but silently applauded her smart thinking. I could feel my cheeks warming at the shadows of emotions long-dormant, but suddenly awakening again. *She's an odd bird, all right.* "Hey there, Alex. I'm an old friend coming to visit, and I promise to be cool - no worries. Okay?"

He nodded shyly, and I took the opportunity to hand the girl her beloved book. "Thank you for hearing me out. Here's your book back."

She snatched it back from me with all the intensity of a starving hyena, and her eyes bored holes in my skull. Definitely not one to cross, I made sure to keep a healthy distance as not to upset her further as I followed her and her friend back to her house. And to avoid being recognized too easily, I donned a stylish pair of sunglasses and a strategically-placed scarf around my neck where I knew the tattoo on my collarbone might reveal a bit too much about me. Good thing I always kept basic accessories in my purse.

I knew exactly where I was, so following the kids was just a formality - a way to get into the scene I needed to be in without too much questioning. Feigning confusion to really sell my character, I almost took a couple wrong turns down side streets I knew were the wrong ones, just to re-route to follow my unnecessary tour guides through the cushy suburban residential outskirts of LA.

A car passed by us, blaring the *Camp Rock* movie soundtrack, and I forced myself not to sing along even though I knew every word. The kids leading the way in front of me seemed to notice it too, but they just kept walking - which I found repulsive. One does not simply *ignore* the musical stylings of one of the best Disney Channel original movie franchises of all time.

Four: Twice Baked

Jet spit his mouthful of lasagna back onto his plate, much to our mother's disgust. "What do you mean he's *back*?"

Our grandmother folded her hands calmly on the table in front of her, as her husband scratched the back of his neck nervously. "He's in town, rumor has it. No one really knows why. But I wanted to let you know."

I managed to place my water glass back onto the table while processing the shock. "Well what does he want? He never shows up unless he wants something - everyone knows that." I immediately regretted the vinegar in my words and tone, but it's difficult to give anyone the benefit of the doubt when your entire family is made up of enough plot holes and missing persons to cover a milk carton. Glancing over to the waning evening sunlight through the sliding glass door leading to the back porch, I couldn't help but wish that maybe just for once, my life could be simple and drama-free. Apparently, that's far too much to ask, especially with a family like mine.

"Vera, I'm sure he has his reasons. Let's hear out Grandma and Grandpa, and see what they've heard." Mom reached across the dainty pale-blue tablecloth to grasp my hand gently. Her warm brown eyes have always calmed me down even when I'm freaking out, even though they were always so full of pain themselves.

I relaxed my expression enough to allow them to speak, but I crossed my arms defiantly in front of my chest as a last-ditch effort to keep my heart from breaking into a million little pieces. Again. "Okay Grandma, what's going on?"

She took a deep breath before continuing. A quick glance at my grandfather revealed that he was equally concerned as - if not more than - my grandmother. "Well, he called us last week to say that he wanted to… 'reconnect' with the family, I suppose is what he said? I'm not terribly sure what that means exactly in the context of everything that's happened. We'll welcome him with open arms, of course. But something about this feels very…"

"...off." Grandpa finished her pained sentence, stating the word that she either couldn't think of, or didn't have the heart to say.

A stuttered silence suffocated our family sitting around the kitchen table at that moment - anxiously awaiting the next words, but also dreading the truth that would come out of them. Grandad piped in just before I started to really sink too far inside my own damaged psyche. "But we don't have many facts yet, all we know is that Edgar is in town and he wants to see us. He's renting a house not too far from here - or so he said, anyway."

Silence, again. I opened my mouth to break it, but the syrupy texture of the air mixed with the lingering aroma of the twice-baked lasagna made me a little sick.

"So what are we gonna do?"

Ever the take-action-now-and-worry-about-consequences-later type, Jet piped in with an obvious question that no one seemed to have the answer to quite yet.

"We're going to talk to him. Give the guy a chance."

Jet slammed his fist on the table in response to Mom's calm suggestion. "And why should we do that? He *abandoned* us, just like Dad did. He doesn't *deserve* to be a part of this family." His flared nostrils and wide eyes gave away the not-so-subtle fact that he was less than pleased with the situation.

Mom sighed sadly, and patted him on the shoulder. "Jet, you know that family isn't something a person can earn - even if they do everything in their power to mess it up, family is family. There's just no getting around that."

Jet turned to face our mother, with flames in his eyes. "You don't mean to tell me, for *one instant*, that you've never once hated his guts and wanted to see him die a violent death? We needed him, and he *left*. We don't really have anyone else. And we especially didn't, after..."

Unable to finish that sentence, Jet unceremoniously got up from the table and stomped upstairs to his room, completely disregarding Mom's protests. She followed him to the foyer, but to no avail. Turning back to the kitchen, she shrugged her shoulders.

16

It was rare and disconcerting to see Mom this helpless. I didn't like it one bit, and I could feel the heat in my belly writhing into a ball of resentment toward my brother for throwing a tantrum when we most needed him to be calm. Dad wouldn't have wanted it to happen like this. At least, I assumed he wouldn't have - if he hadn't disappeared.

Five: Man-spreading on the Subway

The younger girl opened the door to her house about as unceremoniously as any young teen. Alex followed her, holding the door open for me with the sole of his high-top. I smiled politely and closed the door behind me, following their casual chatter through the main hallway toward the kitchen area. The door shut behind me, with noticeable black marks where his foot had just been.

"Lynn, I still don't get why she's here."

"She said she wanted to hang with us, I dunno. At least her mom knew my mom, so she's not a complete stranger."

The girl shrugged and reached into the fridge for a drink. She handed a can of soda to Alex too, who broke the seal with his teeth and then took a sip.

"I can hear you guys, just saying." They blinked at me wordlessly while I nervously tapped on the granite countertop. "Really, it's fine. Just do whatever you'd normally be doing on a Saturday morning. It *is* Saturday, right?" I rubbed my head as I tried to remember what day it was. The most recent events had really screwed up my perception of everything. The younger kids stared back at me as if I suddenly grew a third eye. Without a better option available, I decided to just seat myself on the nearby couch. "You guys wanna watch cartoons or something? I'm down with that."

Their eyes continued to follow me with scrutiny, but then both kids shrugged and plopped down on the couch next to me. My plan was to slowly train this girl to recognize her own awkward habits before they cemented themselves in her brain and isolated her forever. It felt a bit too late for me, but maybe helping her would change things for me too - one could only hope, after all. *Okay, what's the first thing I would change?*

"So my mom won't be home for a while, hope that's okay." She turned to look at me, and I pulled a complete and total blank.

"Uh, sure? Whatever."

Lynn and Alex stared at me for probably the hundredth time today - and it was only about eleven o'clock in the morning. "You said you were hanging out with us because your mom knew her? Isn't that why you're here?"

My stomach dropped at the realization that I might have just walked into my own trap. "Well, yeah. But like, I'm closer in age to you than your mom, so I don't *have* to meet her. I'd really rather just chill with you guys."

The blank stares continued for what I was sure was a completely inordinate amount of time, but they soon subsided long enough for my heart rate to eventually slow down. Then Lynn turned her attention back to the TV. That's when I noticed the first major thing I wanted to correct. When I saw it, I had to force myself not to laugh at how cringe-worthy the moment was. Alex ever-so-slightly, inched his left hand closer to Lynn's, and right when he was about to gently graze her pinky finger, she moved her hand absentmindedly. She didn't even see the way he blushed and immediately turned away, but I did. Oh, thirteen - an age I surely didn't miss in the least. But watching it unfold from an older perspective was fascinating, to say the least. And unlike this girl, I knew how that particular story ends - and it wasn't pretty. Especially now, with Lynn sitting sprawled out like a fat guy man-spreading on the subway. A closer look even showed me that she also had half-brushed hair that looked fine enough from the front, but featured a growing bird's nest in the back hard-to-reach spots. I wouldn't consider myself to be superficial, but this girl could use a little intervention. It's a miracle Alex saw anything in her at all, but not surprising that she never caught onto it.

"Hey Lynn, wanna grab something to eat from the kitchen?"

"I'm not hungry, thanks."

I grabbed her hand a bit more forcefully this time. "Well I am. Come on."

Lynn sighed and then got up. Alex didn't seem to budge, obviously engrossed in the very deep philosophical matters of *SpongeBob Squarepants*.

19

"What?" She crossed her arms and waited for yet another explanation that I barely had the wherewithal to piece together without arousing further suspicion of my mission.

"What was *that*?"

"What was what?"

"You sit on the couch like that, you completely miss brushing the back of your head, *and* you don't realize that Alex totally has a thing for you?"

"I'm perfectly comfortable, thank you for asking. And I just met you this morning, why would I care what *you* think?"

I opened my mouth to deliver a witty retort worthy of the collegiate degree I was getting soon, but nothing came to mind. This chick had a decent point.

"Yeah, that's what I thought. And Alex is just a friend, I swear! No one believes me and it drives me nuts. Even our classmates say things. It's stupid. And they're so rude to me all the time. That is, when they're not completely leaving me out of games at recess and stuff."

I sighed to myself, remembering my own unfortunate social life in middle school. I finally found some great friends in high school and college, but it took an entire childhood to get there. Ideally, it'd be nice to speed up that process for Lynn. "Well, there's gotta be other people you can talk to."

"Not really, my class is tiny."

I sighed. "Well, yeah, that totally sucks then."

"You bet."

Another silence filled the room, and then Lynn headed back to the living room.

"Hey Lynn?" She turned around just long enough to hear my next thought - and by the look on her face, she was none too happy to comply. "Just, um, maybe don't write off Alex so fast. He's so nice to you, and you're young now but you never know… what could happen later."

She wrinkled her nose, and then shook her head while heading back to the couch.

20

"I'm still hungry!" My words reverberated to no one in particular. But luckily, I had a hunch where I could find the potato chips, so I reached for a bag in the cabinet next to the microwave.

Six: Freeze-Your-Ass-Off Alaska

"I have no idea what's gotten into him. He's been pretty agitated lately, sorry guys." Mom's attempt at a proper apology for Jet's behavior to our grandparents fell flat, even though she meant well. She moved her laptop and work articles onto the coffee table instead of the counter to make room for the large bowl of Caesar salad she grabbed from the fridge. "Almost forgot about the salad. Eat up guys, it's pre-mixed."

"It's a tough age, being mid-twenties and not quite knowing what you're doing with your life yet." Grandpa tried to smooth over some of the awkwardness, but Grandma just shook her head while poking at a sliced cucumber on her plate, almost as if she wasn't surprised to see him meltdown that way.

"He *has* a job, Grandma." I took a little pity on the guy - after all, he was my big brother - no matter how distant he felt sometimes.

Pursing her lips in a polite fashion - probably to keep words from flowing out without a filter, Grandma nodded as Grandpa pulled her affectionately closer to his side. "Yes, well, I guess so."

The rest of dinner consisted of my tense family eating lukewarm lasagna trying to avoid stale conversation filled with far too many questions lacking answers. After the silence started to practically suffocate me, both with sheer frustration and curiosity of what Grandma and Grandpa had already mentioned about our uncle coming back to town, I broke it without remorse. "Is anyone going to explain *anything* about Edgar? Or are we just going to keep the silence about him forever?"

Mom immediately gave me *that* look - the one that basically meant "shut up now or you're grounded" - but Grandma calmly patted her arm and then cleared her throat so that Grandpa would get the hint to continue.

"Vera, it's been... a long time. Do you even remember what happened?"

I slumped back in my seat. These are among the things I most hated remembering. Obviously, this entire conversation was going to bring up some painful things, so I resolved myself to just suck it up. The sooner it was done, the sooner it would be over. Or so I hoped. Suddenly the sunny-yellow kitchen walls seemed useless in cheering up the gloomy mood descending over the room.

"Dad left when I - I mean, when me and Jet were younger. I remember Edgar was also pretty upset, but I figured that was just because he lost his brother. I know if Jet suddenly wasn't around, I'd... miss him a lot too." I could feel tears swelling under my eyes, threatening to pour out, but I tried to gulp them down as if they were leaking into my throat. I doubted that would work but it was worth a shot. Dabbing my face with a nearby tissue did the job better. Either way, I hated where this discussion was going. Of course Grandma and Grandpa never really came by without a good reason, so I totally knew something was up since Mom mentioned their visit.

"That's true. And we never really knew what happened, or why he wasn't here."

I nodded slowly, and felt my face heat up – there was no use hiding it now. Grandma gently grabbed Grandpa's hand in solidarity, clearly hiding her own discomfort with the biggest mystery my family has ever tried to bury in the sand.

"It's been almost a decade since he's been gone, you know."

I nodded again. That was basically all I could manage.

"So, it seems, Edgar is determined to find him."

Mom dropped the plate she was washing in the sink. Everyone turned around at the harsh metallic sound of the porcelain plate hitting the stainless steel of the basin. "It didn't break. Keep talking." She continued scrubbing the lasagna pan, extra vigorously now. Some people used a punching bag to get out extra aggression, but Mom always took it out on the dishes.

"How do you know this? Did you see him?"

"Edgar?"

"*Yes* Edgar! Did you see him recently?" I was literally on the edge of my seat, inches from tumbling onto the cold gray kitchen tiles.

"He came to our front door last week. Said he wanted to talk."

Mom had abandoned the dishwashing at this point and sat down across the table from me, with her brow furrowed in a painful-looking grimace and her fists clenched on the table. "Milly, what... did... he... want?"

"He wants back in."

"Into what?"

"The family."

Mom got up from the table, calmly but deliberately, and made her way to the bathroom, slamming the door behind her. I stayed at the table, alone with Grandma and Grandpa. I was shocked too - but somehow, my butt was glued to the wooden dining room chair. I guess my butt knew that there was more to this story - and I intended to hear all of it.

"But... he left after Dad did, right?"

My grandparents exchanged glances, and then Grandpa picked up the slack. "Well, keep in mind, Sweetie, that we don't have any idea why your father up and left the way he did. In all fairness, I don't think we'll ever know. I've never been able to make peace with that myself, but we have to try. And that includes extending grace and understanding to your uncle."

"Even though he hasn't been around since then? By *choice*?" I no longer cared about hiding the bitterness seeping through my words. It's bad enough to disappear, it's even worse to disappear when your family needs you to help process that loss. My uncle had become a bit of a myth to me - sure, he was my dad's younger brother, but he'd always been labeled the black sheep of the family, while Dad was somehow seen as a victim. None of it made any real sense, but it was easier to make up reasons when there was no real explanation to go on. It's part of being human – so we made up what we couldn't explain but also couldn't forget.

24

"I agree that his absence has been... poorly timed. And that his reasoning of going to Alaska for dogsled racing all those years ago was a bit... uncalled for. But he's back, for better or worse. And as his family, we *are* going to welcome him. Isn't that right, Vera?" Grandma's response forced its way out of her pursed lips and crawled its way over my crossed arms and up into my reluctant ears. A quick read between the lines told me that her question was more of a demand than a suggestion, so I resolved myself to keeping the peace - but still refused to fully admit defeat.

"Fine, I guess."

Grandma sighed and leaned back against her chair. "I know it's hard, Vera. What I'm asking - what *we're* asking, is no small matter. It doesn't make a lot of sense, and it hurts all of us. But what choice do we have? Besides, you barely know your uncle. Why not give him a chance?"

"I know all I need to know about him - that Dad disappeared and then he *chose* to leave us too. Edgar traded us for the huskies. So why not send him crawling back to freeze-your-ass-off Alaska where he belongs?"

They exchanged an exasperated glance, and I wasn't even the least bit sorry. I got up from the table without giving them the satisfaction of having the last word.

Seven: Ugh, Boy Hormones

"You guys hang out often?" I plopped down next to Vera on the couch, and started munching on the chips I managed to find in the kitchen. I might've tried to be a little quieter, but they were *really* good chips.

"I dunno, sorta." Alex remained glued to the TV screen, and Lynn resumed her less-than-elegant couch posture. I resigned myself to the potato chips until I could think of my next plan of attack. "Could you be a little quieter? Geez. You're worse than my little cousin."

I blushed as I realized Alex was irritated by my munching. I guess some habits die hard, and even though I'd like to think I was a little more mature than Lynn, we might not be all that different after all. "Sorry. But yeah, it's nice to have a close friend to hang with." I pause to swallow the triple-layered chips I stuffed in my mouth, and then continue. "But you gotta have other friends too. Are you guys in any clubs? Those are a great way to meet other kids with similar interests, ya know?"

Both of them angled their heads slightly in my direction, with the same blank stare that I was already starting to hate.

"I mean, it's just a suggestion. You sit on this couch forever watching Spongebob or you could actually meet new friends and live a little. It's your call."

They both turned back to the TV.

"It's just... hard. Our entire grade is like ten people, and they're almost all jerks."

Alex shrugged his agreement. I rolled my eyes, because I knew this all too well but had to ask anyway.

"I get that, but you can't just isolate yourself. Maybe you can bond over something simple, like a band tee you both like or something."

The kids looked at each other with eyebrows raised something like "who even is this chick" and then rolled their eyes in synch. "That'd only work if we didn't have lame school uniforms. Which we do."

I almost smacked myself in the face for that one. Of course. "Well yeah, okay that sucks." I carefully rolled up the remainder of the potato chips, and then marched back to the kitchen to put then back where I found them - upper cabinet to the right of the stove. Then I drank some tap water to wash down the salt, and rejoined the pint-sized misfits back in the living room. And that's when an idea hit me like a perfectly folded stack of Old Navy khakis.

"Guys. Turn the TV off."

"No - this is our favorite episode!"

"Watch it another time. Trust me, this is good."

"No!"

I practically had to arm wrestle Alex for the remote, but I got it from him. *Thank you gym membership.* Luckily, thirteen-year-old boys are still pretty scrawny. At least this one was, anyway. Then I wedged it down the front of my shirt where I knew neither of them would dare snatch it.

"Ew, gross. You can keep the remote."

I continued with my rampage, unfazed by his disgust with my chest. I didn't think I looked *that* bad, geez. "Okay. Here's what we're gonna do."

"Do about what?"

Clearly my indiscreet placement of the TV remote had distracted him a bit. Ugh, boy hormones. "I have an idea to get the bullies off your back."

Lynn and Alex shrugged in unison. *These two are practically joined at the hip and it's gross - but kinda cute too.* "Yeah, you and every other adult within a five-mile radius. There's nothing you can do - they won't change. That's why we just keep to ourselves whenever we can. Talking to them's not worth it."

I felt myself exhale and then I sat on the closest armchair. It was a quick fall off my high horse when I realized that to a very sad extent, they were right. In a system where nasty kids went full-boar tearing into each other, and adults let it happen without effective consequences - or worse, mass-punishment - then things just continued as they were. Then the good kids felt paralyzed and unable to defend themselves for fear of worse punishment than the bad kids who actually deserved it but never got any flack at all for their puke-worthy personalities. And no, this wasn't *The Hunger Games*, but it might as well have been for all the good adults did for the situation.

"Let me ask you guys something - is it really true that *all* the kids in your class are awful? Or just a few that seem to dominate everything?"

"Um, I guess... there's a few at least that are neutral, I guess? Like, they're not bullies, but they don't really do anything to prevent the bullying either." Lynn scratched the back of her neck and looked off into the distance behind me, deep in thought.

"Have you ever realized that maybe, just maybe, those neutral kids are as frustrated as you, and also have no idea what to do to fix it?" I shook a few strands of stray hair out of my eyes and then resumed eye contact with Alex and Lynn.

Alex nodded, and then Lynn stared down nervously at her feet. "Yeah, I mean, maybe?"

"I think that's the key. All you gotta do, is stage a resistance. A *massive* one."

"A what?"

"A fight. Sort of. Show the bullies they can't rule the roost anymore. Their reign of terror, is *over*. Maybe the teachers won't be able to stop them - but you can."

"Oh really? How? We've tried everything. My mom wrote a bunch of notes to my teachers. Heck, she even brought me on this ridiculous ice-cream outing with the mean girl and her mom, just to smooth things over. I mean, I *tried* to have an open mind, but it was just, *weird*. Like there's no way that's actually going to do anything for the situation. Can't fix that with watermelon sorbet, no matter how good it is."

Oh Mom, you meant so well but yeah, that was quite the blunder, let me tell ya. "Right. Yeah that's definitely an odd idea. But it doesn't matter. I know what's gonna work."

"Which is?"

"First, I need the name of this bit- uh, girl."

28

"Summer - her name's Summer."

"Okay, so you're going to prove to Summer, and her lackies…"

"Huh?"

"I mean her minions. Henchmen? All the worst villains have them."

Alex smirked, and then supplied me with the other names I needed. "Oh okay, yeah that'd be Chloe, Sue, and Wyatt. They're kinda useless without Summer, but they all royally suck on their own too."

"Oh I bet they do." I flicked my hair over my shoulder to keep the sweat on the back of my neck from seeping into it. "But you're gonna start sucking right back. My mom gave me some great advice once. She said that sometimes, you gotta be a little witch. Don't be so nice, because then they think they can take advantage of you."

"Haha that's great! I've wanted to do something about this. I *hate* the way they treat us." Alex grinned, and shyly glanced at Lynn to catch her reaction too.

"My mom said something similar, except she said that it's time I be a little bitch right back to them, haha."

I felt my cheeks heat up as I smiled, because now I probably seemed like the prim and proper one, even though that couldn't be further from the truth. "Okay great. So here's what I'm thinking. Step one: recruit the other neutrals to join your side of the battle. You'll need their support. There's strength in numbers, and if you can get them on your side, this is gonna go over like gangbusters. Tell me about them." I crossed my legs and then rested my chin on the palm of my hand.

Lynn sat down across from me on the other armchair, and Alex leaned against the armrest, noticeably close to Lynn. She didn't react to it this time, though. "Okay, so basically…" Lynn started to work down her mental shortlist of the new members in her bully-crushing armada. "There's Bert, who is always purposely weird to get their attention. He like, mixes random food together at

29

snack time and makes a whole show of it, just to give them things to bug him about. And since we were in elementary school, he loves talking about his hunting trips in detail and telling me how he kills cute little lambs and stuff. Bert just likes to see me squirm, I guess. It's super gross though! Then there's Ricky, who is really good at basketball and… seems pretty cool actually." Lynn turned to Alex after this latest mention. "Remind me again why we don't hang out with Ricky? He's nice."

Alex shrugged. "I dunno. I mean yeah, he is cool."

"See? There ya go. Just gotta think of other people who aren't jerks. Now we're making progress!" I clapped my hands together, and the kids just stared at me.

"Remind me why you care so much about who we hang out with?"

Again with the questions. These kids could be private investigators someday. "I just… heavily relate to what you're going through. I want to help because I've been through it too. *If only they knew how much I relate.* "Okay, so you've got Bert, Ricky, anyone else?"

"Not really. I mean, there's Hazel, but she's kinda hard to classify." Alex looked over at Lynn, and I noticed him divert his gaze slightly, avoiding eye contact with her. That reminded me there's probably something more going on with that particular story. I felt my own body recoil at the thought. This was starting to mess with me too.

"What's up with Hazel?" That was a straight-up bluff. I knew exactly what was up with Hazel, but I needed them to admit it to me first so I could speak about it openly.

"She's a back-stabbing jerk, is what's up with her." Lynn filled me in while I nodded slowly, trying to keep my own composure. "Hazel used to be cool. We were… sorta friends for a while. We both liked Taylor Swift. She stayed over at my house a few times in the summer and hung out in the pool, it wasn't… all bad."

Alex hesitantly patted her on the shoulder with all the awkwardness you'd expect from a pre-pubescent teenage boy. But it didn't matter - I knew he had her back.

"Then she started talking to the bullies. It was a slow change. I barely noticed it, until she did stupid things that were so obviously not cool."

Alex ran a clammy hand through his shaggy hair. "There was this time, Lynn used this big vocabulary word in class to insult them that they didn't know. It was pretty genius, actually. They didn't know what it meant, which made them look even dumber. Lynn, what was that word again?"

Lynn's face started to turn red, and her eyes began to water. Rubbing a stray tear on her sleeve, she looked at me through slightly puffy eyes, the kind that you get right before you cry. Then she stifled a small nervous giggle. "Imbeciles. I called them 'imbeciles'. And then Hazel got the big old dictionary off the shelf by the classroom door, and looked it up for them. I was so terrified the teacher would give me a green slip if I didn't apologize, so I did - over and over again. I felt weak, but most of all, I hated that she *wanted* me to feel weak." She pulled her knees up to her chest and stared at the floor. That realization was probably a breakthrough for her.

"Tell her about Evergreen Lake." Alex reached for his glass of water on the side table, and nodded his support for Lynn. At thirteen, he was already much more sensitive and caring than most college-age guys. *I just hope he stayed that way.*

"Ugh, that was the worst of it." Lynn bit her bottom lip, shifted in her seat, and then exhaled. "Okay so, I was griping to Hazel in the van about how I was glad she was there, since everyone else, was just 'kind of stupid'. Then she told them I said that, even though it was just an off-handed thing. I didn't really get in trouble or anything, but I was terrified that I would. The rest of the trip was insanely awkward. I was pretty much alone for the next couple days. I just read quietly the whole way home. But most of all, I was just so upset that she'd hurt me like that just to be in the 'in-crowd'. I made it clear I didn't want to see her again after that."

"But you're still in school with her?"

Lynn shrugged. "Yeah, but she actually keeps her distance, mostly. It's the other jerks that bother me the most right now." Alex nodded his agreement.

"It was so stupid, you know. Like, the teachers wouldn't really do anything about the mean kids, but if me or Lynn ever try to defend ourselves, they come down hard on us. It's not fair, and it doesn't make any sense."

I listened intently to the narrative they shared with me, and tried not to react, even though I related more than they could ever imagine. Then I pulled the TV remote out of my shirt and set it back on the coffee table because I was starting to sweat, and there's something just universally wrong about getting boob sweat on someone else's TV remote.

Eight: Moms are Humans Too

I tried to slam my door shut to punctuate my frustration with clueless grandparents, but the door closed far too softly for my taste. Yet another sign that I'd better get myself back to the gym. I buried my face in my polka-dot pillow, and deadened my cries enough so that no one in the house would worry I was dying or something - at least not physically, anyway. When I got tired of the tightness building in my chest and the tears clogging up my eyes, I slowly sat up and felt a warm breeze wafting from my slightly ajar window. I walked over to it, and looked out onto my quaint and peaceful neighborhood below illuminated by the warmth of the streetlights breaking up the darkness. It felt like home, and grounded me in my own reality even when life seemed like something out of a low-budget sci-fi film.

Right when I was about to turn away, an all-too-familiar head of light-brown hair floated by my house, bookended by a pair of red high tops and a pear-shaped redhead. My stomach churned, and I felt immediately sick. Hands unconsciously clenched and knees locked, I managed to actually slam the window shut and turn away. For a split second though, that familiar face whipped around to see what caused the noise, and I saw the look on his face. Thick brown eyebrows nearly halfway up his forehead, and his mouth rounded into a soft smile. The redhead pulled him away almost instantly, but I saw it. I saw the *longing*. Maybe he's got a weird thing for houses with gray siding.

Crossing my legs on my well-worn purple carpet with stray fibers poking out of it like mid-summer weeds, I couldn't decide whether I wanted to stay in here for the rest of the night, or go find Mom to make sure she was okay. *Nope, couldn't do that - she was crying in the downstairs bathroom, and I bet Grandma and Grandpa were still here, probably cleaning up after dinner. I'd have to go through the kitchen to get to her - no thanks.*

Out of sheer boredom, I found myself wandering toward the hazy blue light glowing from Jet's room. *Must be working on a late night programming project again.* I knew how annoyed he gets when he's interrupted, but I was desperate to talk to someone who understood this particularly complicated mood from this particularly dysfunctional family. Calling one of my college friends just wouldn't cut it, I didn't think. I bravely knocked on his half-open door, and braced myself for the yelling. But none came. He just sighed, nodded while keeping his glassy eyes on the screen, and typed a few things on his keyboard before removing his headset.

"What's up, kid?"

I shrugged, still shocked at the softness he showed even though I interrupted what I bet was an important work thing. "Well, the sky hasn't fallen yet, so I guess... that?"

Jet ran a tired hand through his overgrown hair and rubbed the slight day-old stubble on the lower part of his long, angular face. "That is true, but I think we both know the sky falling on us wouldn't even be the worst thing this family has gone through." I felt a sad smile tugging at the corners of my own very stubborn mouth, but I gave into it after I saw Jet doing the same thing. Mirror neurons, they called it in AP psych. *Cool.*

"True that." I plopped down onto his unmade bed behind his desk where he still sat in his swivel chair.

"Think Grandma and Grandpa are still here? I couldn't hear if they left or not. Definitely not going downstairs to find out though."

I shrugged. "I was just wondering that too. Was gonna check on Mom but didn't want to have to walk through the kitchen."

Jet nodded, and we sat in a comfortable silence for a few minutes.

"You didn't yell at me."

"What?"

"I mean when I knocked. You hate being interrupted. Why weren't you mad?" It didn't really matter so much, but I was curious. And it was nice to have thought of something to say that wasn't *the thing* that was so uncomfortably revealed at dinner.

"I think..." He stood up from his office chair and sat down next to me on the end of his bed. "There are worse things than being

34

interrupted by my kid sister when crap like this happens. Don't get used to it though. This was a one-time thing." He smirked at me, and then ruffled my hair exactly the way I told him I hated even though I knew it was his way of showing affection.

"Oh of course, wouldn't dream of it." We sat in another long silence, just darting our eyes around the room.

"Jet?"

"Yeah?"

"What do you think is gonna happen?"

He shrugged. "How should I know?"

"Can you make a guess?"

Jet grunted and fell back on his bed dramatically. "I dunno kid. I honestly have no clue. But what I do know is, things are about to get crazier. It could be good, or it could be bad."

"I have a bad feeling about it. I don't want to see... him." I couldn't even bear to say the name of our strange and off-putting uncle. I didn't have the most vivid memories of him, and I'm sure whatever I did remember was repressed like a lot of things from that awful year.

"Me neither. But I don't think we'll really have a choice."

It might not be a bad thing. Maybe it'll be okay. Or maybe it won't. Either way, there's no real use getting all worked up about it. We were quiet enough to hear some muffled voices from downstairs letting themselves out. I'd bet good money that Grandma and Grandpa cleaned the kitchen before leaving. We didn't deserve them, even if they did do some stupid things sometimes that caused more pain than good.

"Yeah, I guess you're right."

"I think they're gone. Maybe we should go check on Mom now?"

I nodded. "Sometimes I forget that it's all really hard on her too."

"Well gee Vera, moms are humans too!"

I punched him gently in the arm. "Well, at least *mine* is. The jury's still out on what alien being gave birth to the likes of you."

"Well at least I was *born* and not *removed* like a malignant parasite." His commentary on my more difficult c-section delivery compared to his relatively uneventful birth was a favorite punch line of his.

"Dude that's such a lame comeback."

"What can I say? I've been programming for hours, my brain is mush."

"Sure, blame the programming for that."

He shook his head and rolled his eyes above a smile forming on his face. "Well you know I gotta blame something."

I ended up smiling at his pathetic but always funny jabs, and then I finally followed him out his bedroom door and down to the kitchen to assess the current situation. Mom was teary-eyed and puffy, but had her feet up on the couch.

"It was nice of Grandma and Grandpa to clean up before leaving. They didn't have to, of course. But I always appreciate it." She blew her nose onto a Kleenex from the tissue box on the side table.

"Mom, are you, uh, doing okay? With all this?" I eased myself onto the couch next to her, and tried not to bump her with my notoriously bony knees and butt.

"It's not your job to worry about me, Vera. That's what I do for you guys."

"Sure, but I mean, it's impossible not to be at least a *little* concerned when someone leaves dinner to lock themselves in the bathroom." I forced a small smile, but Mom just stayed stoic and calm, kind of like the way the air always felt charged with energy after a thunderstorm.

"I guess that's true. But I still don't want you guys worrying about me. I'm Mom, that's *my* job."

"Just uh, don't forget that you can't do your job if you're not doing too well yourself either." Jet jumped in, much to my relief. He's not always a pompous jerk - usually, he's somewhat thoughtful when it comes down to it.

Nine: Lumped in Just for Existing

"Well that's pretty messed up." I kicked my feet up on the nearby coffee table and crossed my arms over my chest.

"Duh. We know." Alex shook his longish light brown hair out of his eyes. "But you said you had some... ideas?"

I grinned, all too ready to enact some justice. "I have some thoughts, yeah. It's rough, but I think there could be some ways to get the justice you've been craving."

Lynn grinned at Alex, and they both stifled what I could only imagine as the most gleeful evil cackles straight out of a Disney movie villain. "It seems that what you've been needing, is for the authority figures to see how completely wretched your classmates are, right? Because up until now, it's really just hear-say. Right?"

My question was met with emphatic nods and wide eyes energized with the promise of bringing on the bully apocalypse. "So if we can correct that, the mean kids will finally be met with the appropriate consequences for their heinous deeds."

"But we gotta make sure they just don't punish everyone. Because that's just annoying and lazy, I think."

"Wait, so you weren't kidding? They really do that? Like if one kid screws up, you *all* get hell for it?"

Alex sighed and scratched the back of his neck. "Yup, basically. Like a month ago, Chloe made up this stupid, disgusting rumor, *about herself*, and the teachers made us all sit through a conference telling us why that's not funny. No crap, Sherlock!"

"Oh, and they said we couldn't use our lockers in between classes, so we had to pile up all our books for the day and carry them. Like, what kind of actual bull crap is that?"

Alex huffed. "They thought it was a worthy punishment to keep us from starting stupid rumors at the lockers."

"But of course, I have mild scoliosis, so I wasn't gonna carry all that. I used my locker *anyway*." Lynn crossed her arms and grinned proudly. And who could blame her? She stood up to the twisted authority figures when she could. That was refreshing to hear. But even that victory would pale in comparison to what I had planned.

"That's definitely ridiculous." I shook my head and then opened my mouth to ask what the rumor was, but then I heard a door slam outside. *Someone's home.* "Hey uh, is someone here?"

"That's probably just my older brother. He comes home during the day sometimes."

No no no he can't see me. Crap. What do I do now? Gotta think of something! "Hey, um, I gotta take this call so I'll step outside for a sec." I grabbed my cellphone and mimed answering it, even threw in an extra "hello" just to really sell it. Then I eased myself out the front door as gracefully as possible, and not at all like my life depended on it. Or so I hoped.

"Oh, uh, okay."

"Did her phone even ring? I didn't hear it."

"Me neither. Whatever."

I managed to slip out the front door and hide out in the bushes until I thought the coast was clear. I also pulled my light scarf over my head and replaced my sunglasses onto my face for extra privacy. *Great, now I'm the freaky sunglasses lady hiding in the bushes and stalking a house. Just fabulous.* Not that I had that much of a choice anyway.

I heard voices inside the house, and managed to spy on them a bit through the secluded front window. Chills ran up and down my spine as I experienced what could only be described as that really uncanny Gothic doubling that I learned about in my college Lit class. They were discussing something, I'm not sure what. Not that it was really my business anyway. Well, it sort of was. It's complicated, I guess. When I saw the shadow of the brother disappear up the stairs, I waited an extra minute or two, and then took that as a cue to reenter.

38

"Sorry guys, had to take a business call. What'd I miss?" *Way to play that off believably.*

"Oh nothing, my brother came home to get some schoolwork done. Anyway, what were you about to say?"

"Um, I can't totally remember. Oh, right - what was the rumor about?"

"Oh it was - "

Alex shushed her with his hand over her mouth. "It's, awkward. And it doesn't really matter now anyway." He blushed awkwardly and then pulled his hand away from her face. Lynn's eyes were wide. I'm gonna take a wild guess and assume that never happened before. *Ah, to be young and clueless again.*

I shrugged. Whatever, they didn't have to tell me anything they didn't want to anyway. But I did find it odd that he reacted that way. Eh, teenage boys - always impossible to read. I should know that better than anyone else in this room. "Well, okay then."

I shifted uncomfortably in the armchair again, and then remembered the plan. As in, the ultimate plot to bring down the bullies once and for all. I felt heat spread over my face and scalp, and then rubbed my palms together in excited anticipation. "Gather 'round, children. We're taking them down one by one. And I know exactly how we're gonna do it."

Alex and Lynn looked at me with an equal amount of excitement, or perhaps more, since they were going to be the ones exacting the revenge - er, I meant, justice. Yeah, that's it. "First things first, befriend the neutral kids. That'd be…" I paused for dramatic effect. "Ricky and Bert, right? And your targets are Hazel, Summer, Wyatt, Sue, and Chloe."

They nodded their heads.

"You guys ever watch any spy movies? The target, or, 'mark', as they call it there, is always super important. If you can isolate that person, you're golden."

"But in this case, there are five marks, right? Like, I really hate Summer the most, but the other ones deserve to be punished as well. And for once, I don't want to be lumped in just for existing."

"Absolutely! You will not be held accountable. I still can't believe that's the way they handle it. After all, in such a small class, you'd think they'd be able to figure out exactly who the problem kids are. It just boils down to laziness, really. I know they think they're trying, and that's all fine and good, but the current system is utter bull crap. It shouldn't take a rocket scientist to figure that one out."

Both kids seemed quite pleased that I've taken such a personal and proactive stance with their mission, and it already felt like they forgot I only met them earlier today. "So talk to Bert and Ricky as soon as you can. Tell them it's going to be great but you need their help. When will you see them next?"

"Uh, there's a spring arts show tonight. All our artwork gets pinned up and displayed in the gym. It's actually kinda cool." Alex jumped in, and Lynn seemed excited as well.

"Yeah and I even got a blue ribbon! 'Best in Show' for a painting I did of a beach scene."

"That's great Lynn! Which reminds me, the next part of the plan, is boosting your confidence."

The kids looked at each other quizzically, and then back at me. "Uhm, okay, but how?"

I smirked, thinking of what a treat they were in for. "Well, you gotta feel like total badasses! You gotta walk in there like you rule the joint. Ya catch my drift?" I smiled at them like a proud mom - because at this point, I basically was.

"Clothing. There's no dress code for the spring art night, right?"

"Only if you're in the play, which we're not." Alex smiled out the corner of his mouth. "It's not exactly the coolest thing to do. I'd barely even call it a play. I'm glad it's only mandatory for the elementary school."

Lynn rolls her eyes. "Yeah, okay, but I *like* my clothes."

"Just for tonight, let me help you look just a *little* cooler. It'll be some really subtle changes, but I swear I can help. If you let me help you, I think this will all feel even sweeter. You'll see." I could see the gears turning behind their skulls. Inquisitively considering it, I even saw the pieces practically lock into place.

Ten: Snail Mail Surveys for FedEx

I didn't remember much of what happened after dinner that night. I talked to Jet, then Mom, and tumbled back into bed next to the open window letting in the warm spring breeze. If it weren't for the family drama threatening to uproot my life as I knew it, this would have been a perfectly pleasant evening. Well, perfectly pleasant aside from tossing and turning all night. I had this weird dream that there was some kind of sharp object stuck in my bed, like a spider or something that kept biting me. It's extra unsettling when you're half asleep and can't escape this thing with all these legs trying to attack you while in a sleep-deprived state. But somehow, I doubted that my mattress was the reason for the tossing and turning.

My alarm went off the next morning, as the latest pop song slowly increased in volume from my pink speakers on my bedside table. I reached over to kill the volume a bit so Jet didn't yell at me from his room next door (he sleeps late because he stays up most of the night coding software to accommodate his colleagues in Japan). Problem is, once the volume goes down, I always had so much trouble getting out of bed. With a class at ten o'clock, I didn't have to get up super early, but it was still earlier than I would have liked. That heavy-eyelid feeling is always a hard one to shake any time before noon, I'd say. I grabbed the nearest pair of ripped skinny jeans and a light sweater previously laid out on my desk chair, and then ran a brush through my hair as I tried to get downstairs to scrounge up a quick breakfast before heading out the door. I was halfway through my gluten-free bagel when Mom padded down the stairs in her mint-green bathrobe and slippers.

"Mornin' Vera." She yawned and headed to the coffee maker.

"Morning. How are you feeling after all... that stuff?" I stuffed a big bite of my breakfast into my mouth because I had to leave in five minutes and still really had to pee. I got up from the table mid-conversation to handle that, but I heard Mom mumble something nearly inaudible under her breath. "What? Didn't hear ya."

Mom shrugged. "Don't worry about it, I'm sure everything will turn out fine. Have a great day." She smiled at me, and then sat down at the table with the TV remote in hand to check the weather channel.

"Uh, okay. See ya later." I headed out the door to get to my marketing class even though I really didn't want to leave her after everything that went down last night. Jet was probably still out cold - sometimes he didn't even get up until two o'clock in the afternoon if he had an especially important Skype meeting or something in the middle of the night. It seemed like a pretty annoying job if you asked me, but he really seemed to love it and claimed that it paid well enough. Mom always worried about him not socializing enough, but he's always been an introvert, just like me. I guess that's a typical trait in the Bartlet family.

I plopped my sorry butt into the Volkswagen and turned up the volume on my favorite alternative rock channel. A nostalgic Greenday tune fueled my inner emo and I sighed as the angsty, iconic lyrics filled the sonic space of my little car. Turning down my quiet neighborhood, I waved politely to Mr. Johnson walking his dog and adjusted my mirrors to avoid the morning glare of the sunlight hitting my still-tired eyes. And that's when it hit me: No matter what I did, Edgar was going to screw up my whole family. There was no way to avoid it.

And in a strange way, it was comforting to realize that there was nothing I could really do, because that meant panicking about it was useless and unnecessary. At this point, a rational person would take a deep breath, mumble 'que sera sera', and go on with their day. But I never claimed I was rational - and I wasn't about to change that now. True to form, I pulled over to handle the tightness in my chest because I knew it could turn into a full-on panic attack if I wasn't careful.

Chill out, Vera. Can't be late for class again or Professor Melendez is going to chew you out. That thought just freaked me out more though. I've always feared authority figures, probably due to my problematic past with teachers who never seemed to treat me any better than my less-than ideal classmates. Plus this particular professor was just intimidating in general anyway. It's extra hard to please a teacher who glares at you for being late one too many times no matter how perfectly you did your homework. I enjoyed the class - just not the vibe I got from it, I guess. Regardless, I steadied my heartbeat enough to get back onto the road, and let the Fleetwood Mac lyrics floating out of the radio wash over my frayed nerves as I passed by Santa Monica Pier. My hands still shook a bit, but I was driving again, the ocean was pretty, and I would probably make class on time after all.

I parked, and heaved my heavy backpack over my shoulder. My hair got caught in the car door though, so I had to unlock my car door to fix that before walking to class. *Thanks a lot, windy Los Angeles.* I freed myself from the clutches of my car and then headed over to the building I needed to get to.

"Hey 'sup girl!"

I turned to my left to see Willow running toward me, her long auburn hair flowing behind her in the breeze, mingling with the straps of her simple beige burlap backpack. "Nothing much." *And by nothing much, I meant everything.* I shrugged off the unpleasant feeling of lying through my teeth and plastered a cheesy grin on my face to sell it even more. She casually threw her waist-length hair over her shoulder and straightened the fringe on the bottom edge of her boho-chic crop top. Always a bit of a hippie, Willow marched to the beat of her own drum, even inventing her own veterinary and agriculture double major. I had to admit that was precisely what I liked the most about her - and her freshly grown veggies were always the best.

"Did ya finish that case study yet? Melendez is gonna go ballistic on our asses if it's not in his office by four." She tossed her hair over her shoulder and kept pace with me as we both entered the classroom.

44

"I, uh, started it. Just not finished. I'll probably have it finished just before it's due."

She nodded her agreement. "Same. It's such a dull assignment. After all, why should I care about the relevance of snail mail surveys for FedEx?"

"Can't argue with that."

Willow loved radio pop tunes more than anything, but she put up with my punk obsessions once in a while. We met during orientation freshman year and have been tight ever since.

"Got any fun weekend plans? I was thinking of spending Sunday at the pier with Zander to stress-eat my way through corndogs and shaved ice before we gotta hunker down to study for finals. Wanna come with?"

I sighed and yanked my class binder from my bag. Mom would tell me to go and have fun with my friends, but I'm not sure if I even have the capacity for fun right now.

"Vera? Earth to Vera, are you free or not?"

She tapped my arm to get my attention, and that's when I realized that I totally left her hanging there. *Oops.*

"I mean, I'm not sure how fun I'll be, but I'm technically free I guess."

"Um, of course you'll be fun! What gives?" She crossed her arms, waiting for an explanation. I needed to figure out how much would be appropriate to gripe about right before class starts. I opened my mouth to offer some kind of excuse, but Melendez slammed his massive textbook on his desk and started scribbling furiously on the smart board with his stiff, pointed finger.

"I'll tell ya after class," I whispered in the hopes that she wouldn't worry too much about me in the meantime. I might worry about me, though. Not much I could do about that.

Eleven: Face Full of Sticky Goop

"You really think you can fix me?" Lynn looked up at me with the most desperate pleading I had seen in a while. Her eyes were wider than usual, and her lips were turned into a slight frown mirrored by raised eyebrows trying desperately to scale her forehead. She was originally pretty hesitant, but after a brief talk about how looking cooler would also make her more confident - and this victory all the more sweet - she relented and put herself into my very capable hands. I wasn't always the fashionista visible here today, but I think it's fair to say my past inspired me to get to the point I was at now.

"Well, I'll do my best. It's just a bunch of really subtle things, really."

Alex rolled his eyes. "So you're telling me, that you have this 'epic' plan for us to get revenge on our stupid classmates. But first, a makeover? Barf. What am I supposed to do?"

I just grinned at him with a knowing smile. "You can start phase one of the plan - the technology." His eyes widened at the sheer idea of being important - in reality, I just needed him out of my hair long enough to make Lynn the drop-dead bombshell I knew she could be. Well, as much as any thirteen-year-old can be without looking like an overgrown *Toddlers in Tiaras* contestant.

"Okay, what do I gotta do?"

"To catch the bullies being, well, bullies, we'll need tiny spy cameras. Can you borrow the ones your dad bought off Amazon?"

He nodded his head excitedly, until an uncanny chill crept over his shoulders. "Wait, how did you know my dad had spy cameras?"

I froze in my tracks. *Come on Vera, you're better than that.* "Um, lucky guess? They're so popular these days." Well, no they weren't, but that's the best cover I could think of on short notice.

Thankfully he was thirteen and still impressionable enough, so Alex's pinched facial expression relaxed into a smile.

"Yeah, I'll go grab those and make sure they have fresh batteries and stuff." Happy to be helpful, he ran out the backdoor to get to his own house, I assumed.

"Well, guess it's just you and me now. Ready to be drop-dead gorgeous?" I motioned to Lynn to go and head upstairs, and she nodded slightly and then hesitantly jogged upstairs. I followed her as un-creepily as I could and entered a room painted in garish lime-green paint, with a bright pink bedspread covered in a butterfly and flower pattern. Underfoot was a wall-to-wall gray rug, accented by a somewhat stylish rectangular green area rug with pink flowers littered across it. The room was even smaller than I expected, and her closet was tiny as well.

"Okay, so here's what we're gonna do. You're going to wear exactly what I tell you to, and then I'll help you with your hair and makeup."

"Makeup? Nah that's not my thing. I've just never liked it. Ever since I had to wear a ton of it for dance recitals, I hated the way it made my face feel."

I smiled to myself, and then remembered she's just thirteen. And a very *young* thirteen, I might add. She could easily pass for ten, I'd say. Then again, that's not half as bad as being twenty-two and looking fifteen on a good day. I blame that for why I haven't actually dated, since I'm sure most guys my age worry I'm not even legal yet. Fun times. "Okay, well how about some lip gloss at least?" I pinched the air in front of my face to emphasize the small amount I wanted to apply to her face.

Lynn hesitated for a moment, and then warmed up to the idea. "Deal."

"Great. Can I check out your closet now?"

She nodded slowly. "Sure, yeah I guess."

I gingerly opened the white sliding door and let the nostalgia wash over me like a warm summer rain. I shuddered slightly and then continued. "Okay, how about these cool pink capris? These are super cute. Then, uhh, maybe this pretty white blouse?" I held them up to her for a minute and then smiled to myself. "Yes, these are perfect! Okay. Go put these on, and then I'll do your hair."

Lynn shrugged and then walked to the bathroom, leaving me momentarily alone in her room. It's so odd to be someplace foreign and yet, so familiar. I guess that's just something magical about any teenage girl's room - there's just a vibe of brightness and hope in it that any other girl can relate to and feel on a spiritual level. You know, the been-there-done-that sort of relating that comes from being of the female gender. I looked at the framed photos on her bureau, covered with a light layer of dust and the cute jewelry haphazardly laid out between them. I took that opportunity to find something that would go with her outfit. Finding all of it to be a bit too straight-laced, I ended up thinking that the edgier choker I was currently wearing might be a perfect fit. I was just taking it off of my neck and removing my scarf, and then I heard the bathroom door open, so I quickly covered my collarbone again before Lynn came back.

"Aw you look so cool! Great outfit!"

"Well you picked it." She shrugs, avoiding eye contact with me.

"Yes, but you agreed to wear it. And in fact, I have one more thing that might go well with that." I handed her the choker I just took off, and she looked at it like I was handing her a gross sea slug.

"Uh, what's that? A choker necklace?"

I nodded. "Geez girl, we're fresh out of the 2000s, aren't chokers all the rage or something? Just try it. Here, I'll put it on you." I motioned for her to turn around, and I gently lifted her hair out of my way. Then I fastened one of my favorite thick, woven black chokers to her throat, and she looked pretty badass, if I did say so myself. But she was still missing something.

"Ah, so cute! You look totally punk."

"What?"

"I mean you look... cool! I am gonna have to help you with one more thing though. And I have a feeling you're not gonna like it."

Lynn shrugs. "Whatever. I guess it's worth a shot."

"Great!" I opened my purse, and removed my favorite liquid eyeliner from the small zippered compartment on the side. "With that choker, you need a little eyeliner. It'll feel a bit weird but I can apply it for you. Okay? Just trust me."

Her eyes widened, and I could tell she desperately wanted to say 'no', but she didn't. For some odd reason, she nodded and closed her eyes. But then they popped open again just as I uncapped the eyeliner. "But wait, Mom said you're not supposed to share makeup. It's germs and stuff." *Great, how am I gonna get through this one? I guess it's not super important, but I think it'll boost her confidence.*

"Trust me, in this isolated instance, you'll be fine. I, uh, just bought this brand new. Haven't even used it yet." That last part was a lie - I've already been using it. But I knew that I wouldn't be infecting her with any weird bacteria.

"Oh, okay. I guess that's all right then." She closed her eyes again, and I made quick work of slathering the makeup on the edges of her eyelids. I smiled to myself thinking of how great this was going to look.

"You're all set. Take a look in the mirror!"

She slowly turned around and looked at her reflection, with my additions of the choker and the eyeliner. Somehow, she looked more confident, sure of herself, and even a bit attractive. *Wait until Alex sees her now.* "Well, what do you think?"

"I think I look... good. It's good right?"

"Yeah, most definitely. Now add the lipgloss." I handed her the tube I saw sitting unused on her nightstand, and she applied it liberally. A bit too liberally, I'd say. "Um, you might want to rub a bit of that off. Your mouth is dripping wet, here." I handed her a tissue to wipe it off with, but she rolled her eyes.

"Look, I know you seem to know what you're doing, but it's just lip gloss. What's the big deal, really?"

I sighed. "Well, I guess it's not, really. It's just that... boys don't wanna kiss a face full of sticky goop."

All the color drained from her face at that precise moment. "Uhm, that's fine since I don't wanna... kiss boys right now anyway. Ew." *Oh, to be young again and without relentless hormones.*

"Fair enough." I obviously didn't want to push her *too* fast in that direction anyway.

Twelve: The Famous Miss Vera

Melendez droned on especially annoyingly today. Maybe it was the fact that I was super uneasy about all the crap that was about to happen with my lame excuse of an uncle. Or maybe I was just hungry again.

As soon as he closed the ginormous textbook he ordered for the class, I packed up my stuff and headed out the door, but Willow followed me with her brow furrowed and a tense frown spreading over her face. "Hey! Vera, you gotta tell me what's up. You're like, totally off today. What's up?" Her tone skipped right over concern and straight to frustration. Who could blame her though - in my haste to get out of that boring class, I totally brushed her off.

"Oh man, there's just... family drama happening." I forced my footsteps to slow a bit as she fell into step next to me. "I swear I didn't mean to ignore you. It's all just... very odd."

Her face relaxed a bit, and I took that opportunity to fish my car keys out of my bag.

"Heading home already?"

I nodded. "Yeah, Wednesdays are pretty chill, just Melendez to deal with. And since that case study is due later, I'm glad I have time to work on it." She patted me calmly on the shoulder, obviously unsure of what to say.

"Well, if you want to talk about it, you know I'm here for you. I'm pretty damn curious but I respect your privacy. I mean, I *am* your closest friend but I can't exactly force you to spill it. No matter how much I desperately want you to."

Turns out, Melendez wasn't the only one who enjoyed rambling. "Look, Willow, I appreciate your concern, but I just really have to head home. There honestly isn't much to tell yet, but I'll keep you in the loop as much as I can, okay?"

Somewhat satisfied with that, an exasperated sigh escaped her lips, but she shrugged and smiled at me politely. "Sure, yeah,

51

whatever. Talk to ya later, chica!" Then she blew me a kiss and headed in the opposite direction, to the large glass-and-steel building where I knew her other least-favorite class was held. It's pretty insane to think any class could tie with Melendez for being the least fun, but it was true. And since Willow avoided a couple of her gen-eds until the very last minute, she was stuck taking them in her very last semester of college. Typical Willow, gotta love her.

I marched all the way back to my very inconvenient parking spot where my beloved black Volkswagen bug was being held hostage by the asinine commuter parking location. Thanks to all the construction going on at school, the commuters had to pay the price - as if our tuition dollars didn't go straight to lawn maintenance as it was. I started the car and then blasted the AC, trying to steady my mind as I headed back home, where I knew I had measly four-and-a-half hours to turn in that case study. Fantastic. Of course, I didn't mean to leave it until the last minute, but sometimes, life just happens. And happen, it really did.

The blue ocean flashed through my windows, and I opened my window to inhale some of the soothing sea breeze. If it were any other day, I'd probably take a detour to the beach to stick my butt in the sand and down a lobster roll or two, but I had this tugging in my gut that was dragging me home. Plus I developed a weird rash on my left thigh, probably from my fitful sleep last night - but it looked like something bit me, oddly enough. Consciously, I knew I probably wanted to get home because I had to finish this important assignment for Melendez, but when I got to my driveway and had to park my car on the street to avoid hitting the unfamiliar beat-up pickup truck parked in my spot, my stomach dropped. I shook it off, thinking maybe Mom was just entertaining a friend or maybe Jet got a new car - again. He's the worst driver I've ever seen, and totals every car he buys. For the car's sake, I hoped it wasn't his. I smirked about the mysterious owner of the unfamiliar vehicle as I grabbed my bag from the passenger seat and made my way to our front door.

It was when I opened that door that I suddenly wished I hadn't. I mean, I could have closed it, but that really wouldn't change what - or rather, who - was on the other side of it.

"Vera, come greet your uncle." Mom's strained voice entered my ears without an invitation, but I squirmed even more at the face that met my gaze next to her.

Edgar freaked me out just by his vibe alone. Visually, he looked like a creepy, older stunt double of my dad. They were brothers, after all. But this was just another level of creepy. His vivid green eyes pierced my gaze, and seemed to be sunk deep into a familiar oval face that was taken up largely by a prominent nose that looked almost comical in its size. His lips parted to breathe my name, bringing back to life the person that I had worked so hard to forget. His plain outfit of work boots, muddy jeans, and a wrinkled, faded flannel seemed extra bizarre in Los Angeles. *Did he not notice that it's always like, a bazillion degrees here?* I tugged nervously on the hem of my shorts, and avoided eye contact at all costs. Suddenly, my mechanical pleasantries became a desperate plea for help, which completely went over my always-polite-no-matter-how-awkward-it-was mother's head.

"Hey Edgar. It's nice to, uh, see you. I have a ton of work that's due later today, so I better get to it." I tried to push my way through the unwelcome crowding at the front door, but Mom's curt hand on my shoulder stopped me. The slight squeeze was code for 'don't you dare question me now', and coupled with her plastered smile, I knew I was done for. *Now I really wish I stayed at the beach for an hour or two.*

"Vera, why not ask for an extension on your homework? Your uncle just got here."

I sighed. If only getting extensions from Melendez was that easy. Although, maybe he'd make an exception if I pulled the long-lost-uncle card. Oh well, I guess that would have to do. "Yeah, I can try."

Mom relaxed some of the tension accumulated on her face, and then patted the shoulder she just squeezed. "Good. Edgar, why

53

not come in for some coffee or lemonade? I'm sure you have a lot you want to catch up on."

Edgar nodded, and followed me into the kitchen. "Vera, you've gotten *so big* since I've seen you. How old are you now?" His gravelly voice, mixed with the curious lilt of his tone, made me more than a little uncomfortable.

"Older than I should be since I've seen you last."

Mom gave me a characteristic silent scolding, with her eyes wide open and her mouth rounding out the words "be nice" behind Edgar's turned back. "She's twenty-two, Edgar. Just about to graduate from college."

His slow whistle increased my discomfort. "My my, time sure does fly. And how about your boy, Krystal? How old is Jefferson now?"

My mom smiled politely again, and brought the pitcher of iced lemonade to the kitchen table. "He would be three years older than Vera, so twenty-five. He's probably upstairs working on his programming again. I can go get him if you like?" Her question hung in the air like the smell of burnt rubber in a boiling parking lot.

"No need to bother him if he's busy. I really came, to speak to the *famous* Miss Vera." His knowing smile and increasingly leaning posture toward my side of the table increased my discomfort tenfold. Plus, I was jealous that he wasn't going to interrupt Jet's important work, but my project was suddenly going to be pre-empted. Double standard much - and for what exactly?

"Uh, famous?"

Edgar nodded excitedly. "Oh yes, my dear. There is just so much, I want to catch up on."

This guy really gave me the creeps. *How was Mom possibly okay with this?*

"Uh-huh. So... what do you want to know?" *And how quickly can I get through this before my homework is due?*

Edgar paused for a moment, so Mom jumped in to kill the awkward silence. "Edgar, it was very nice of you to bring this very generous and unnecessary gift basket." She motioned casually to the large and imposing mound of bread and artisanal cheeses taking up unwelcome residence on our kitchen counter.

"Oh it was my pleasure! My buddy owns the deli nearby, so I told him to throw a little something together for *ma familia*. I knew you'd like it." He pulled his grimy lips into a pleased smile, and crossed his arms across his chest while leaning back in our aging kitchen chairs. The dull groaning that burst out of the wood matched my current mood to a T. "So anyway, Vera…"

He paused for dramatic effect, and then leaned forward. Mom absent-mindedly started washing the already-clean dishes by hand the way she always did when she was nervous, and then paused for a moment to place the giant cheese basket into the fridge. How there was space for it in there, I'll never know. "I have to know, what have you been up to all these years?"

I scoff. "You mean besides hating you?"

Mom dropped a dish into the sink, which luckily didn't break but still sounded with a moderately noticeable THUD. "Vera, that's not very becoming of a lady…"

I rolled my eyes. "Sorry. But it's really just been high school and college. Pretty uneventful, I guess." *Aside from the bullying, and nearly debilitating stress and anxiety. Also still don't have a boyfriend, thanks for asking.*

"Really? That's it? Hmm, I was sure a girl of *your* caliber would be practically ruling the world by now."

"My caliber? You don't even know me. I'm nothing special." *And you're a freak.*

"Oh I know plenty about you! You're little Charlie's kid. Besides, I got enough dirt on that kid to make you laugh 'til you pee yourself. There was this one time, when he was about ten, that he -"

I raised my hand mid-air to stop him mid-boring story that I honestly had no desire to hear, especially about my dad who I missed so much. "Save it. It's not like it's gonna bring him back. Besides, I have things to do." I got up from the chair I was in, and decided to head to my room and turn my work in on time, no matter how much that pissed off my mom. It's far more important than

55

whatever useless drivel my should-have-stayed-lost uncle wanted to spew at me.

Thirteen: Potential Busting Time

I followed Lynn out of her lime-green bedroom and back down the hallway stairs. Sitting back down on the couch, I smiled at her as she caught another glance at herself in the mirror. "Like what you see?"

She smiled back at me. "I kinda do. Wouldn't normally put these pants with this shirt, but I really like it."

"You're gorgeous, Lynn. Believe it." If only someone cool had ever said that to me at her age. Sure, my parents always said I was beautiful, but that was likely just because I was their kid. It's not like a parent could ever tell their own kid they were ugly - the worst they might say is that they have a great personality, or some B.S. like that.

Her brace-faced smile beamed back at me, and it was at that precise moment that I knew I was making a difference in her life. And after all, that's what I came here to do. It felt pretty damn great. She shrugged, but continued smiling. "You really think so?"

"Hell yes! You're confident, stylish, and look like a total badass now. Can't go wrong with that mix."

"Thanks. You know, it's kinda crazy how I just met you this morning, and yet it feels like... I've known you forever. It's like you're inside my head, or something."

Oh, if only she knew... "I guess we've become fast friends, huh? Well I for one, am very glad about it. And tonight, we're going to get those bullies off your back for good."

"I seriously can't wait. They're so obnoxious and mean. I'm convinced they're just bad people overall. Do you think we could get them expelled?" The excited lilt in her voice suggested that getting them expelled would be the ultimate success - this kid's got a dark streak. And as much as I would love to see that happen too, I had to tell her that we shouldn't get our hopes up. Better throw in some morality and crap too, just for kicks. *Ugh, I am so becoming my mom.*

"I mean, we'd have to think of a pretty good set-up to get that to happen. If you guys have any ideas, let me know. I currently have no idea though. Do you happen to have the school handbook?"

Lynn smirked. "Finally, it's gonna be useful for something…" She yanks out the bright yellow handbook from the magazine rack near the couch. "Literally there's this whole range of offenses, and the jerks in my class have committed most of them but never get into trouble, I don't get it. I bet the teachers know something is up, but they just don't ever do anything about it."

"All right, let me at it." She hands me the handbook and I flipped through until I landed on the section about discipline. "Repeated bullying? Level 3. Beginning student friction? Level 2. And you're sure they never get in trouble? This sounds pretty obvious to me." *I can't believe how lame this is. Literally this handbook may as well have their stupid little names printed in there along with all the offenses. And nothing happens to them? Ridiculous.*

Lynn shrugged. "I never claimed any of this was logical."

"I guess you're right." *All this is me pretending to be surprised. I knew about this all too well.*

"So, what are we gonna make them do on camera?"

I started to respond to her question when the back door flew open and Alex reentered carrying a sizable black bag on his shoulder. "Okay, so I've got the spy cameras and… woah."

Clearly he noticed Lynn's little makeover, and he did not seem at all displeased. *I think his little crush is becoming even more obvious and harder to hide.* I smirked as I noticed Lynn smiled at him normally, while Alex's jaw remained in danger of full-on dropping to the kitchen tile. The kids stared at each other in silence until I decided that someone's gotta break it up, in the name of justice. Puppy love can be handled later. As in, *I'll* handle that later. Ugh, middle schoolers - too young to do anything cool and too oblivious to have any fun.

"Lynn… you look… cool." Alex cleared his throat after his voice cracked and then looked away awkwardly, settling himself on the couch.

"Uh, thanks." Lynn sat next to him on the couch, nearly putting him into cardiac arrest by the sheepish look on his face as her shoulder brushed his.

"Alex, we were just looking through the school handbook to think of ways to get their scrubby little asses out of your hair for good."

"What?"

"Expelled. I mean, we're trying to get the jerks expelled."

"Oh, yeah. That'd be good."

Lynn smirks. "You do realize, that the bullies are basically more than half the class? What if they really do get expelled? Would the school enroll more kids to take their place?"

I shrug. "Who cares? That school is just ridiculous anyway. I doubt you'd miss it."

Both kids looked down, and smiled, but their faces seemed flushed. With either excitement at what's to come, or hormones, I guess I'll never know.

"Alex, what kind of cameras do you have? The kind that you can wear, or the kind that you plant in different hidden locations?"

Alex broke out of his haze and grabbed the zippered bag he brought from home. "Both, I think. What's your pick?"

"Both I think? You guys should definitely be mic'd, and hidden cameras would definitely help. But we can put recording devices around the room as well. You said there's the art show tonight, right? Do you know if there would be an instance where you'll be in a room with the bullies long enough for crap to go down?"

Lynn looked at a still-blushing Alex, and then comes up with an idea. "Well, typically everyone hangs out in the classrooms before the play starts. Teachers are around, but they never notice anything, of course. Either way, I'd say that's a solid half an hour of potential busting time."

"Perfect. So, let's start by wiring these microphones under your clothes. Except, I don't know much about how these work. Alex, are you more familiar with these?"

He nodded. "Yeah, so they're attached to these power packs here, which I just freshened up with new batteries to be sure that they're gonna work. Then, you just put it under your clothes." He placed one under his own shirt, dropping the larger pack into his pocket and positioning the clip on the inside of his collar. Then he motioned to Lynn to do the same thing. His hands froze awkwardly at her collar bone, clearly afraid to get too close or make things awkward. I stifled the laugh threatening to explode from my throat – it was all just so cringe-worthy. And then I took the microphone pack from him and wired it into Lynn's shirt.

"Great. So now you guys are all wired up. What about the other cameras to plant in the room? Can you smuggle those with you and hide them on a windowsill or something?"

Lynn nodded her head, but Alex shook his.

"Why not, Alex?"

"I just think someone would notice us trying to hide them. We're probably better off doing that before we have to be there."

I huffed. "Well of course you would get caught, why didn't I think of that? Seems those teachers are way too quick to punish the good kids, isn't that suspicious..." There wasn't really any other point to that statement, but I felt myself trail off mid-thought as if there was.

"So how are we gonna get them in there?" Lynn stuck her hands on her hips, clearly agitated - because she knew Alex was right.

"How about we sneak over to the school a couple hours beforehand, and plant them?"

"Without keys to the classroom, how?"

"Oh Lynn, you really think keys are the only way into a room? You poor, innocent girl. Lucky for you, I've got a plan. But

60

first, can we get something to eat? All I've eaten today were those potato chips earlier."

The two kids smiled, and nodded their heads. "Sounds great, let's go. I know just the place." I grabbed my purse off the couch and followed them out the garage door.

"Is it within walking distance? I don't have my car with me today."

Lynn nodded. "Of course - that's how we get there all the time. Come on!"

Adjusting my scarf over my shoulder again, and grabbing my sunglasses out of my bag, I followed the kids down the street to their favorite eatery, even though I once frequented that very spot when I was their age.

Fourteen: Screw You. Happy Now?

Despite the surprise visitor, I was still able to turn in my case study to Melendez on time. No guarantees that he'll like it, but at least I did my best. Whether or not I aced it was probably the least of my worries as of late. A solid day had passed since that initial rendezvous, and Edgar had luckily stayed away. Maybe he got the hint after all. But I still had the sneaking suspicion that this would not be the last I'd see of my *dear* uncle. I was about to head downstairs to catch up on some reality TV on this relatively uneventful Saturday and munch my way through a bag of chips or two, when I nearly collided with Jet at the top of the stairwell. He had a sort of distant look in his eyes - I could tell because he wasn't able to make eye contact with me. Jet also barely reacted to my klutziness which was odd, since quite literally stepping on his toes usually resulted in me getting treated to some choice words that would make Mom scold him thoroughly if she heard.

But instead, he just mumbled an apology as if it was his fault, and then shuffled back into his own room. I followed him, curious what was bugging him because he definitely wasn't acting like himself.

"Jet? Everything okay?"

"Huh? Yeah, why wouldn't it be?" His face was still glued to his desktop screen, clicking away on some important software program.

"You didn't swear at me when I walked into you. You always hate when I'm a klutz."

"Oh, well in that case, *screw you*. Happy now?"

"If there's no emotion behind it, I won't feel any better."

Jet paused his work long enough to swivel around in his desk chair. He looked me in the eyes, waiting for more of an explanation. "Look, I'm like super busy and I have no idea what you want from me. Can I at least have a hint?"

I ran my fingers through my dirty-blonde hair. "I just wanted to check on you, that's all."

"Well I'm fine."

"You don't seem fine, Jet. Is this about Edgar coming by?"

His palms smacked the surface of his wooden workspace. "Edgar was here? Why did no one tell me?"

I tried to say something more, but he just marched downstairs in a big huff. "Mom. Mom! Why didn't you say anything about Edgar being here? *What* did he want?"

I peeked around the corner of the foyer, waiting for any reaction to his frustration.

"Jet, he was only here for maybe an hour. I was going to call you down, but he said not to bother you about it. He brought by a nice cheese basket…"

"I don't want any part of Edgar or his cheese, I just want him to stay *the hell* out of this house. Since Dad left, I'm the man here, and no one is going to undo the life we've built here. I mean *no one*." His words seethed, carrying their intensity up the stairs and into my ears.

"Jet, it's really okay. He just stopped by, no damage was done."

Jet remained silent, and I imagined that Mom was hugging him, doing her best effort to calm him down after such an outburst.

"If at any point, things are not fine, you gotta tell me so I can beat his sorry ass to a pulp, okay?" His words sounded muffled, likely from resting his head on Mom's shoulder.

"Jefferson, you will do nothing of the sort. But yeah, I'll let you know if anything gets out of hand. Okay?"

Jet mumbled some thinly-veiled expletives after nodding politely and making his way back up the stairs. He shook his head in disbelief and walked right past me, as if I wasn't even there. I found myself following him back into his room to finish the conversation we had started a few minutes ago.

"Okay, so now you know. Big whoop. Can you answer my question now?"

Focusing his tired eyes back on his screen, Jet shrugged. "What question?"

"I asked if you were okay - you don't seem like yourself." I eased myself onto the side of his nearby bed, and crossed my ankles tightly as if the pressure I applied would compel him to spill the beans.

"Vera, I really am fine. Just tired, really. I'm always tired."

"What's that programming company called again? The one you work for, I mean."

"Captain Tus, 'the premier leader in digital communication for gaming and entertainment'." He slurred the company's slogan in a sarcastic sing-song voice as I saw their ridiculous digitized aquatic mascot in a sailor's hat open and close its giant mouth at the corner of the screen. I guess it was supposed to be a play on words, with 'Tus' sounding a bit like 'Tusks' or something like that.

"You don't sound thrilled about it."

"Well, it's very dry, rather boring work and all the other programmers live on the other side of the planet. It pays well enough though."

"Not as fun as *playing* video games I bet?"

"Oh you know it." He continued clicking away on his monitor, always engrossed in his work. "I still do that sometimes though."

I watched his screen for a moment, watching him type endless amounts of code and then merge various groups of data together. None of it made any real sense to me, but I couldn't shake the feeling that the repetitive work was sucking the life out of him. "Well, okay. I guess… I'll just be around - don't want to bug you."

"You're not bugging me." My older brother reassured me pleasantly, but remained glued to his screen, almost in a trance.

"I just know you're busy, so I'll leave you to it." I let myself out of his room, and made my way downstairs. Mom was busy marking up some articles by hand, so I snuck out the front door to avoid interrupting her. I swear, my entire family was a bunch of workaholics. Thankfully, that gene must have skipped me.

It was late afternoon now, and the sun was well into its steady descent. The warm Los Angeles suburban air was calling me, so I decided to take a walk outside by myself. Had to clear my head - there was just too much going on. I grabbed my purse and walked straight out the front door, never looking back.

I wished it was as simple as just Edgar being in town and complicating everything - theoretically it'd be easy to just avoid a person, right? But it wasn't even close to that simple. Beyond all the family drama, I had my own future to worry about. I knew that graduation was only the beginning, and that it would all fall into place eventually. But that didn't do jack squat to help me figure out the here and now.

Making my way down to my favorite local neighborhood park, I saw other locals passing through, often with young toddlers in tow. Some kids my age or even a bit younger were out with their significant others, holding hands and kissing in the waning daylight. I popped a squat on a nearby large rock that was my favorite spot to sit, given its convenient location directly in front of a large palm tree. The still-warm surface made contact with the back of my thighs, and I sighed as I tried to erase the negativity and worry out of my mind. Easier said than done, of course.

And that's when I saw it again. Or, *him*, rather. The longish, light-brown hair ruffled lazily in the warm evening breeze. A grabbed hand, connected to a redhead. They pull closer, holding each other and gazing out over the cliffside and the bustling nightlife growing below. My stomach churned, with a sick, sort of nauseous desperation.

It wasn't jealousy - couldn't be. I was better than that. I *wanted to believe* I was better than that. But I was starting to think I might not be. Judging by the way I had to swallow a scream when I saw them kiss, I was definitely *not* better than that. I could've sworn for a split second that the boy made eye contact with me while hugging his girlfriend. His brown eyes met mine, and I almost saw recognition fill his face, but then the girl captured his surprise with her lips, and he was suddenly engrossed in that. Heck, who wouldn't be? I peeled my eyes away to give them privacy.

I've never actually dated. Not by choice - I'm not some weird celibate nun or something. But heck, for the amount of experience I've had in that particular area, I might as well be. I didn't know why it hasn't happened for me yet - but it just hasn't. Not like I haven't tried, of course. I really have. It's just never gone anywhere. I did all the right things, but I guess I'm just not conventionally attractive enough. Or something. I don't know. Maybe my desperation was showing too much. Although I hope I wasn't too desperate. Nah I definitely was - had to be.

I think a lot of it was due to my rather unconventional childhood. I never did have a lot of friends my age growing up. I also spent a lot of time around mostly adults, since my mom dragged me to just about every nursing home and funeral within a five-mile radius if it involved anyone in our family or even family-adjacent, 'to pay our respects' she said about the latter. But really, that just meant a lot of time spent sucking down hard candy mints and nodding politely while the adults talked. Needless to say, that was a lot of time spent not socializing with kids my age. Add that to my less-than-stellar social scene in elementary through middle school, and I was a pretty awkward twenty-something. I've tried to play catch-up, but it's a scary thought: pushing your mid-twenties and having never even kissed a guy.

I found myself staring at the happy couple again, clenching my fists, and wishing I had what they had. At least, I told myself that was what I wanted. But in reality, I knew that what I wanted was *that* particular boy.

He was a good friend to me, growing up. He lived on my street - still does, actually - and I have so many memories of us spending summers together, throwing family cookouts, going down to the pier to get corndogs and slushies, and just generally being kids. I think the only reason I survived my less-than-ideal childhood was because of him. I don't think I totally realized my feelings for him, until more recently - when it was too late.

66

There wasn't any particular reason as to why we parted ways. I think we just sort of grew apart, as people often do when life gets busier than they can keep up with. It was so subtle at first, maybe six or seven years ago. It was definitely during high school, anyway. It was because he got into music and technology, and I pretty much always had my nose in a book. But that didn't really matter now, and if I could go back and change anything, I'd tell myself to slack off a little more, hang out more with the one friend I actually had, and keep a more open mind in the romance department.

And now I was the pathetic, lovesick overgrown teenager sitting on a rock fighting tears. Of course *this* would happen. I thought a little walk and some time away from my family would clear my head a little, but I think it actually just dug up all the dormant pain instead.

My emotions and memories were really starting to eat away at me. That is, until my tears were dried by a potato sack being pulled over my face.

Fifteen: Punkin

Entering the pizza place was, quite literally, a blast from the past. The grayish carpet covered the entirety of the small room, and the meager handful of tables were grouped together haphazardly depending on how many people were dining at the moment. I saw the main counter wrap its way around the back of the room, and the small door behind it leading to what I assumed was the kitchen where the cook was likely working his way through the mid-afternoon late-lunch rush. The rich and savory aroma of fresh pizza dough, calzones, and pasta filled the air.

"Do you need to look at the menu? Alex and I always get the same thing so we're set to order." Lynn looked up at me politely, and I shook my head. I had my favorite already picked out as well.

"Nah, I'm good to go, thanks. Let's eat, lunch on me." The kids smiled, and I panicked for a sec when I realized that my credit card might arouse some suspicion, so I couldn't use it. I'd have to opt for the cash I had on hand instead.

"Welcome to Luigi's. What can I get for you today?" The perky brunette at the register smiled politely at us, and I started fishing my wallet out of my purse.

"I'll have a small pepperoni pizza, and these two both want buffalo chicken calzones. Add three iced teas to that as well."

She keyed in the order and then told me the total, which I luckily had just enough cash on me to afford. "That'll be out in a bit, please take a seat anywhere."

"Hey, how'd you know what we always order?"

I froze, caught not quite in a lie, but I also had withheld more of the truth than I probably should have. "Uh, lucky guess?" I shrugged to sell my point, and luckily, the very-impressionable middle schoolers bought it - hook, line, and sinker.

That's when I saw him. My - I mean, Lynn's - dad. He was unmistakably standing next to the takeout counter, in his typical construction garb, probably waiting to bring lunch back to his coworkers. My pulse quickened and as the happy tears started threatening to roll down my cheeks, I quickly wiped them off and forced myself to keep my composure. Hugging him like a crazy person would absolutely not do. I steadied myself by grabbing onto the nearest table and breathing deeply.

I smiled stiffly at the kids and handed them their drinks. I had another mission to attend to, besides the obvious one. "Go ahead and pick a table, I'll be right there." They turned away to do just that, but then Lynn saw her dad before I got a chance to say anything to him.

"Hey Dad! Whatcha doing here?" Lynn greeted him pleasantly, giving him a hug. He smiled at her, his face less time-worn and exhausted than I remembered.

"Just grabbing lunch for me and the guys, Punkin. I see you have a new friend?" I shivered as I felt his brown eyes digging into my face for an explanation. At first, it was a cursory glance, and then it grew deeper. His eyes widened in what I assumed was a silent freak-out, but he probably didn't have the means to make sense of his shock anyway. And out of context, it was unlikely that he figured me out anyway. I could feel my whole body relax once his face resumed a normal expression, but his eyes were still glued to me like a moth to a lightbulb.

Lynn paused for a second, and then whispered in my ear: "What's your name again? I think you told us but I forgot." She giggled a bit to herself. That was close - I actually never told her, but she luckily forgot about that. I had to think fast now to keep the wild truth from hitting their ears - before I could adjust it enough to make sense in this bizarre reality.

"Uh, call me Vee." *Not a total lie, just a clever nickname. Perfect.*

"Dad, this is Vee. She said her mom knew Mom, or something. She's visiting us today and took us out to lunch. Cool huh?"

I held my breath, hoping that he wouldn't pry any further. I didn't think he would, but you never really know. To my relief, he

69

just nodded and smiled. He extended his hand and I grasped it firmly, slightly shaking from his close proximity.

"I'm Charlie, Lynn's dad. Nice to meet you, Vee." His face remained relaxed until he saw the scar on my wrist, the one I totally forgot to hide that I got from a scalding cup of tea when I was twelve years old. *Crap.* His mouth rounded into a soft "o", but I pulled it away nonchalantly before he could analyze it any further. My poker face served me especially well in this particular moment, and since I didn't react any further, he didn't either. Instead, he just responded to Lynn's introduction of me. *Phew.* "Okay, that's nice. Have a good time, and don't forget to be back home so we can leave for your art show thing. That's tonight, right?"

He clicked away on his phone next to me, and I noticed a goofy-looking aquatic animal appear on it. It was oddly familiar, but I couldn't pinpoint where I had seen that before. *Where had I seen that logo before?*

Lynn exchanged a quick glance with Alex, and nodded. "No worries, I promise I won't forget. But Vee might take us by a little early, just so you know. Maybe you and Mom can meet us there instead?"

"Oh sure, that'll be fine. I'll let Mom know too. See you guys later."

"Bye, Dad." He smiled at her, picked up the stack of to-go containers and a lone pizza box, and made his way out the door. I exhaled the breath I didn't know I was holding, and turned back to Lynn and Alex who had settled themselves comfortably at a table close to the window overlooking the small parking lot. *I forgot how easygoing he always was. My gosh, I miss him so much.* I caught another tear threatening to fall, shook off the rest of my emotions, and rejoined the kids at the table. They were giggling loudly about who knows what.

"What's so funny?" I smiled at them and took a sip of my peach iced tea.

"I mean I can't wait to see Summer's stupid face when the teachers realize how mean she really is." Alex grinned maniacally - well, as maniacally as a very friendly and sweet-as-pie-all-

70

american-thirteen-year-old-boy could possibly grin. Lynn smiled as well, and I patted her on the back to show my support of their efforts. I had a *very* good feeling about this, and every minute that passed felt closer and closer to the moment of reckoning for those good-for-nothing scumbags that I - I mean, Lynn, was forced to share the classroom with.

"Oh yeah, it's gonna be pretty sweet for sure. I think it's safe to say that I'm really going to enjoy seeing those jerks come to justice too." I winced as I suddenly worried that they might read too far into what I meant by that, but then I remembered that I wove a pretty decent web for myself, so they'd likely just assume that I was rooting for their success. And that was true - I *was* rooting for them as well. It didn't hurt that I also had my own reasons for wanting to see those exclusive snobs get their comeuppance.

Maybe I'd better say something to smooth over everything, just in case. "So um, your dad seems cool."

Lynn nodded. "Yeah, he's pretty great. Comes to all my school things too, even though I know he feels a little out-of-place with all the preppy private school parents."

"Plays sick b-ball too." Alex chimed in, excitedly munching the calzone the waitress just placed carefully in front of him. I winced as a drop of piping hot cheese narrowly avoided scalding his chin.

"That's so great. You're lucky to have him." *Really, truly, very lucky. Hold onto that feeling. You'll miss it later. You'll miss him.*

I dug into my pepperoni pizza, and closed my eyes as the dough hit my taste buds and mixed with the perfectly-blended cheese and meat. *I forgot how good this place was. Way underrated, obviously.*

"So Vee, you said we should get to school early, right? Just to scope it out?"

I nodded and winced as I swallowed a too-large and still-scalding bite of pizza. Putting out the heat with a swig of iced tea, I managed to answer his question. "Yeah, I mean I'd like to sneak you into the classroom and get the external cameras placed. Hopefully the doors are open, but if not, I'll hike you up through the window. We'll figure it out. Just get ready for your, just desserts…" I cringed at my own joke, and the kids were a little slow on the uptake, but then eventually got it.

"Haha, nice one Vee." Lynn rolled her eyes, but she was unable to completely hide the smile poking through her cheese-covered grin.

"What time does the show start again?"

Alex shrugged. "I dunno, seven o'clock I think? But we gotta be in our classroom by six thirty."

"Okay, so let's finish up here, and then maybe hang out at the park until then? It's so nice out." The two kids nodded at my suggestion, and then we continued eating and laughing.

Sixteen: Two Birds Short of a Cuckoo's Nest

"It's just me, don't freak out, okay?"

The potato sack over my head made it significantly more impossible to see what the heck was going on. Looking back, that *was* probably the point though. The burly arms wrapped around my mid-section and expertly pinned my arms to my sides, until the familiar musky scent hit my nose and my heart dropped to my feet.

"Edgar? What the *fudge* are you doing?" While freaking out, I didn't exactly say "fudge" - I actually said something else that would horrify my mom. But it doesn't matter, he deserved it. My whole body was paralyzed with fear, and I didn't know how to process what was going on. My brain was whirring a million miles an hour, and all the self-defense training Mom made me do pretty much went out the window as he carried my useless body to an undisclosed location. I tried to find his face to claw his eyes out, but he was wearing protective goggles. I also tried to kick him hard where I knew it would hurt, but he had me angled just over his shoulder in a way that kept me from reaching that critical area with my foot. My blood boiled, wondering if maybe Edgar was a bit too precise about this for a reason. I tried to get fresh air to my lungs, but the potato sack made that difficult. Plus it reeked of sweat and desperation - or, maybe that was me.

I continued to writhe and wriggle my way out, but my uncle's vice grip on me was just too strong. And the craziest thing about it, was that being carried on his shoulders kind of reminded me of my dad. They were brothers, after all. But the memories flooded back, and I started to feel my face heat up as the tears fell. Everything that had been swirling around in my head started to combust in those tortured moments. And then in the blink of an eye, I found myself seated on a surprisingly cold metal stool, with an odd lingering scent of something dying. Or maybe something already did. I hoped like crazy I wouldn't be next. With my arms free, I tore the potato sack off of my head and looked around. My uncle sat on a wooden chair directly across from me, in what appeared to be a garage with some kind of object covered by an old bed sheet yellowed with age. I saw the door behind him, and I immediately bolted directly to it, trying to get out. It was shut tight, and it didn't take a rocket scientist to figure out who locked it and that he didn't want it to budge. That door was meant to keep me in here. *But why?*

After settling my nerves enough to make eye contact with my should-have-stayed-lost uncle, I exhaled the air I held in my chest and tried to figure out a way out of this creepy, musty, garage. There weren't any cars in here, and I could see the waning evening light outside the glass windows in the large metal panels. I grabbed the nearest golf club and hit a home run on the glass, but it didn't even crack. All through this, my uncle sat in his chair, calmly tapping his calloused hands on his grease-stained knees.

"It's bulletproof, don't even bother." His words crawled out of his face like vermin out of a trash heap - fluidly and without emotion.

I dropped the golf club in frustration, let it clatter loudly on the concrete floor, and looked at my hands. *Maybe I could choke him? Nah, then I'd still be stuck in here. He's gotta stay alive, and conscious, if I ever wanna get out of here.*

"My family thinks I'm just out for a walk. If I don't come home soon, they'll probably call the cops. And guess who the first person they'll think is responsible for it." Deadpanning my logical approach, I hoped to appeal to his better nature.

I expected that to rattle Edgar, but it didn't. He just pulled an all-too-familiar bedazzled gadget out of his pocket. "That would be logical, yes. But they actually think you're staying overnight with a friend. Willow, is it? While you were taking a little nap, I took the liberty of letting them know she invited you over."

My eyes widened, as my uncle's insanity continued to reach new, indescribable heights. I opened my purse and looked for my phone, in utter disbelief that he dug around and found it. "You... you're freaking nuts!" (I didn't say "freaking" though.) "Why the hell did you kidnap me? Like, if there was something you needed to talk about, you know where I live!"

"You refused to talk to me at your house! This was the last resort, I swear. And I'm not going to hurt you."

"Oh really?" I paused for effect. "Then why was I out cold, as you said? You drugged me, didn't you!"

Edgar shook his head, and the slightly over-grown tendrils of straight salt-and-pepper hair mingled with his bushy beard. "I would never do that to you, Vera. It seems you panicked and fainted. I got you to come to with some handy gym socks I found nearby."

Oh so that's what I thought was a dead rat. Dude needs to shower more, or something. Gross. "Well they did the trick. I'm awake now. So *what* do you want, asshat?" My murderous thoughts seemed to slowly melt away as I realized that he didn't intend to cause me any harm - he was just clinically crazy. Regardless, the words seeped out of my mouth like congealed blood, staining my skin as it dripped out.

An off-putting giggle escaped Edgar's throat, causing his beard to jiggle creepily and his oddly-perfect white teeth to stick out like a sore thumb. "Oh, my dear. It's not at all what *I* want; it's what your family wants."

"What kind of bullshit is that?" That was a *bit* more vulgar than I usually was. But I had good reason to be - this guy was two birds short of a cuckoo's nest and he had every right to know that.

"Haven't you noticed, how much they miss my dear brother Charlie? Your father has been absent for too long. Heck, you miss him too, don't you? You don't even have to answer me, I've seen that look in your eyes. I already know."

I shrugged, and crossed my arms across my chest. "Oh really? What look? You come back into the family for a few days and suddenly you think you know me? Fat chance of that."

Edgar stood up, and walked the two feet between the stool I sat on and his wooden chair. "I don't need to know you to know that you miss him. I do too, Vera. And the best thing, is that I've devised a way to prevent him from disappearing *before* he actually does."

"And what makes you think you can do that? Have you been hitting the sauce, Edgar?" Apparently, I get extra sassy when I'm scared out of my mind. Edgar remained unaffected, and simply yanked the old bed sheet off the mysterious object in the middle of the room. It was a metallic cylinder, more round than flat, and seemed to be oddly balanced on the floor. There wasn't a visible stand holding it up, so I found myself staring at the bottom of it, perplexed by its symmetry and spotless stainless-steel exterior.

"No, Vera. I simply accomplished what I've been wanting to do for a very long time." He folded his hands on his lap, and grinned at me with sheer joy - which creeped me out even more.

"Oh? And what's that?" I was starting to be less scared and more curious. Also, listening to the nutcase was beginning to be pretty entertaining. *Who the hell does he think he is?*

"I built a time machine."

And that's when I completely lost it laughing. It felt like something straight out of a sitcom. Either that or I was scared again and decided to process it with humor. "Yeah, right. Did you buy that on eBay? Some kind of movie prop? Congrats, Edgar. You can add that to your geek collection. Very impressive. Next thing you're probably working on is getting your hands on a DeLorean, right?" I started the typical slow-clap, and nodded my head in false approval with my lips pursed together in a distinguished frown. He remained silent until I got tired of clapping and nodding.

"You done yet?"

"I dunno, are you done being delusional?"

"It works, Vera. I tested it."

"Oh yeah, I'm sure it does. You threw a ball through one end of it and it teleported across the room. Gotcha. That's *real* useful."

"It is useful. But that's not what it does. And you're going to see for yourself."

"I'm *what*?"

"I'm going to send you back in time."

76

Then I giggled again, and couldn't stop. "You're really something, Uncle. You know, since the dogsledding thing didn't work out, you could totally be a comedian. I bet you'd sell out the pier on Saturday nights or something..." I continued laughing until I felt my uncle's gross sweaty hand covering my mouth and I suddenly wanted to vomit.

"Vera, *shut up*." He pulled his hand away from my mouth after those venom-filled monotone words oozed out of his lips.

"Gross, you know, there's this new invention called soap, you could use some."

"Vera, I'm serious. I know how you can keep your dad from disappearing."

"Yeah, okay, I'm sure you do."

"I do though. It's quite simple, I've calibrated the machine to molecularly transport you back in time to maybe about a week or so before he left. If you can find out what happened, or even stop it from happening, you could change this reality and your family wouldn't have to know a life without him anymore. Isn't that what you want?"

"Yeah, sure, in some alternate universe with a new set of physics that would accommodate it, then sure. That'd be nice."

"You could enact some revenge on your unpleasant classmates as well, while you're at it."

I still didn't buy the hogwash he was putting out, but I figured that as long as I was stuck here, I might as well humor him. Tilting my head back to let the fluorescent overhead lights wash over my frayed nerves and my lingering fears, I paused to let my brain come up with a decent response to his bizarre ideas. But then a question popped into my head that needed to be answered immediately. My head snapped back to normal posture again.

"How did you know about that?"

Edgar smirked. "Vera, you must have forgotten that I was still in the picture for your rather... tumultuous middle school years."

Recalling those years made my insides hurt, like they were being squeezed over and over again by a juicer or something. But as the memories trickled, and then completely broke through in a gushing current, I did remember how my dad had told Edgar how difficult school was for me. Not academically, just socially. And how there was really no explanation for it. I nodded my head slowly, somewhat relived to be understood, but also terrified that he had a very clear look into my past that could tangibly affect me even now.

"I think the two might be linked."

"What?"

"I think that the close proximity of the bullying you sustained that year, to the day your father disappeared, suggests they could be linked." In hindsight, he couldn't be more wrong about that, but the theory was a decent one.

"Okay. But what does that have to do with me?"

Seventeen: Carrot Sticks Dipped in Frosting

I followed the kids out of the restaurant and we made our way back to the park where we had all met this morning. It was an odd feeling of double deja-vu, but I shook it off and tried to just soak in the excitement of what we were going to pull off. I settled back onto a familiar wooden bench, and watched as Alex and Lynn ran around on the wooden play structure together. I envied their carefree mindsets, and was comforted to see that their connection was one that appeared to be lasting. Appeared, I mean. Because I knew the end of that particular story, and it wasn't what I would have hoped.

I cringed for a moment as Lynn almost fell off one of the platforms, but Alex's quick reflexes caught her before that could happen. She smiled at him, and I noticed him blush considerably, and then let go of her, crossing his arms shyly over his chest and then suddenly staring at his feet. *I've gotta figure out how to solidify that whole thing for them before I go home. It was meant to be, and neither of them can see that at all. Hard to believe I was ever really that clueless.*

"Hey guys, do either of you know what time it is? Maybe we should head over to the school?" I patted the bag next to me on the bench full of Alex's dad's camera and other tech. Which reminded me - hopefully it was okay that Alex had borrowed it for our purposes. Given how proficient he seemed to be with the gadgets, I doubted this was his first time using them.

Lynn checked the bright pink watch she always wore on her left wrist. "It's almost five-thirty, just about an hour before we have to check in with Miss Sullivan."

"Perfect. What do ya say we head on over to school? Hopefully, you can find Bert and Ricky and let them in on our little plan while you're at it."

Alex smirked at Lynn and they both climbed down to meet me at the bench, and then we started walking down the street toward their school. I hiked Alex's bag over my shoulder and the two kids walked slightly ahead of me, whispering excitedly and sharing secrets. They turned back to make sure I was right behind them, which I was. I couldn't get lost on this route even if I tried, but they didn't know that. As we approached the brick building with all the outdated, tiny windows and dandelion-covered grass, I felt myself get even more creeped out by the memories that kept flooding back.

"Okay, so do you guys wanna see if the door's open?" Lynn nodded and tried the big, metal storm door under the overpass.

"Looks like it's locked."

"Maybe we can try another door?"

Alex motioned for us to follow him to the main door that was completely glass, and there appeared to be an intercom system. "I'll ask if they can let us in." He stepped up to the intercom machine and held a button. "Uh, hi, Alex Halliday here. Can I be let in to get a book I left in the classroom?"

I panicked as there was a bit of hesitation, but a nasal female voice granted his wish and buzzed the door open. "Come on in."

Lynn and I rushed in behind him, and tried to discreetly get up the stairs. I had to remind myself to let the kids lead the way to the classroom, even though I knew it all too well.

"Here's the classroom." Alex pointed to a cheerfully decorated wooden door in an otherwise dreary hallway. Trying the doorknob proved fruitless, however.

"It's locked. Now what?"

I sighed. "I mean, we could get back outside and try the window. Is there a tree you could climb?"

Lynn nodded her head. "No problem! I love climbing trees."

I shook my head vigorously. "Not in that outfit you're not. Any tree sap will show on those pants and blouse. Have Alex do it, he's wearing darker colors anyway. Do you feel up to it, Alex? You don't have to though, your concealed microphones might be enough anyway."

Lynn shook her head. "Oh no, we really need video footage as well. I'm not sparing any chance for them to not see exactly who the problem really is." Alex agreed.

"Yeah, I guess you're right. Okay Alex, I'll help you get into the tree. From there, hopefully you can open the window. Or at least, maybe attach the cameras outside the window to catch what happens in the classroom."

We made our way out of the hallway and down the stairs, and that's when we saw Ricky And Bert. I recognized them immediately, but had to pretend I didn't.

"Hey guys, whatcha doing here so early?" Ricky smiled politely at Alex and Vera while absentmindedly bouncing a basketball under his palm, and Bert remained relatively silent digging around in his lunchbox for something to munch on. That is, until he addressed the elephant in the room.

"Who's she?"

Lynn stepped in to clarify before things got too confusing. "Her mom is a friend of my mom's, so she's hanging out with us today. Or something like that."

Both boys seemed satisfied with that, and then I slyly elbowed Alex to remind him to let them in on our genius plan.

"Oh yeah, um, we're sort of... working on something. Something important. I'll uh, tell you outside. Come on." Bert and Ricky followed us back outside. "What were you guys doing here early anyway?"

Bert shrugged. "My mom was helping the sewing group with something."

"Yeah and my mom was reorganizing the gym closet, or whatever. I dunno." Both boys were often stuck at school at odd hours due to their moms being involved in various different capacities as teachers or classroom aids.

We got outside and Lynn pointed out the window leading into their classroom. "It's that one, with the blue curtains."

"Wait what are you doing?" Ricky stopped bouncing the basketball just long enough to get the gist of what was going on.

Alex smirked as I boosted him up to the closest tree near the second-story window. I handed him the bag as carefully as I could once his footing was secure. "We're going to get cold, hard, evidence that our classmates are jerks, once and for all."

The two boys' eyes widened, but their smiles grew even larger. "Amazing. How do you plan to do that though?" Bert was enthused, but not totally convinced our idea could be anything more than just that. Meanwhile, I did my best to keep any onlookers from sabotaging our carefully devised plan. Alex was busy climbing now, so Lynn picked up the slack.

"We're wearing hidden microphones that will pick up the stupid things they say to us, and then the camera that Alex is going to plant in the windowsill will get visual footage of what they do. That way, even when Miss Sullivan isn't in the room, or isn't paying attention to us, we'll have proof that Hazel, Chloe, Summer, Sue, and Wyatt are just awful people that need to be punished."

"Or maybe even expelled!" Alex yelled excitedly from the window, where he managed to ease it open enough to clip the hidden camera on a nearby potted plant. He carefully made his way back down, and then gave everyone a big thumbs up.

"I dunno, that seems way too easy. Do you think they'll buy it?" Bert gnawed casually on a carrot stick dipped in vanilla frosting.

"Of course they will! They can't ignore what they see with their own eyes." Alex dusted off his jeans and grinned. In my heart, I hoped he was right, but I honestly doubted it. I've seen some pretty asinine things in my time, and I had a sinking suspicion this could be one of those things. But there was still a chance it would end the bullying. We'd find out soon enough, anyway.

"Okay, well, I'm in. What do I gotta do?" Bert polished off his carrot sticks, and then reached for some Oreos to dip into his Thermos of clam chowder.

"Nothing, except try to angle the stupidity toward the window where the camera is. And if you'd like to wear a hidden wire under your shirt, we've got extras of those too." I motioned to Alex's bag, which he promptly opened and grabbed two more wired mics. Bert put his oddly-paired snack away and reached for one, as did Ricky. Alex showed them how to fasten them properly, and then they were ready to go.

"So when anything obnoxious starts happening, try to click that red button right there, and then it'll record everything you say and everything they say to you. After tonight, you'll hopefully have multiple recorded examples of them being asses to you." I smiled gleefully at my younger compatriots. "I've got a very good feeling about this, guys. I hope you're ready for your life to change for the better."

"Vee, it's six-fifteen. Maybe we should start heading back in?"

I nodded. "Sure thing. I'll hang out in the gym where the art is. See you in a bit, and good luck!" I gave Lynn and Alex a hug, and noticed that Alex clung onto me just a *tiny* bit too long. Oh, the irony - if only he knew.

Eighteen: Slumber Party With a Scorpion

"You are the one in the middle of it all. Theoretically, you would be able to do the most good for the situation. And as his daughter, you have enough incentive to actually go through with this."

I crossed my arms over my chest. "That *may* be true, but you can't force me to do this. That is, assuming by some freak accident that you actually did figure out time travel. And I'm still not buying it."

Edgar tapped his gritty fingertips on the stainless steel exterior of the machine. "It doesn't matter if you believe me or not. You're going to want to do this - I just have to figure out how to make you aware of that fact."

One of the many weird things about Edgar, was that he always functioned as if he lived inside someone else's head. His ideas were never internal - or completely external, for that matter. But rather, he processed the world like his consciousness was a traveling virus infecting those around him and allowing him to see their most private thoughts and ideas. There was something almost occult about such a sensation, and I didn't like it one bit. I found myself subconsciously looking for some kind of tarot cards or something, but there was nothing like that in the garage I found myself imprisoned in. Just, me, Edgar, and the machine. Or rather, the big hunk of steel that he *claimed* was a time machine. Fat chance of that.

"I can prove it to you."

"Oh really? Be my guest."

Edgar smirked with glee and yanked another sheet off of a nearby terrarium on the counter. I didn't see anything in there at first, until I got a closer look and screamed.

"That's... that's a scorpion. What the hell are you doing with a scorpion? Are you gonna torture me?" And that's when the panic settled in again, full-boar. But Edgar remained pretty calm. I mean, of course he would be - no one trapped *him* in a garage with a mysterious hunk of metal.

"It's not what I'm doing with it - because at the moment, nothing at all. Except using it to prove to you that time travel is real - because I've already done it many times."

"Uh-huh, sure. Okay. You still haven't convinced me though, because I haven't seen it."

Edgar covered the terrarium again, and then sat on the stool directly in front of me. "You didn't *see* it, but you *felt* it." His rank breath hit my face, but I was too creeped out to wince too much this time.

"You're going to have to be more specific."

"You didn't sleep very well the other night, correct?"

I shrugged. I had no idea how he knew that, but it wasn't the weirdest thing he's said to me since he's been back home. Not even by a long shot. "Correct. But how do you know that?"

"I suppose I should apologize for that actually, Vera. I went back in time and interrupted your slumber, solely for the purpose of using it for proof later."

I could feel my blood running cold and congealing in my veins. My head also felt light, as if it was about to detach itself and float away from my body. "You what?"

He lifted the covering off the terrarium again. "My little stinger-laden friend here and I are the first time-travelers this world has ever seen. This morning, I brought him into the machine with me, and set the time and location of your bedroom at approximately midnight the other night. Then I carefully let him into your blankets to uh, *cuddle*."

"Yeah right, of course, like I can believe..." And that's when it hit me - the other night, when I couldn't sleep, I could've sworn I felt something with legs crawling all over me. I had assumed it was just a bad dream from all the stress I'd been under... but now, it turns out it was a time-traveling scorpion from my crazy uncle. "Oh my gosh... that *was you!*" I stood up quickly from my stool, pointing my finger in his crusty face. "Why... how... what?" Suddenly I felt the spindly legs all over me again.

"Don't worry, I only let him stay at your little slumber party for a couple hours. I quickly collected him and then returned back to the present time. I knew it would have a better effect if I made you think you had imagined it the whole time." He slapped his knee and cackled in my face, as if this whole thing was just absolutely hilarious.

My mouth had long-since fallen open, and despite Mom always reminding me to breathe through my nose instead, I just let my jaw hang slack until I realized how freaky this whole thing was. After I got over the initial awkwardness of my weird uncle creeping in my bedroom at night though, I found myself wondering how that proved time-travel was real after all. "Oh my gosh it bit me! I gotta go to the ER, that thing might be poisonous! I have this ugly rash." I grabbed Edgar by his greasy shirt collar, but he calmly shook his head.

"Nope, you're fine. I bought him from the local pet store down the street, and they remove the venom before selling these little guys. He still can sting with his tail though, which leaves the nasty gash you probably noticed. Don't worry your pretty little head about it."

I let go of his shirt collar, but not to be polite. "Okay, you're officially a freaking weirdo, just in case there was any doubt before. Newsflash, you still are. But that still doesn't prove that you time-traveled. You could've just brought the scorpion over in the present time and left it in my room."

He shrugged. "Well, perhaps that could be true, except the receipt from the pet store says that I made my purchase earlier this afternoon." He held the small slip of thin paper in front of me, and my eyes widened when I saw it. My freaking uncle bought a scorpion this afternoon - but tortured me with it like two nights ago.

I felt silence crawl down my throat without permission, and his smug grin reflected off the sheen of his immaculately polished garage floor.

"Then I traveled two days in the past, to your room."

86

"That's not sketchy at all." I crossed my arms again feeling pretty damn violated after all this. And still super freaked out, but lacking words to properly lay out this guy who desperately needed his scrawny ass kicked.

"No, of course it's not. You see why I did that now." My sarcasm clearly went right over this dipstick's head.

"No, not really."

He sighed with frustration, not totally unlike my math teachers over the years while explaining a concept to me for the umpteenth time. "I need you to go back in time before your father disappeared, maybe then you'll be able to stop him. Geez Vera, how hard is that to understand?"

"Well you know, it's totally logical until you factor in the laws of physics. But it seems you somehow… broke those?"

"Haven't you heard? Rules are meant to be broken."

I shrugged. "I guess that's one way to look at it." I couldn't shake the feeling there was more I should say or do to get myself out of this situation, but I continuously kept pulling a blank. "And you're still convinced I'm going to *want* to do this? Hah - as if."

Edgar didn't even flinch at my caustic words - it's almost as if he knew all my angles before I even took them, and then knew exactly what to say to mess with my resolve. Easily the most unsettling dynamic I'd ever experienced. Zero out of ten, would not recommend.

"You will *want* to do this because you miss your dad too. And now, you might be able to bring him back. This is an opportunity most people would sell their souls for, Vera."

"Oh, that explains it then - so you're the devil. Okay, yeah that lines up then."

Edgar chuckles. "No, I can assure you I'm not. He's much more efficient and delegates better than I do."

He was kidding, but nothing this guy said was even remotely funny. Then again, nothing is funny when you're trapped in a garage with your crazy uncle.

"I just mean, you'd be foolish to blow this."

"Well then, call Barnum and Bailey, measure my feet for giant shoes, and stick a ball on my nose because I must be a clown." Even though I had nowhere to go, I found myself marching to the corner of the garage and facing away from him, moving myself as far from that freak as possible. Which, was only about ten feet at most, but it was better than nothing. I heard his footsteps creep closer and closer to me, and I froze until a massive crunching noise filled my ears and I turned around to see the instant bulging of the garage door, gaping at the blunt force collision from a vehicle of some sort. I backed away from it, feeling my back hit the rear wall of Edgar's garage, completely shaking at this point.

Edgar screamed some expletives and grabbed the very same golf club I used to threaten him with minutes ago as a weapon. Squaring his feet, my uncle was equal parts perplexed, but also ready to fight. Strong fingers reached around the edge of the broken garage door, and peeled the pliable metal open enough to sneak through. Edgar marched right up to the offending figure, but stopped as soon as he saw who it was.

My brother's characteristic tanned skin and overgrown sun-bleached blonde hair just like mine emerged from the opening, obscured only by the motorcycle helmet he wore.

"Vera, get on my bike. We're out of here. Edgar, go to hell." I quickly followed his simple instructions, squeezing through the forced opening of the garage door, grabbing the spare helmet out of the bike's compartment, and buckling it on as Jet revved the ignition. I placed my hands around his waist just as he peeled out of there, leaving Edgar watching us through the broken garage door. I felt my blood pressure steadily rise and fall, both with the anticipation of getting home in one piece, but also with the insanity that I had witnessed from our certifiably deranged uncle. And the worst part of it all was that I no longer doubted him as much as I did.

The guy was definitely crazy, but he had an alarming amount of cold, hard, proof that was hard to counteract in my own head. I tossed around these ideas amongst the anxiety of being kidnapped, and let my eyes settle on the crisp, clear night sky flying past us like a swarm of lightning bugs. Familiar ocean air caressed my face in a comforting embrace, but the salty taste of it reminded me to stay alert even in the face of familiarity.

The stars twinkled above our heads as we made our way home, but all was not right in our world.

Not by a long shot.

Nineteen: Pink Slip

I told them I'd wait in the gym with the artwork, but somehow, this moment was far too entertaining to miss. Instead, against my own best judgment, I found myself slinking stealthily back up the stairs after my younger counterparts. They went straight down the hall, back to their classroom. The trap was set, and I knew that within the next thirty minutes or so, they'd have all the proof they'd need. The idea was thrilling, to say the least. And at this point, I was far too invested to maintain a healthy distance - emotionally or otherwise. So I found myself seated on a bench in the hallway as discreetly as possible. If anyone asked, I'd just say I was someone's older cousin or something. After all the craziness that'd been happening, this excuse was the least of my worries at the moment.

The familiar smell of paper, books, and sweat filled my nose as I sat and waited in this stuffy middle school hallway, not so unlike a hunter setting their trap or a fisherman relaxing with a baited line. Overly positive posters and motivational classroom decor littered the walls - what a load of good that did. *Maybe they ought to invest more time in enforcing kindness instead of throwing some thumbtacks at the situation and calling it a done deal. There's a wild idea for ya.*

I crossed my legs and tried to busy myself with my phone, until I realized that the model of my iPhone might not look like it belongs here. Without a better option, I covered it with my hand and pretended to tap away on it, even though it obviously didn't get service here. And that's when the pint-sized miscreants started to roll in.

Summer appeared at the end of the hallway first - her dirty blonde, stringy hair flopped like straw over her forehead, and she walked over to the classroom with Sue, Wyatt, and Chloe in tow. I felt somewhere between hot anger and lukewarm hilarity at the way they carried themselves - it felt like something straight out of a teen movie. You know the one - the typical cool kids who are convinced they can do no wrong no matter how wretched they actually are to

90

the main character. I forced myself to stop staring so intensely and went back to busying myself on my temporarily useless phone.

I felt their eyes flit over me absent-mindedly, and then they marched into the classroom like they owned the place. Heck, I wouldn't be surprised if they did - the way they so conveniently avoided punishment on a consistent basis implied there had to be some favoritism involved. I followed their strides with my eyes and waited for the real fun to begin. Lynn and Alex were casually chatting near the very window we bugged earlier, just like we had discussed. And just when I started to worry that maybe the classmates would decide to behave themselves on a total fluke for once, Summer did what she does best and started being a little "witch with a b".

I couldn't hear what she was saying from my vantage point, but I saw Alex's eyes widen a little and then look away toward the floor. Lynn rolled her eyes and flipped her hair in Summer's direction, while Wyatt feigned shock and started to call over their teacher. His still high-pitched yet-to-change boy voice reverberated over the dingy wall-to-wall classroom carpet and garish pastel blue painted concrete walls.

"Miss Sullivan, *she* just rolled her eyes at Summer! *And* flipped her hair. That's *so rude* right?" He rolled his eyes and smirked at Lynn with a knowing glance, once again trying to get her to panic. Much to my distaste, it worked. His smug brown eyes sparkled maliciously under his dorky haircut, punctuated by the metallic gleam of his braces on his rounded, plump face.

"She did, we saw it too." Chloe chimed it, letting her words lilt in an over-confident slang, taking a step closer to Lynn as if to throw her meager skinny weight around. Her tan complexion was only the tip of the iceberg in regards to how different she was from Lynn and Alex - with the main difference being, Lynn and Alex weren't bullies.

"Yeah, that wasn't nice." Summer adjusted her black-rimmed glasses to the edge of her nose, as if pretending to be the teacher herself, and Sue crossed her arms, refusing to take an obvious side even though we all knew where her loyalties layed.

"I'm sorry, I uh, didn't mean to, I just… felt bad." Lynn stammered her words, and I could see her face reddening from the hallway. Her subtle glances toward her teacher showed she was bracing herself for the impact. Her anticipation for the backlash was palpable, even from where I sat. The poor girl was paralyzed by fear. That pissed me off to see that again. But I was even more pissed off to *feel* that again.

Luckily, Miss Sullivan seemed too busy organizing folders in the back of the room by the filing cabinet to care. She brushed a stray piece of auburn hair out of her eyes. "Guys, can you just relax for a bit? The spring art show will be starting soon. I gotta tidy up these folders, okay? Gotta have the room looking nice for the parents and grandparents. Lynn, be nice, okay? Slip up again and I'll have to send a note home." I sighed, relieved that she didn't give Lynn hell for that, but I also felt giddy that whatever the stupid kids had said to her, was caught on camera. But then I realized that their teacher had not-so-subtly implied that Lynn had done something wrong too, and my blood boiled all over again.

"You're all too fatuous to realize how mean you're being." Lynn mumbled that under her breath, but it was still loud enough for me to make out from where I was seated in the hallway. It also helps that she had since moved away from the window and more toward the center of the room. I was glad to be able to hear more, but also knew that the cameras would only reach so far. Good thing she and Alex, as well as the other kids, were wearing concealed microphones.

"What was that?" Hazel piped in, having just walked past me and into the classroom as Lynn mumbled that last thought. Her tight ponytail bobbed as she drew attention to Lynn's feeble attempt to grow a backbone.

"I dunno, I think she called us *fat*." Wyatt smirked again, and put up a pretty convincing front that he was genuinely upset.

"No she didn't!" Bert jumped in, trying to get the bullies off Lynn's back. But their personalities were too strong even for him to dilute - like a tall glass of vodka left out in the sun to ferment past its prime.

"RUDE!" Summer and Chloe whined in unison, as I could see Lynn shrinking into the corner again. Alex sat by her and patted her on the back in support as Bert and Ricky calmly positioned themselves nearby so their microphones could pick up the audio.

"Hang on, I'll look it up. How do you spell that?" Hazel grabbed the big dictionary by the door, her pale face emphasized by a ponytail pulled so tightly that it seemed to make the skin of her face appear almost translucent. The plainest of the bunch, the girl could've used a little makeup. Or a truck load. Her only "lipstick" was an occasional spaghetti sauce stain outlining her lips - and even that was uneven. But regardless, her backstabbing tendencies made her appear even uglier from the inside out, no matter how much her ears protruded from her boring skull. "Okay, I've got it. It means… stupid. Stupid? She just called us stupid!"

"Oh my *gosh* Hazel, not again…" Alex didn't even try to hide his distaste.

"Alex! We do not use the Lord's name in vain." Miss Sullivan reappeared from behind the filing cabinet door just long enough to chastise Alex for a truly *heinous* crime, apparently.

"But I didn't! I said *gosh…*"

"Doesn't matter, close enough. One more time and I'm giving you a pink slip. This is your last warning."

He mumbled an apology and then stared out the window, mumbling something about them being too stupid to recognize the different synonyms for the word.

Hazel stared at him with a smug, closed-mouth smirk.

Lynn shrugged, and tried to drown out the stupidity around her. But then, and I almost missed it from my vantage point - Alex smiled at her. And then she smiled back. He quickly squeezed her hand, and their shared realization that the bullies were unknowingly sealing their own fate was pretty comforting.

"Ooooh you like her!" Sue pointed at them, and then adjusted her purple headband. "Look, they're holding hands."

"No we're not." Alex stood up to emphasize his point. "We're just friends, you know that. That is, you *would* know that if your head wasn't so far up your-"

"That's it! Alex, I'm writing you a pink slip. Pretty pathetic to get one outside of school hours, but that's on *you*." Miss Sullivan always seemed to jump into action just when the good kid finally got agitated enough to slip up the slightest bit. Her staccato reprimand reverberated off of the uselessly golden-rule covered walls.

His face fell visibly, with his prominent eyebrows sinking down his face, but it wasn't surprise that registered on his face. No - it was expectation. Business as usual in this place, I'd imagine. And from what I've heard from Lynn and Alex, it wasn't just Miss Sullivan who seemed to catch all the wrong things - it was all the teachers. "Okay, whatever." He begrudgingly took the slip from her and shoved it in his pocket. My heart went out to the kid, and I hoped that this plan would do the trick for them both.

I felt myself settle into the uncomfortable bench I was in, trying to process the tension that seemed to bleed out of the open classroom door and into the hallway where I was casually camping out for the time being. It seemed that things had mostly settled down, until I saw Wyatt put his hands on Lynn's shoulders out of nowhere.

He wasn't hurting her, just asserting improper dominance. And Miss Sullivan's head was deep enough in the filing cabinet again that she didn't even notice. That's when I silently hoped that Alex would slyly be able to angle the hidden camera from the window at him. As if reading my mind, he grabbed the small potted plant that he placed the camera in, and angled it at Wyatt. *Atta boy.*

"Get. Your. Hands. Off. Of. Me."

Wyatt didn't budge. "Oh yeah? And what are you gonna do about it?"

Lynn shoved them off alarmingly fast, and then Wyatt placed them there again, onto her shoulders, but pushed her back into the wall. Her eyes widened, and Alex looked back over at their teacher, who was far too engrossed in whatever was on her desk to care.

Lynn ducked out of his grasp and walked to the other side of the room, and sat down wordlessly. Alex followed, but strategically placed himself in between her and Wyatt. Summer and the other lackies seemed to be whispering about who knows what, with their grimy fingers blocking their lips and staring at Lynn and and Alex intermittently. Things were silent aside from their idle chattering, and luckily Wyatt scampered away to join them. But this time, he reappeared with a mechanical pencil. He handed it to Summer, and she marched over to Alex.

"Give me your hand."

"Why?"

"Just do it, moron."

"No."

Seemingly another word she'd have to look up in the dictionary to understand, she grabbed his hand anyway and forcibly drew a heart on it with the mechanical pencil. He tried to pull away, but not before she scrawled some very specific letters on his skin.

"Hey! Not cool, Summer." Alex tried to grab some nearby hand sanitizer to scrub it off, but it wouldn't budge.

"Why are you always bothering us? Do you *really* have nothing better to do?" Lynn tried to stick up for Alex, but it didn't take a rocket scientist to know this wasn't going to go well.

"Well now everyone who sees Alex's hand will know you guys like each other." Summer sung the words like the latest annoying pop song on the radio - long, drawn out, and endlessly peppy.

"But we don't! I don't like him…"

The bully's smirk oozed over her face, and her glasses seemed to punctuate her superiority complex with their noticeable frames outlining her murky gray eyes.

Even Bert just started nibbling nervously on some pizza pockets dipped in a strawberry protein shake. "Yummy, strawberry shake and cheesy cheese!" *Definitely not helping our case with the added weirdness, buddy. I can see from the hallway that you're a bit odd.*

"Back off, jerk." Alex tried to ameliorate things with that mumbled attempt at defense, and seeing how he already got a pink slip anyway, it's not like he had much more to lose.

"That's bull!" Summer rolled her eyes and looked back at her entourage, hoping they'd back her up, ironically for rolling her eyes just like Lynn did. Double standard, anyone?

"Did you just swear at him?" Lynn caught the blunt end of that exchange, and probably hoped like heck that it was caught on audio, video, or both.

But before any of that could escalate more than it already has, Miss Sullivan looked up from her desk work. "All right, it's almost time for the show. Everyone line up, and we'll head over." I took that as my cue to get out of the hallway before anyone could see me. But before I could turn around, something truly asinine started brewing.

"Hey, Alex, what's in that plant you're holding?"

Twenty: A Disconcerting Metamorphosis

Jet pulled into our driveway, and sat wordlessly for a moment. I'm sure he had a million questions about what happened, and my available answers were definitely limited. He took his helmet off revealing his sandy blonde hair and dismounted, probably waiting for me to start talking. The comfortably warm spring nighttime breeze soothed my frayed nerves as my pulse started to return to a normal rate.

"What. When. How. Feel free to jump in anytime."

"I'm okay, thanks for asking." I didn't mean for that to sound as sassy as it did - I was grateful that he rescued me, but something in my gut was keeping me from kissing the ground he walked on. I appreciated my brother, but there were just too many ideas fighting for dominance in my head.

"I know you're okay - it's because I figured out you needed help and busted in there to get you away from that psycho. What the hell did he even want with you anyway?" Jet lowered his voice as his face turned slightly red. "He didn't... touch you, did he? I'll kill him."

"No! I mean, of course not. He just... needed my help with something." *I have no idea why I'm defending him right now. This is nuts. Maybe I'm nuts. Something weird is going on.*

"Oh yeah? And what was that? Did he call you on the phone like a normal person or drag you there by force?" Jet crossed his arms, clearly wanting to settle this matter before we re-entered the house.

"No yeah - that part was definitely weird. He threw a potato sack over my head and brought me to his house where he keeps his time machine. I guess I passed out from fear. Crazy huh?"

"No, he's crazy. It's a good thing that I noticed your text message was a little weird. The dude used way too many emojis. Like a whole text of them. Hearts, sparkles, puppies, unicorns, you name it. And you never do. So then I tracked your phone to his house, which was an address I didn't recognize, and realized something was off." He paused for a second as my explanation took root in his head. "Wait, a time machine? What the hell?"

I felt myself exhale. "Yeah, I dunno, the guy's a freak." I let that last part escape my lips to appease Jet. In reality, I knew that machine was the real deal. He proved it to me, after all. But for some reason, I didn't want anyone to know about it yet. Maybe I was still processing it all. "Thank you, Jet." I ran over to hug him, and his body stiffened like lead weight.

"What's eating at you now? I'm okay - Edgar didn't attack me. It's okay, really."

Jet's eyes widened. "No, but you were kidnapped. I think we gotta file this, Vera. The guy needs help. He crossed way too many lines."

My own back stiffened, and something in me felt the odd need to prevent that at all costs. I tried to push past him toward our front door, but his hand lightly touched my shoulder, keeping me away from it. "Does Mom know?"

Jet shook his head. "I didn't want to worry her until I was sure, she's got enough going on with work and all the other family stuff. But I gotta tell her now, sis. We gotta do something about this."

I shrugged. "Whatever. Can we go inside now?" I finally got past him.

"Hey, you're welcome for saving your life."

"I wasn't dying."

"Yet."

"Whatever."

Jet followed me in the house, and we found Mom asleep on the couch with the news still on the TV.

"She's asleep. We should tell her tomorrow."

Jet swore under his breath. "No, we should tell her *now*. This is important, Vera!" He raised his voice slightly above a whisper, but Mom was still sound asleep.

I checked the clock on the wall. "It's past midnight, Jet. We'll talk to her tomorrow, she needs her sleep. It'll be okay for one day."

"What if that psycho attacks you in your sleep or something?"

I definitely avoided mentioning the whole overnight scorpion fiasco, because I knew Jet would absolutely flip out. And yeah, flipping out was definitely warranted. But since I'd been on the business end of the brotherly interrogation, I thought it was in my best interest to avoid it.

"He won't. At least, I don't think. Heck, camp out on my bedroom floor if it makes you feel better. But I think it can wait until morning. We'll talk to Mom then and see what she wants to do. Okay?"

Jet reluctantly nodded, probably only because he had worked all day and was pretty exhausted himself. "Alright, kiddo. Get some sleep, we can handle it in the morning. But I'm still gonna worry, that's what I do." He then made his way up the stairs, finally leaving me to my own devices.

After draping a light blanket over Mom, I climbed the stairs to my room and nearly collapsed on my bed from the adrenaline. Being kidnapped could do that to a person, I guess. I still hated the way it sounded though - I mean yeah, 'kidnapped' was the operative word, but it felt far too serious for the situation. My uncle didn't mean any harm to come to me, he just felt that I was the best person for the job. Plus, he did claim that he tried to talk to me about it and I ignored him. Yeah there are still better methods than abducting a person, but at least his heart was in the right place. *'Heart in the right place?' What? Okay, now I'm losing my mind. That's not actually valid. Is it? Could it be?*

I forced myself to take a shower, mostly to scrub the remnants of my uncle's sweat off of me. And then I realized it - I left my purse at his house. *My purse, with my phone, wallet, and everything. In Edgar's garage. Fudge. I'm so screwed.* I knew that Jet was ready to divide and conquer, crime and punishment style.

Which is all good and fine, except that I still needed my stuff back. And in the very back of my mind, I could feel a sort of buzzing. I was curious - deathly curious - about that machine. It seemed so real to me - too real. And although the scorpion thing still has some margin of error, I know that I saw that receipt. And it would be hard to fake that, especially paired with my night of tossing and turning that was still vivid in my head.

Maybe I can sneak out in the morning and get my stuff from Edgar's house. The thought solidified in my head - a ton of bricks weighing down my better judgment. Venturing back to his house filled me with dread, but the curiosity outweighed it by a long shot. *I'd collect my things and get another look at that machine. Maybe then I'd be able to put my curiosity to rest.*

As I resolved myself to that plan of action, I found that sleep came comfortably this time, thankfully without any spindly creatures crashing the party. Sinking into my bed, I closed my eyes and seemed to open them mere moments later to the early Sunday morning light shining through my window - a sure sign of a good night's sleep.

Then I found myself getting dressed and grabbing my car keys - luckily, they weren't in my purse when I went for that walk last night, so they were still on my dresser. After throwing on some jeans and a comfortable tee, downing some orange juice and a large piece of banana bread, and heading out to my car, I turned on the ignition and realized that without an address, I'd have to find his house based on backtracking from memory. From the back of Jet's motorcycle last night in the dark, I wasn't able to take any clear mental notes, but I figured that I could do my best from memory. After all, I really had no other choice. I turned out of my driveway slowly as to not wake Jet - ideally, I'd hope to be back here before he or Mom even noticed I was gone. At seven in the morning on a Sunday, it's a pretty safe bet that they'd both still be fast asleep. I did leave a note for Mom on the kitchen counter saying I had to run an errand though, just in case.

I started driving leisurely down my street, and then had to stop the car for someone crossing the street. I paused for a moment

100

and then I saw him - that familiar mop-top brown hair framed by thick eyebrows and an athletic physique made even more attractive by his musician status. His brown eyes met mine and I kept the car in park while rolling down my window. Trotting up to my open window, he shyly smiled at me.

"Uh, hey there Lynn." He stared down nervously at his shoes, adorably. I could feel my skin melting just at his closer proximity. You know, from inside my car while he stood outside my window. Yeah, I definitely didn't get out enough.

"Hey Alex. So uh, what's up? It has been a while, yeah. Oh, and it's Vera now. I switched back to my first name."

His face darkened slightly under the weight of being out of the loop for so long, but then recovered. "Right right, I did hear about that from my mom. Guess I forgot. Anyway, I just..." He swallowed his words before he even spoke them. Half of his lower lip disappeared under his upper teeth - a new nervous habit he must have developed over the years. "I saw you last night in the park and you seemed upset. I know we haven't talked in a while but I was concerned anyway I guess. You're good though, right?"

My face heated up as I remembered what I saw in the park last night - Alex, with the pear-shaped redhead and the magnetized state of their faces seemingly unable to stay apart for too long. Okay, that was probably just my jealousy talking - the guy wasn't a man whore or anything - far from it, actually. Dude should be able to kiss a girl without getting the riot rant for it.

"Vera? Went quiet on me again. You good?" The left corner of his mouth tilted up the same way it always used to.

"Yeah, yeah, I'm fine. Just some family crap going on. I'm running a quick errand, and then I'll be home. Thanks for asking though." We both paused for a minute, and then he asked me again.

"Okay. Like, I know this is probably pretty awkward, but I've always been around, you know. If you... need me. Or something."

"I know."

"Okay, good."

"Yep."

Another awkward silence washed over us. "Well I should get home, I'm sure my mom is wondering where I went and she's going to yell at me for making everyone late to church again. It's always nice to take a morning drive though." I felt bad lying through my teeth since we haven't gone to church in years, but I went with it anyway as a convenient excuse.

"Yeah, I guess."

"Okay, well I won't keep you. Don't be a stranger." He smiled at me with that kilowatt grin again, and sauntered away. As much as I appreciated him as a person, I liked the way his gray skinny jeans flowed over his trim body. The black tee-shirt he wore this particular morning only increased how attractive he appeared. When did my elementary-school buddy grow up into this gorgeous male creature that I only recently appreciated? Talk about missed opportunities. I forced myself to stop staring at him as he walked away, and I continued down the road toward where I vaguely recalled Edgar's house being located. The church thing was definitely a fib. But at the time, it just felt like the best way to gracefully end an awkward conversation.

I took a few turns down some side streets until I found it - it's a good thing my sense of direction kicked in when I really needed it to. It also helps that his garage door was still totally jacked up from Jet's hasty rescue mission last night. *He'd be so pissed if he knew I came back here alone.* But I quickly pushed that out of my mind because I knew this was worth it. The excuse of getting my belongings back was what I used to rationalize my rogue mission - but in the pit of my gut I knew that I just *had* to get to the bottom of that machine. It was the only way to satisfy my obsessive curiosity with all things of the fantastical and sci-fi variety. Plus, even a really unlikely chance of seeing my dad again this side of eternity was enough to make me at least want to investigate.

Pulling into his driveway filled me with dread, but I ignored that nagging worry and just pushed ahead anyway. *Should I ring the doorbell? Nah, that'd be way more polite than he deserves. I'll just duck into the garage through Jet's crash landing zone and find my*

102

purse and phone - I bet it's right there. Then maybe I'll get a closer look at the time machine, and then head back out to my car.

Satisfied by that plan, I killed the ignition and exited my car. Slipping into the garage through the banged-up door was easy. When I found my purse and my phone perfectly laid side-by-side out on the worktable, I really shouldn't have jumped out of my skin when I heard an all-too-familiar gravelly voice enter the room from behind me.

"I knew you'd be back."

"Edgar! You scared the crap out of me!"

"Why? This is *my* house. If I wasn't expecting you back so soon, you'd be the one 'scaring the crap' out of *me*."

"How did, how did you know I'd come back?"

He chuckled to himself, sipping his coffee lazily while wearing an old stained bathrobe. "Your eyes gave you away, my dear. They sparkled far too brightly at the prospect of time travel to just dim at the sight of your vigilante brother."

"Yeah, or maybe it's because I left my stuff here."

"Sure, that too, I suppose." Edgar remained where he was in the doorway likely leading to his kitchen from the garage, sipping his coffee in silence and staring at me.

"You're not gonna throw me in a potato sack again, are you? Because that was *really* not cool."

"Duly noted. But no, that wasn't the plan this time. Besides, I doubt it would work more than once anyway."

"It shouldn't have worked the first time!"

"Well, it did."

I ran my hand nervously through my hair and shrugged. "Sure, yeah, whatever. Congrats, you successfully hefted a petite beanpole of a girl who weighs ninety-pound nothing over your shoulder. You're the new heavy-weight champ."

"I'm not keeping you from leaving, you know. The exit is right where your brother left it. It's not like there's an overnight garage door repairman I could've called."

"I know."

"So, go then."

I took a step toward the broken garage door to make my exit, but then I turned toward him again.

"I will, but show me how that machine works first."

A sly grin spread across his face lighting-fast. "I knew you'd warm up to it."

I shrugged. It's not like I wouldn't have questions about a mysterious hunk of metal. But I was starting to think that I was the first person either crazy or curious enough to ask more about it. He walked over to it before I could change my mind, and the lid of it smoothly opened up with a loud *hiss*. He pushed a bunch of buttons and I saw the machine fully come to life as he activated it.

"This time machine scrambles molecules to make them pliable enough to travel inter-dimensionally. Then they join back together at the chosen moment in time - all within the blink of an eye. The solution for such a feat was, surprisingly simple, I'd say. I'm honestly surprised that the real scientists haven't figured this out before I did. After all, I'm just a bum garage-dwelling hack." He smirked, and ran a calloused hand through his frizzy, thinning gray hair. "I dedicated the better part of the past decade to this project, because I know Charlie didn't just disappear. He loved you kids too much, and your mom too. It wasn't like him - and when I realized that, I knew something was fishy about it – and it wasn't just my leftover tuna tetrazzini going moldy in the fridge."

I found myself absorbing what he had to say, more readily than I was comfortable with. But it all made sense - it lined up with all the questions I had been battling for years. And the potential for answers was significantly attractive to me. "And you think I can find him?" The words scraped my throat as they left my chest, but I knew they just had to be said.

"No. Actually, I *know* you can find him. The key to any theoretical idea is that you need two things to accomplish your goal: a butt load of chutzpah, and an emotional connection to motivate you. And you, my dear, have all those things and more. Plus, your relatively young flesh should reanimate perfectly - sometimes, with

104

older folks, it takes longer for everything to uh, come back together the same way."

"What?"

Edgar raised his hands in defense. "I'm just telling you the facts, Vera. When I journeyed with your little leggy friend there", he pointed over to the scorpion terrarium again, "my left ear lost some hearing, I had a little trouble breathing deeply, and my abdominal muscles were very upset. It all went back to normal a few days later though - and that was only the stuff I noticed. At my age, there was probably much more that was temporarily out of order. External organs always transfer visibly, but the internal mechanics can sometimes be off due to the way the machine scans your form. That won't happen to you though - it's the extra collagen and stem cells that prevent that from happening in younger folks. They conduct the scan straight through so everything gets copied just right."

I nodded, carefully considering how much of this to believe. At the moment though, it was getting near impossible to question any of it. Edgar was no longer a frightening stranger to me - now he seemed a bit like a Byronic hero - inherently problematic at his core, but smart and powerful despite that fact. "Wait, how do you know that? Were you... testing on anyone?" I crossed my arms, ready to run out of here again if I heard he was kidnapping people for some nefarious scheme.

"What? No! Well, uh, a little. But they're already dead, so it's technically ethical."

"Huh?"

"Corpses, Vera." He lowered his voice, as if his own garage was bugged. Heck, maybe it was. "I had a deal with the local morgue in Juneau - they gave me access to any unclaimed bodies under the age of thirty in exchange for me sharing my classified information with them about where to find... the goods."

"The what?"

"Plutonium, Vera. They use it for rapid freezing, rather like cryogenic suspension, but for the dead. The point is, I had many young test subjects that were only too happy to let me send them back and forth in time, and then test their bodily structure - and that's when I realized that age was the defining variable. My point is, you'll be fine, Vera. At your age, you won't feel a thing before, after, or during."

My face felt like it wasn't even mine anymore, because I could sense my own head nodding, but this whole thing was getting ridiculously dark. I wasn't sure how serious I could take him, but I was buying it hook, line, and sinker anyway. Then my mouth opened, seemingly of its own accord, and I starting actually considering this craziness. His explanations were a siren song, steadily and carefully leading my logic and sense of reality into disaster. And yet, I let him keep talking.

"So uh, if I went, and that's a big *if*, how would I get back?"

Edgar moved a few feet over to his tool bench, and grabbed a small, silver wristband with a small flip-cap not unlike a fire alarm cover. "I set this bracelet to act a bit like a remote - because the machine stays here, in this room since it isn't equipped to move through time. Rather, it functions more like a slingshot, projecting your body to whatever time you desire to visit. When that button is pressed, your body will be absorbed back into this machine and you'd end up here, feeling as if no time had passed at all."

"Show me how you'd do it. Where, I mean, *when*, would I go?"

Edgar grinned. Flipping open one of the panels on the metallic machine, he started to type furiously for a moment, and then paused long enough to explain. "That depends on what you want to accomplish. To find your dad, I'd suggest some time in early-to-mid 2010. He disappeared the following January, right?"

I nodded slowly, as the pain from old wounds started to reappear on the surface of my brain.

"Okay, so that seems to point us logically to maybe the preceding April of that year? Just because the weather is always so balmy in April, perfect for time traveling. Then, there was something else you wanted, yes? Some unfinished business with your classmates?"

106

I nodded again, hating that he knew so much about that dark time in my life, but also a bit touched that he remembered and wanted to help me, in his own twisted way.

"So I'd have you reanimate in a nearby park, that should give you enough of a baseline to get your bearings. Then, I'd have to track your younger self, and place you somewhere near her so that you can make the desired changes in her life as well - which, would, in turn, affect yours as well. Which reminds me - it may be easier if you keep your identity a secret. You wouldn't want to complicate things by telling your younger self who you really are."

"Huh? Oh, um, yeah, I guess."

"So you're going?" His eyes sparkled with an excited gleam, which made everything feel all the more off-putting. But even then, I still couldn't make myself walk out through that bent garage door.

"I... don't know quite yet. I'm just thinking."

Edgar continued typing away on the hidden keypad, probably putting in the right credentials for the journey I still hadn't completely consented to yet. "Fine, it's your life. Change it or don't. But one day, you'll regret not taking the opportunity to chase what you should have had from the beginning." He winked at me and I immediately thought of Alex.

Sweet, boyish Alex who always had cared about me in some capacity, even if neither of us thought it would ever turn romantic. Or, at least at the same time. Heck, I still doubted that it would. But now that I was older - now that *we* were older - I realized how much I actually wanted that. So I'd think changing the past could only help? Maybe I could convince my past self to give the kid a chance. But my main reason would have to be to find my dad. Secondly, maybe make sure those bullies get their just desserts. And if something could happen with Alex in the middle of all that, then I guess I'd be pretty jazzed.

These three things are what I told myself as I voluntarily sat in the surprisingly plush leather seat of the machine. I reminded myself of these things as Edgar handed me my purse, phone, and metal bracelet I would need in order to come back. I remembered my all-too-important reasons as I reclined on that oddly plush leather seat, and allowed Edgar to strap my arms and legs into the restraints. I breathed in these feelings as he closed the door in front of me, sealing me off completely from the outside world and making me feel trapped in my own insanity.

I exhaled the fear, and the judgmental attitudes I held of myself for agreeing to this - this absolutely bonkers, ridiculous foray into the unknown, the white-washed borders of my mind melting away as a tingling sensation covered every inch of my skin and I thought my skull would literally explode. I held my breath while I remembered my seemingly important reasons, that were suddenly not so important now that my whole body felt simultaneously blisteringly hot and freezing cold and I was pretty sure I was going to quite literally die. I held onto the hope that these reasons were worth it, even if I had walked into a trap and Edgar really was killing me. And then I remembered that although finding my dad, revealing the bullies as the scum they really were, and reconnecting with an old friend in a new way was worthwhile, none of it was worth having my whole body pulled apart. I momentarily reached for the door, having second thoughts and hoping to maybe jump out. But that last part I remembered just a moment too late, as I had already begun to feel myself melt away through a painless yet disconcerting metamorphosis punctuated only by a swirling light, and then nothing at all.

Twenty-One: Eat a Piece of Humble Pie

"Uh, some dirt?" A smirk played at the corners of his mouth, and although the pun was probably only apparent to me, Lynn, and our other accomplices, it was pretty good. The stifled giggles that escaped from their mouths only exacerbated their teacher's distaste.

Miss Sullivan was not enthused - I could see her all-too-familiar fighting posture from the hallway. Hands on hips, feet staunchly splayed shoulder width apart. Though her back was turned to me, I could vividly remember her slightly widened eyes and pursed lips, waiting for either an explanation or an apology - either way, outcomes would not be good for whoever ended up in her crosshairs. Then she reached out her curt hand and picked up the offending substance - the small, hidden camera with a short wiry-tail attached. Bits of soil stuck to it, but Miss Sullivan's face resembled that of an angry sea sponge - pinched, and a little red. Not the kind of surf and turf I'd order.

"Alexander, what is the meaning of this? And what is *that*?" Her resolute finger pointed directly at his collar, where undoubtedly, his microphone wire had begun to slip out and the microphone itself was also slightly visible.

He opened his mouth to speak, but the words were lodged in his throat. Lynn stepped in, and with a subtle nod, reassured him it would be okay. He visibly relaxed, because we were all so sure that the real fun was about to begin.

"Miss Sullivan, those are hidden cameras and microphones that we used to get actual proof that we've been victims of chronic bullying for years. No one would believe us, until we found a way to get proof. We - I mean, me, Alex, Bert, and Ricky, are all wearing hidden microphones. And we planted that camera in the uh, plant, so that you'd have audio and visuals of what was going on."

Her face continued to expand, like a dehydrated blob fish, but remained silent, as if determining what angle her tirade should take. We had a precious few moments before she went on full rampage mode. Listening in from a slightly nearby portion of the hallway, I was *so proud* of these kids. I had to keep myself from positively beaming. Bert and Ricky stood nearby with their hands jammed in their pockets, but also revealed the wires they were wearing. The bullies were about as amused as their teacher - as in, not at all.

"What? They *framed* us. This was a set up!" Summer - always the whiny and dramatic one - put on quite a show. With a grimy hand covering her supposedly aghast mouth, she had a pretty convincing front that she was hurt. Never mind the hurt that she inflicted on Lynn and Alex for years, but somehow, she was bent on showing this was somehow light years worse. Newsflash - it wasn't even close.

"How dare you?" Chloe shifted her meager weight toward me again, and crossed her arms. Hazel tilted her head slightly to the side, her tight ponytail hanging awkwardly from her oversized head as if she were a demented antique doll. Wyatt just watched what happened silently, as if he had some actual guilt for once. As Alex removed the data chip from the tiny camera and placed it in the disk reader of Miss Sullivan's laptop, all was revealed - the ugly words that she never noticed from across the room, the exclusions, the whispering, and the forced pencil tattoo that Summer had inscribed on Alex's hand. He took the liberty to hold it up as extra proof in the off chance that the actual recording wasn't quite enough. Miss Sullivan remained silently glued to the screen, and I saw Alex and Lynn's faces totally light up. *Finally, they got them. Those bastards deserved what was coming to them.*

Their teacher reviewed the video silently, and I was so sure they had won. But just as she opened her mouth to speak, the principal walked right past me and popped her head into the classroom door. "It's almost time for the musical, why aren't you guys heading over?" And then her eyes landed onto the offending substances - the wires, the camera, and the audio and visual footage still wafting from Miss Sullivan's computer screen. "What's all this?" Crossing her arms like it was her job, Principle Raca was not one to be trifled with - her policies were pretty messed up but they never failed to raise a ruckus.

Miss Sullivan had remained relatively silent until this moment, when the words I never thought I'd actually hear bubbled up from her throat. "These students have employed the use of unauthorized surveillance for the detriment of their classmates. I'm not even sure if that's legal." Her words tumble out, almost mumbled in a monotone fashion, and before I could process what was happening, I saw Lynn's eyes widen while Alex looked at her with shock on his face. His eyes sparkled with some residual hope, but the light behind them started to visibly fade.

"Miss Sullivan, those aren't toys or anything. We just needed proof that we were having a rough time. You didn't believe us before so I just thought it would help -"

A quick shake of her head and a hand on her hip silenced him far faster than I thought it would. Then Principal Raca stepped in. "This is unacceptable, Alex. Lynn, I'm not sure how much of this you were involved in but it appears you, Ricky, and Bert are in a boatload of trouble." And that's when Lynn absolutely burst into tears. Alex tried to comfort her a little with an arm around her shoulder but his face was bright red. The bullies shrugged and laughed gleefully at the appearance of their demise, even adding in their typical teasing - calling Lynn and Alex a couple and then gawking at them. As for me, I stood dumbfounded in the hallway, shocked that the inanity of my old teachers would really extend this far. It was my idea, after all, to stage this little stunt, and I was so sure it would work because I lived in this hellhole for so long, I thought I would know its weaknesses.

"But look! She wrote on my hand. With a pencil. By force!" Alex held up his hand to Miss Sullivan, where Summer had essentially branded him with her own blunt force and relentless cruelty. "It's even captured on the tape, we got that recording, and it's on the screen, look!" He pointed with his other hand to the laptop, which still played the covert footage in the background.

Principal Raca didn't budge, not even a little. Lynn was an absolute puddle at this point - her face was a puffy pink, and her eyes were barely holding in a barrage of tears threatening to trail down her cheeks. In full panic mode, she was barely even able to coherently speak. Meanwhile, the bullies just laughed, smirked, and snapped their fingers at their classmates while the teachers had their full attention on the good kids. Fan-freaking-tastic.

Throughout all this insanity, I still hovered nearby in the hallway, and I really wanted to intervene. But for some odd reason, a dull feeling in my gut told me to wait. So wait I did, and that's precisely when it all hit the fan.

"It doesn't matter, you caused friction between your fellow classmates deceitfully with intent to harm their reputations. We're going to have to discuss some disciplinary options with your parents. All *four* of you." Her eyes full of daggers set to kill landed on Ricky and Bert as well, and they didn't cry at all like Lynn - but based on their downturned glances, it was easy to see that they were upset. But their lack of challenging the matter showed me something even more upsetting about this toxic dynamic - they weren't fighting it anymore because they actually *expected* this sort of ridiculous treatment on the regular. Even at their relatively young ages, they had seen enough of this happen over and over again to be convinced it wasn't worth the fight.

Miss Sullivan nodded her head in agreement. "This is pretty serious, guys. I can't believe you'd actually pull something like this. There will be severe consequences, just so you know." Her auburn hair bobbed in place, seemingly invigorated by her caustic words and bitter reaction to some broken kids' very human need to prove that their miserable existence at school wasn't all in their head. "We're running pretty late now, you guys better all head over to the chapel. We'll follow you in a minute."

And that's when something in me snapped. All the rage that had been taking up space in my brain came completely unglued, and

112

before I knew what I was doing, I took the extra few steps needed to enter the classroom.

"Absolutely not. You can't actually be serious." I passed over the doorstep incredulously, feigning surprise for the moment. But like Ricky and Bert, I wasn't actually surprised at all.

"And who are you?" Principle Raca turned to look at me, her dark eyes boring holes into my resolute skull.

"Who am I? I'm someone who put up with your crap much longer than I should have. And you obviously can't see that what you're doing is *toxic*. It's toxic to all your students - but it's toxic especially to the good kids who can never properly kick some ass when they need to." I crossed my arms to punctuate my point, and the teachers just stared at me like a deer in headlights. I could practically hear their eyelids blinking like in the cartoons. My fists started to curl inside my pockets, and I could feel the venom leaking from my mind and just under the smooth skin of my face. The students locked their eyes on me, while Lynn and Alex stood agape with their jaws practically hitting the floor. For just a second, I thought I saw a slight grin pull at the corner of their lips. That warmed my heart to see right before I divided and conquered this mother-freaking mess of a classroom.

Another teacher heard some of the commotion as the other classes were all making their way down the hallway to the chapel in a mass of shuffling feet and whispers for the spring arts show. And yet, this class wouldn't be going anytime soon. I was a ghost who had far too much unfinished business to attend to.

"Rhonda, Lucille, everything okay here?" My former music teacher stepped out from the hallway, and was noticeably perplexed. "Oh, who is this?" Apparently, I was unrecognizable after almost ten years - and in this case, that was actually an advantage.

"We don't know yet, Barb. We're just trying to figure out an appropriate consequence for students engaging in advanced espionage techniques to deliberately exploit the others. Shocking, I know."

"Okay, listen up people. I'm going to lay this out, and you're gonna listen."

Miss Sullivan was not at all enthused. "What gives *you* the audacity to tell us what to do here? This is none of your business, and these are private school matters. Please leave before you make a scene." Her curt hands made their way onto my shoulder, and I shoved them off fast just like I did to my bullies years ago. What I realized then was that the bullies were led by example, and these cronies were nothing but bigger versions of them with dollar-store framed credentials on a wall of lies.

"You will take your hands off of me and hear me out, okay? I don't want any trouble. Or at least, I don't want to see the trouble continuing that *you allow* in these classrooms." I stepped forward further into the room, much to the chagrin of the teachers.

"Rhonda, do something about this! The show is starting in five minutes." Barb the music teacher was noticeably upset, but I didn't actually care. I continued with my point anyway, even hoisting myself onto a chair so that they couldn't help but notice me. A quick whistle with my thumbs in my mouth got their attention surprisingly well, considering how densely useless they usually were in this department.

"No, Rhonda, *you* will give me a few moments of your time so I can tell you how royally screwed up this whole school system is. And you two," I motioned to the other two teachers that I had been wanting to scream at for years. "You will both listen to me too. Now shut up, sit down, and eat a piece of humble pie or we're all gonna be here a while." Much to my surprise, they begrudgingly sat down, probably either out of terror or because they were at a loss of what to say to get rid of me. Spoiler alert: nothing could possibly get me off that high horse once I was on it.

"And what gives you the right?" Miss Sullivan glared at me especially, which freaked me out but I have to admit, I also kinda enjoyed the head rush.

"You may have taught them all about sentence diagrams, spelling, adverbs, and gerunds, but you left out the part about actually having personal agency and calling out the jerks before they can take advantage of you."

"Excuse me? We do not encourage bullying here, we had a whole seminar on it -"

"Oh and what a load of good *that* did. See, by never punishing the obvious problem kids, you perpetuate their power." I took this moment to grab Summer by the earlobe and drag her over to the principle. "Particularly, *this little bitch* has been leading the pack for years, so you gotta take her down a few notches before you can even hope to fix this mess. I mean yeah, there are some ambiguous little buggers like Hazel and Sue, who pretend to be friendly until they backstab the nice kids for a shot with the 'popular' kids who are actually the bullies. Then after you do that, her devilish little posse should disband quickly enough, because they're weak and only do what they do because they can hide their secrets behind their hands, keeping you completely out of the loop and the other kids at the mercy of their stupidity."

Summer growled at me, and I just flared my nostrils in her direction and rolled my eyes. "Yeah yeah, whine all you want jerk. But this is what you get. Suck it up, buttercup."

"Who the hell even are you?" Summer didn't bother to sensor her words anymore, perhaps because she realized that her ship was sinking - fast.

"Summer! Language please." Miss Sullivan was trying her best to exert some last-ditch control over the situation.

"See? You see this, but you don't do anything. You give the bullies a warning, which means next to nothing, in the reality that exists outside of your little private school bubble. Meanwhile, when Alex, Lynn, or any of the other kids react at all to this insanity, you come down on them like a brick wall. This is a ridiculously stupid double standard. It. Needs. To. End." With each word of that last sentence, I butted my head rhythmically in the personal space of the teachers, meeting their steely gaze with the crazed sense of power in my own eyes and the added use of dramatic air quotes.

All the teachers remained silent, and I finally thought I had gotten through to them. But then the principle opened her mouth.

"The spring art show is starting, and we all need to get over there. Thank you for your yet unsolicited advice. We will be going now." She started to get up from her chair, and I did something I never thought I had the guts to do - I grabbed her shoulder and shoved her back down into the dark blue, plastic classroom chair.

"Not quite yet, *Rhonda*." I rolled the 'r' of her name like the sexy Latin lover on my grandma's favorite soap opera, seducing the powers of good and evil, and showing the powers that be how absolutely assholic they've been. Her eyes bugged out in response, and I think I shocked the other teachers into compliance as well. All the students just stood around us in a small crowd, observing what I imagined was a pretty wild scene while rounding their mouth's into 'o's".

"I'm not convinced I've been totally clear yet."

All three cronies remained silent, searching around the room with their eyes, looking for a worthy distraction from their own shame.

"So let me break this down for you - the bullies in this classroom, are bad news. You know they are, don't even pretend you don't. So when they're being stupid, punish them. Take the other kids' word for it - they're suffering a lot and it's just unnecessary. And then when they try to defend themselves, you yell at *them* for it. Otherwise, you're quite literally defending the actions of the bullies when you do that. You've even seen recorded proof of it, and yet you still don't believe them. So you will not punish Alex, Lynn, Bert, or Ricky for this - it was their last resort because *you* wouldn't listen to them. And you *will* create a better, healthier environment where the bullies get punished until they decide not to be bullies anymore."

The teachers remained silent for a full minute after I stopped speaking, and I just stared and stared at them. I thought for a second, some kind of recognition flickered in the principal's eye, but it seemed to dissipate as quickly as it came. But it didn't matter, because it wasn't about who I was or what I had done - it was about the difference I hoped to make in these kids' lives.

"Who are you *really* though?"

Ah, screw it.

"Who, me?" I paused to soak in the delicious moment of reckoning that I had been romanticizing for literal years. My borderline evil villain laugh almost shook the perky laminated classroom decor right off the baby-blue painted cement block walls.

"I'm Vera Lynn Bartlet, graduating class of 2011. I'm from the future, and I may be older now, but I was done with your crap a *long time ago.*" I saw her eyes widen, and I could've sworn she was totally shocked. Maybe she even thought I was certifiably nuts. The other teachers did too - I could see the almost the full whites of their eyes gleam in the fluorescent lighting as they were probably mortified to be talked down to this way. Gasps and whispers filled the room as I hopped off the chair I was standing on.

"You're insane!" Hazel yelled at me from across the room, while the other bullies simply stared in shock.

"Oh, am I?" A crazy amount of boldness I didn't know I had coursed through my veins as I undid my scarf to reveal my initials tattooed on my collarbone - a beautiful script rendering of the letters 'VLB'. Then I grabbed Lynn's wrist with my own to show off the identical scar we both bore from the scalding tea incident of 2009. "See? We are *the same.* That's your proof. So clean up your act, treat these kids better, and punish the ones who actually deserve it. Their lives will be all the better for it, and maybe, just maybe, Lynn won't grow up lonely and miserable like me, because she'll learn her worth far sooner than these disgusting excuses for classmates can steal it from her."

I looked once more at Lynn and Alex. "Oh and you guys? It's okay to be more than friends, you know. Don't let these idiots shame you for finding what most adults wish they had early on in life. Just embrace it, okay? And if they give you any more trouble," I paused to glare at the bullies with as much venom as I could muster up from the bile growing in my stomach, "tell them future

117

me will come back here *again* and personally kick their little scrawny asses into next week, 'kay?"

Then I spun on my heel, and after a brief goodbye glance at Lynn and Alex, who were rendered absolutely speechless with their jaws on the floor and their eyes bugging out twice their size, I exited the classroom and ran down the hallway and out the main door. Invigorated by the adrenaline of finally finding closure for past woes that I never even dreamed I'd have a second chance at, I bolted outside and hid behind a tree. Sitting down to catch my breath, I gingerly pressed the silver button on my wrist so I could return home, and the familiar tingling filled my body as I could feel my body being absorbed into the void. I was ready to return home to a life I hoped would be enriched by the adjustments I had made in my own past. As I felt my body weightlessly leave the ground I sat on, I could hear echoes of police sirens and voices from that day I had voyaged to in my past, but I felt so enveloped by satisfaction that I couldn't help but smile as I left this realm for my own, ready to see what the next chapter held. Lynn and I may have had the same genetic makeup, but we had become drastically different people. And that was okay - it was good and necessary to grow up and evolve. Now I just had to use what I learned to fix everything before Edgar made everything messier than it already was.

Twenty-Two: Thank   You, Youthful Stem Cells

"Welcome back to the year 2019, stranger." Edgar's words flooded my ears as I found myself reassembled in his garage. Pretty groggy, I felt like I was waking up from a vivid dream. Heavy eyelids and slight dizziness greeted my consciousness as I sat up in the plush leather-like seat of the machine.

"Uh, how long was I gone?" I rubbed my eyes and cringed at the splashing sound that reverberated inside my head.

"From my point of view, maybe about ten or twenty seconds. But I'm guessing where you were, it felt a *lot* longer."

I opened my eyes more completely and looked around, wondering if there was a chance I actually imagined all this in some kind of crazy fever dream. "Did I imagine that? It feels so... impossible."

Edgar chuckled and smiled at me as he offered his grimy hand to help me sit up. "Nope, you really time-traveled. I monitored the whole thing. Nice work, kiddo. Find anything interesting?"

I shrugged. "I mean, maybe? I just feel... really weird. Like my head is spinning, in more ways than one. You know?"

Edgar nodded. "I sure do! I'm really glad you did this though. I think you'll find that even just a short amount of time in a previous era of your own life can make things change favorably."

My eyes widened as I could only imagine what I may have accidentally altered without meaning to. Edgar had warned me that things could shift and move with time travel, then affecting the present. "Did I... is everything okay?"

Edgar shrugged. "Well, as for you and your friend, yeah everything's okay. For your teachers, not so much. They claimed they met a time-traveler, and no one believed them so they ended up losing their jobs and getting thrown into the loony bin. You don't mind though, do you?"

The breath was sucked out of me with that news - I definitely didn't consider that possibility and if I'm being honest, it really did scare me. "Uh, yeah I mind! I gotta go back, I gotta- " I feverishly started grabbing at the lid of the machine to pry it open again and return to the year 2010, but his firm hand on my arm stopped me.

"No, I'm sorry, but you can't. Your bodily makeup is pretty unstable after time travel, even after just a short amount of time. If you went now, you'd explode upon impact and that would mean certain death. Besides, I don't know that anything you did would matter anyway. Because you did what you had to, right?" He tilted his head to the side, and I mused to myself that he looked a bit like a pigeon.

I shrugged again, still reeling from my most recent venture and trying to make sense of everything I saw and did while I was there. "Hey, how did you know that about my teachers?"

"I read up on it online, apparently it was all over the news in 2010."

"All because of me showing up."

"Yeah, pretty much."

"Woah."

"Indeed."

I sat back on the wooden kitchen chair in Edgar's garage, trying to make sense of everything. I still felt a bit woozy, but my skin and everything was perfectly intact, just like my crazy uncle had promised. *Thank you youthful stem cells.*

He pulled up an article on his laptop, and let me see it. Even though I already knew about it from our brief conversation, the shock of what I had caused through my time traveling still left me pretty shocked. In front of me, in giant letters, the headline "Local Private School Teachers Claim to Have Met Older Student From The Future" splayed across the screen. When I clicked on it, the article went on to say what Edgar had pretty much already mentioned - that whole thing about how the teachers lost their licenses and jobs because no one believed them, and they appeared to be certifiably crazy. Of course, they weren't actually crazy at all,

120

even if their classroom disciplinary policies were. Although I must admit the picture of Principle Raca in a straightjacket was pretty convincing.

"Wow - they really bought it, huh?"

"You bet, kiddo. Have to say, I'm impressed."

I smiled to myself, but then instantly felt bad. Aside from the crazy ineffective way the bullies were handled, I did like my teachers. Yeah I had a bit of a rage trip back there, but who wouldn't? It was pretty insane what was going on and I just had to step in. After all, that is partially what made me crazy enough to even try time travel in the first place. And that's when I remembered what I else I had come to find.

"Alex? Do you know what happened with him?"

Edgar shook his head. "Kid, I'm not psychic. I only heard what happened to the private school harpies because of the news records. What do I look like to you, a freakin' genie or something? Hang on, let me grab my gold wristbands, lamp, and turban."

I shrugged. "No, but you're definitely not a *normal* uncle." I managed to stand up, and get my bearings a bit while he closed down the machine I had just traveled through.

"Well, thanks I guess." He smirked as some various lights and gadgetry shut down, and then plopped down on a rusted, rickety old folding chair in front of me. "So what's next on your to-do list, kiddo? Fight crime? Pull a bank job? Defy gravity?" Tapping his grimy fingertips on his thigh, my uncle always seemed oddly calm in the midst of crazy. Then again, that's probably because crazy was what he lived in.

"Honestly, I didn't think too much farther than this. I, well, I just wanted to come to retrieve my things, and then, well, I guess a lot more happened than I thought."

"That happens sometimes, ya know. Life is crazy - better hold on tight, kid."

"Yeah, and if you add in time travel, it gets… pretty bloody bonkers." I cringed as I slipped into my British slang, which was a habit I was trying to kick. Hey it could always be worse, I guess.

Edgar sipped his gritty coffee cup with remnants of previous drinks and other food clinging to the surface, and we just sat in silence until I realized that if I waited too long to return home, Jet would start to seriously lose his shit.

"Hey what time is it? How long have I been here?"

Edgar shrugged his sleeve down to get a look at his watch. "In this dimension? I guess about an hour. Overall, about a day, right?" He winked at me. "You'll be fine, kiddo. Just head home before anyone starts asking questions. And by anyone, I mean that wild motorcyclist brother of yours." He gestured again to his mangled garage door, proving he must still be pretty salty about that. I mean, heck, who could blame him?

"Yeah, he's um, a character all right. I guess now that I have everything I need, I better get going." I paused to grab my purse and phone, and then wondered what the polite thing to say would be after time traveling. In itself, it was a marvel that I suddenly felt obligated to be polite to my weird uncle who kidnapped me, but I guess time travel changes a girl. "Um, thanks for…" I motioned awkwardly toward the machine, hoping he got what I was getting at. "You know."

"I do, kiddo. And you're welcome. I hope you found what you were looking for."

I nodded shyly and then turned away, toward the broken garage door. I'm sure the place had a real door, but there was something uncannily familiar and comfortable about entering and exiting through that unlikely doorway now.

"Hey kiddo?"

I paused, only slightly worried he was gonna sack me again. "Yeah?"

"If anything, anything at all, comes to mind about… Charlie, you'll tell your uncle, right? Sometimes things that you may have seen in your journey can come back in your head stronger as you continue to re-acclimate to this time. It's a slow absorption process, ya dig?"

I shrugged, only half believing what he was saying. After all, I really barely saw my dad at all besides just for a minute in the

122

pizza shop with Lynn and Alex – and that really wasn't enough to go on. "Uh, yeah, sure. I guess." But then, as I saw the way his eyes were a bit glassed-over and his eyebrows raised ever so slightly, I could sense that my inclusion in this journey brought him hope. In some very twisted yet understandable way, it wasn't just my dad who was missing - it was *his brother* too. And Edgar missed him - a lot.

"Good. Safe travels back home, kid." He got up from his chair and ambled his way back to the kitchen door, one foot shuffling sadly after the other. Seeing him this way now, I wondered how I was ever so afraid of him. When he disappeared through the door, I made my way through the broken garage door once more and walked to my car. In some ways, I wondered if that mangled garage door mirrored the hole I probably just tore in the space-time continuum or some sci-fi geek lingo like that.

Hopefully it's legal to drive after time travel. I mean, I'm not drunk or anything so I should be fine. I would think, anyway. Pulling away from Edgar's mysterious house, I found my mind whirring a million miles an hour as my car ironically went a measly thirty in the heavily settled neighborhood. *I really just time traveled. I went somewhere I had been before, and really just met my younger self. Okay, now back to real life. Hopefully I still know how to do that. Or at least fake it believably enough.*

Driving in my black punch buggy seemed so familiar and surreal after what I had just been through. I legitimately felt the enormity of time travel on my shoulders - both what it meant for my past and my future. And yet, everything felt normal enough. My car was still here, my uncle was there, and as I got closer to my house and surveyed the surrounding areas, I realized that everything seemed to be more or less the way I left it. The digital clock on my dashboard read 10:30, so I guess I could still make it back before Jet worried too much. But just to be safe, I opted to stop for coffee on the way home so that I had an excuse for my early morning errand.

I parked the bug in my typical spot, and then entered the coffee shop to see the familiar faces of the people there that knew my order by name - triple mocha latte with extra almond milk. The attractive blonde barista caught my gaze, and I felt myself smiling back at him shyly. Gavin always noticed me too, but I never really did anything about it because well, I'm a wuss and I'm terrified of rejection even though this has been going on for at least six months. Social anxiety is real, my friends. Or maybe that was just a side-effect of having my molecules scrambled and then standing in the presence of a really cute member of the male species shortly after. Either way, I wasn't feeling too hot and just needed to get my latte and get out of there. I blushed noticeably when it was my turn at the counter regardless - the heat rushed to my cheeks and the way he smirked a bit while biting at the corner of his soft, pink lips told me he felt something too.

"The usual, Vera?" His slightly imperfect smile seemed to catch the light from the overhead lamps, and his small silver gauges winked at me from their perch under the shaggy hair reaching to the tops of his ears.

Oh crap - he remembered my name. Great.

"Yep, the usual. Thanks." I fumbled in my purse for my wallet, but his curt hand on mine stopped me.

"Nah, don't worry about it. It's on me today. Hell, you show up enough." He winked at me, and then turned around to fix my drink of choice. I had hoped to say something even remotely suave and appreciative, but unfortunately, things rarely went the way I planned.

"Huh? For me? Wow, um thanks!" I smiled at him shyly, and tried to steady my heartbeat as my mind whirred. *There's no way he likes me. He's just being nice, right? Yeah, he's just a nice guy. That's gotta be it. Okay. Phew, dodged that bullet.*

His hand lingered on mine just a moment longer than it had to as he handed me my coffee, made exactly the way I liked it. Just like always. And as I wished I could say something insightful or earth-shattering, I just smiled, nodded, and walked right out of there. Then I proceeded to cringe as soon as I got to the safety of my car. *Why did I always have to be such a derp?* It was obviously not a good feeling.

Starting the ignition took my mind off of things as I took a sip of my drink and started driving home again. Small, excited tingles of adrenaline flooded my arms as I settled myself in my seat, letting my mind wander at the scenery flowing past my windshield. An old Blink-182 song was playing on the alternative station, and I took some comfort in the familiarity of the music. Tapping my fingertips lazily on the steering wheel to the beat of the song, I tried to exhale the weirdness of everything that just happened.

As I pulled back into my own driveway, I grabbed my coffee cup and noticed something scrawled hastily toward the bottom rim of the paper sleeve. It was a phone number, and it took me a measly fraction of a second to figure out whose it was. Gavin wanted me to call him, apparently. And I was trying to figure out how I felt about that. No one said life was any easier than time travel, after all. In fact, it might actually be harder and more complicated - hence the reason why time travel has been romanticized basically since forever.

It was also the reason why I legit sat in my car for a solid ten minutes wondering what to do next, when Jet knocked on my window, scaring me out of my pro-and-con lists. I rolled down my window, still in a daze for many reasons - and only one of those reasons being time travel.

"Jet? What's going on?" I shielded my eyes from the late-morning sun as he crossed his arms and stood over me, clearly upset with me.

"We gotta tell Mom about our psycho uncle, and you make a leisurely coffee run, disappearing for a few hours? It's important, Vera. I dunno why you're so calm about this." He paused, waiting for me to react, but I just couldn't.

I felt suddenly numb to the fight he apparently wanted to start, which was probably a good thing even though I didn't have a specific reason as to why. I inhaled sharply, trying to figure out a way to get my brother to calm down enough to not get my uncle arrested. I mean, he definitely went about everything in the worst way possible, but something in me hesitated to go along with my

125

brother's obvious ploy to get Edgar incarcerated. Maybe it was the time travel hangover but I really felt that maybe it wouldn't be fair to just yell first and worry about consequences later. Granted, I kind of just did that with my middle school classmates and teachers, but something about time travel felt improbable enough for the laws of courtesy to go right out the window. Like, time travel wasn't supposed to be possible anyway - so on the off-chance that it suddenly was, I felt oddly empowered to divide and conquer exactly the way I wish I had years ago.

"Vera! I'm talking to you, geez. Let's go talk to Mom, come on!"

I shrugged my way out of the car, still clutching the coffee cup and strategically covering the digits scrawled on it so my brother wouldn't ask questions I didn't have answers to. He wasn't *that* much older than me, but he always took his brotherly protective role seriously - especially since Dad wasn't around.

"Okay, um, can I talk to you first?"

"Yeah, whatever. Just get in the house. Mom just finished breakfast and now's a good a time as any."

"That's the thing, I don't think she should know about it."

And that's when I could swear Jet's face turned beet red again. His eyes rolled back into his skull and he threw his head back dramatically, obviously feeling defeated. Resting his hand on the roof of my car, he looked equal parts defeated and angry, with his face puffed out but his head angled slightly toward the ground.

"My gosh Vera. You may be in denial, but a sketchy member of our family abducted you. It's not something that should go unnoticed. He's got to pay the price for that. Heck, you might even be traumatized. For all I know, this whole mass of bull crap you're feeding me right now just proves that you've got some weird Stockholm syndrome thing happening and we gotta handle that too. And if you think for one second that I'm gonna let that bastard hurt my little sister, you'd be quite mistaken. Heck, it's all I can do not to ring his neck myself."

Jet's tirade went on like that for at least another ten minutes, and I just stood there, sipping my coffee, pretending to listen, and

126

planning my next move - both for Gavin and for this fiasco. And at the moment, neither of them seemed to have any clear answer. I took a deep breath, and let him finish getting through all the angst. And then I waited. When he was completely silent, and I was sure Mom was busy enough typing on her laptop not to hear us, I decided to tell him what really happened. I told Jet how I went back to get my phone and purse, and how I ended up deciding to time travel without being coerced in any way. I mentioned how I laid out my teachers pretty good for the utter bullshit they put me through, and how I kinda accidentally got them thrown in the loony bin because of it. Naturally though, he didn't believe me. Not yet, anyway.

Twenty-Three: Retroactively Pissed

"Yeah see, I just don't buy it." Jet's crossed arms and furrowed brow didn't fully cover the wonder slowly bubbling in the back of his eye sockets. My mention specifically of our matching scars though, and the way Alex was always awkwardly flirting with younger me, definitely caught his attention even though he hesitated to admit any of it.

"See, I think you kinda do though, actually." I crossed my arms to mimic his ridiculous posture, and let the smirk bloom over my lips as I still clutched my now-empty coffee cup with Gavin's number on it strategically covered by my fingers.

"Oh really? And what makes you say that?"

I paused, looking for a chink in my brother's always-so-damn-sure armor. "You're a sucker for anything sci-fi. I know that because I found your hoard of books under your bed when Mom made me vacuum last week. You know, along with plenty of even more mortifying literature." For once, I was grateful for the unpleasant chore.

His resolve weakened as his face softened, but his arms remained crossed and a slight rouge of embarrassment spread over his skin. "That proves nothing."

"Oh really? Collector's editions of *Divergent* and *The Hunger Games*? Yeah, okay, sure. It's not like you'd be picking out all the chick-flick sci-fi books unless you just really liked them."

He shrugged. "I dunno. I guess work has just been... really stressful lately. They help me unwind, okay? Don't judge me."

"What helps you unwind - the teenybopper sci-fi books or the magazines with the big boppers?" I smirked at him, quite amused with my little joke. Jet however, was not enthused, so I continued on with my spiel. "So whether or not you 'buy' my report of actually time traveling, you're far too intrigued to actually challenge it. At least, that's what your face is showing me."

He sighed, and looked at the ground. So that's when I told him about the time-traveling scorpion that I ended up cuddling with the other night.

Jet stared at the ground while I explained what I could and then looked at me, his eyes bugging out as he totally lost his cool. "Oh. My. Gosh. You really time-traveled, huh? What was, how did it feel? Was it crazy? Oh man, our crazy uncle actually did it. Do we gotta report him to the Feds or something?" He started pacing around, trying to make sense of what should have been impossible and placed his hands on my shoulders, as if the answers could be shaken out of me.

"Uh, I dunno, honestly I didn't even think about that."

"Well you *gotta* think, Vera! This is, the biggest thing to happen, like ever!" He paced around in small circles, and kept rubbing the back of his neck and muttering to himself. "We gotta start by telling Mom."

"No."

"What do you mean, 'no'?"

I exhaled sharply, trying to think of a way to contain the situation before it got bigger than either of us could handle. The last thing I wanted was for our uncle (or even us, for that matter) to be captured by the government and kept locked up like radioactive guinea pigs or something. "I mean it could easily get out of hand, and I'm not actually mad at Edgar anymore. He's actually, kinda okay - once you get to know him."

"Oh so you guys are all buddy-buddy now?"

"Well, no - but I've seen he's not a psycho looking to actually hurt anyone. He actually just wants to find Dad."

Jet paused mid-pacing. "Really? You're telling me he just wants to find Dad? That Edgar actually built a whole-ass time machine just to find him?"

"Look, I know it sounds crazy. I just... I have no choice but to believe him. He hasn't actually scared me wrong yet."

Resting his hand over his eyes to block the sun, Jet shook his head, trying to process the absolute craziness that had become our life in the blink of an eye. A four-letter expletive burst from his lips. "Honestly I don't really care how cool he supposedly is. I just really think Mom should know."

"Sure, maybe once we get a handle on everything. But not yet."

He shook his head. "Vera."

"Jet, she's just gonna freak out and call the cops or something. Plus, she might not even believe us."

"Still, she's *Mom*. She has to know." He started walking toward our front door and despite my best attempts to pull him back with my meager strength, he made it all the way to the porch before I had to resort to a petty but effective blow.

"Open that door and I'll tell Mom all about those very *interesting* noises coming from your room whenever Shelby Roberts came to 'study' pre-calc with you in eleventh grade." I added air quotes to fully emphasize how bogus the studying excuse really was and winked at him.

Jet immediately turned around, as the absolute embarrassment registered on his face. "I didn't... think you knew." His cheeks turned bright red and I could swear a bead of sweat threatened to fall from his forehead.

"Oh please, I'm not an idiot. Plus, we share a bedroom wall. I got very good at popping in my headphones on Friday nights to keep from having to hear all of that '*studying*' going on." I grinned at him, knowing that I had him beat. Our very conservative family wouldn't take too kindly to that news - one of the many reasons I myself was still very much a virgin. Not like I've had the option to change that anyway, but hypothetically, even if I did, I'm not sure I'd want to defy them that way.

Jet kept opening and closing his mouth like a fish gasping for water, trying to think of something to counteract what I threatened to say. He knew that even as a full-fledged adult, Mom would be retroactively pissed if she found out about those times he was going all the way with some ditzy high school cheerleader years ago and never looked back.

130

"Fine. I won't tell her. Yet." He rolled his eyes to punctuate his point, and then headed upstairs tossing me some kind of excuse about needing to work on some programming deadline for work and not to bother him or else. It wasn't the warmest of agreements but it was one I'd happily take regardless.

After that ordeal with Jet, I clicked my key remote again to make sure my car was locked, and then went into the house myself to process all that had happened - both with the time travel, and also Gavin. I was so shocked that he'd even want to see me so out of the blue, but obviously, it was actually a long time coming, and I was just oblivious.

Heading back into my house after time traveling felt oddly familiar but also wrong - almost as if I now existed in two separate worlds. Or times, perhaps? In my head, I just needed a leisurely Sunday to relax, but I knew that was highly unlikely given how bizarre things had suddenly become.

Nodding politely at Mom, who was on the phone with someone from work, I made my way back to my room, trying to ignore the gnawing in my chest and the irrational fear of not belonging in my own house. Straddling the cross-section between two worlds, I re-entered my present state trying to make sense of what I had experienced both in the past of this reality, and the past that I just revisited. Grounding my feet in the soft throw rug on my floor, I collapsed on my bed, still a bit wary of any spindly creatures sneaking in there with me. I knew that likely wouldn't be the case, but I still felt uptight about it.

The early-afternoon sun was careening through my windows like a beam from a UFO - it was all-encompassing my line of vision and demanded to be acknowledged, one way or another. I lazily rolled away from it, shading my eyes with my fuzzy blue throw pillow. And that's when my phone buzzed with a text from Willow. She was still planning on heading to the pier today with her boyfriend and invited me to come, even as the pathetic third-wheel that I always was. Don't get me wrong - I always appreciated her invites, but time-travel messes with your head in new and unfamiliar ways. Timelines were starting to move and blend, and what Edgar didn't warn me about was the uncertainty of whether I was awake or asleep. Maybe something in my brain didn't reassemble quite right - or I really was just being neurotic.

My coffee cup with Gavin's number rested on my bureau, so I figured I might as well input his info into my phone before I forgot and threw it away. Still had no idea what would come of it, or even if I wanted anything to happen, but I decided it was definitely worth considering. It's not every day a very cute boy who knows exactly how you like your very complicated latte order gives you his number. Correction: actually, that has literally never happened to me before. Still in disbelief that it did, to be honest.

I was about to text Willow back to say I wasn't feeling up to it, but hesitated. Something about the idea seemed like maybe a good distraction from everything that I had going on. But even that thought seemed to be an inadequate incentive for me to agree to the outing. As my fingers hovered over my touch screen, I saw the three little dots appear under Willow's previous message, and I waited for her to say something else to get me to cave.

"Come on Vera. It's a beautiful day out and I miss hanging with you somewhere besides class."

I sighed to myself. It had been a while since we did something fun. And even though my whole body still seemed to be buzzing from the molecular scrambling, I considered it.

"I'll come provided I don't have to sit and watch you suck face with your BF all day." I added a sassy emoji for good measure, just in case the message came across snarkier than I intended. Again, the little peppy dots appeared on my screen.

"Hey come on I've never done that in front of you! Not a lot, anyway." Her winking emoji acknowledged that there would likely be some kissing going on, but maybe not enough to make me want to vomit. As much as it pained me to admit, anything would beat moping around in my room all day.

"K fine, see you in twenty."

Willow sent me some sort of animated GIF of Taylor Swift smiling at the Grammys giving me a thumbs-up, and then I flopped

132

back on my bed to stare up at my ceiling. I didn't really want to be reminded of my single status, but what choice did I really have? I grabbed my purse again and ran a brush through my hair to look slightly less gross. In a short ten minutes, I felt presentable enough to get in the car and head to the pier. I waved to Mom on my way out, since she was still on the phone with who I assume was a very important phone call. The doorknob of the front door clicked as I opened it, and I glanced quickly upstairs to make sure Jet was safely distracted with his programming or whatever. I just didn't want to keep talking about what we were and weren't going to tell Mom, and I could tell this conversation was far from over.

I drove straight to the pier and inhaled the salty ocean air amidst the smell of corndogs and fried dough floating on the fresh air. Parking my Volkswagen on the street next to the cheesy tourist shops, I tossed my keys into my bag and tried to find Willow and Zander. But I didn't actually find them - instead, I saw a familiar tuft of longish brown hair move in the breeze next to the shaved ice cart.

Is that Alex? What's he doing here? I mean, of course the pier was just a favorite hangout spot for locals and visitors alike, but the timing of this kid was impeccable. My feet started marching right over to him, likely out of sheer disbelief and curiosity. I mean, I had just seen him this morning on the way to Edgar's house before my little time-travel experiment. *Was he stalking me? Nah, of course not. Why would he be? It's just Alex - sweet, thoughtful Alex who you're so close to. Well, were close to before life happened and you grew apart.*

Musing a bit as to why that all happened in the first place, I decided against getting his attention, for fear that he'd think *I* was stalking *him.* Turning on my heel, I tried to get away from there before he noticed me.

"Vera? Hey!"

Crap, I'm too late. "Oh, um, hey! Long time, no see right?" I coaxed my face into a smile, hoping he couldn't see too far past my surface.

"Yeah! I guess so." He took a sip from the red plastic spoon-straw sprouting from his cup of blue-raspberry shaved ice. It always was his favorite. *I guess some things never changed.* We stood in a pretty awkward silence until I got a strong whiff of chamomile shampoo and Willow appeared next to me with Zander a few paces behind her.

"Hey girlfriend!" The casual title rolled off her tongue like a singsong rendition of a pop song. "I see you've decided to get some vitamin D outside of your cave for once, huh?" She placed her arm around me, and Alex raised one of his bushy eyebrows.

"Girlfriend?" His face contorted into a surprised look, with a slightly rounded mouth and wide-open eyes as I quickly realized what he probably thought was going on.

"What? *No*, not like that. We're pals - this is *her boyfriend,* Zander." My face blushed, because you would think that Alex would remember that I'm completely straight. Then again though, we hadn't been talking very much over the years beyond a cursory "hey" so I can see why he might question it in this *one* isolated context.

"Hey Vera, who's this?" Zander smoothed out the stray wrinkles of his cotton button-down shirt and reached out to shake Alex's hand.

"Yeah Vera, who's this cutie? Were you so sick of being a third wheel that you finally brought a date with you?" Willow waggled her fingers and giggled at me as my face turned beet red. Again.

"I, uh, this is Alex. He's… an old friend." I smiled, trying not to make Alex think I was ashamed of him or anything. Actually, quite the opposite was true, even though I was still figuring out what that meant for me in my real life and not just my diseased imagination.

"Nice to meet you, uh?" Alex paused as I guess I forgot to supply him with Willow's name.

"Willow, and her boyfriend Zander. They're my college pals. And they're dating, even though they were in denial about it for like *ever* until I called it."

"It's true! My girl Vera has a sense for these things!"

"Except when it comes to herself." Zander piped in and raised his eyebrows, much to my embarrassment. I wrinkled my nose as he smirked at me. He's always been a great friend to me but still knew just how to push my buttons. His perfectly-ironed khaki shorts and Dockers flaunted the epitome of his preppy aesthetic, but at least he walked the talk. After all, his parents did have a yacht - I would know, I've been on it before.

Alex's lips pursed together awkwardly and I noticed his gaze shifted past me and toward the vast ocean and beach behind us. The accidental irony of the situation was palpable - Alex always liked me throughout our younger years, and I just never noticed. It was more than likely that he related to Zander's statement more than he'd probably like to publicly admit.

"So, um, we were just gonna walk around and graze a bit at the various fried-food carts while Vera rattles off about how we're destroying our kidneys with all the sugar and carbs we're consuming, but you're welcome to join us if you want. Right Zander?" Her boyfriend shrugged, and winked at me. His short-cropped, sandy blonde hair was tousled slightly by the sea breeze.

I dunno what they're thinking, but if it's what I think it is, they're wrong. Alex doesn't like me that way anymore. We never were great at timing, I guess.

"I, uh, Alex, you don't have to if you don't want to, I'm sure you're probably super busy and -"

"Nah, actually I'm free all day. I finished running errands this morning so I'm just chilling anyway." He slurped a bit more of his blue slushy, which had lowered a bit in his paper cup both from melting in this warm weather and his routine sipping. Pushing a larger chunk of ice around with his straw, he raised it to his lips, dyeing his pinkish skin slightly purple.

"Perfect! Now you don't have to third wheel with us!" Willow clapped her hands excitedly, and grabbed Zander's hand to drag him to the corndog cart while Alex and I just stood where we were, avoiding eye contact in the wake of that hasty implication.

135

"You don't have to, it's okay if, uh, I don't know what she meant by that." I started rambling as Alex just stared anywhere except at me.

"It's all good, I don't mind really. It's a nice day out, might as well enjoy it." He paused, seemingly searching for an excuse to hang out with me. *Gee, have I really gotten that disgusting?* "Been a while since we got to catch up, anyway."

I longed for him to say he missed me, or wanted to tell me how he felt, or something to that degree, but it didn't happen. *What'd you expect, Vera? This is real life, not some cheesy chick flick.* "Oh um, okay then."

"Hey Vera, Alex, you gotta try this fried dough, it's *to die* for."

I shrugged and started walking over to where Willow stood at a nearby cart as I felt Alex fall into step next to me. His presence never felt imposing - rather, it always felt *comforting*. Even though we hadn't been talking as much as we used to as of late, his energy seemed to be recognized by my body like a remembered device to a seldom-visited WiFi system. No password necessary - this guy always had the all access pass just by being himself.

If only the connection was really that simple to diagnose.

Twenty-Four: She'd Eat You Alive

"So then I had to run all the way to the dry cleaners to get my dress and Zander was like, *so pissed* but I had to have it or else I just flat out wasn't going." Willow's recount of her near-disastrous date outfit last week seemed to be only interesting to her, which was fine since I was too busy trying to not get powdered sugar all over my face while eating fried dough. Sitting at a table near the water clogging our arteries, I was next to Alex on a picnic-style wooden bench with chipped paint poking irritatingly at the insides of my bare thighs. Zander nodded politely at Willow's story, being the sweet boyfriend he always had been.

Alex didn't avoid my gaze, but he didn't initiate it either. His presence felt like the definition of social limbo - we were barely friends at this point, but there still existed (at least for me) an undeniable spark that suggested we might be something more. I didn't actually expect anything to happen really, but my thoughts continued to spin through my head at an increasingly rapid rate. So it made sense that I was pretty tuned out of the conversation right in front of me. That is, until Zander popped the bubble of blissful meditation around me.

"You're taking the same class as Willow, right Vera? How's that going?"

"Huh? Oh yeah, um, it's okay. Melendez expects a lot from us but he's nice enough, I guess."

"I bet! My roommate had him last semester, said he was a royal pain in the ass."

I smirked a little at his word choice, and shrugged. "I dunno, I like a good challenge sometimes."

Alex tapped my shoulder and I nearly jumped. The electricity from even that cursory touch was enough to send me through the clouds. Blushing was inevitable, but I took a swig of my iced lemonade before anyone could notice. Well, Zander winked at me but it was subtle enough I don't think it mattered - he just liked to tease me a bit, not unlike the brotherly way Jet sometimes did.

"I forgot to ask - what are you majoring in?"

"Communications, I guess."

"What do you mean, you 'guess'?"

I swallowed an especially large bite of fried dough that I probably shouldn't have, especially while sitting within three feet of a *very* pretty boy. I felt the mound slide down my esophagus and cringed at the amount of sugar it probably contained. "Well I mean, I know I want to work in entertainment in some capacity - I just haven't figured out exactly what I specifically want to do yet. So I chose a fairly versatile major until I know for sure."

"Seems logical."

"Yeah." An awkward silence hung in the air as Zander and Willow exchanged glances with each other and with me. Their eyes gestured subtly toward Alex, and I shook my head as imperceptibly as I could while Alex stared out at the ocean. His slightly pouted lips were still stained slightly from the slushy he had earlier. *Is it weird that I find that strangely attractive?*

"So you guys went to school together, right?" Zander snapped Alex back to the table, and he responded with a nod.

"Yeah, kindergarten through about seventh grade."

"Must've been a good time." Willow said it off-handedly, the same way one might suggest that going to a ballgame or a concert was a fun experience. I never opened up about this part of my life to her - that is, the part about the bullying and how alone I felt all those years. Alex must've felt my discomfort because I felt him subtly give my hand a small squeeze under the table. *What the hell was that supposed to mean?*

"Well actually, it sucked." Alex's face dropped, and I realized what that sounded like. "No, I mean, not you, Alex. I was glad to have you around. I meant, the bullying royally sucked." Alex nodded in understanding, but his hand remained holding mine - and I let him.

"You were bullied?" Zander's eyes bore into mine, as if searching for more hidden answers in my very plain irises.

138

"We both were, actually." Alex removed his hand from mine to brush his longish brown hair out of his face, and I hated the way I desperately wanted him to put it back.

Willow and Zander frowned in exactly the same way, their facial features making them appear almost like siblings - which would've freaked me out if I wasn't so close to them. But in reality, I just suppressed the giggle that threatened to burst out of my throat and shrugged for the umpteenth time today.

"Oh, uh, I'm sorry to hear that." Willow tossed her long hair over her shoulder. "Now I feel stupid."

"No don't!" Alex jumped in, hastily wanting to preserve the otherwise good vibes of the fun day. "I mean, it was rough but I'm okay now."

I nodded. "And I'm, uh, working on being okay about it."

Alex looked at me quizzically, with his head tilted slightly to his left and lips pursed. "Vera, I didn't know it still bothered you."

I shrugged. Again. "It's, not a big deal. Just a thing to live with." I slurped my lemonade loudly just to have something to do. I didn't usually choose something so sugary but it felt like the outing warranted something properly saccharine to compensate for the sourness of my time-tossed mood.

The conversation lagged a bit after that - nothing like recalling childhood pain to put a royal damper on a day at the pier. Alex meshed surprisingly well with Willow and Zander - it was impressive how quickly they took to him, actually. Zander found that they had similar interests in programming and graphic design, which resulted in Willow and I sharing bored glances while the boys chatted endlessly about various technology that we would never be able to understand. Alex talked endlessly about his music mixing software while Zander nodded happily as my ears tuned in and out of the conversation. Instead, I looked out at the ocean while the skin on my arm warmed with Alex's close proximity next to me.

We all convened again while chatting about school, since we're all in college (even though Alex didn't attend our school).

And over some stories about the hilarity of dorm life and quirky professors, I found the two halves of my life melting together into an interesting new brew.

"So Alex, are you seeing anyone?" Willow directed the question directly at him, and he blushed. Meanwhile, I pretty much wanted to kill her and made that obvious by kicking her under the picnic table we sat at.

"Uh, no, not currently. I was, but it didn't work out." He shrugged. I inhaled sharply, trying to hide my excitement in the midst of his vulnerability. The last thing I needed was to seem like a narcissistic weirdo.

"I'm sorry to hear that." Willow smiled at him politely, and Zander nodded.

"If it makes you feel any better, Willow and I didn't get together for a long-ass time even though we'd known each other most of our lives. Point is, shit happens." He shrugged, and Alex nodded, still clearly processing whatever went down between him and that mysterious redhead I never met.

Aside from that temporary tension, today felt like effervescent foam in the air of the future, bubbling noisily inside my brain with my newfound perspective since traveling back in time. Alex was my past, but maybe there was a chance he could be my future too. It was presumptuous, I know. But I could swear that when he wasn't holding my hand under the table, I could feel his arm resting casually behind me on the stone railing, or the stone wall, or whatever structure was nearby and eligible to hide obvious affection. At least, that's what I assumed it was. Correction: that's what I *hoped* it was. I was starting to want my past to congeal with my present in a way that would allow for a possible new romance with a very familiar face.

All afternoon and into the evening, I nodded along and smiled. Anything to avoid properly acknowledging the many feelings I experienced from seeing my dad again, and from hanging out with Alex (both this version of him and the younger version). It was honestly all just too much to take in, and I found myself subconsciously pulling away from it for as long as I could. In the moments between chatting about the typical everyday struggles of college and social life, my mind kept pulling me back to my journey through time. Although nothing seemed too important, I kept worrying that things would be different. Maybe in a good way, or maybe in a bad way, it would all just be inside my own head. Regardless of how it was different, my life had been altered. Not the cheesy stuff like in *Back to the Future,* thank God. That's just a movie, after all. But even a change in mindset can be a ripple-effect, and I found myself still wondering what I felt about that, if I even felt anything at all.

"Vera? I was asking what you have going on this week." Willow snapped her fingers in front of my face, trying to get me out of my emotional stupor and back into reality. This reality, that is - not the past reality that my head seemed to be stuck in.

"Oh uh, just classes I guess. You know I'll see you in marketing with Melendez."

"Girl, you have *got* to live a little. That's it, you're coming clubbing with me and Zander Thursday night." Then she said something that made me blush to my core (literally, I bet my lungs and bones were red with embarrassment). "Bring Alex too. You guys need to get out more."

Alex's bushy eyebrows nearly hit his fringed hair when they rose in surprise. "Uh, um, I'm not really into that whole party scene."

"Well that would be fine, except I wasn't *asking* you." Willow winked at me, and shared a very knowing glance with Zander. "I was *telling* you. I better see you and Vera at The Blue Pelican, together, on Thursday night. And just to make sure of it, I'll expect you to swing by my house around seven so we can all go together. Sound good?"

I sighed. Willow always meant well, but she came off as pretty intense more often than not. "Alex, I'm not a dancer either. We can just go with them, sort of hang out? If you want to." I whispered those words in his ear to keep Willow from making some other mandatory announcement and scare him even further away from me.

"Yeah, um, okay. I guess, seven it is."

Willow clapped her hands like the valley girls we always made fun of, à la *Clueless*. "Sweet! That'll be so fun."

I glanced at my phone, noticing that it was almost six. "Well, as fun as this has been, I should probably head home. Mom hates it when I miss dinner, especially without telling her first." I paused, and then spit out something that could easily sound very date-ish, when in reality, it was just for convenience, I swear. "Alex, want a ride home? Just because you live down the street, and it'd be easier than walking and nicer than taking the bus." *Oh crap, 'nicer'? You really just said that, didn't you Vera. Just great.*

"Sure, that'd be great. Thanks. It was cool meeting you guys." He got up from the rock wall we'd all been sitting on after walking around all day, and I marveled at how much my butt hurt from the rough, hard surface. *I wonder if his butt is sore too. What even am I thinking - that's weird, even coming from you.*

"It was really nice to meet you, Alex. Vera speaks so highly of you." I cringed at Zander's words but he just smiled at both of us, as if we were already a couple.

"She does?" His eyebrows did that thing again while I mentally wished I could sink into the sand that had accumulated on the boardwalk.

"Yeah. You guys were obviously very close as kids." Willow jumped in trying to smooth over any awkwardness, but she's still Willow, so she only emphasized it.

"We are - I mean, we were." I caught myself trying to overcompensate for her awkwardness, which just made it even more intense. Alex didn't seem to mind though - or if he did, he hid it *really* well.

"I guess we just sort of... drifted apart. Life got busy, you know?" Alex scratched an invisible itch on the back of his neck after acknowledging the elephant in the room, probably feeling every bit as awkward as I did. Willow remained oblivious to the tension building in the air, casually fishing her car keys out of her

142

trendy suede purse. Zander just put his arm around her and stared out over the water to our left.

"Yeah I mean, it just happens sometimes, I guess." Drawing unidentifiable pictures in the sand with the toe of my sneaker, I turned my body awkwardly toward my Volkswagen bug and hoped that Alex would follow me without making a big deal of everything. "I'll see you guys at school." I breathed a sigh of relief when I sensed his light footsteps following me and then coming to the passenger side of my car. Waving at Willow and Zander, I closed my car door and started the engine. My breath hitched tightly in my throat, practically suffocating me in the midst of the tension just being in his close proximity created.

"Hey um, sorry that they were so... forward. I love my college pals but they can be a bit... much if you're not used to them." I started turning out of the parking lot and started the short drive toward home. I turned the radio on softly to play some music to soothe my nerves.

"Don't sweat it, they were cool. I definitely wasn't uncomfortable."

"Well that's good to hear then." He tapped his fingertips nervously on his thigh as we continued down the highway, and I racked my brain for something to say, anything at all to make myself believe that we didn't just barely even talk for the better part of a decade. Nothing came up - this boy had me completely silent, for the first time ever. But it's not that he was boring - far from it, actually. I'm just of the belief that sometimes silence can come in the moments when there is just far too much to say. Then you just end up saying nothing at all as if you could preserve the words for a seemingly better time that will likely never come. It's the socially introverted version of the tomorrow that's just never here, or the procrastination that you used to rationalize putting off your homework.

I wanted everything, but got nothing. And I was starting to see that it might all be because I couldn't manage to squeeze out those all-too-important words when they were needed the most.

Rounding the bend in front of Alex's house, I swallowed the knot that formed in my throat from the rush of nostalgia that came back in full-force. I didn't live far from here, but I hadn't gotten a good look at his house in ages. Same blue shutters, but the house itself was gray now instead of the lemon yellow we grew up with. His mom's handwriting was still on the side of their sensible mailbox in green lettering. She's always been pretty artsy, so it made sense that she took it upon herself to decorate their mailbox with 'The Hallidays'.

"Thanks for the ride back." He paused, looking for something to say to kill the silence that had been plaguing us off and on most of the ride here. "So, I guess I'll see you Thursday? Mostly because I'm terrified that your friend is going to kill me in my sleep if I don't show." He smirked, obviously kidding.

"Well lucky for you, Willow is more enthusiastic than she is vicious."

"About what?"

"The better question would be to ask what she *isn't* enthusiastic about."

And then we lingered in that awkward moment when maybe a hug would have been a normal thing to do, but we were both sitting down in my car. So Alex just let himself out and nodded at me. "So, I'll see you then, I guess. Your house at quarter of seven or so?"

"You don't *actually* have to go, you know."

His face dropped, and then I worried I disappointed him when I was actually just trying to take some of the pressure off. "I mean, Willow's just being a goof. If you don't wanna come, you don't have to."

Alex jammed his hands in his pockets and glanced at the ground in front of my still-open car door. "Well I mean, you're going, right?"

"Totally. I have to, she'd eat me alive if I skipped out."

"Well that would definitely suck. But being there alone would also equally suck. So I really don't mind coming with you. It's only polite, after all."

144

I couldn't help but notice the sweet smile pulling at his lips, and I felt my stomach flip a little at his reaction. *Chill out Vera, he's just being nice. He's always been so sweet but it doesn't necessarily mean anything now.*

"I guess you're right. See ya Thursday." I smiled back at him, and then he closed my door and waved as he jogged over to the side door that I knew led into their garage and mudroom.

Twenty-Five: What are You Looking For?

After that whirlwind day or two of time traveling, apparently wooing Gavin at the coffee shop, and hanging out with Alex for the first time in literal years, I completely crashed. Both physically and emotionally, I was a disaster. My whole body felt mixed up inside, like someone stuck a blender down my esophagus and clicked it on full blast. There was no real way to tell how much of that was just my mental state, or if my reanimation after time traveling really did screw things up, but I was fairly confident it was the former.

I couldn't sleep very well - I just kept waking up over and over again seeing random snapshots of what I had experienced while time traveling. So when my business professor emailed cancelling class with a bad cold on Monday morning, I wasn't even the least bit sorry. I literally checked my email and then drifted in and out of sleep for the entire rest of the day. That would've been my only class for the day, and I was in sore need of a personal day - or two, since I always had Tuesdays off as well. Or maybe just a day to process the insanity that had become my life since Edgar arrived on the scene. Waking up around dinnertime after sleeping just about all day is especially odd when you think about circadian rhythm and all that jazz, but that's what my body needed. Mom noticed I was not feeling myself, but when she asked I shrugged it off, mentioning some BS about being stressed about school and graduation. Although looking back, I guess that wasn't a complete lie, because those things were definitely on my mind in one way or another.

Edgar was keeping his distance so far, but I quickly found that he was the one person I could talk to about my experiences. Jet was still processing the news of my time travel, and of course I hadn't told anyone else. I think a lot of the reason I chose to keep it to myself was because it was just damn crazy. That brain space to handle it on my own was crucial to me, and I couldn't see myself letting anyone else in on such a wild and borderline insane thing that happened to me.

I also hadn't quite figured out how the firing of my teachers had made the newspaper headlines, but then that Jet (or anyone else, for that matter) didn't believe me initially about the time traveling. Probably because the teachers were branded as crazy by the media - yeah, that could be it, I guess. And maybe the guilt of what happened was haunting me now, breathing down my shoulders with the chilled air of my past after having collided with the warmth of the present. A thunderstorm was brewing in my mind, and my body seemed to follow suit. Equalizing that would be tricky - not impossible, I'm sure, but I could already tell it was going to be really hard.

I've heard of post-traumatic stress disorder, and I wanted to believe that this wasn't it. But for all I knew, it easily could have been. And that was likely why I did something impulsive and insensitive, just for the hell of it: I texted Gavin.

My feelings had barely processed anything about him - heck, I didn't even know if I had feelings. But for a fleeting moment, I just needed to feel normal and do something a typical college girl would do. So I started a conversation I wasn't even sure I wanted to have, even though I had a pretty good hunch as to where it could lead.

"Hey it's Vera"

Pretty bland, I know. But something in me seemed to require that initial contact to be made. Maybe I was craving attention. Or maybe it was a back-up plan because I didn't actually believe Alex would ever really think of me the way I needed him to. I put my phone down to go watch TV or something - anything to slow down the thoughts that wouldn't stop spinning out in my mind - but it buzzed less than five minutes later.

"Hey yourself ;)"

I felt like I should respond somehow, but bargained with my internal control freak that he had my number now, so mission accomplished - and I should chill out until I figured out what I wanted. And that plan would have been fine, until my silence seemed to encourage more messages from him.

"Whatcha up to today"

"Taking a personal day because I'm not feeling that great"

The three little bouncing gray dots told me he was typing again, and although his interest was flattering, and I thoroughly enjoyed the adrenaline building in my gut, I was running out of things to say.

"Aw that sucks hope you feel better"

"Thanks"

Then I literally walked my phone upstairs so I could exist in peace and quiet without any more buzzing - at least for right now. I sorely needed the brain space to process what I couldn't properly explain. Clicking through the channels proved fruitless though - daytime TV was always either the annoying ankle-biter cartoons or cringe-y soap operas, so I gave up on trying to find something to watch and just ended up conking out on the couch for a while instead.

The images I saw as I drifted in and out of consciousness were striking, and nearly impossible to recall clearly. I kept seeing spidery legs, bright colors, faces of my younger self, classmates, my dad, the pizza place, my old school, younger Alex, etc. None of it made sense, and it was starting to really irritate me because sleep was becoming damn near impossible.

By Tuesday evening, I was running on no sleep but realized I hadn't actually done any of my homework yet. So I skimmed over a few chapters of my textbooks and hoped I could BS the rest. Luckily, I didn't have any exams scheduled for this week, so I was pretty confident in my ability to just coast through hopefully undetected. Closing up the last textbook, I was about to get ready for bed when I heard some irritated grunting coming from Jet's room. Pausing at his door to investigate, I was worried I might walk in on something I'd really rather not see, but felt like I had to knock anyway.

"Jet? Everything okay in there?"

Shuffling footsteps rubbing lazily over the wall-to-wall carpet made their way to the other side of the door, until it opened revealing my very-disheveled older brother. His hair looked like it was caught in a tornado, and his eyes were red - either from repeated rubbing or crying. Chewing on his lower lip, he crossed his arms and looked at me through eyes sadder than any I'd ever seen. They were glazed over like half-melted ice, reflecting my own face so clearly I wondered how much of Jet was still present in there, or if I really was staring at a miserable shell of my older brother who had overworked himself practically to death.

"Woah. What... what happened to you?"

Jet shook his head and looked down at his feet, seemingly unable to string words together. "I don't... I don't know how to say it. Work has been... rough. Really rough. It's... different than I expected it to be."

"You probably just need a break then. When's the last time you took a shower? Or ate a meal that didn't come in a box?"

"You're not Mom, Vera. Don't worry about me, I'll be fine. Just go to sleep." He tried to shut the door in my face, but I stuck my foot in the doorjamb just in time. The force of the door probably left a bruise through my fuzzy green socks, but I didn't care.

"Jet, you're my big brother, I care. Deal with it. And let's face it, Mom's been so busy with work lately, if I didn't check in on you, who would? It's not like you have a girlfriend -"

And that's when I realized I should have just quit while I was ahead because his face instantly dropped and turned red, probably with both anger and embarrassment. His eyes flashed daggers at me, and I could feel myself shrink down to my sock-clad feet. "Jet, I, I didn't mean -"

"Just go, Vera. Leave me alone." This time, I let him shut the door in my face because I knew I deserved it. Maybe it was the lack of sleep, or the way I had far too much on my own mind to be able to filter my thoughts before saying them. Forcing my sorry ass into the shower, I tried to steam away my stress but it obviously didn't work. Tomorrow was Wednesday, and I had to pretend that everything was normal even though it couldn't be further from the truth. Then again, the jury was still out on whether or not my life was ever normal even before the time traveling. When I closed my eyes in the shower, I kept seeing the images again, over and over again. This time, the images became clearer and more varied, almost as if they were growing and evolving. I wondered if maybe I should ask Edgar about it, but tomorrow was pretty booked with my classes. I guess a phone call would have to do.

It was crazy how fast my perception of my uncle had changed. Initially, I saw him as someone wild, crazy, and dangerous. But now I knew that he was the only one who could possibly understand what I was dealing with, so I had to let him into my life for that reason alone. I was starting to trust him completely, and while it was nice to feel a bit closer to my dad through him, I found myself craving the real thing. Sometimes, a girl just really wanted her dad around, and I was robbed of mine when I probably needed him the most.

I guess it just wasn't in the cards for me to have my dad around during my formative years. And honestly, I think I had managed pretty well given the circumstances. Trying to shake off the loneliness I felt, both for losing contact with my dad all those years ago and also for fear of losing Jet in a similar way, I turned off the water and dried off, pulling on an oversized band tee and the comfy shorts that I always slept in. Marching back to my room, I saw my phone glowing from my desk, but I was about to go to sleep, so I just decided to leave it until morning. My mind had been so overwhelmed with processing everything that I had just been through, I wondered how long it would be until I would be able to tackle anything else new in my life.

A quiet knocking on my door woke me from a partial slumber, and I sat up in bed as my mom cautiously opened my bedroom door. "Hey Vera. I know it's late, I just wanted to check on you."

"I'm fine, Mom. No need to worry."

Her pursed lips suggested this conversation was far from over. "You seem like you have a lot on your mind lately, I just wanted to ask if there was anything I could do? Even if you just need someone to listen, I'm here for you, you know." Easing herself onto the side of my bed, her weight displaced some of the mattress and I felt my body lean slightly toward her. I readjusted myself to compensate for her presence and tried to formulate somewhat convincingly coherent thoughts despite my drowsiness.

"It's just school stress. I'll be fine." I could see my phone glowing again in my peripheral vision, but I promised myself that I wouldn't look at it until morning, and that was a promise I intended to keep.

"Are you sure that's really it? Is it… boy troubles?"

I cringed, probably more outwardly than I wanted to. Luckily, the lack of light in my room probably hid my less-than-amused facial expression. "No, it's not that." I felt pretty crappy lying through my teeth, but it was at least partially true I figured, since 'boy troubles' implied actually having a relationship with a boy with whom to have such troubles with. And I've always come up with a deficit on that front - for better or worse.

"Okay." She paused for a moment while rubbing my shoulder, as if trying to look through the darkness in my room to read my psyche below the surface. "I'm sorry things have been so busy with work. You know you can interrupt me anytime if you need me. Well, not if I'm working on an important celebrity edition, or a news article, but you get the idea. Even then, I can drop those if I really have to. As long as I meet my deadlines for Melissa, it really doesn't matter."

Obviously, the rambling gene was genetic. "I know Mom, and I appreciate that. I'll let you know if I need you. But right now, I really gotta get some sleep." I yawned for real now, silently grateful that my body allowed me the opportunity to punctuate my statement with some tangible proof of exhaustion. You know, as if the clock on my nightstand's display of half-past midnight wasn't enough.

"Right, of course. I'm always up late editing so I forget how you like to crash earlier. I love you." She planted a kiss on my

151

forehead like I was six years old again and breezed out the door, turning on the foyer light no matter how much I groaned and buried my face in the pillow. I loved my mom, but most of the time she was pretty incapable of going more than ten minutes without doing something at least slightly irritating.

I closed my eyes and let sleep overtake me, even though the thoughts and the images kept coming. When I woke up, I recalled that the images seemed to increase in their speed, like someone was flashing a desk of cards in my face and I could barely make out the visuals as they flipped by at warped speed. The effect was equal parts dizzying and off-putting, since I was unable to escape them unless I was awake. Sleep with the images flashing wasn't at all restful - so the tiredness remained while my day unfortunately had to continue.

The sun that shone through my window was beyond irritating to my already frayed nerves. It seemed to force my eyelids open, no matter how much I tried my best to clench them shut. Before long though, my alarm clock assaulted my ears and I was forced to get up before I ended up being late for class. As I shuffled my way down the hall to brush my teeth, I remembered that I hadn't checked my phone since last night and I probably had some messages from Gavin to answer. My stomach did that little flip thing at the thought of him texting me, which irritated me because I felt like my hormones were acting in direct defiance of my emotions. I still needed time to process the whole time travel thing - unless, maybe carrying on with life would be just the thing to get my mind off of it. Unless I wasn't *supposed* to get my mind off of it.

Chill out, Vera. These thoughts are far too deep for having been awake less than ten minutes. I've never been one to wake up well rested, but my brain never seemed to wait for me to fully function before bombarding me with the typical slew of what-ifs and regrets. I spit the minty froth into the sink and washed my face with the cotton candy colored blue washcloth I always kept on the towel rack. Looking at myself in the mirror elicited some groans, because I wasn't looking so hot. But who could blame me? I was sleeping but not resting, and my life was good but complicated. All

152

that would take a toll on anyone - at least, that's how I managed to rationalize my less-than-stellar appearance. If I really wanted to, I could cover the dark bags under my eyes with concealer but I lacked both the energy and ambition to pull that off.

Exiting the bathroom, I could hear Jet clicking away on his keyboard on the other side of his bedroom door, still covered with the teenaged hormone-laced "keep out" signs and other angsty adolescent things. He had been a legal adult a few years longer than I had, and yet, he always seemed to appear much older than me. Perhaps it was his lack of a social life, or maybe it was the way he was always glued to his computer working for that software company.

After grabbing some clothes from my bureau, I got dressed and then bit the bullet and answered the messages left on my phone since last night. But to my surprise, none of them were from Gavin. Rather, they were from Willow.

"Your friend is cute. I ship it."

I cringed, but also didn't mind hearing that she approved. Funny enough, it actually made me think I actually had a slightly better chance with Alex.

"Lol thanks. We'll see."

"So you're gonna try?"

I bit my lip, wondering how much I even knew the answer to that question.

"You only live once."

She responded with a GIF of some character from *The Office* nodding in approval. Then I slid my phone into my backpack and made my way downstairs to grab something I could eat somewhat safely while I drove to school.

Turning on the radio only drowned out some of my thoughts - most of the images still remained, flashing through my head like a perpetual slideshow I couldn't turn off. It got so bad when I was about halfway to school that I did something that surprised me - I cut class to go talk to Edgar instead.

153

Looking back, I guess I could have gone to see him after my class, but my brain felt so invaded by these repetitive images and ideas that I just couldn't piece together. And I noticed that with the passage of time, they only seemed to intensify. It was all just very, very strange.

After I took that "wrong" turn to see him instead of going to class, I mentally started thinking up ways to get notes from class or something. *Maybe I'll text Amy from the group project a few weeks ago.* Turning onto Edgar's street filled my whole body with dread, because I knew he'd have answers that could help me stitch together the shattered remains of my past with my new perception of the present. But those answers would probably not come without a lot of pain in the process. Plus, I had no way of knowing whether or not he was even home - for all I knew, I just cut class for nothing.

Luckily for me, I recognized his beat-up car in the driveway right away, so I parked behind it and made my way to the front door. *Looks like he had that garage door fixed pretty quick.* The opening left from Jet's rescue attempt was completely repaired, such that no one would ever know what had occurred behind those metal slats. Maybe that was the point, after all - to increase privacy from the prying eyes of the neighbors.

The doorbell appeared to be broken, so I just knocked on the door instead. I was about to turn away in defeat, thinking maybe he was unavailable for some reason. *Maybe I could go to class just slightly late, that might be okay.* But as soon as I reached the bottom step of the landing, I heard the lock click as the doorknob turned and he peeked out at me.

"Patience, my dear Vera. I was only pouring a cup of coffee." He must have deduced what I was just thinking from my unsteady stance and worried facial expression. "To what do I owe this pleasure on a typical Wednesday morning?" He sipped his coffee out of a mug with "I heart mermaids" printed on the side in a psychedelic scaly blue font. I wanted to ask him where he got it but thought better of it, given the way my head was spinning and how desperately I needed it to slow it down.

"Well uh, my head has been... spinning."

"Spinning? Maybe you've just had too much to drink then."

"No, I don't drink."

"No? Hmmm. Well I'm really not sure why you're here anyway - "

"There are images flooding my head all the time now. I don't know what they mean but they won't stop and I can't sleep."

The smug smile dropped from his face, but he nodded as if he knew exactly what I was talking about. "Yes, okay. I had a feeling this would happen. Come on in, let's chat."

"You can help me?" I asked as I squeezed past him through the front door.

"Possibly. Tell me what you've been seeing." The stubble on his chin seemed to scratch against the tension in the air around us, and I eased myself onto a surprisingly normal-looking couch in an average living room. As time went on, the mystique surrounding my uncle dissipated like a rogue fog, taking with it any doubts I had about the quality of his character. At least, that's how I rationalized the way I found myself opening up to him. He sat in an armchair across from me, and sipped a mug of coffee that was placed on a perfectly-sensible side table next to him.

"They flash far too quickly to know for sure. Do you know what that could mean? Like, why is that happening?"

He scratched his chin and looked out the window to our left. "Vera, when you returned from time-traveling, do you remember what I said to you?"

I shrugged. That whole morning was such a blur and in the handful of days since then, I've barely been able to sleep long enough to recover both physically and mentally from the ordeal. But then my next thought appeared like a light bulb might over a character's head in those cheesy old cartoons. "Hmmm something about ideas coming to me in fragments? Oh crap - that's totally what this is, isn't it?"

"That's what I'd wager."

I felt the couch under me swaying - or maybe, that was just my head processing the reason for my most recent source of unease. "Why is it happening that way?"

"From my limited research, our brains weren't wired to exist in any time except the present. We can think back on the past or imagine the future, but it's not something that our minds can process in real time. That's why no one talks about the way time traveling can mess with your head beyond the emotional way - logistically, your mind is struggling to make sense of the reanimation in different times that should have been, theoretically, impossible."

"But, but it wasn't impossible."

"Correct, it was quite possible. But that doesn't mean that your mind was properly equipped to handle it."

I rested my head in my hands, wishing this nightmare could end. "That might have been nice to know, before I agreed to this." The words seethed as they left my mouth, their latent heat practically searing the sensitive skin of my lips.

"No Vera, I didn't want to scare you. Besides, I doubt it will last forever. More likely, the images will start to disappear from your consciousness once you address them in one way or another. Really, they're functioning as a sort of quest, or snapshot, from your journey. Handle what they're asking you to observe in your present life, and then they'll leave you alone."

"But, what if it hurts? What if it screws up everything?"

Edgar sighed, and the room was so eerily quiet that I could hear him sipping his coffee across the room while tapping his fingertips on his armrest. "Vera, have you ever considered the possibility that these images, and ideas, might be the antidote for the problems you've been dealing with? That maybe by going back in time, they've made themselves fully available to you? Yes, it will be hard, and complicated. But you can work through this - and I'll help you."

Staring up at the textured plaster of the ceiling, I wondered how all of this would affect my family and friends. It might be best to keep them more or less out of it, until I was sure they could handle what I may need them for.

I shrugged. "Jet knows. I told him, because I thought he could help. He didn't tell anyone as far as I know. But I needed to let him into the equation. It was terrible on my own." I waited for my uncle to be upset with me, but he just continued sitting quietly in front of me, as if I had said something completely mundane about the weather or school.

"I can only imagine how hard that was for you."

"You - you're not, mad?"

Edgar shook his head slightly, and shifted his weight in his recliner. "Why would I be mad at you, my dear? You can handle this however you choose. And I will do everything in my power to help however I can."

"But, but, the government could arrest you! Or something. I dunno. You could... end up as a lab rat. Or be labeled clinically insane!"

"I trust you, Vera. You have a lot of your father's intuition in you, and that will serve you well."

"I do?"

"Very much so. Jet reminds me a lot more of your mother than you - he's always hunched over that laptop, after all. Workaholics, the two of them. If they don't stop to enjoy life once in a while, they're going to miss it." He winked at me, and I found myself warming from the inside at his confidence in me. Of course, Uncle Edgar was very much still a pariah in our family, but to me, he was a genius. Sure, the guy still drove a beat-up truck and lived in scrubby overalls, but he had a richer mind than anyone I'd ever met before. I wonder if this is how Yoda's friends must have felt.

"Yeah, I mean, I guess so."

"So what've you been seeing? You never told me, explicitly."

"You mean, the flashing images? Oh, they change all the time. But I suppose there's a good handful, that seem to continue all the time. Maybe those mean something?" He nodded.

"Okay. Let me think." I closed my eyes and leaned back on the couch for a moment, trying to trick my body into thinking I was trying to sleep - that's when the images were the strongest and clearest. Helpful for me now, but quite unfortunate for my depreciating energy level. And that's when they started swirling in my mind's eye. Picking apart enough bits of the debris was tricky, but I managed well enough.

"I see... insect-like legs, my younger self, my old classmates, the pizza place, my dad, and some kind of aquatic tail flipper. There's a lot more than that but it's all I can make out right now."

"Hmmm... okay. And do you have any idea what those things might mean? What do you think your subconscious is trying to tell you about their importance?"

I ran my hands through the knots in my half-brushed hair and exhaled. "I have no idea. I haven't been able to sleep so my analytical abilities are probably at an all time low right now, honestly."

"Well, here's what I think all that means - you have very strong emotions tied to your less-than-agreeable classmates, yes? And your father, well, I assume you saw him in the past? Those things hold much emotional significance for you as a person. The answers you are likely looking for, lie in those things. So my next question, Vera, is - *what* are you looking for?"

I inhaled sharply, frustrated by the way he seemed so sure of what he was saying even though nothing he said resonated with me. I couldn't link his suggestions to the experiences I've had, and my head started to swim with the information overload. "Well, I know we both wanted to find my dad."

"Yes, that would be wonderful, don't you think?"

I nodded. "Seeing him, in the pizza place, was surreal. He talked to me. I kept my true identity a secret at that point, but talking to him, after all those years, was... incredible." Glancing wistfully at the rugged and faded carpet at my feet, my uncle let my voice fade into a comfortable silence, as if to treat the moment with the reverence it deserved.

Edgar finally broke the silence with another question. Although the words itself seemed vague, the feeling I got from them seemed to blossom into a completely new idea in the pit of my stomach. "Given that feeling that you had, from seeing Charlie... do you think perhaps the other images you've been seeing are tied to your emotions similarly? That would make the most sense, I suppose. What are some other things you hoped to accomplish by traveling to your past?"

I shrugged. In my head, I knew that improving my chances with Alex was part of my reasoning, as was exposing those bullies to the useless faculty harpies. But those things seemed to pale in importance to finding my dad - and therefore, far too silly to admit right now.

"Well, why don't you go think about those things and let me know if you need anything else?" My uncle got up from his armchair with his now-empty coffee cup, likely to bring it to the sink. "And Vera, you can call me too, you know."

I nodded as he settled back into his well-worn armchair.

"I know things have been ... tense, for our family, and for that, I truly hope... you can forgive me. It'll probably take time, but that's okay. I'm back for good now, so hopefully things will get better with time."

I thanked him for his time, and then he hugged me. I mean, a complete bear-hug situation. It was a bit unexpected, but sweet, I guess. He really was trying to make amends and I totally respected that, even if I felt stuck in the middle of a war.

"I believe in you, Vera. You're going to figure this out - just like your dad would have."

"Thanks. I'll try my best."

I made my way back to the front door, and marveled at how earlier this week, I was terrified of being trapped here. But it was really just a quaint house like any other, and my uncle wasn't a psycho kidnapper like Jet believed.

Lucky for me, Jet always seemed too wrapped up in his work to worry Mom too much about it. Might not be the healthiest thing for him, but it was definitely a plus for me in this isolated situation.

Twenty-Six: A Cute Little Smol Smush

Leaving Edgar's house after we had that heart-to-heart put me in a weird mood. Not in an especially bad way or anything - just that talking about the things I was sure were just in my head seemed to make them all the more real and scary to me. My uncle had explained what may be causing my relentlessly spinning thoughts, and realizing that it was directly linked to my brain failing to process time travel was definitely unsettling, to say the least. But I'll admit it was also nice to know I wasn't going insane or something.

Looking at the clock on my dashboard, I realized that if I went home now, Mom might ask what happened with class since I'd still be expected to be there this time of day. And although she was always knee-deep in an article, she always had a pretty accurate memory of my class schedule. *Maybe I'll just kill some time and grab a coffee.* That idea seemed good, but then I realized that Gavin might be working, and I was still pretty unsure what I was feeling about him, if anything at all. Would he expect me to make a move about what he had implied? Would it be awkward? Can I go into the coffee shop and remain somewhat ambiguous throughout the ordeal?

A sane person might just get coffee elsewhere, but I was craving specifically *that* coffee and getting a cheap knockoff was just not going to do it for me today. After all that I've been dealing with, I needed the real stuff. *Maybe for once, I'll just have to wing it.*

Without any other ideas, I begrudgingly drove to my favorite coffee shop. *I'll just get my latte and leave, no biggie.* But I was wrong about the no biggie part - yep, as soon as I walked in, Gavin looked up from the whipped cream he was swirling onto a drink and waved at me, smiling like an idiot and blushing. I definitely wasn't *uninterested* in the guy - I was just still sorting out *how* interested I was. I think the ordeal I had been through with the

161

time traveling had scrambled up my emotions. Or maybe I was just hormonally out of whack - who knows. It could be anything.

"How's it going, Vera?"

Crap, he's staring at me. "Oh, I'm okay."

"Sorry I didn't text you back, I had a mandatory family dinner thing last night so I had to be off the grid. Anyways, what can I get for you today? The usual, I assume?"

Dammit, that smile is so cute. He's such a cute little smol smush.

"Yeah, that'd be great. Thanks."

He turned around to get that ready for me, and I backed away from the counter so the next person could order. But then I realized that I was the only customer waiting for their drink - probably since it was an odd time of day to be here. Eleven in the morning on a weekday is definitely not a peak coffee shop hour - too late to be the morning rush and too early for the afternoon slump. I ended up browsing through the specialty mugs and other merchandise when Gavin materialized right in front of me to hand me my drink.

"Here ya go, and it's on me today." He flashed that killer smile again, and I'd be lying if I said my knees didn't totally melt at least a little.

"What? But you did that just the other day, you don't have to..."

He shook his head defiantly, with that smile still plastered on but replaced with a knowing grin. "I never *have* to do anything. I just *wanted* to, that's all."

Gavin winked at me, as if the smile wasn't enough, and my stomach did that little flippy thing it always does around ridiculously cute guys. I mean, usually they don't notice me, so this was uncharted territory.

"Well uh, thanks so much!" I smiled at him, nodded, and turned to leave, but his hand gently touched my shoulder. I turned right around, as if struck by lightning. Or at least, I felt sparks from his touch even through the fabric of my t-shirt.

162

"Vera, would you, um, maybe want to go out with me sometime?"

There it is. And I was so close to getting out of here without having to decide. And that's the precise moment where I felt my head and hormones running a hundred miles per hour in opposite directions. It happened so fast that it felt like an out-of-body experience watching myself smile, blush, and nod.

"Yeah, totally!"

His smile immediately doubled in size and he walked back around the counter with a little extra bounce in his step. I noticed it because the silver pocket chain poking out from the side of his apron caught the light from the window as he moved. "Okay, I'll text you when I get off work. Have a great day Vera." He waved at me again, and I walked back to my car. Ideally, it would have been nice to sit for a bit, but Gavin had to work and I felt awkward and excited enough without sitting there staring at him. I mean, I would have *tried* not to stare, but I'd make no promises about the success rate of that.

"Looks like I'm actually going out with Gavin." The words were deadened by the fabric seat covers of my car, and saying it out loud seemed all the more surreal. I had time traveled, and yet I believed that was happening far more quickly than I believed this. And in a very strange way, I was still thinking about Alex a lot too. *Chill out, it's not like anything is exclusive yet. A date is a date, not a formal proclamation of undying love and devotion.* I chuckled to myself, and then started the engine to get home. The clock read eleven-twenty now, but it still was too early to go home after cutting class, so I figured I might as well head to the park to clear my head and sip my coffee.

I parked my Volkswagen bug and exited, heading toward the cliff area overlooking the water. It was my favorite spot, even though now it was accompanied with the odd chill of remembering that I sat in this very spot when Edgar captured me and I was so sure he was going to kill me or something. Obviously, that was not the case, even though it was terrifying at the time. Life is just nuts sometimes.

Landing very unceremoniously on my favorite sitting-rock, I sipped my coffee and closed my eyes. Breathing in the salty ocean air, I silently tried to coax the images in my mind out of wherever they hid during the day, but they outsmarted me. They seemed to continuously appear in my mind's eye throughout the day, but then were much clearer at night when I was either trying to sleep or actually dreaming. I did catch some new glimpses of them though, and even though I had been seeing a handful of the same ones for a while, I started to manage to pick through the whirlwind and find a few others that seemed to appear in a very blurry and disorganized fashion.

Now, the spidery legs, faces of my former classmates, my own face, and my dad were accompanied by pizza, the school, Alex, and the tail of some aquatic creature. In a classic case of "one of these things is not like the others", I was pretty stumped. Maybe my head was glitching - what does a random tail flipper have to do with anything I had recently witnessed? Newsflash: nothing. It had nothing to do with anything I had just been through and seen. But there it was, the scaly surface of the scalloped edges emerging from the water in my brain. It flashed by quickly like the other images, but somehow, it seemed to linger in my vision just *slightly* longer than the others. I found that especially ironic because it was the least relevant of them all.

I mulled over everything for the next hour or so, and once I determined enough time had passed for Mom not to question whether or not I actually went to class, I headed home. While I was driving, my phone beeped, but I resisted the urge to look at the screen. Instead, I made it safely into our driveway and checked it once I was parked. Of course, Gavin had texted me - he must've finished his shift shortly after I left.

"So looks like we're hanging out soon. Lunch on Saturday maybe?"

Inhaling sharply, I paused to try to think about what I wanted to do here. Of course, I already said 'yes' so it wasn't so

164

much that I was questioning, I just had to mentally check to make sure I was free Saturday afternoon.

"Yeah that works! Pick me up at noon?"

"See you then ;)"

Slipping my phone back into my pocket, I felt simultaneously excited and nervous. Suddenly, it all felt very real as I realized that I had an actual, real-life boy who was going to take me on an actual date. Had to shake it off long enough to get back into the house without making a scene, though. Mom was amazing at a lot of things, but I've never been comfortable chatting about boys with her, no matter how much she lovingly poked and prodded me for insider info.

Realizing that I probably shouldn't skip tomorrow's classes too, I'd better do my reading and homework to stay on top of everything. But the images continued to make it harder and harder to focus. I started to notice that whenever I was just passively living my life, they dissipated, and then condensed at the most inopportune moments when I was clearly trying to focus.

After a few more minutes looking through my textbook fruitlessly, I closed it and decided to make myself a cup of tea. Padding past Jet's room with the eerie light of his monitor illuminating the gap between the carpet and the bottom of his door, I made my way down to the kitchen. The house was pretty quiet, as Mom was in her office editing, so I was alone with my relentless thoughts. I wanted desperately to be excited about my date with Gavin, but somehow all the more important things on my mind seemed to steal my attention from anything happy like that.

Grabbing a chamomile tea bag from the package Mom kept in the cabinet with the birthday candles, I filled a teacup and waited for it to boil. Absentmindedly, I found myself doodling on a piece of scratch paper that was left on the counter. At first, it was a bunch of random doodles - just the typical swirls, smiley faces, flowers, and anything else that was relatively easy to draw without being a professional artist. But then, something weird happened - I found myself drawing that tail flipper in my mind's eye that just wouldn't

165

quit. I wondered why I chose that, but then realized that most of the other images were of faces, which were quite a lot harder to draw.

When I looked at what I had drawn, it was almost as if I was seeing it for the first time. In my head, the images were often blurry at best. I was able to determine this one was a tail of some sort, but until I saw it on the opposite side of my eyelids, I could barely make out any details of it. My hand seemed to know what I was seeing better than my brain did. Dropping the pencil I held and shivering as if some cold breeze had nipped at the back of my neck, I inhaled deeply and felt a buzzing in my brain. Then I realized it was just the teakettle notifying me that it was ready to pour. Transferring it to my favorite mug with the words "boss bitch" embossed on it in glittery lettering, I sat down on a nearby barstool and let the tea steep.

The sketch that appeared on the paper moments ago was unclear - it reminded me a bit of some demented mermaid tail. The scalloped edge seemed inverted, as if someone had taken a bite out of it. It also had these ridges that made it appear very gothic in nature, and definitely not something friendly. The level of detail in my little doodle kind of blew my mind - it looked like something that could appear in an academic journal or something. Unfortunately, it's not like I could easily search the Internet with nothing but a doodle from my time-traveled half-baked brain, so I'd have to hang onto it until maybe the pieces fit themselves together in my head over time. I'd never been one to be very patient though, unfortunately. And now I was really feeling the effects of that as I sipped my still-too-hot tea and winced as the very warm liquid burned my esophagus all the way down.

As I sat trying to make sense of all this, the other images continued to swirl relentlessly in my head, and I mumbled some choice words under my breath wishing that I was better prepared to deal with these kinds of confusing side effects of time travel. Anxiety reared its ugly head as I remembered the fact that my teachers were fired for being labeled clinically crazy. What else had crumbled as a result of my feeble attempt at rebuilding the life I felt I deserved from the beginning?

The aquatic tail refused to reveal anything to me about itself, so I stuffed it in my pocket, turned off the stove, and marched myself back to my room with my mug of tea in hand. Determined to get at least a bit of my homework done, I struggled through the distracting images flashing through my mind and threw myself into my marketing case study reading. My past may have been pretty messed up, but that didn't mean my future had to be. Just when I was finally getting into my reading, my phone buzzed on my nightstand and my concentration was completely broken.

"Hey you ;)"

It was Gavin, apparently flirting his tail off - no pun intended, given my most recent discovery. I didn't have time to chat so I let my phone go dark even though I saw the message on my lock screen. *That kind of stuff would just have to wait until I finished my reading.*

I had only the highest hopes for my homework, but it couldn't have been more than two or three minutes before I gave up and grabbed my phone to text him back. And the funniest thing was, I couldn't even pinpoint why. Was it a feeling of obligation, hormonal desperation, or loneliness? I'll never really know.

"Heyyyyyyy"

The little bouncing dots signaled his next response was soon-to-come.

"You looked beautiful today. Definitely distracted me at work."

I nearly choked on my own saliva - I wasn't at all used to this kind of attention from a guy. I think my inexperience made me fall into either one of two extremes. I either was too cynical to take him seriously, or I was far too lonely and hungry for affection that I would eat it up like a starving hyena. Unfortunately, at this moment, I was the latter.

"Thank youuuuuuu :) I'm really not used to hearing that"

"Why? You really are gorgeous."

I wasn't sure what more to say after that, but my hands were shaking from the excitement of it and the butterflies in my gut were

167

about ready to burst out of my belly. I just responded with a heart emoji and then decided to call it a night.

Throwing my books into my book bag, I turned down my bed and brushed my teeth. My cheeks were a little extra rosy as I saw myself in the mirror, and I silently cursed my pale skin for always revealing my deepest secrets. If I was this obvious now, what would happen when I saw Gavin on Saturday? Or for that matter, what would happen when I saw Alex tomorrow night for Willow's well-meant but ridiculous club outing?

Only one way to find out, just gotta suck it up. My shoulders tensed up as I noticed how everything in my life became its own kind of struggle lately - even the things that should be fun, like going out with friends, had become stressful in their own way. Given what I had been through though, I guess it made sense. Now I just had to be careful to avoid resenting the current state of myself.

Twenty-Seven: The Gothic Mermaid Tail

The staccato beeping of my alarm clock woke me up on Thursday morning, and I rolled out of bed even more tired than the days before. My exhaustion was quickly starting to pile up, between all the stress I was carrying and the images in my brain that seemed to fly through my head at a dizzyingly fast rate. Luckily, it was nothing a little coffee couldn't fix, at least for a short while. Mom was already up and working, so I just grabbed a travel mug and filled it up from the batch she already made. Since I was running a bit late, I just stuck a bagel between my teeth and grabbed my car keys and book bag.

The drive to school was pretty uneventful, so I tried to occupy myself with the latest alt-rock tune to play on the radio. It's pretty rough when your own brain starts to self-destruct from the inside out and there's no way to escape it. I wasn't going crazy - at least, I didn't think I was. But this perpetual state of anxiety was definitely doing a number on me.

I sat through my marketing class, and then my business class. After those, I met up with Willow for lunch because her class was cancelled and I desperately needed any kind of distraction I could get from my cluttered head.

"Hey girl! Ready to tear up the club tonight?" She brushed her long auburn hair over her shoulder, and flashed her pearly-white smile at me. The girl was always the picture of beauty, but not in the superficial California it-girl way. Rather, I swear on my grandmother's grave that Willow must roll right out of bed ready for Coachella.

"I mean I said I'd be there, I never said I would be 'tearing it up'."

She crinkled her nose like a frustrated bunny rabbit and swatted my shoulder playfully. "Yeah, okay. We'll just see about that now won't we." Willow winked at me and then chose a pre-made kale smoothie from the refrigerator in the café.

I shrugged, just to get her off my back about it but I knew this was far from the end of the conversation. After grabbing a veggie wrap and lemonade, I followed Willow to the card scanner to pay for lunch and then settled down at a sunny table by the window.

"So Vera, what's the latest? Give me the deets, the four-one-one." She speared some lettuce onto her fork and dug into her caesar salad.

"About what, exactly?" I tried to hide the tremor in my voice as I popped the cap off my lemonade, wondering what she knew and what I would be comfortable admitting to.

"Oh anything! I just feel like we haven't gotten to chat in a while, just you and me, ya know?"

I shrugged. "Oh, yeah, um okay."

Willow's eyes blinked impatiently, and she rested her fork on her plate and crossed her arms. "Well? Geez Vera, you seem really out of it lately."

"I'm sorry, I haven't been sleeping well. Just a lot on my mind." *You have no idea how much.*

"You haven't? Hmm. Any idea what might be causing it?"

Don't spill too much Vera. She might not be able to handle it - if she would even be able to believe me at all.

"I have um, very *vivid* dreams."

"Oooh anything… *dirty*?" She slurred that word like every letter was intensely pleasurable and smirked at me like we were about to get caught by my overbearing teachers in grade school. Or maybe it was the idea of me actually dealing with that sort of thing that she found hilarious.

"What? No. I just mean, I keep seeing very vivid images that repeat over and over again, but I can't figure out what they mean, or why I keep seeing them." *Okay that was a partial lie - I had a pretty good hunch as to why I was seeing them. I just couldn't figure out what they meant though.*

"What kinds of images?" Luckily, Willow had returned to her salad, and her voice was normal again, lacking her salacious tone.

"Well, most of them are pretty straight-forward. I've been seeing my dad, Alex, our old classmates, and teachers. It's all pretty logical because those people were really significant in my life, for better or worse. But, there's something else that I can't make sense of."

Willow raised her eyebrows, silently encouraging me to continue.

"I think it's easier if I just show you." I shoved my hand into one of the tiny pockets inside my book bag, and showed her the sketch from last night. "I've been seeing this... tail flipper, or something. But I couldn't really grasp it until I tried to sketch it out. Looks like a mermaid tail, right?"

Willow took the wrinkled-up paper from my hand and smoothed it out on the table we were eating lunch at. "I don't think it's a mermaid tail, the edge of it looks too gothic, kinda creepy, actually. You're sure it's a tail?"

"Yes? No. Oh I don't know. For some reason, my brain kept telling me it was a tail, so it probably is. Maybe my art skills are just lacking."

Willow stared at it for another agonizingly slow few minutes, and I nibbled at my veggie wrap punctuating the silence with sips of my drink. While I was reaching for a napkin across the table from the plastic dispenser, she touched my forearm and nearly scared the crap out of me.

"What?"

"It's a walrus tail."

"How do you know?"

"I've been studying lots of animal tails in my zoology class. That, my friend, is definitely a walrus tail."

"But I don't think I've really seen a walrus before. How would that pop into my head, repeatedly? It doesn't make any sense."

171

Willow sat back in her chair and crossed her arms with a sly grin spreading over her lips. "Seems you have a very *vivid* imagination then."

"Seriously, why is everything dirty with you? I think Zander's rubbing off on you."

"Probably." She kept smirking at me, just so I would squirm a bit. But today, I felt myself tensing up for completely other reasons that had nothing to do with raging hormones and R-rated dreams (which I don't really ever have, by the way).

"Okay, think what you want. I gotta get to my last class." I picked up my trash and threw it away, while I heard Willow's flip flops excitedly hit the tiled flooring behind me to throw away her trash as well.

"Vera, I'm sorry - I didn't mean to upset you. I just wanted to lighten the mood a little, you seemed pretty overwhelmed."

I exhaled, and forced myself to slow down before I chased away one of my closest friends. Gems like Willow were few and far between, and I wasn't about to let my internal battles kill off one of my best relationships.

"I know that." My voice felt small, like the knots in my throat were constricting it.

"So uh, you and Alex'll be at my house tonight, right? Seven o'clock sharp. Can't let all the good bar seats get taken!"

"Yeah, see ya then." I accepted her hug and then speed-walked to my ethics class because I really was about to be late. Luckily, I ended up getting through the door just in time, and the class itself actually flew by since my professor just gave us the time to research our paper topics. Admittedly, I used probably half that amount of time to look up images of walruses - and consequently, their tails. And Willow was right - my cruddy, half-asleep sketch matched almost exactly with the results of my Internet search - and also with the foggy images in my head.

Nice one, Willow. I knew your major would come in handy eventually. I smirked to myself, thinking about how cool it was she was blazing her own trail, even though it was often inconvenient and uncertain.

172

After BS-ing my way through the rest of my class and researching just enough to have something to show for it should I be asked to report back, I walked across campus and back to my car to get ready for my evening out. I wanted to be excited about hanging out with Alex and my two closest college friends, but my mind was just everywhere. I was still thinking about Gavin, and hoped that things were still casual enough that this outing I was on tonight wouldn't seem rude or slutty in any way. This whole dating thing was super new to me, so I found myself treading lightly more often than not. The butterflies in my gut and chest were nice, though. Really nice. A girl could get used to that.

For once, Jet was out of his room and parked on the couch, apparently having fallen asleep with his non-dominant hand resting comfortably in a bag of cheese puffs. The orange cheese-dust was still noticeable around his mouth mingling with his five o'clock shadow, and I tiptoed through the kitchen as not to wake him. My brother was working so hard lately, I could only imagine what that company had been asking him to do. If you asked me though, what good was a high-paying job if there was never any time to enjoy some of that money? All he did was work twenty-four-seven - or at least, it appeared that way.

I've stopped wanting to know what he's been up to since those *interesting* noises started coming from his room every week in high school. Our relationship wasn't strained usually - but lately, yeah, I'll admit, it had been complicated. Jet seemed to be pushing me away, but I could sense there was something happening under the surface that he wasn't letting me see. Brothers are just notoriously hard to read, I guess. Or so, that's what I've heard from some of my other friends who also have brothers. And then you factor in all that wild stuff about birth order and you've got yourself a real conundrum.

Returning to my bedroom-turned-sanctuary was always my favorite part of the day. Unfortunately for me today though, I couldn't stay. It was five o'clock now, and I had to get ready to be at Willow's house by seven. I mentally kicked myself for not

173

getting Alex's cell phone number from him the other day, but I thought that he knew where Willow's house was, so I figured he'd probably just meet me there.

I set my iPod dock to play my latest rotation of favorite songs, and then resigned myself to picking something at least somewhat attractive from my closet to wear tonight. After a solid twenty or so minutes, I settled on my short leather skirt and white halter top. I wouldn't typically pair them together, as I thought they were extremely flirty on their own. Wearing them together, I'd look a little *extra* attractive. Which was definitely not a bad thing - I just wasn't used to it. In case my confidence crapped out on me mid-evening, I decided to grab a light blue cardigan to pull over my slightly more revealing top. Then I grabbed my favorite black pumps and a cute black handbag to hold all my essentials - phone, wallet, lip balm, and hand sanitizer. After running a brush through my hair, fixing my eyeliner, and choosing a choker necklace, I made my way downstairs to grab a quick snack so I wasn't gonna be starving all night until we got food later.

Jet woke up from his cheese-dust coma long enough to take one look at my outfit. His eyes widened in surprise. "What are you all dressed up for?" He ran his hand through his hair, and I cringed thinking about all the cheese dust he just accidentally deposited in it.

"I'm going out with Willow, Zander, and Alex. I should be back around midnight, maybe."

He raised an eyebrow. "On a weeknight? What is this, a quarter-life crisis or something?" He smirked, and then got up to wash his hands in the sink. When I didn't answer him and just started grabbing some cheese and crackers to nibble on instead, he shrugged and started heading back upstairs. But he paused in the foyer, and I could feel his brotherly stare locked onto me.

"Hey Vera? Just be careful, okay? And uh, I'm glad you're hanging out with that Alex kid again. I always thought he was pretty cool." I couldn't quite read his expression and tone - it was surprisingly brotherly and sweet - vastly different from the perpetually tired, overworked, cranky Jet that I've been seeing

174

lately. Maybe a couch nap was all he needed - I'll have to remind him of that next time he gets all uptight. Although, I could still palpably sense some significant pain. His eyes crinkled slightly at the edges and then became tensely furrowed.

"Oh, okay. Um, yeah. I will." I smiled at him casually, and he made his way back to his room, probably to work on more software stuff or something. I never did have a clue what his work required of him, but I knew it must be stressful, based on the way he snapped at anyone who got within ten feet of him.

Settling down to eat my pretty boring snack, I tried to calm my thoughts and look forward to tonight, even though I was definitely not the clubbing type. Far from it actually, despite the surprisingly trendy outfit I managed to throw together. At six-fifteen, I was just about ready to head over to Willow's house when the doorbell rang. I wasn't expecting any visitors today, but I went to answer the door since I knew both Jet and Mom were working - workaholics, the both of them.

And let me tell ya, I *really* wasn't expecting to open the door and see Alex Halliday staring back at me.

Twenty-Eight: Some Tall Fruity Blue Disaster

"I hope it's okay, I didn't exactly know where Willow lived. Figured we could just drive over together." He ran his hand through his perfectly shaggy longish hair and stared into my soul with those deep chocolate brown eyes. In the evening light, tones of honey and amber seemed to peek out of his warm irises, and I caught myself staring at his slightly-unbuttoned dark blue shirt and black skinny jeans.

"Vera? You ready to go?"

I shook myself out of my hormone-laced haze and nodded. "Yeah, I was just getting ready to head out. Come on in for a sec." Stepping aside, he moved quickly past me and his cologne hit my nose - seemingly a mix of musky sandalwood and sage. It was intoxicating, but I pushed it aside, reminding myself I was hanging with an old friend tonight. Totally just a casual thing. Besides, I had a date with Gavin on Saturday. *I had a date with Gavin on Saturday.*

"I was just grabbing my purse, then I'll drive us on over to Willow's house."

"I parked on the street, is that okay? I don't think I'm blocking anything." I glanced out the window, and sure enough, Alex's car was safely stowed out of the way.

"Yeah, you should be fine there." I nervously flipped my hair over my shoulder, and then grabbed my keys and bag. "All set?"

"Ready as ever." He smiled at me, that familiar smile that colored my periphery for most of my childhood. Everything about Alex was familiar - and I couldn't tell if that was what attracted me to him, or really what I was feeling at all. I really liked Gavin too, but it was hard to say what was going to happen with that. With Alex, I felt safe - familiarity made me feel like I knew everything I needed to know to be comfortable.

"Hey, so I should be upfront about some stuff."

176

"Oh?" As I pulled out of my driveway, I felt my stomach plummet down to my ankles in two separate pieces. *Was he about to address the elephant in the room? Or dash some of my feelings? Could he tell how I was feeling?*

"I'm really not a dancer. Never really been to a club before."

Oh okay, that's not so bad. "No worries! I've only been a couple of times with Willow and Zander. They're super into it and try to get me out of the house because I'm such a homebody. I guess when they met you they figured they could rope you along too. Sorry about that." I adjusted my cardigan that had twisted around a bit and kept driving in the direction of Willow's house. The late evening sun was just about setting now, and the golden glow had become a deeper rum-hued tint over the asphalt.

"Nah it's all good. I'm happy to be able to hang out with you again, it's really been too long."

I nodded. "Yeah, I mean I always asked myself why we just... stopped talking. I never wanted to, you know. I guess it just happened." Then I had another thought. "I also just realized that I don't actually have your cell number because I always used to just call you on your house phone when we were younger. Do you wanna go ahead and text me?"

"Oh sure! What's your number?"

I rattled off the digits as I drove and then felt my phone vibrate in my purse next to me. "Got it."

We sat in a comfortable silence for the remaining few minutes it took to pull into Willow's driveway. Her cozy house sat on a quiet street shaded by a lot of mature trees and friendly neighbors.

The digital clock on my dashboard said it was seven o' two, and Willow came marching right out of her front door with Zander in tow behind her. She wore a sparkly green bodysuit and a slinky black shawl framed by her freshly-curled, long hair. Zander pretty much wore what he always did - typical khakis and a button-down

177

shirt. The evening was cooler than the day, but still pretty warm. This was springtime in California, after all.

"Vera you gotta be punctual to the par-tay! You know this." Willow feigned distaste but then smirked as I exited my car and Alex followed me over to her.

"Oh please, two minutes is nothing! We have all night for you to try and drag me onto that dance floor."

Willow jingled her keys in my face. "That's the spirit! Now let's go. I'll drive."

Zander snatched the keys from her. "And *when* you drink just a little too much, I'll drive us back here safe and sound."

"Well I haven't had a drop of alcohol yet so hand me my keys!" She playfully pried them out of his hand and then strutted over to her car and opened the doors. "Into the party bus, people!"

Zander sat in front with her while Alex slid into the back seat, with a comfortable bubble of space between us partitioned by a folded-down cup holder and armrest. I took a deep breath, hoping that this night wouldn't be too crazy - after all, I was still trying to read him. I was pretty sure I still wanted something, but I was still a bit uncertain. And as for Alex, his warm personality seemed to have stood the test of time. Still didn't really know what that meant in my context, but it was certainly nice anyway.

Some cheesy pop music played softly on the radio, which I only tolerated because I knew that was what Willow liked the most and she was nice enough to tow our sorry club-hating butts around all night. Still cringed internally though. Although based on Alex's smirk next to me, I'm guessing it wasn't quite as internal as I thought - oops.

"So when we get past the bouncer I wanna head straight to the bar to get liquor'd up. Who's with me?"

Zander rolled his eyes and looked back at us, shaking his head. "Easy does it, babe. You don't wanna scare away the rookies. Besides, I don't have the energy to put up with drunk you tonight. Let's just grab a table and chill, 'kay?"

"Okay but if the music sucks and isn't danceable enough, I'm getting booze right away." She let out a giddy laugh and pulled

178

into the already packed parking lot of The Blue Pelican, which featured bright neon light-up signage of a large-billed bird sipping tequila or something illuminating the increasing darkness of dusk. After parking, we exited Willow's garish purple car and walked toward the entrance. We easily made it past the bouncer since we're all over twenty-one and actually had "proper identification" on us for once. He stamped our hands with a little cartoon pelican so we could re-enter if needed. So far, so good.

The music was loud, and the lights were strobing, as expected. The one good thing about being dragged to a club with an old-friend-turned-sort-of-crush was that little to no conversation was expected, and there were no awkward silences. Or any silence at all, for that matter. As promised, Willow agreed to claim a table for us all to sit at as our central hangout spot for the night, and Zander got up momentarily to order some appetizers for us to share. Or at least, that's the best I could make out from reading his lips and hand gestures - the music really was that loud.

Willow's voice, however, boomed over the speakers, much to my embarrassment.

"Vera! What the hell are you doing wearing a button-up sweater to a club? Take that off, *duh*. You're gonna overheat anyway."

I froze like a deer in headlights, suddenly regretting wearing the slightly more revealing top than I was used to. But to avoid making a scene, I found myself absentmindedly unbuttoning my sweater, and after laying it neatly on the back of my chair, Alex's eyes locked with mine. Or, perhaps slightly *below* my eyes. *Well, that's new.* I smiled at him shyly, fighting the urge to cover my chest with my arms.

"Damn girl, you look hot!" Willow patted me on the shoulder, and then turned away in search of something alcoholic to consume. I blushed, and hoped that Alex wouldn't just stare at me like a horny middle schooler all night, even though it was secretly kinda flattering. Okay - it was actually *super* flattering, to be honest.

As words seemed to be more or less useless in this particular environment, I sat next to Alex and just laughed at the erratic dancing of the obviously drunk people our age. When Zander returned to the table a moment later, he was facing away from the dance floor but immediately turned around and started laughing at them too while sipping his artisan whiskey. Willow sat down with some tall fruity blue disaster in a giant glass, and I hoped she wouldn't drink it too fast. It was going to be a long night and drunk Willow is no picnic to deal with. Trust me, I had stories to back up that claim.

Willow sucked down about half of it in like ten minutes, which was equal parts impressive and concerning for my straight-edge self to witness. I just nibbled on a mozzarella stick and sipped my Shirley Temple and tried to look like I somewhat belonged here. Alex got a beer, but it was only one bottle and he seemed to be able to handle it - at least, I hoped. Once in a while, he nudged my arm to point out an especially hilarious dancer and I laughed. As the night wore on, we both seemed to get tired and naturally scooted a bit closer to each other, leaning on each other absentmindedly. That is, until Willow was properly boozed up after finishing her drink and dragged us onto the dance floor with her and Zander. We managed to bounce around a bit to some faster songs, but when things slowed down a bit, things got… interesting.

Zander pulled Willow close like the sweet boyfriend he is, and as a nostalgic Nickelback song blared over the speakers, Alex and I just stood there awkwardly for a minute. We were standing about three feet apart, but the drunk and tired crowd around us seemed to naturally push us closer together as they swayed to the music. Seeing as how it'd be extra awkward to just be standing in each other's personal space, I found myself hesitantly resting my hands on Alex's broad shoulders. I could smell the beer on his breath still, and his eyes seemed a little glassed-over, but he was still pretty coherent. Willow on the other hand, was a wild girl. I glanced over at her very obviously sticking her tongue down Zander's throat, which he only tolerated for like a minute before gently pushing her away. The guy was never that big on PDA -

heck, neither of them were. But drunk Willow was quite another story.

Alex followed suit, placing his hands on my waist and swaying slowly to the music. I whispered in his ear something about not having to dance if he didn't want to, Willow can't actually force us to, etcetera, but he just shook his head and smiled, even encouraging me to twirl a little by shifting his grip on my hand and raising it in the air. His hands sent shockwaves through the thin fabric of my halter top as I faced him again, and being this close didn't actually feel as awkward as I expected it to. Maybe it was the beer keeping him calm and loose - but whatever it was, I was grateful for it. His brown eyes reflected the strobe lights of the room and sparkled, be it from the beer or the moment - I'm still not sure.

By the time the song ended, our bodies were pressed about as close together as possible without sharing the same skin, and my head rested on his shoulder as another faster song hit the airwaves. I moved to separate from him and maybe head back to the table, but his fingers found the back of my neck, and they guided my head toward his lips sharply, filling me with a longing I didn't know he felt. I was shocked, so I barely reacted at first even though his mouth moved softly, like a whispered promise.

After that initial contact, I responded by even opening my mouth slightly, but my heart was threatening to break right out of my ribcage. His lips tasted like the beer he just drank, and I soaked in his cologne and his scent as the flashing lights seemed to increase my pulse rate while his hands wandered a bit over my back. I dared to let my tongue touch his, and he deepened the kiss as electricity passed in between us. He pulled away after probably five or six seconds, but I must've looked like a deer in headlights because I smiled slightly but my eyes were wide, and I could feel blood rushing to my cheeks. I chanced a glance at our table where Willow and Zander had sat down for a break and their eyes were wide.

They totally saw. Dammit.

I turned back to look at Alex, but he disappeared. That is, until I saw him across the room, running out the front door. He probably needed to get some fresh air after what just happened. Who could blame him, after all - the air in here reeked of hormones, booze, and desperation.

I ran past our table where I saw Willow mouth a certain four-letter expletive after the words "what the" and I just blushed and shrugged. Then I followed Alex right out the front door. I was still shaking from his touch, and the slightly chillier night air raised goose bumps on my exposed skin, snapping me back to reality.

Alex just kissed me. Voluntarily.

I saw him leaning up against Willow's purple scion with his head in his hands. He seemed to be breathing hard. He tilted his head up to the night sky, looking for answers in the cloudless atmosphere. I wanted to figure out how he felt about what just happened, but then it hit me like a wall of bricks: maybe it was an accident and he didn't actually want to kiss me at all. He *had* been drinking, after all.

Okay, gotta play this cool Vera. Don't seem too needy or expect anything. Just say you wanted to check on him to make sure he was okay.

I eased myself over to where he was crouching down on the ground now, with his face in his hands. He heard me before he saw me, because I wasn't able to sit down on the concrete very gracefully in my heels and tight leather skirt. I sat next to him, leaning against Willow's car, with a strategic couple of feet of space left between us. The words that I previously rehearsed in my head only moments ago had completely vacated my brain, so all I managed to squeak out was a very inadequate "hey".

He looked at me with his face still very red and his eyes still a bit glassed over, perhaps from either beer or adrenaline. The air around us seemed to be thick with expectation and tension, and neither of us really knew what to say.

"Vera, I can't believe I just did that. I'm so sorry."

"No, it's okay. It was... good, actually."

"But I promised you I wouldn't try that again."

"Alex, don't worry about it. Wait, *what?*" The confusion of his words hit me like a wall of bricks, and I suddenly experienced something like deja-vu's slutty goth cousin who makes you worry that you missed random, important chunks of your life that you should have experienced but didn't. Like FOMO but skankier.

Alex exhaled and avoided my gaze, looking off into the distance at stray cars passing by on the main road. It was only a bit past ten o'clock, so for most of us, the night was just getting started. The hands that held my hips only minutes ago were now curled into fists and sitting resolutely on the paved black surface of the parking lot.

"Vera, a few weeks after our middle school teachers were fired because your future self time-traveled to see us-"

"Wait hold up." I raised my hand to pause the conversation. "You knew about that? Even now?"

He raised one of his prominent eyebrows. "Well uh, yeah, I was there. So were you - *both* versions of you."

I pinched the bridge of my nose, trying to make sense of all that he was saying. "You, you believed that whole thing? I just... I just time traveled last week. How did, what?"

He calmly waved away my question. "Vera, it was *real*. And I remembered it. I don't understand it, but I did remember meeting this version of you years ago. It was weird - heck, I was pretty weird then. Still am now, actually. Which is probably why I pulled a stunt like that. Well, that and the fact that I'm... still a *little* buzzed right now."

My head was spinning, and there wasn't a drop of alcohol in my blood so I knew it wasn't that.

"Okay, so you know about the time traveling. Then... why did you never mention it to me? Or better yet, why didn't I remember it?"

He shrugged. "Well, we just... grew apart, I guess. And I dunno, maybe you repressed that whole thing along with the other bullying. You always took it pretty hard."

"I have no idea, whatever. I'll ask my crazy inventor uncle about that later" I paused, as my train of thought was totally lost at this point. And then I remembered it again. "But you just said...

183

'again'? Alex, have we kissed before?" The question hung in the air like heavy smog.

He nodded slowly while avoiding eye contact with me. "As I was saying, I guess you don't remember, or something. I'll try not to be too insulted about that." Alex smirked, clearly just an attempt to bring some levity to the conversation.

"Okay but seriously, *what happened*?" My eyes widened again, and I stared at him, wishing he would just get on with it. My heart was still thrumming from his touch, his hands, and his scent. Everything about my childhood friend had completely intoxicated me, and even though I didn't consume any alcohol, I was pretty drunk off him.

He sighed, exhaled, and leaned back on Willow's car while I braced myself for the truth.

"Vera, a few weeks after we met the older version of you from the future, I thought a lot about what she said about... us. If you recall anything about middle school, you might remember that your old friend Alex wasn't subtle. And you know, I was just starting to notice girls. So since I spent most of my time with you, it was only logical that I might... start to fall for you."

I nodded, remembering the way I had observed younger Alex constantly flirting, albeit badly, with younger me and how she never noticed. "Sure, okay. Then what?"

He exhaled, and ran his hands through his gelled hair. "I really wanted to kiss you, just to see what it would be like. I cornered you after school, and just went for it. We were thirteen, Vera. I didn't know what the hell I was doing. I'll never forget the look on your face. It was a bit like your face just now, actually. Except I'm pretty sure you were the one to run away, and... you were crying." His voice trailed off after that, his throat choked up with regrets that I had no recollection of as tears collected at the corners of his slightly puffy eyes.

"Alex, I really don't remember that at all."

He started sniffling a little, and he wiped his eyes on his sleeve. "Well you know, I'm actually glad to hear that. It wasn't good - I mean, *I* wasn't any good, I guess. And well, I wasn't

184

exactly discreet either. Our asshole classmates happened to see the whole thing, and they tortured both of us relentlessly for that. And then of course the remaining teachers and our substitute teachers caught wind of all that and did this whole stupid anti-kissing seminar that we had to sit through. Vera, I made you go through hell. And I think... I think that's why I slowly sort of faded away. I didn't wake up one day deciding that I was going to just stop hanging out with you."

"I never thought that you did that." At this point, Alex was balancing precariously on the brink of tears, so I started to casually rub his shoulder a bit and scooted closer next to him on the asphalt so our sides were touching.

"But I did. Vera, I started to avoid you, at least subconsciously, because I was so ashamed at myself for what I did. Now that I'm older, I realized that an innocent kiss is such a normal thing, especially when you're thirteen. But our school was just so effed up that they made even something normal seem like the end of the world. I never forgave myself for that look on your face, and I promised myself - and you - that I'd never try that with you again."

"I appreciate that, Alex. But I really can't believe I would have minded so much."

"Oh trust me, you did. Your face was so similar to the way it just looked tonight, that I was transported back to that terrible middle school moment, and I ran out here to process it all over again. Besides, I know we just reconnected last week, but our history is so... significant, and part of me felt like we just picked up where we left off. And then tonight, you just looked so beautiful, and I couldn't help it, I guess. I don't know what I was thinking, must've got caught up in the moment."

"That's okay, I really didn't mind. I didn't have any memory of you from kissing me before, so I'd say that was pretty good, honestly." My words felt like a pathetic consolation prize as my friend bared his honest soul in front of me. What could I possibly have said to even the score?

"You don't understand though, I promised you that I wouldn't, and I broke that promise."

I shrugged. "It was nice, honestly."

He blushed, and looked away from me. "Maybe so, but I just have too many memories connected to you. Plus, I *just* broke up with Emma. I'm just... not in the best headspace right now. I really shouldn't have done that, Vera. You didn't ask for any of this and I just complicated everything."

"Oh so *that* was her name?"

"You saw us." It was stated like a fact, not a question.

"Yeah, a few times."

He rested his face in his hands, obviously distraught and probably a little embarrassed - not for the first time tonight.

I tried not to let his words hurt me, because I knew he obviously didn't mean to do that by admitting all this stuff. But I'd be lying through my teeth if I didn't admit that I was half-hoping that something might happen with him eventually. Of course, I still had Gavin on my mind, but Alex was definitely on my radar too, and I rationalized that I didn't have to actually decide until things became exclusive with either of them. I guess Alex had decided for me, so it wouldn't matter anyway now.

"Alex? This is a lot for me to process too. It sounds like there are some gaps in my memory that I'll never get back."

"Trust me, you wouldn't want to remember those events anyway. It wasn't a fun time for me either."

"Okay well, whether or not I can remember any of that stuff, I'm really glad you were the first kiss that I actually remembered. *And* the one I didn't remember, even if it didn't seem like I appreciated it at the time." At this point, I was leaning my head on his shoulder, trying to get him to see that I wasn't pissed off at him at all. Quite the opposite actually - in many ways, his honesty and care for me through it all seemed to trump even the glaringly obvious fact that we wouldn't be dating anytime soon. I thought that realization would break me, but it didn't.

"Wait, you mean you haven't kissed anyone besides me, ever?" His eyes were a bit bloodshot at this point, but they pierced mine with the same intensity as they might've if they were well rested.

I lifted my head off of his shoulder just enough to be able to shake my head. It wasn't something I felt comfortable verbally admitting, almost as if the act of saying the words would make them all the more true.

"Oh man, Vera, I'm sorry I'm such a pathetic loser who can't respect his friends better than this." His head landed in his hands, which rested on his propped-up knees. "Dammit. I just, man. I wanted better than this for myself. And for you."

Alex quietly sobbed while I just sat there with my arms around him, my heart breaking where it was nearly going to explode mere minutes ago. I'm a firm believer that some people are in your life for different reasons. Even if those reasons seem similar sometimes, they really might not be. And I was working on being okay with that.

"Shh, it's okay. You're okay, I'm okay. Don't worry about me. I'm sorry you've been carrying this for so long." I felt myself calming down a bit as the realization that this reaction he was having wasn't because of anything I did - but rather, it was a flashback to our shared and very complicated past. Maybe he was starting to realize how much our awful school experience had affected him even now. To be honest, I was starting to notice the same thing in myself. The poison pumped into our young veins seemed to linger in our bloodstreams long after we moved onto high school and college. And there might be parts of us that will always resent those very frustrating things that happened to us.

"Vera, I really do care about you, very much. It just might not be... in a romantic capacity. I'm sorry I couldn't figure that out before tonight."

I rubbed my bare arms and nodded, and then I reached around to hug him again. "I totally understand, Alex. Please don't worry another second about me. It's all going to work out."

He shrugs. "I spent all those years pining after you, and then when we're finally old enough to actually date like the adults we are, we're just in different places emotionally. Of course that's the way it would be. Why would I expect anything different?" He laughed sadly, and then slowly shifted his weight to his feet and stood up. Offering me a hand, he helped me up off the concrete as well and I brushed the pebbles off of my black leather skirt, hoping it didn't get too scratched up.

"If it brings you any comfort at all, I think I might have actually met someone."

His eyes lit up in the darkness illuminated only by the garish Blue Pelican sign and the streetlights in the parking lot. "Really? Who?"

I blushed. "Just a guy who knows how I like my coffee. He works at my favorite cafe and I guess we sort of hit it off. His name's Gavin. We're going out for lunch on Saturday."

"Vera, I'm so happy for you! Honestly. And I'm not just saying that. You deserve someone great, even if it can't be me." He winked at me, and a sad smile spread over his face. I imagined that the beer buzz he had was already starting to wear off. He wrapped his arms around me and pulled me close.

"Really? So you're sure you don't feel weird about it? That's probably not the coolest thing to say to a guy who just tried to make out with me in a club - 'oh, by the way, I have a date in two days'." I smirked at him, and he laughed.

"Nope, I'm the one that said I didn't actually see it going that way for us. Yeah, I may have spent most of our childhood thinking that, but we're older now and I just don't feel like this bond we have is romantic."

The energy of that touch was different now - it wasn't laced with hormones and pheromones. I mean, those things were logically still there, but they didn't affect us anymore. We had reached a sort of mutual understanding about a lot of things that even I had no idea were going on, and for the first time in literal years, I felt like Alex and I could be friends again, without the awkwardness that was present after everything hit the fan in middle school.

Twenty-Nine: Don't Be a Stranger

Alex and I stood in a surprisingly comfortable silence as the streetlights flickered and the heavy bass beats reverberated from the nearby club entrance. My mind was whirring fast with all that he had admitted. I was a little disappointed about his ironic lack of romantic interest in me - especially after all we had been through together. His arm was still draped around my shoulder while we leaned against Willow's car, and we both looked off into the distance, wondering what would happen next for both of us.

"Hey, maybe we should head back in? You know, to check that Willow hasn't blacked out yet."

Alex's eyes widened, but my light giggle reassured him that I was kidding. Mostly.

"Yeah, sure."

He offered me his hand, probably more for himself than for me, but I gladly took it. Alex was careful not to interweave our fingers, as that might feel a bit too intimate. We weren't in middle school anymore, but I appreciated his sensitivity.

As we re-entered the club after showing the bouncer our hand stamps, we were met with a very tired and frustrated looking Zander walking toward us. He was carrying a very-drunk Willow bridal-style, with my cardigan and both our purses sitting carefully on her lap.

"Guys we should go, hope you don't mind - Willow's pretty out of it."

Alex and I both nodded, maybe a little too excited to leave this noisy and crowded club scene.

"No worries, we're a little tired too."

We all went right back out the way we came, and I grabbed my cardigan and purse off of Willow's lap, hopefully lightening Zander's load a bit.

189

"Can you grab the car keys out of her purse? My hands are a little full."

Willow's head lolled back, her eyes closed in a drunken stupor.

"Yeah, sure thing. I'll drive, since I'm the only one who didn't drink, I guess. Hey, does she need to go to the emergency room or something? I've never seen her *this* out of it."

Zander shook his head as he set Willow down comfortably on the back seat of her car. "Nah, this happens every once in a while when she's especially stupid, and also very tired. I think she just needs some water and rest. I've checked her pulse - it's there as strong and irritating as ever." He rolled his eyes, and then buckled her in. Their relationship was sweet and sour, calm and sassy in its own way. But their love for each other was undeniable. Scooting in next to her, he closed the car door and waited for me to start the engine. Alex was sitting in the front passenger seat with me.

"You ever driven the scion before? It can be a little finicky. Train wasn't kidding about this car." Zander rested his chin in his hands, clearly as tired as the rest of us. "I keep telling her that she can just have my Porsche - since I'm getting a new one anyway - but she won't accept it. She loves this purple piece of shit."

"That's Willow for ya - always conserving and thinking ahead. Except when it comes to alcohol. I think I can manage, thanks Zander." I pulled out of the club parking lot, waving goodbye to the neon pelican sign. The accelerator hesitated a little, but it came through just when I needed it to. There's something equal parts charming and obnoxious about older cars that still hold on for dear life.

Alex silently watched the other cars go by out his window, but I knew he wasn't upset with me. Our little talk was great - and I had peace after handling all the stuff I guess we had been holding in for so long. I chanced a quick glance in the rearview mirror and noticed Zander gently stroking Willow's hair as she started to wake up a bit.

"Hey there, sleeping beauty. We're almost back to your house, and you're gonna need some water. A *lot* of water."

190

She rubbed her eyes with the heels of her hands, and her head lolled back onto the headrest again. "Drink... too much?"

"Yes, yes you did. But you'll be fine, you always are. Although I do worry about the hangover you're going to be nursing tomorrow. You might want to skip your morning classes." He rubbed her shoulder, and tried to keep her more or less pretty calm after such a self-medicated ordeal. I never did understand why Willow couldn't control herself around alcohol, but it did worry me quite a bit. She's usually fine, but bring her to a club, and forget about it.

"Alex..."

Alex turned around in his seat to face her while I drove. "Uh, yeah?"

Willow giggled ecstatically, and slurred her words as the alcohol still coursed through her veins. "Y-you... k-kissy kissed... Vera..." Her laughter continued, and he turned right around in his seat, and sat in silence. He knew she was drunk, and probably didn't mean to bug him. But pairing Willow's loud personality with booze was never a good mix, and someone was bound to be at least a little pissed at her.

"Willow, shush. Sleep, babe. You gotta just relax."

I was grateful for Zander's willingness to calm her down, but I caught his quick wink at me in the rearview mirror. My cheeks heated up, so I just turned up the radio a bit to drown out my thoughts and Willow's drunk rambling.

Thankfully, the crappy purple scion ambled down Willow's street just around half-past eleven - a relatively early night for hitting the club, which I was grateful for. I killed the ignition, got out of the car, and handed Willow's keys back to Zander.

"Will you be okay getting her in the house, or do you need help?"

Zander shook his head. "Nah, I got it, thanks. It wouldn't be the first - or the last - time this has happened. Got it down to a science by now. I'll make sure she's hydrated and gets to bed in one piece." He winked at me, and balanced Willow's half awake body between himself and her car.

"Hey Will, you're home now."

She was only half-awake, able to stand with some support by her boyfriend and her car.

"Home? Okay." Willow yawned.

"It was, uh, cool hanging out with you guys again." Alex made a move to shake Zander's hand, but realized his hands were, once again, busy keeping his intoxicated girlfriend from face planting onto the asphalt.

"You too, Alex. I'm sure we'll see you again soon." Zander nodded at him and smiled pleasantly at me – a silent goodbye for a night that was filled with a lot more excitement than I think any of us were expecting.

And with that, Zander balanced Willow on his hip as she wobbled next to him, depending on him to brace her torso and prevent her from falling. She really found a keeper in Zander - he was fun, thoughtful, and stepped up to take care of her when it mattered. I was so sure Alex might've been that for me. And maybe he still could be - just in a slightly different context than I would've initially expected.

As soon as her front door closed, Alex turned to me with a wistful look on his face.

"Hey Vera?"

"Yeah?" We had started walking to my car that was parked at the opposite end of Willow's driveway. The slightly cooler air of the night hit my shoulders, and I tugged my cardigan on while I fished my car keys out of my purse.

"Do you think, that maybe, if I wasn't so stupid, we could've…"

"What?"

He hesitated, trying to find the right words. "Maybe… we could have had what they have?" He gestured loosely toward Willow's house as I clicked my key fob to unlock my car doors. It answered back in a major-key chirp, zapping me back to reality.

"You want to carry my limp, too-drunk butt home after we get back from the club?"

I inhaled sharply after I realized he didn't respond to my humor. I was pretty sure he wasn't changing his mind about me, but the question opened up some new tabs in my mind that I had pretty much closed for good over the past couple hours or so. "Uh, can you rephrase the question?" I cringed as my speech reminded me far too much of the annoying spelling bees we both participated in during middle school. One such occasion involved Alex and I being the top two spellers of our class - but that's not too much to shake a stick at, since our class was tiny and the other kids were actually pretty dense.

"I just, I feel like we - you and I - are close like they are. But maybe in a different way? I really do wish things were different, Vera."

I paused, meeting his gaze with eyes like a deer in headlights. Everything in me wanted to scream at him something about how we could totally be that, I wouldn't mind at all. But somehow, the situation didn't seem to call for that. My gut and my heart waged a war against my brain, and I quickly lost track of the score so I just sat in silence, waiting for him to say something that I could respond to without sending our recently resuscitated friendship back into a coma.

"Vera? Sorry, I'm probably confusing everything. Just go ahead and drive back to your place, I guess."

I started my car. "What? No, you're fine. I mean yeah, tonight has been... a lot to think about for both of us."

He blew some air out of his mouth. "You can say that again."

"Alex? I gotta be honest with you."

"Shoot."

I took a deep breath, choosing my words carefully as I followed my headlights into the darkness of the night. "These past few years, I *have* started to think of you as potentially more than just my friend. But I understand you've been through a lot lately and aren't looking for that right now. Basically, I'm just really happy to be able to say we're friends again."

"I figured that was the case, since you've been staring at me and Emma for months." His voice had a gleeful lilt to it - he wasn't irritated with me, just a bit amused.

"What? You noticed?"

Alex shrugged, and I tried to keep my eyes on the road - killing us both wouldn't solve anything. We weren't the Thelma-and-Louise type. "Well, yeah. You weren't exactly... subtle." He smiled at me, and brushed a stray piece of his hair out of his eyes.

I giggled nervously, and just kept on driving. We were almost back to my house when he said it.

"You're okay with this though, right?"

I froze, honestly not sure what to say. I wasn't *not* okay with it, but not totally thrilled either. Plus I was very interested in Gavin - at least, I thought I was. "Yeah, it's no problem. Don't worry about it, Alex. I'm glad you were honest with me. But for all it's worth..." I paused, wondering if this was going to cross an unwritten line, but I went for it anyway. "You're a really great kisser."

"Oh am I now? Well, that's good to know." He blushed, and shifted his gaze to look out the window as we pulled back into my driveway.

"So uh, thanks again for being cool with my goofy college friends."

"Willow and Zander are rad. I'd hang with you all again sometime if the opportunity presents itself." He smiled at me, and then leaned in for a sweet but awkward hug.

"So we're good?"

"Totally", I said into his shoulder, finding an odd sense of peace with the arrangement. I was grateful for that, nonetheless. "So uh, don't be stranger, right?"

"Wouldn't dream of it."

Another nod and smile, and he was heading over to his car parked at the curb in front of my house. I let myself into my front door, and found myself staring out the window at him as he drove

194

away. If tonight taught me anything, it's that some connections aren't romantic, but that fact doesn't make them any less real. Maybe that's what growing up is, after all - learning that there are different versions of the things you thought were only one thing or another. Maybe getting older lets you finally see all sides of the dice - not just the ones that are facing up.

He disappeared down the street, and I marched upstairs to get ready for bed. Jet was sitting in front of my bedroom door though, and that's when I realized that tonight was probably far from over.

"Hey sis. Just getting home?"

The question wasn't overly protective or sassy - it was just that, a question. Small talk, probably leading up to a bigger conversation.

"Yep, Willow and Zander dragged me and Alex to the Blue Pelican. We left after Willow had a bit too much to drink - not really my kinda scene."

He nodded. "I figured as much." His eyes were bloodshot again, and his face was slightly puffy, as if he'd been crying. Even his sandy blonde hair seemed a bit lackluster as of late.

"So uh, what's up? Just decided to take a break from programming to camp out on the floor in front of my room?"

"Well, I wanted to catch you before you went to bed. I've been... not feeling so good lately about a lot of things involving my job. And some of that stuff was making me worry about Edgar."

"Nah he's chill. I've been getting to know him a bit more lately, he's actually a pretty normal dude. You know, aside from the obvious eccentricities." I lowered my voice for that last bit, not sure whether or not Mom was in earshot.

"You don't have to whisper, she's taking a late-night conference call in her office downstairs. But Vera, I really think we should tell her."

I chewed my bottom lip, accidentally reminding myself of Alex's kiss even though there were currently more important things to think about. "And I really think we shouldn't."

"Look, Vera. I think our mother deserves to know that her kid time traveled thanks to her weirdo uncle." He got up from the floor and gently placed a hand on my shoulder, probably a last-ditch attempt to calm me down. Unsurprisingly, it didn't work.

"That's valid. I just don't think right now is the time."

"Okay, so if not now, when?" He crossed his arms in front of his chest, and leaned against the nearest wall.

I exhaled, trying to buy myself time to figure out what my answer to that question might be. "Well, I'm still working out a bunch of things with Edgar, and I really need his help to mentally process what I've seen and experienced. Can I have a little time to talk to him before we bring Mom into this? She's gonna go all Mama-bear on his ass and frankly, I just can't deal with that right now."

Jet stared at me for a minute, probably trying to search for a decent rebuttal. But he didn't seem to find one. "Consider yourself lucky that I'm way too tired right now to question that logic. But you gotta be careful Vera. Sometimes you might not know what you're getting into until it's too late."

That last thing he said left an unwelcome chill running up and down my spine. "Jet, what do you mean by that, exactly?"

He ran a hand through his hair. "Work has become... a lot of things I didn't expect."

"More work than you were expecting?"

He hesitated to say yes or no, which worried me quite a bit. "Sure. Something like that."

"Well, okay. I'll figure it out soon. Goodnight, bro."

He rubbed his eyes with the palms of his hands. "Night, sis."

I watched him turn around and shuffle down the hall toward his ever-glowing bedroom-turned office. Something was definitely up with Jet, and it wasn't just his fixation on telling Mom about Edgar's antics that worried me. But after a long night surviving the club chaos, including the emotional ordeal that Alex had put me through, I found myself stumbling toward my room, my trendy but uncomfortable heels long since abandoned by the garage door.

Thirty: Emo Catnip

"Why can't I remember Alex kissing me in middle school?"

I sat across from Uncle Edgar after my classes on Friday. I managed to get used to blocking out the repetitive images long enough to muddle through my classes. Plus, I couldn't rationalize any more absences. I was getting dangerously close to falling behind on my reading and coursework, and I knew Edgar would be home after I got out of class for the day, because he always was. Who knows what he even did for work.

"Vera, you *do* realize that you altered your own timeline, right? Luckily in this case, it's a relatively subtle change, and nothing particularly Earth-shattering-"

"Well maybe to *you* it's not. But to me, my best friend in the whole world was affected by this pivotal moment in our lives that leaked into the present. And when he was recounting that whole thing to me, I just completely pulled a blank. You've got to explain it better than just this 'changed timeline' bull crap." I leaned on the edge of his couch, staring into his cloudy eyes for answers that could calm the storm brewing in my psyche.

He folded his hands neatly in his lap, probably searching for the words that would help me understand this incredibly complex and frustrating element of time-travel.

"I did tell you this was a possibility, right?"

I shrugged. "I think I would have remembered it if you did."

"Ever seen *Back to the Future*?"

"Yeah, but that's a movie! This is real life, Edgar. And I'm still having trouble processing that my reality was... changed."

"It's such a minor thing though! Count your blessings, my dear."

"I beg to differ, but okay whatever." I crossed my arms, waiting expectantly for his explanation.

"Vera, since time travel is fairly new to the world - as in, I'm the only one I know of who actually fabricated a working device - there isn't much written up on the subject in the way of

197

academic journals. But here's how I understand it." He paused again, probably trying to formulate the explanation as comfortably as he could for me to take in. "So when you went as your older self to visit your past, you brought with you your enlightened perspectives as a result of living longer and thinking things differently, correct?"

I shrugged. "I mean, I guess."

"Okay. So when you encouraged your younger self to pursue a more romantic relationship with Alex, you changed the course of your past and future, aka your present."

"Oh, right. That. But why don't I remember it though?"

Edgar sighed again. "The reality that existed before you time-traveled is gone now, but up until then, you existed in the other reality, with the other past where that awkward event didn't happen. Once you time-traveled, your memories of the original reality remained even though your future now is the future that you incurred by speaking up the way you did while re-existing in the past. Is this starting to make sense, my dear?"

Edgar spoke very slowly and patiently to me about these difficult matters, and I found myself needing his help more and more often as the days wore on (one of the many reasons I didn't actually want Jet to rat him out to Mom).

"I think it's... starting to." I leaned back on Edgar's well-worn couch, and tried to process the power that I had unwittingly stepped into. It was a lot for me to process - it would be a lot for anyone, I'd wager.

"It doesn't have to be a bad thing, you know. Maybe over time, you'll find that the choices you made were for a reason."

"I just wish I lived it. There's no way I can get that moment back, is there?"

"Nope, not in the same way. If you wanted to see it happen, you could travel back there again to observe from the outside, but I wouldn't recommend it. From what you've told me, it doesn't sound like a good time to relive."

198

"Yeah, I guess you're right. I'll try to make peace with that, I guess. It's a small price to pay for at least knowing how Alex feels about me."

"And if I do recall, that was one of your reasons for traveling back in time in the first place, correct? So I'd call that a win then."

I nodded politely, letting that realization wash over my frayed nerves. Then another thought occurred to me. "So how did Alex remember that I time-traveled? I mean, I kind of said it when I visited that time... but he recalled it after all those years?"

"Well that's not so odd - wouldn't that kind of experience be pretty permanently embedded in your memory if an older version of one of your friends showed up on the street? Pretty wild stuff."

"But how did... I dunno, the government never get involved?"

"No one would believe a middle schooler, and the teachers were the only other adults to witness that event. And we know what happened to them." He smirked, clearly still enjoying some of the satisfaction of those cronies getting their just desserts, the same way I was up until a few days ago when I realized how I pretty much ruined their careers. They were decent people, even if they fell prey to some pretty outdated and obnoxious disciplinary methods.

"Yeah, I guess we do."

"And how are the images? Still spinning around in there?" He pointed to his temple to illustrate his question.

"Uh yeah, although I'm getting better at mostly blocking them out when I'm in class or something."

"That's good to hear, I know they were really bothering you a few days ago."

I nodded. "They really were, but I'm slowly trying to sort through them. You were right, I think that's what they want me to do."

"They?"

"Oh, I meant the images. But yeah, I was describing one of the less obvious ones to my friend, and since she's into nature and

199

stuff, she helped me identify it." I held up the sketch I had from the other night - now dog-eared and wrinkled - and told him all about how Willow said it was a walrus tail.

"Interesting! I have no idea what that means for you though."

"Same. I'm guessing it's important though, since I see it the most frequently out of all the images. Well, that and my dad's face are probably the ones I've been able to isolate the most."

Edgar stroked his chin, and looked out the dusty window across the room. He breathed slowly, as if searching for the answer buried deep in his lungs.

"Well my dear, I'd say to just keep at it, and keep investigating. Your brain has had more of its potential unlocked than most humans have ever experienced. You ever hear how we only use about ten percent of our brains? I'd wager you're dangerously close to twenty percent functionality at this point."

"Would that explain the images as well?"

Edgar rubbed the stubble that had grown on his chin. "That's very possible, yeah. Why not? I'll just say yes for now."

A casual silence fell into the room we sat in, and I took it upon myself to get up off the couch and start making my way to the door. "Thank you for your help, once again, Edgar. I think I should probably head home before anyone starts wondering where I've been."

"Sure thing. I'm always here if you need me, Vera. I'd do anything for one of Charlie's kids." He nodded at me from his armchair, and then I let myself out of his house and made my way back to my car. It was so comforting to have a resource like this - I wondered if I might literally have gone crazy otherwise. And it was also comforting to hear my dad's name in such a positive context. I never gave much thought to how his disappearance would affect my uncle, but the sadness hiding just behind Edgar's eyes gave it away.

I headed back to my house, only a bit later than I usually would have on a Friday evening. Now it was officially the weekend, and I had a lunch date with Gavin tomorrow. *I guess this is really happening.*

200

In the midst of all the nightclub drama, I had somewhat convinced myself that I was really ready for a relationship. And Gavin seemed really great - he checked all my boxes, and seemed really sweet and pleasant. Not to mention, he also had really great hair. And he rocked that slightly alternative aesthetic that I always went crazy for.

The dude was catnip to my emo ass - all I had to do was convince him I was as normal as any other girl and totally *not* a time traveler. That fact was strictly under wraps - plus, it probably wouldn't do anything helpful except paint me as one of those tin-foil hat weirdos on the *Discovery* channel. Not a cute look.

I marched back up the stairs to my room with all my school stuff on my back. Plopping it all down on the floor next to my lamp, I felt my phone buzz in my pocket so I picked it up. It was a text from Gavin - and a very sweet one at that.

"Hey cutie, text me your address. I'll pick you up tomorrow at noon ;)"

I did as he requested and texted back a smiling emoji. For some reason, I was hesitant to flirt back. But that might have been me still coming down from the whirlwind that was last night - and I still didn't know Gavin quite well enough to feel too strongly about him yet. At least, that's why I rationalized that I was still unsure. I had known Alex for most of my life, after all - so of course, it would take a lot longer to warm up to a less familiar - albeit equally desirable - guy.

I was about to take a shower and put on some sweatpants to lounge around the house, but I suddenly heard a crashing noise from across the hall. I opened my door and saw Jet's door wide open.

A very distraught-looking Jet was standing in the middle of his room, staring down in disbelief at his monitor with a shattered screen at his feet.

"What the hell happened in here?" I walked right into his room, totally ignoring the signs plastered over his door telling me not to. It's not everyday you see your typically calm workaholic older brother look like he's on the edge of a breakdown.

He met my gaze with a pained look in his eyes, and then backed slowly away from the debris on the floor. Only a whisper emerged from his quivering mouth.

"I, I threw it."

"And why would you do that? That's your *work* computer. Aren't there some Japanese video game moguls who are gonna be pissed at you now?"

"No, I quit."

"What do you mean, you *quit*? You *love* your job!"

He shook his head, and then crouched down on his stained wall-to-wall carpet and rested his face in his hands. "No Vera, you don't understand. This job... it's not what it looked like. It took years for me to see that. It's... it's just *wrong*."

"So you voluntarily broke your computer over it? Oh man, Mom is gonna flip."

He shook his head. "I don't give a shit, Vera. I really don't. I just, I just can't. Not anymore."

"What actually just happened though?"

"I don't want to talk about it. Not even a little. Just, just go." He got up from where he sat and leaned against the opposite wall of his bedroom. Then I'm pretty sure I heard him starting to openly sob, no longer even trying to hide it anymore.

"Well, uh, okay. If you need me, I'm here." Then I did something he probably hated. But in some ways, I think it was equally for me as much as for him. I walked over to where he stood and I hugged him while he cried. I still had absolutely no clue what happened to make him lash out that way, but I hoped that whatever happened wouldn't scar him. Wrapping my arms around my distraught brother was probably similar to trying to calm down a hysterical giant. He wasn't abnormally tall but his body was so much stronger and bigger than mine - most people even questioned how my scrawny butt could be related to him at all. But we were family, regardless of our seemingly unrelated appearances. Our life experiences were also quite different, what with me being a college student and him being a software programmer, but our roots ran deep. I thought about how lucky I was to have my brother here with me, since Edgar was probably missing his brother a lot.

When I hugged him for as long as I felt I could without him swearing at me, I backed away and went to get the dustbin out of the hall closet for the glass shards of his monitor. When I came back, he had collapsed onto his bed and seemed completely dejected - from what, I still had no idea. I carefully swept the shards off of the carpet and into the trash so that he wouldn't step on them, and then scooted the now-useless remains of the monitor to the side of the room.

I wanted to say something to him, but no words came to me. Instead, I just took the trash bag of debris with me out of the room and down to the kitchen. Mom was still busy on the spring issue of the magazine - one of her quarterly all-consumer editorial missions that ate up all her time about four times a year.

"Hey Mom?"

She turned around to see me leaning awkwardly in the doorway of her office. "Vera? Is something wrong?" Removing her glasses from the bridge of her nose and straightening a pile of articles on her desk, I could tell she was hard at work, and that my interruption was poorly timed. But what could I do? My older brother was having a meltdown and I didn't know what to do.

"I'm sorry to interrupt you, I can see you're busy-"

"Well, a little, but don't worry about it. What's going on? I can take a quick break." She placed her smartphone back down onto her desk as the screen glowed through a myriad of notifications in the dim light of her office.

"It's Jet, he's having some kind of freak out about his work or something. Actually, I think he quit his job."

"What do you mean 'he quit'? Vera, what happened?" Mom crossed her arms and started getting up from her chair, clearly upset with both having to pause her editing and also that Jet was dealing with something uncomfortable.

I shrugged. "Now you know as much as I do, you'd have to ask him. He ruined his computer though. I heard a crash, and it was just on the floor. I left the glass shards in a bag in the kitchen. You'd have to ask him."

She immediately breezed past me like a hurricane. I tried to tell her that now probably wasn't the best time as he wasn't really all that talkative, but she either didn't listen or didn't hear me. By the time she was halfway up the stairs, her footsteps had seemed to grow in weight and emphasis as she planted them on the floor, and running through Jet's bedroom door elicited some groaning and hushed expletives that he no longer tried to censor. Mom must have been able to tell that whatever happened was really, really bad because when I followed her up to his room again, she just sat on his bed cradling his upper body in her arms while swaying softly and humming something almost imperceptibly. It was almost like he was seven years old again - except he was a very strong grownup who spent any time not programming lifting weights. The image of our mother trying to console him was almost comical in its disparity, but I noticed a comforting smile spreading over my lips as I witnessed the innocence in that scene.

Any happiness I felt was replaced by curiosity when I picked up a crumpled-up piece of paper on the floor. Opening that piece of paper was both the stupidest and smartest thing I ever did, because it shook up my whole world, even though I didn't know it at the time. On that piece of paper, was an image that chilled my blood. There was a bunch of numbers and digits that I didn't understand at all, but above it all, in the upper left corner of the page, was what I now knew as the unmistakable curved and scalloped edge of a walrus tail, just like the one that'd been flashing through my head since I time traveled.

Thirty-One: French-Kiss with a Vampire

It took me hours to fall asleep Friday night for two reasons. One - I was worried about Jet's meltdown, and two - I had that lunch date with Gavin on Saturday - aka, *tomorrow*. I felt so stupid and girly to let myself get hung up on butterflies around that stupid boy, but I guess that's just how it is sometimes. Whatcha gonna do? Whereas Jet seemed to be dealing with something positively cataclysmic, and yet, it didn't seem to affect me in quite the same way. I wanted to worry about him, but I just didn't.

Once I saw Jet relatively stabilized the next morning, I started to worry even less. He sat downstairs and ate cereal while I blended up some fruit for a smoothie. That all seemed normal enough, except he was pretty quiet, still staring intently at nothing in particular. Whatever he found out or noticed in relation to his job must have really upset him - although he hadn't told Mom or me anything about what actually happened.

But even though Jet seemed okay for the time being, the image of that creepy-looking walrus tail on the crumpled paper in his room scared me. What if the image that kept floating in my head was related to his software company? I wanted to believe it was a coincidence, but the possibilities haunted me as I tried to calm down enough to process everything. I had a date today though, so any sleuthing would just have to wait until later.

Outside the window, the sun seemed to be obscured by a bunch of angry-looking clouds. I guess that forecast about it being rainy today wasn't lying. The idea of potentially frizzy hair on my date irritated me, but seeing how there wasn't much I would've been able to do about it, I just ran a brush through and hoped for the best.

My strawberry protein smoothie slid down my throat softly, but the nerves in my stomach made it hard to relax. And yeah, I definitely was still at least a little concerned about Jet - but understandably, my mind was currently elsewhere, I guess. I took

205

the rest of it up to my room so I could start to get ready while I finished it.

As I started to make my way back upstairs, my phone buzzed in my pocket, making my stomach lurch again excitedly. It wasn't guaranteed to be Gavin, but I'd wager it was a pretty good chance. Upon a closer look though, I turned out to be wrong. Texts from Willow were blowing up my phone because she had a "disastrous" hangover and apparently needed help with a class assignment. Unfortunately, my brain was temporarily rendered useless by my excitable hormones.

"Willow I can't meet up today for the case study, I have a lunch date."

I hit send and braced myself for the barrage of questions that I was sure were going to follow. But instead of the little bouncing gray dots showing me she was typing, my messaging app closed to allow me to respond to an incoming call.

"Hello?"

"What do you mean you have a lunch date? Who is it and why didn't you tell me? If my head wasn't in throbbing pain right now, I'd yell at you a heck of a lot more for that."

I sighed. "I thought I mentioned it, I guess I didn't. Sorry about that, Will."

She groaned loudly on the other end of the call, and I couldn't tell if that was about me or because of her hangover. "You didn't mention it at all! And now I'm so damn curious! So, what time is Alex picking you up?"

"Uh, I dunno. It's not Alex."

I heard something like a sitcom-worthy spit-take over the speaker, and I hoped that was water that Willow likely spewed - both for her health and for the sake of her bedroom decor.

"And *why* the hell not?"

I chewed on my lower lip, hoping that I could explain this in a way that she would accept as truth. Sometimes Willow's overly positive personality made it hard for her to understand that sometimes things were not as they seemed, and that it was perfectly okay when that happened.

"We both realized that we just don't view each other in *that* way."

"Pfshhhhh tell that to your epic lip-lock at the club the other night."

Now it was my turn to groan, and I was grateful that she couldn't see me rolling my eyes. "So you saw that, huh? I was hoping that maybe you didn't."

"Oh yes, I did. And it was *glorious*. So I'm skeptical that you're not pulling my leg right now."

"I swear I'm not!"

I heard Willow clear her throat on the other end, and I assumed that she shook her head in disbelief because I heard the jingling of her long beaded earrings. "Yeah, sure. Okay, whatever you say Vera."

I swallowed both my excess saliva and some bitter words that probably wouldn't entice her to believe me any more than she already was. "His name is Gavin, we met at the coffee shop. Well, actually, he works there. And he asked me out. That's all, I swear! I don't exactly have any salacious details to share."

"Yet."

The single word hit me with a nerve-inducing realization that anything could happen today. And it might be really, really great. But I wouldn't get my hopes up - that never ended well.

"Oh so *now* you believe me?"

She must've shifted her weight, because I heard the unmistakable crinkling of an icepack on her forehead. Like I said, this wasn't the first hangover Willow's had, so I knew all her methods of nixing it. "Luckily for you, my head hurts too much to question you much more than I already have. But once I'm feeling better, I gotta hear all the details. Every single delicious, jaw-dropping second." She paused while I cringed at her implication. "He's cute, right? He must be cute, or else you wouldn't even entertain the idea of dating him."

"Oh um, yeah. He's... very cute."

"What *kind* of cute?" I could picture Willow thrumming her nails on her chin, awaiting a more detailed response from me. It was this kind of question that made me grateful Mom splurged for the unlimited minutes phone plan. I sifted through the garments hung in my closet while we chatted though, because unlimited phone minutes unfortunately did not equal unlimited primping minutes.

"Well let's see... he's got short blonde hair, a nose ring, gauges, and wears a pocket chain."

A sugary-sweet giggle filled my ears. "Sounds like he's *perfect* for you then!" The words rolled off her tongue with all the surety of a drunken sailor - or, a drunken friend, in my case, I supposed. But I was starting to feel a bit drunk on the possibilities. In any new relationship, half the excitement is just finding out where it's going to go - at least, that's what I assumed, since I've never actually really dated. Until now, that is. And I had a feeling in my gut that I was going to find out quite a lot about what this whole dating ritual is really like.

"Hey so, not that I don't wanna stay and chat, but it's nearly ten thirty and he's gonna be here at noon. And I still haven't picked out what I'm going to wear, so I better get to it. I'll fill you in later?"

"All right. I'll just be here nursing this headache. Oh and vomiting - lots of vomiting. Next time I try to down something half my height, will you remind me how positively dreadful I felt the last time it happened?"

"Sure, but you usually drink whatever concoction you want anyway."

"Well, it's worth a shot. Have an awesome date, Vera. I'm so excited for you, even if it's not with Alex. That boy is a tall glass of water, ya know?"

I chuckled to myself as I pulled my favorite skinny jeans from a hanger. "I'll try not to tell Zander you said that."

"Hey, cute is cute! I didn't say Zander wasn't cute - I just meant he wasn't the only one ever to walk the face of the Earth."

"Fair enough. Talk to you later, Will."

208

I ended the call and found myself pacing in and out of my walk-in closet, searching for just the right thing. After grabbing the skinny jeans, I settled on a cute, lightweight, flowing pink blouse that I figured was equal parts edgy and sweet. A quick glance out the window told me it was still raining a bit, so I grabbed a small foldable umbrella to take with my purse. I also chose my favorite pair of Doc Martens, because I knew they were waterproof and would keep my feet dry, while keeping with the aesthetic I wanted to portray for the day.

As noon approached, I did my best not to stare out the window like a forlorn puppy waiting for its owner to return home after work. I did glance out of it a few times though. And then, as his signature blue Jeep ambled down my street, I took a deep breath and let myself out the front door. I could've waited for him to come and get me, but I didn't want it to seem too formal before I knew where we stood.

He exited his car as I walked out of my house, and his immaculate blonde hair seemed to withstand the light rain that fell around us, while his kilowatt smile sent lightning bolts through my chest.

"Hey Vera. Ready to grab some lunch?"

I nodded. "Totally. Where are we headed?"

He gave me a quick hug and then opened the driver's side of his car. "I know this great little spot. You'll just have to wait and see." I heard the smile in his voice even before I turned to my left to see it.

"Okay, sounds good. If it's as good as the coffee you always make, then I have no doubts that I'll love it."

Lunch was delicious at the quaint little cafe he brought me to, and I actually managed to not be a total idiot conversationally for once. Plus the small vase of tiny purple flowers on the table made me smile.

"So I mean, we could hang out at my place for a bit if you want? Been wanting to check out this new show that looks good, and I could make some coffee. Since ya know, I know exactly how you like it." He winked at me, and punctuated the suggestion with a sweet smile and a slight bite on his lower lip. He tugged nervously on his gray beanie, and I thought my heart might legitimately burst all over the concrete sidewalk we were standing on. This guy was starting to really worm his way under my skin and into my heart - and fast. It wasn't the ongoing unrequited romance that existed completely in my head with Alex. This was natural, organic, and actually seemed to be mutual for once (I know, shocking).

"Yeah, that sounds great." I returned his smile, and wondered why I hadn't caught on to his interest ages ago. I mean, I was pretty oblivious, I guess. I never quite knew how much I missed out on.

He grabbed my hand and gently led me back to his car on this rainy afternoon as electricity danced on the surface of my palm. I could argue that maybe it was just the increase of ionic energy in the air with the rain falling but I knew it was chemistry - and a lot of it. Climbing back into his spotlessly-clean blue Jeep, he turned the key and started driving. Tuning the channel to the very same alternative channel I consistently listened to, I could feel myself falling in love faster than I could process. It was pretty scary and great all at the same time. The way my breath hitched in my chest felt like something between a heart attack and a rollercoaster - so I loved it and hated it all at once.

This boy was gorgeous - he had traded out his silver gauges for black ones, which made him appear like an even edgier, kind of punk rock version of himself. His gray beanie rested over his ears, and his button-down flannel was rolled up to his elbows - probably the only way to pull off the look while staying comfortably cool in this very warm Los Angeles spring air only slightly cooled by the intermittent rain showers.

After the accidental kiss with Alex that was never actually supposed to happen after my actual first kiss that I totally forgot - thank you, time travel adventure - romance had become a complicated case to crack, and I was still pretty dumbfounded that the answer was as easy as frequenting the same coffee joint.

"So, Vera?" His mid-range voice was a welcome interruption to the complicated thoughts brewing in my head, and I answered back.

"Yeah?"

"I'm just, really glad you finally got the hint." He smirked at me out the corner of his eye while he kept watch on the road ahead of us. Not only was this guy sweet as all heck - he was also a responsible, and conscientious driver. Dad would be so impressed with him if he was here.

"I'm actually really embarrassed that I've always been so clueless. I've never uh, gotten this kind of attention before." And then as soon as the sentence left my mouth, I immediately felt stupid all over again because Alex had loved me our entire life, and I never noticed that either. How many opportunities had I missed because I was too much of a dope to realize them?

"Eh it's okay. I guess that's on me for not getting the guts to make a move faster." The corners of his mouth tightened and turned up a bit at the edges while the butterflies in my gut seemed to make a run for it.

"Well it's better late than never." I awkwardly winked at him with both eyes since that's a skill I just never mastered, but he didn't actually seem to mind even after my face probably turned completely red.

The music continued to play on the radio, and even though it all felt like a complete dream, I couldn't shake the feeling that it was going to crash down at any minute. I honestly felt like I didn't deserve a guy like Gavin - sweet, thoughtful, and cute? Yeah no, there's no way. Of course, I also acknowledge how very unrealistic that perception is but still, I found myself struggling to make sense of how this cute hipster hottie landed in my lap practically out of thin air. Tapping my fingertips on the armrest of his car, I tried to create at least an illusion of calm even though I was pretty much freaking out.

"So uh, this is my place. I've been trying to save up and it's not much, but it's mine, I guess." Gavin pulled the car into a quaint little neighborhood with small but neat houses in uniform rows. His was navy blue on the outside with off-white shutters and a basic concrete walkway. A pretty decent starter home, I'd say. And from my pathetic perspective of still living with my parents, I had to admit I was impressed. The rain had mostly let up at this point, but the air still felt charged with the crisp energy of the recent rainfall that had darkened the hues of the grass, trees, and asphalt.

"It's nice! I still live with my parents so I'm easy to impress." I closed the car door and followed him to the front door, where he unlocked it with a key he had been keeping in his pocket. Holding the door open for me, I followed him into his house, and marveled at how it was actually pretty clean - for a guy, anyway. Sure, there was a stray sweatshirt left on the sofa and some magazines and mail on the kitchen counter, but it was nothing excessive.

"Ha - good to know." He threw his keys on the counter with the mail and washed his hands at the sink. "Can I get you something to drink?"

I shrugged. "Well, I've already had my coffee for the day, so what else ya got?"

He smiled at me and opened the fridge. "Luckily for you, I just went shopping so I got the good stuff." Turning around happily, he brought a glass bottle to the countertop. "Sparkling water?"

"Sure, that sounds great."

He grabbed a couple glasses from a nearby cabinet and poured. "I'd offer you something a little more fun but it's like two in the afternoon and I'm really not a day drinker myself. Plus I forgot to buy more since my friends cleaned me out the other night."

"Oh that's fine! I don't actually drink at all. Well, besides lattes."

"Really? So like, you never kick back with a beer? Or wine, if that's more your thing?" He slid my glass of sparkling water across the counter, and I caught it before it took a cataclysmic detour to the white-tiled floor.

212

"Nope, it's just not for me. Call me straight edge, or whatever, but I've just never liked how it made me feel. I like to experience life without that stuff clouding my head."

He chuckled quietly, and then took a sip of his water. "Fair enough! Honestly, I haven't really met a lot of girls like you. I think that's pretty cool, actually."

I felt the skin of my cheeks warm again under his complimentary gaze. "Really? Oh good. I mean, not good that you haven't met that many girls, I meant like, good that you don't mind it. Sorry, I know I'm rambling, I just, um, really like you."

The butterflies seemed to be staging a complete war against my insides at this point. I tried to appease them by drinking the sparkling water in a way I hoped was dainty and feminine, and not at all like Jet downing beer with his buddies at poker night. I had a sinking feeling that I likely resembled the latter.

Luckily for me, Gavin didn't seem to notice. Or if he did, he didn't care. Instead, he walked around the counter and grabbed my hand, pulling me closer to him. I could feel his strong chest under his flannel pressed against mine, and his other hand gently but firmly held my lower back. His heartbeat became the staccato rhythm to my own increasingly ragged breath as his musky cologne filled my lungs.

"That's really good to hear because the thing is - I really like you too, Vera."

I opened my mouth to squeak out something pathetic like "what, why?" or something like that but instead, I just felt the warm metal of his nose ring touch my cheek, and then his lips covered my mouth. I found myself leaning into him a bit more, wrapping my arms tightly around his neck as I hungrily placed my mouth around his lower lip. His smooth skin tasted like coffee, and the warmth shooting through every inch of my body was electric. Shifting his stance to better support my weight, I found myself leaning slightly against the countertop behind me as his fingertips traced my back. I pulled away after maybe about a minute, not because I didn't like it

213

- quite the opposite, actually - but because I needed to process what the hell actually just happened.

"Well uh, that was nice." Real smooth, Vera.

A familiar smirk played at his pink lips. "Yeah, it was." His eyes sparkled in response, as if he charged off of my essence or something. I blushed for the millionth time today, because I still couldn't believe this was actually real life. My real life, that is. This kind of thing seemed to always happen to everyone except me. Or maybe just in books or movies.

"You - you're really good at that."

"Well gee, thanks. I guess practice makes perfect. I mean, not that I'm sitting around kissing girls all the time - that isn't my style."

"I didn't think that at all, you're fine!" I smiled at him, still standing on the same four small kitchen tiles he was. The close proximity was beginning to feel like I belonged here - no longer a foreign place, his arms were surprisingly familiar. Without anything more in mind to say, I found myself glancing over at the living room searching for a smooth diversion. "Uh, you mentioned something about a show you wanted to watch?"

As if being awoken from a spell, Gavin's eyes left my gaze and widened slightly, shaking off the excitement we both undoubtedly felt after that first really electric kiss. "Yeah, right, a show. You said you hadn't seen the third season of *Stranger Things* yet, right? I figured we could watch?"

"That sounds great, sure." I smiled at him like a thirteen-year-old and made my way over to the couch in the other room. Sitting politely in the far corner by the window as not to assume anything, he plopped right next to me, about as close as he possibly could without sitting on my lap. Grabbing the remote, he expertly called up the show and let the first episode start playing. We watched the entirety of that one, and by the iconic dark piano intro of episode two, I noticed that I was leaning on Gavin completely. My head was on his shoulder and his arm was around me. I would have thought it to be pretty cozy any other time of year besides now - springtime in California was usually pretty warm. Luckily, the air

214

conditioning provided a climate a bit more suitable for cuddling - and I definitely wasn't complaining about it.

In a lazy sort of contentment, I felt my hand find his completely by itself. What was happening to me? I marveled at how much I craved his touch - any touch at all, really. It was like Gavin was the power line and I was the suburban neighborhood - he powered everything in my world, and I suddenly felt unable to function without him. It wasn't even a conscious thing - I've always been the go-getter kind of girl. But this boy - this beautiful, kind boy, had basically arrested all my resolve. It was scary, and stupid, and I loved it.

I'm convinced that's why I didn't pull away when I suddenly felt his mouth on my neck. Never being the type to romanticize the erotic vampire young adult book craze, I was surprised by the way I didn't shirk off his advances, or even challenge them. Instead, I leaned slightly across him on the couch, feeling a soft moan escape from my lips as his mouth moved to my own lips and I responded again, just like in the kitchen a couple hours ago. But this time, I was hungrier for it. And the couch was just so comfortable, so I barely realized what was happening until it was almost too late.

I crashed back to reality when I felt him ease himself over me gently and suddenly become very preoccupied with the zipper on my jeans.

"Gavin? Gavin."

"Hmmm? Vera?" His breathy mention of my name floated over my ears like a lullaby, almost lulling me back into subordination. I faltered for a moment, but then snapped out of it when his hand got *under* my jeans. His touch repulsed me. I didn't fully understand why, but it did.

"Gavin, I can't do this. I'm sorry." I managed to edge my way out from under him, and his face was flushed with expectation and a slight shade of what I knew had to be disappointment.

"What do you mean, you can't? Is there an issue with - "

I must've hesitated to answer quickly enough so he made a very graphic gesture to illustrate his question. "No, no, that's not what I meant." My face flushed beet red, realizing that I accidentally made him think I had some kind of weird deformity.

"Okay good, then come here." He remained in the same position he was in moments ago, but now he patted the area of the couch that was likely still warm from my presence on it only moments ago.

His tone wasn't at all authoritative, and he wasn't forcing me. He was being sweet, and romantic. Or at least, that's probably what he thought he was doing. It's probably what he most likely intended, I'm sure. But that's not at all how I received it.

"Gavin, that's not happening right now. I think... I think I should get home." The words spilled out of my mouth before I could stop them. Lips that only moments ago wanted to taste every part of him, suddenly were casting him away.

His face remained stoic, but he furrowed his brow and pouted a little while sitting up from his reclined position. Smoothing down my own shirt, I found it nearly impossible to make eye contact. It was mortifying - disappointing him this way when I so desperately wanted him to love me. I knew I couldn't - shouldn't cave, but this was... heartbreaking. I could feel lingering butterflies still flapping around in my gut, but most of them had begun to lie dormant again, not expecting to see the light of day any time soon. Resentment of my own upbringing started to bloom in my own chest, wishing that for just one day, I could be one of those other girls that accepted Gavin's advances. He was damn good at romance, and after just a taste I wanted it all. But I knew I couldn't allow that. Not now, anyway.

"Oh. Okay."

Those two words were all he had to say about it, apparently. He wordlessly turned off the TV and grabbed his keys. Following him to his car was filled with tension - even the air itself seemed to quiver with the disappointment of what almost was, what should've been, for any other girl who didn't have very specific limitations the way I did. Any normal girl would have been fine with anything this boy wanted - he was lovely in every way, and smooth and refreshing as a finely-cut lemonade slushy on a hot summer day. I knew it wasn't my fault, but I still felt like being swallowed by the ground would be a preferable alternative to whatever this was.

The rain had un-ironically resumed outside, so I rushed into his car hastily smoothing down wet strands of my hair to create the illusion of being at least somewhat presentable, since I was too distracted to bother with my umbrella. I had a sinking feeling that none of that would matter now though. The car ride featured probably the most uncomfortable dynamic I've ever seen - and that's coming from a girl who watched her younger self get hit on by her childhood best friend. He wouldn't talk to me, or even look at me. He was just being responsible and staring at the road ahead, but the dull aching in my gut told me that was most likely not the case. I tried to ignore the echoes of sadness taking over my lungs, but they wouldn't quit. No matter what I did, the ache continued, and seemed to grow in strength and volume as the minutes and miles ticked by.

I've never been so happy to see my mom's obnoxious, embarrassing mermaid mailbox appear in my passenger window. The blue painted sequins glittered with rain droplets, as if she had just voyaged out of the ocean to explore dry land for the first time. I guess there was a first time for everything - just not for me today.

"So uh, thanks again for lunch and... everything." I cringed at my own word choice, but I doubt he noticed. He nodded at me politely, sighed, and then drove away. I found myself staring longingly at the place on the pavement where his car had previously occupied, but then I reminded myself I was being stupid and just needed to get home, shower, and curl up with a good book or something.

I never did see Gavin again in person after that day. Looking back, I was pretty sure he even transferred to a different coffee shop just to avoid seeing me.

Thirty-Two: Nachos and Salty Tears

I walked back up the stairs to my room after that very abrupt ending to my date, wondering what I did that was so wrong. My brain told me I did the right thing, but my heart was telling me I was an idiot to let a guy like that get away. Or, maybe it wasn't my *heart* saying that. I didn't even know anymore.

My feet may as well have been encased in cement for the weight they seemed to carry as I finally got to the top step and took the sharp left across the hallway to my room. Jet was downstairs watching some crime show on Netflix, probably still feeling out-of-sorts after quitting his job for some mysterious reason that he still refused to reveal.

Today was pretty bad. I mean, it wasn't all bad, but it ended badly, I guess. I could feel my chest tightening and my eyes moistening, but somehow, my body was in too much shock to even allow me to properly cry. I immediately went right to the shower, peeling off my clothes to get the last of this date out of my mind. But of course, it wasn't even close to that simple. Part of me still wanted to talk to Gavin, but I wasn't sure what that would really lead to, since it seemed we wanted different things. Maybe it was a stupid thought, but I decided to maybe reconsider after the dust settled, even though coming back after awkwardness like this was probably quite unlikely.

True to form, Willow's name kept glowing on my phone that entire evening after my date with Gavin. I didn't mean to purposely ignore her, but I was so overwhelmed with all the emotions that I was feeling, and I doubted my ability to explain everything without feeling like a total prude. Of course, I knew I had nothing to be ashamed of, but this kind of thing just wasn't something I wanted to blab even to a good friend about. At least, not yet anyway.

Instead, I just curled up in bed with some homemade nachos and a movie on my laptop that I've been wanting to see for a while.

Now seemed as good a time as any, since I needed any and all the distractions I could get. Drowning myself in melted cheese and a cheesy rom-com, I marveled at how momentarily easy it was to forget about my current predicament. But I knew that victory was short-lived, because before I knew it, my damaging thoughts were sure to be back to haunt me, just like everything else in my life that left me feeling scarred and inadequate.

I heard a hesitant knock on my bedroom door just as I was scraping the last little bit of congealed cheese off the plate I pilfered from the kitchen. Assuming it was my mom, I yelled a hasty "come in" but I was surprised to see Jet at the door, his messy shoulder-length dirty-blonde hair a bit unkempt probably from lying on the couch most of the day.

"Oh no, you made nachos?" His frown turned up into a half-smile as he made his way over to my pile of pillows, blankets, and stuffed animals.

"What's wrong with nachos?"

He gave me a knowing glance and then took my empty plate from me, placing it gingerly on my side table. "You only ever make nachos when you're upset."

I nearly choked on the mouthful of soda I was in the middle of swallowing. "How did you know that?"

"Look, I know I've been pretty tied up lately with that stupid job, but I'm still your big brother." He ruffled my hair, messing up my loose bun to further emphasize his point. Never big on showing affection, this sort of thing from Jet meant more to me than I could articulate most days. Today though, with all the thoughts swirling around in my head - both from time travel and just my complicated life - I was pretty monosyllabic.

"Yeah."

"Hey, what's eating you?"

"Nothing."

"I call BS on that."

"Tough."

I rolled over onto my side facing away from Jet. I knew he just wanted to help, but it was hard to let him past my hardened outer shell. We were siblings, but not the kind that typically talked about our feelings. And I was experiencing quite a lot of feelings at the moment.

"I really did quit my job."

"I know."

I wanted to press him for more answers, but he seemed reserved about it. And yet, at the same time, I could feel the answers I wanted nearly tearing at the seams to get out in the open. But instead, I just turned back to the movie I was playing and tried to clear my head.

"So uh, how are you doing with… everything?"

"Everything what?"

"The time travel? Which I still think Mom should know about eventually…"

His approach this time with the whole tell-Mom-thing was a lot more passive and flexible than it had been even just short days ago. I wondered if maybe the lack of job-induced stress had softened him a little.

"Yeah yeah I know, I'll figure out how to tell her soon-ish. And uh, I guess I'm okay. Still seeing the images flashing through my head though."

"Images?" Jet shifted his weight to sit more comfortably on the edge of my bed, narrowly missing my giant pink stuffed bear perched precariously next to him.

"Oh, I guess I didn't tell you?"

Jet shook his head, and I wondered how I had neglected to update him on this oddly residual experience left over from traveling through time. Pausing the movie on my laptop, I turned to face my brother.

"Actually, part of the reason why I've been so uptight lately…"

"You mean more than usual?" He smirked, and punched me playfully in the arm. "I'm just kidding, sis. I know I've been no peach to deal with either."

220

"You can say that again." I shrugged and grabbed my glass of water nearby on my nightstand. The nachos were salty, greasy, and delicious - as they should be, since I made them myself. But that also meant I was craving more water than I could fit in my stomach, producing that all-too-familiar feeling of being parched but too full to down any more liquids at the same time. I swallowed a few more sips of water, regardless of my stomach's feeble protests.

"Anyway, yeah so I've been seeing these random images since I time traveled."

"Images? Like a movie?"

I paused, trying to think of a way to explain this for someone outside my own head to be able to understand. "Sort of? It's like a bunch of faces and things that could be related to what I was looking for when I traveled back in time."

"Okay, so uh, what were you looking for exactly?"

I wasn't about to admit to Jet that I was desperately trying to make my childhood best friend fall in love with me while ratting out my school bullies, so I opted for the other half of the equation. "Well uh, for Dad, actually. Edgar was actually the one who even had the idea that going back in time might give me some answers as to what happened to him."

Jet nodded slowly, clearly still trying to take in what I was saying. "So... what'd you find?" He clutched my pink teddy bear in his arms, perhaps from boredom or absent-minded interest in holding something soft and familiar while I delved deep into the complications of unfamiliar territory.

"Nothing obvious - mostly faces of my old classmates, and Dad, of course."

"Okay. That makes sense - they were probably imprinted in your brain already. You know, with memories, and stuff? I'm no brain scientist though."

"Yeah. But there's been, something else that I've been seeing a lot in my head too." I eased myself slowly off of my bed, stepped over my discarded laundry on the floor, and then fished the

221

crumpled piece of paper from my pocket. "Jet, the other day, when you quit your job and threw your computer onto the floor, I found this piece of paper that matches one of the images that keeps flashing through my head."

Slowly, as if it was made of crystalline syrup and would break at the slightest mishandling, I opened the wadded up piece of paper that Jet had discarded, with his ex-company's logo in plain sight in the corner of it.

"Yeah, that's the Captain Tus logo. But where would you have seen that before? I mean, besides on my computer or something. And why would that matter to your travel through time?"

"Well, those are the golden questions, Sherlock." I sarcastically flipped my hair over my other shoulder, as my neck was starting to sweat from the warm spring air wafting through my window, mixed with the tension in my body I felt head-to-toe. "I really have no clue why it matters, but when I saw this paper scrap on your bedroom floor the other day, I had this indescribable chill down my back. It felt like I'd stumbled over a corpse or something."

Jet's face dropped, and he suddenly avoided eye contact with me.

"Why the long face, bro?" I smirked, trying to lighten the mood with some casual small talk, but Jet seemed to exist in a separate dimension for a few moments. When he snapped out of whatever intruding thoughts he had, his eyes were slightly red like he was on the verge of tears.

"Vera, that company was engaging in some really effed up stuff. Like, CIA-level creepy stuff. When you mentioned that you felt like you stumbled on a corpse, well, I guess that wasn't so far from the truth."

I tilted my head to the side. "You mean, like they have goofy rumors about having their leader's body frozen and kept in a freezer deep in the basement until he can be reanimated later?"

Jet didn't laugh. Not even a little. I inched closer to my brother, trying to read his face for any kind of context clue. But there was none to be found.

"Jet, I'm so lost. What are you talking about?"

He scratched the back of his neck, and stared at my duvet cover. "You weren't so far off from the truth."

"I'm really lost, Jet."

He exhaled. "So uh, you knew that I worked in programming, right? Well, it turns out, the software wasn't actually for video games or media entertainment." A nervous laugh escaped his lips, and then it seemed to almost crawl back into his mouth as the subtle sound was deadened by the uncanny darkness descending over the conversation. Like a black rain cloud overhead, I immediately felt not only blindsided by what I could not know, but also terrified by what I was about to find out.

"What was the software for, Jet?"

"Well uh, looked like some sort of cryogenics."

I sighed. "I mean, that is a thing I've heard of - it's not illegal, just a little odd, I guess. You really thought that was a reason to quit your job?" I tried to keep myself from laughing, which suddenly became easier as I saw his eyes widen and sharpen their gaze on mine.

"Vera, some of the numbers I input... they weren't serial numbers. I think... they were social security numbers."

"Okay, what makes you say that? And so what if they were?" I crossed and uncrossed my legs nervously, and forced down another few gulps of water.

Jet rested his head in his hands, clearly struggling to get the right words out. "The numbers were grouped like social security numbers. You know, like three-two-four digits, and seemed to be linked to data that looked somewhat medical. The data was like, pulse rate, oxygen, etc. Almost like a hospital would have for patients. Pages and pages of this stuff, more than I could count. You would've thought there was a whole city of people in there."

I shrugged. "I'm still not seeing the issue, Jet. Maybe your job was more medical or scientific than you expected. But you liked it a lot and you said it paid well."

"Vera, you don't understand. I figured all of that stuff out by myself. It wasn't presented to me that way. And once I realized that cryogenics was the game, I wondered if maybe... there were people being held prisoner. And if my hunch was right... there could be *hundreds*."

I nearly spit out my water. "You mean like *people*? Being held on ice? Against their will? You're nuts." Crossing my arms, I turned away to hide my disbelieving grin. When I snuck a peak at Jet's face though, I felt like I hit a puppy. His eyes were watery, and his eyebrows were pulled together as if he was in physical pain.

"Okay. Well, I'll just get back to my show. Sorry to bother you, sis. I thought I could talk to you about this stuff, but you don't seem to believe me."

I stood up to chase after him, but he disappeared out my bedroom door faster than I could with all the pillows and things I first had to remove from my lap. *Nice going Vera. Your brother finally opened up to you and you didn't listen to him.*

The critical thoughts started swirling through my head alongside the perpetual images, and the sensation made me dizzy. Coupled with my heightened emotions from my date with Gavin, I just felt totally spent in more ways than one. So instead of answering the many texts from Willow asking how my date went, I turned off my laptop, brushed my teeth, and cried myself to sleep. I couldn't tell if I was finally crying because of my disastrous date, or if it was because of me completely butchering the first good conversation I had had with my brother in literal years.

Waking up the next morning to a sleepy Sunday household, I let myself drift in and out of consciousness as the morning sun continued to shift and move towards high noon. The light blankets on my bed seemed to constrict my body, either with stress or disappointment - I couldn't pinpoint which one exactly.

My phone buzzed, alerting me to more texts from Willow. Don't get me wrong, she was one of my closest friends, but she could be pretty intense without realizing how much I just needed to be alone with my thoughts.

I was honestly too pissed to even deal with her excited rambling at the moment, so I just texted a quick "I'll tell you at lunch tomorrow" since I knew that we always had an overlapping break between classes on Mondays. After crossing my fingers that she would be satiated with that, I hauled my sorry butt into the shower and tried to peel the sleep and congealed tears off of my eyes.

Although the idea of locking myself in my room for the day seemed attractive, I did need to get down to the kitchen for breakfast. I passed by Jet on the couch watching more episodes of that Netflix show he's been into lately, and I cringed as I felt myself avoiding eye contact with him. We'd never been super buddy-buddy but we were still closer than other siblings I knew. Hopefully my stupid misstep wouldn't damage the bonds that we had. But I also could read him well enough to know that now was not necessarily the time to try and fix it.

Mom was in her office, as usual. But when I walked by to get to the kitchen, she looked up at me and smiled while holding the phone receiver to her ear. She worked so hard, and she did it for us - my mom inspired me everyday.

Well, except for today as I fought this indescribably dead feeling deep in my body - I was temporarily incapable of being inspired by anyone or anything. Every limb felt heavy, and I felt my sadness cling to my bones like a thick glue slowing me down with every step, threatening to render me immobile soon if I didn't find a way out.

I scarfed down some pretty bland wheat cereal and some orange juice, and then headed back upstairs to do my homework. Unfortunately though, the images in my mind seemed to swirl even faster today. And that thing which I now recognized as a walrus tail seemed to be the most prominent of all - which infuriated me because I still wasn't sure why it even mattered. There was a chance that it was somehow related to Jet's ex-company, but I hadn't worked out those ideas yet. And even if it was related to that company, why was it getting stuck in my head over and over? I

225

didn't see a connection to the things I searched for when I time-traveled. And no matter how long I sat, trying to do my homework, that image seemed to slowly take over the spotlight from the other images floating in my head. Eventually, it was such a powerful bout of repetition that I had to quit trying to read my textbooks and start lying down with my eyes closed. The spinning of the walrus tail, mixed with the tiny print of my course readings, was enough to give me vertigo. At least, I assumed it was at least a mild form of vertigo because everything seemed to be spinning.

One of the weirdest things about these images in my head was that they seemed to be *alive*. Like some kind of a virus, they would grow and react and evolve on their own. Sometimes I could tune them out long enough to drive safely or study, but other times, like now, they seemed to feed off of my heightened emotions. In this powerful storm, I felt myself steadily crumbling, and I began to see why Edgar mentioned something about potentially going insane. As my pulse quickened and I felt my head trying to compensate for the extraneous motion and sensory confusion, I gave in to the need to just curl up on my bed, and slept fitfully until dinnertime.

"You kids sure have been quiet," Mom remarked as she dished up the turkey sandwiches and pasta salad. "I mean I have an excuse since I have a very demanding job. But you guys are so young still, what could you possibly have to be worried about?"

Jet met my gaze and then looked away. My heart sank immediately, wondering if maybe he deemed me unworthy of even a cursory glance.

"Are either of you going to say anything? Or am I really going to have to eat in silence?"

Mom waited for a verbal answer, but the best I could do was shrug. Jet took a bite of his sandwich and killed the silence with a handful of potato chips.

"Okay, well I can't force you to talk. But we're going to sit here, as a family, and eat together regardless. And if you won't talk, then I guess I will."

Never one to put up with our shenanigans, Mom took charge of the silence and made it her bitch. Specifically, she injected

226

it with all the latest happenings in the editing world, from the latest lifestyle articles she had been working on, to the rantings of her boss's borderline-neurotic expectations. None of that held my interest but it didn't matter, because the images swirling in my head gave me plenty to think about and puzzle through. As I sifted through it all, I couldn't shake the feeling that the answers would make themselves known to me very, very soon. And when they did, my world as I knew it would be gone forever.

Thirty-Three: Looking for Attention

"Okay, tell me everything, and leave no detail out. Not even one!" Willow smirked at me, wagging her finger in my face to emphasize her need for complete information. The staccato rhythm of her plea for a recap left me shifting uncomfortably in my seat, nervously picking at my Thai garden salad to find the invisible answers buried deep under the romaine lettuce, carrots and peanut sauce.

"Willow, I really don't wanna talk about it too much."

Her face contorted, and suddenly her eyebrows tried to evict her hairline from ownership of primary forehead real estate while her mouth opened slightly to catch any nearby flies.

"And why *the hell* not?"

I sighed. How was I supposed to explain to my friend what happened without her thinking I was totally weird? I understood that I did the right thing - at least, the right thing for me at the time. But my heart hadn't stopped casting blame on me for my seemingly-prudish preferences. Inhaling once more and looking out the window overlooking the green lawn of the campus quad, I carefully picked my words to keep myself from crying in public.

"Um, we just wanted different things. It wasn't going to work."

"What do you mean? Oh, was he one of those freaky types that wanted to get married like, yesterday?"

"Huh?"

"Hey, it can happen!" Willow raised her hands in mock surrender. "My cousin met this total loon at a party once. Cute as hell but he proposed to her after their first date. That's wild - even for LA." She bit into her french fry, the snap of the crispy fried coating punctuating her point while flaunting her regularly-scheduled weekly cheat meal.

"Uh, no. He didn't propose to me."

"Well, what'd he do then? He sounded adorable, and just your type."

"He was. He really was." And then tears pricked my skin, fighting their way to the edges of my eyelids.

"Woah, are you crying? Okay, where is he so I can beat his ass? Or, I can send Zander to do that because I don't exactly know how to fight. But that's a tiny detail, who cares? But like, what'd he do?"

Willow's rambling gave me just enough time to spit out the words that were pooling at the back of my throat and hiding under my tongue, getting ready to launch themselves out into the world.

"He got upset when I wouldn't have sex with him."

Her face went white as a sheet. "Wow. Okay. Geez, I'm sorry Vera. Some guys are dogs. He didn't... force anything, right?"

I was grateful she kept her voice down to a whisper, as I didn't exactly want the entire welcome center hearing this.

"No, he didn't. But I could sense the frustration in his face when I made myself clear. He wasn't even embarrassed, just angry. I asked him to take me home, which he did - immediately. But didn't say anything to me besides a couple of polite grunts the whole way back to my house."

Willow had walked around the table in less than two heartbeats, and wrapped her arms around me. Her touch of solidarity coaxed my tears out of their hiding places, and I didn't hold them back this time. Grabbing a paper napkin to wipe my face and salvage what remained of my eyeliner, Willow smiled at me sadly and patted my shoulder.

"You advocated for yourself, and if he couldn't respect that, that's his problem. At least you talked it out and now you know."

"Well, we didn't exactly talk it out. I just kinda put the kibosh on it when I could sense things were heading that way."

Willow smirked at me once she saw that I had more or less stopped crying. "So he kissed you?"

I sighed. "Repeatedly."

She sighed seductively, and winked at me. "Well how was it?"

"I don't really have much frame of reference, but pretty amazing I'd say." I paused, already regretting the words I was about to say. "That's probably why I'm so upset. I really, really liked him, Willow."

Willow pursed her lips, and took a sip of her smoothie. "Okay, unpopular opinion time. What if, this whole thing was a misunderstanding? What if, he thought your denial of his advances was a personal affront? Whereas the reality is, it was nothing personal, right? You just weren't ready. For anyone. And that's perfectly okay. But it doesn't sound like you made your reasons clear."

I shrugged, and stared at my hands. Stuffing another bite of salad into my mouth to buy myself some time, I mulled over her suggestion and realized that she may have a point. "Honestly I was just too shocked to say anything about it. It was embarrassing and I just wanted to get out of there."

"Okay so, besides that, would you say the date went well? You got along well and were attracted to him?"

"Willow, that's a pretty big thing to just overlook -"

"I'm not saying you should overlook it. I'm just helping you figure this out."

"Okay, then yeah. I found him to be really pleasant, cute, and attractive. So?"

She thrummed her fingertips on the garish dark-green table we sat at. "So, this could be salvageable. I mean yeah, it's gonna need some serious relationship CPR but I think it could work out. What you gotta do, is call him back, address what happened, and reassure him that it was nothing personal and you're just not looking for that specific sort of thing right now. If he understands that and respects it, then you just scored a hot boyfriend. If he doesn't, then he's a jackass and then you don't want him anyway."

"But wouldn't this mean he's already a jackass?"

Willow shook her head. "I can certainly see why it could appear that way to the naked eye, but I really think that relationships can adapt and change. It depends on the person, of course, but it's worth a shot. Seeing how broken up you are about it, I'm convinced you need to breathe some life into the situation. At the very least, you'll have the closure you need to move on."

I took a sip of my water and looked out the window again, wishing for an excuse not to go through with this. But her argument was convincing, and I told myself that being scared just wasn't a good enough reason to back out - especially when something I really wanted hung in the balance.

"Okay. Yeah. I mean, I didn't totally see it that way at first but I get what you mean. I'll call him later. Unless that's too early? The date was Saturday, and today is Monday, obviously. Too soon?"

"Nah, I think that's fine. Just be yourself - can't go wrong that way." She smiled at me, and then her eyes widened as she remembered something. "Did I ever tell you how I used to think Zander was a bit of a geek?"

"What? No, you didn't!" I smiled as she launched into this whole story about them meeting as kids in middle school, and how he allegedly used to fold his gym clothes neatly in his locker organizer, etcetera. Willow was always a free spirit, dancing to the beat of her own drum or whatever muse she happened to come across in her daily travels. Pairing her up with the schedule-loving, steam-pressed Zander would definitely not cross my mind - until it happened, and their chemistry was undeniable. Life was funny that way, and it gave me hope for me and Gavin. Not every love story had to start off perfectly, but it could still end up somewhere great later on. Right?

"So, I hate to ask, but Alex isn't... on the radar? I've been meaning to ask more about that since my head stopped throbbing." Willow sliced through the giant Oreo cupcake we always shared on her cheat days, and then slid one half toward me. I stabbed my fork into the thick buttercream frosting probably more angrily than I really needed to.

231

A sigh escaped from my lips, and I shook my head almost imperceptibly. Willow's mouth rounded into a soft 'o' while she signaled for me to elaborate. "I think he might be one of those people that I'll always love in some capacity. But it doesn't appear to be romantic at this point - at least for him. I have to respect his wishes, as much as it pains me."

Willow nodded. "Tough break, kid. But I'm proud of you! You're moving on, speaking up when you need to, and taking no shit. Mad respect! And hey, at least you got one smoking hot smooch out of the ordeal, am I right?"

I covered my face with my hands. "You really saw that, huh? I was hoping you were too drunk to remember it." A shy laugh escaped from my lips, and I wondered why the memory made my heart so happy even though it also made me really sad.

"Oh I never forget anything that juicy - not even alcohol can wipe that kind of lip-lock from my memory." She smirked and munched on the last of her cheeseburger.

"Well uh, it was pretty good, yeah." I smiled, and checked my phone. "Crap, I have class in like ten minutes, I should start walking over."

Willow nodded and started gathering her trash. "Let me know what happens after you talk to Gavin. I think it'll be really good for you, no matter how he takes it. It's a little ballsy, but I think that's just your style."

I snorted, not even trying to hide it. "Since when am I ballsy?"

"Since today - gotta start somewhere, babe!" Willow blew me a kiss, waved, and started off toward her next class that I knew was across campus from where mine was.

Sitting down in class, I was grateful when I noticed that the images in my head had somewhat subsided in their resiliency, allowing me to block them out long enough to take some notes in class and feel like a normal human being for the first time since I traveled through time. It probably also helped that this particular class was one of the least-boring ones that I got to take, so I kind of enjoyed it.

What didn't help, was the endless thoughts about what my conversation with Gavin might be like later today. After talking to Willow about it, I was convinced that things were far more ambiguous than I realized, so I could logically see it going in either direction. The not knowing was the worst part of the situation.

I told myself that I could handle whatever was thrown at me, but looking back now, that was totally all talk. What I didn't know was that I was in for it - and I was in deep.

After class ended, I got back into my car and made the trek home on mental autopilot. Having driven to school so many times over the past few years, I could get there and back with my mind more or less free to agonize over forgotten reading, my lack of a boyfriend, or a career. Thankfully, the radio was playing a bunch of my favorite songs on the alternative station, so I turned those up full-blast to drown out the loud anxiety in my head. It worked pretty well until I pulled into my driveway and wondered if I should make this call in the privacy of my car, or in the comfort of my room.

If I took the call in my car, there was a good chance Mom or Jet would look out the window and wonder what I was doing out here longer than I needed to be. But if I called Gavin in my room, they could potentially hear my end of the conversation through the walls.

Yeah that second option was definitely worse. I'll bite the bullet and just call him now. I at least turned off the ignition to save fuel - my punch buggy was cute, but I paid for its gas-guzzling habits weekly.

Just call him Vera. You have nothing to lose. I psyched myself to just go for it, reminding myself what Willow said and how smart her reasoning seemed earlier today at lunch.

My breath hitched in my chest as I held my smartphone in my hand and just stared at it until I felt like my head was going to explode from the lack of oxygen. As the screen dimmed from inactivity, I decided it was now or never, so I scrolled to Gavin's contact name in my phone and hit the call button. Raising it to my ear, I was prepared for whatever happened next. Or so I thought, but I couldn't have been more wrong.

"Hello?"

His voice hit my eardrum like a siren song to my ultimate demise - I had to hear more but I had a sinking feeling in my gut that as soon as he answered, the game was already over.

"Hey, it's Vera."

"Oh. Uh, hi." His tone was suddenly sheepish and uncertain, lower in pitch and quieter compared to his initial greeting. Did his mood change upon hearing my name? Did he delete my contact number?

"I just thought... I'd call you about Saturday. I felt bad how things sort of ended and wanted to get a feel for where you're at." I exhaled, feeling quite a bit better about my suddenly-acquired ability to explain my reason for calling.

I was met with what sounded like an exasperated sigh on the other end of the call, so I started spiraling into damage control mode. "I just want to clarify that, it wasn't anything personal. I'm not looking for... that... right now - with anyone."

"Are you even ready to date right now?"

"Excuse me?" *What was that supposed to mean? I'm twenty-two years old, who does he think he is?*

"You just seem like... you're looking for attention."

"Huh? How?"

"Look, I don't have time for this, okay? There are things you'll need to learn about life and you gotta not be a prude. That's the only way to grow up."

I couldn't breathe, couldn't even process what he was saying. I even questioned whether or not I had dialed the wrong number somehow.

"Gavin, you're not making any sense. You can't actually be *that* upset just because I wouldn't put out..." The silence on the other end of the line gave me my answer. "Wow. You really are upset because I wouldn't put out."

"It's not an abnormal thing to expect on a date, you know." His voice had risen slightly in volume and significantly in jackassery.

Did he really just admit to that? On a first date, really?

"You know what you are Gavin? You're a *pig*. I really liked you, you know. But you didn't actually care about me at all." Then I let a few expletives loose that felt really good in the moment, even if I'm not super proud of that now.

"Look, I don't need this. Don't call this number again." He dead-panned his way through that last bit, almost as if it wasn't the first time he'd had to end a relationship that way.

"Oh, I won't." I let those words seethe as I ended the call and deleted his number from my phone. And then *my eyes erupted with tears*. Suddenly I couldn't breathe, and a lump formed in the pit of my belly which started clawing away at my insides. My fists suddenly had the urge to punch something, or someone, and I screamed. Luckily, I was still in my car with the windows closed, so my family probably didn't hear me. It was so hard to pinpoint exactly what I was crying about, because lots of guys are jerks and I shouldn't have expected anything less - especially after what already happened. *What was Willow even thinking? This was a very bad idea. A very, very bad idea.*

After another twenty minutes of self-pity and pure unadulterated rage, I managed to pull the shards of my psyche somewhat together to fake being fine enough to avoid getting the third degree from Mom or Jet. That being said, I totally crumbled again as soon as my bedroom door was shut. People can warn you all they want about how much rejection can hurt, but you can't fully grasp it until it happens to you. I laughed sadly to myself as I realized that I'm never going to be able to drink coffee again. Or, at least not the way I used to, because it would always remind me of Gavin.

I looked up through my tear-soaked face to my backpack that I had dropped near my desk, and wondered how much longer I could get by with just doing the bare minimum. I already hated reading those boring textbooks, but adding time travel and a jackass into the mix made my limited resolve drain to basically nothing.

A couple hours later, my cellphone started vibrating on my bed next to me, and my quick glance was met with Willow's face glowing on my lock screen. *How did she know I already called him?* I shook my head as I assumed she just knew me really well or something - it was a lot less likely that she had suddenly developed psychic abilities, but knowing her, I guess anything was possible.

"Hey girl, how did things go with Gavin?"

"How did you know I talked to him already?"

"I knew you wouldn't wait too long." Her voice had this bubbly tone to it that I was sad to ruin with my less-than stellar news.

"Yeah so he's a total jackass."

"Really? Oh man, so he didn't take it well?"

"Well, I actually sensed something was off when he answered his phone and didn't sound like he recognized who was calling until I said my name. Then he came up with all this utter BS about me not being ready to date, looking for attention, etcetera. It was pretty much even worse than I was expecting." The words tumbled out of my mouth all at once, and I even amazed myself at how quickly I was able to spit them out even though they left the taste of bile in my mouth.

Willow was silent for a moment, but I could hear her tapping her gel manicure against her teeth. "I mean, we did acknowledge that possibility right? So he's a jackass, okay. That means you don't want him anyway."

"Yeah. I mean yeah, you're totally right. I'm just gonna get over him. That's all. I have to, no question about it." My throats started to choke up a bit as the tears began to fall full-force.

"Atta girl! You don't need that kind of negativity in your life." Her voice was triumphant and encouraging. "But uh, you don't have to be a hero either. I can be there with Ben and Jerry's in twenty minutes if you want?"

"Sure, why not. Thanks Willow. I probably won't be all that interesting to hang out with though." My nervous laugh echoed in my room, and I cringed at the awkwardness of it all.

"Doesn't matter. See you in a bit."

I ended the call with Willow feeling slightly better, and figured I'd better get at least a little reading done before she got here, even if my eyes kept leaking all over the pages. *It's a very good thing to have a Willow.*

Thirty-Four: Clues from the Pizza Parlor

"Jet?"

After a few days had passed since our fight and my less-than-deal phone call with Gavin, I had had a lot of time to think through a lot of things. And I felt truly sick over how I treated my brother - but even sicker after considering what his claims could mean.

"What."

I leaned absentmindedly on the baseboard of the living room doorway, letting my toes sink into the plush carpeting. "I wanted to apologize for being, well, stupid the other day. I didn't mean for you to think I thought your ideas were dumb."

"But you did though." He had the decency to mute the TV, but the screen still moved in front of him, holding his attention.

"Well, I mean, maybe."

I stared at him, while he stared at the TV. Then I plopped down next to him, uncomfortably so, as a feeble attempt to get his attention.

"Personal space, Vera." He shoo'd me away with a cheese dust-covered hand, but I already had the remote in my hand. I clicked the TV off, and Jet immediately responded with some choice words, but I didn't let them phase me.

"I need to talk to you!"

He rolled his head in my direction. "Oh, like the same way I needed to talk to you?"

I sighed. "Okay okay, we get it. I screwed up. I apologized. What's wrong with you?"

Jet shook his head. "I'm not doing so hot right now, sis. I quit my job and I don't exactly have any IRL friends to talk to."

Due to his intense work schedule, Jet never really socialized beyond the four edges of his computer screen. Now without work, I guess it made sense that his whole life had been twisted and muddled into this habitual couch-potato alter ego.

"I… guess that's true. Sorry - again - for being insensitive."
I continued to sit next to him, even resting my head on his shoulder
as an attempt at a sisterly sort of affection and support.

"It's… okay. I know you've been going through some shit
too." He ran his hand through his hair, and I cringed as the cheese
dust was deposited on his strands. Silence fell upon us both, and
then it cracked under the weight of the truth fighting to get out. "Did
I ever finish telling you why I quit my job?"

I shook my head. "No, not exactly." I mumbled the words,
as I shamefully recalled how I didn't believe him when he tried to
explain it before. It was still pretty hard to believe, but I really
should have given him the benefit of the doubt, especially since I
could tell it was so important to him. I paused the TV, because I
could sense that whatever he was about to tell me was important.

Jet inhaled sharply, and then turned toward me after
glancing around to make sure Mom wasn't within earshot. "You
know those numbers and medical data that I found? There's more to
it than just vitals. After clicking around a bit, I noticed the
algorithms changed. They started to form strings of data that seemed
to be compressible into words."

"Okay, and?" My eyes were glued onto his while he seemed
to search me for readiness to hear what he was about to say.

"When I analyzed them, they appeared to be distress signals
like 'help'."

I tilted my head. "Are you, are you sure?"

"Positive. I've worked with digital data for a while now and
it behaves strangely at times, but nothing even *close* to this strange,
I swear. The probability of that happening organically by chance is
next to nothing."

What he suggested was ridiculously unbelievable, but I
forced myself to hear him out. Last time, I didn't, and we fought
about it - I definitely didn't want a repeat of that. So when the words
finally took hold in my mind, I felt my whole body start to shake. It
wasn't terror, or anger - but a distinct sense of gothic horror that

was seeping in through my clothes. A slimy rain of blurry truth crept into my skin.

"Jet, you don't think..."

"Honestly, anything is possible. At first, I considered that maybe I was just overtired and seeing things, or maybe that it was a coincidental glitch. But then it kept happening, with the distress signals getting more and more intense, and I was so terrified I was helping the company with this somehow. That's why I destroyed my work computer and quit my job."

I sat in silence digesting the revelation Jet recounted, and the images kept flashing in my head, but most of them sort of fell away. The faces of classmates and various school-related things faded in a pixelated cloud, until only two were left - my dad's face, and that god-forsaken walrus tail. I didn't get why, until those thoughts led me down a sort of mental rabbit hole, and I started replaying the brief interaction with my dad at the pizza place while I was visiting my younger self and younger Alex.

I remembered how I saw him, and how he looked at me with a hint of recognition, but then continued on as usual without missing a beat. And then he pulled out his phone to check on some message from a customer, I'm sure. And how there was some sort of tail-like symbol on his phone. Wait - a walrus tail on his phone?

Oh. Em. Gee. From my lazy vantage point on the couch, I felt all the missing pieces of my mind and experiences meld together. Like a spark was ignited behind my eyes, my entire body awakened to the haunting realization that the answer was in front of me the whole time.

"Jet? Jet!" I started punching his shoulder while he glared at me with daggers even though he had technically already forgiven me.

"What?" He seemed pissed on the surface but I could've sworn there was a hopeful smile tugging at the corners of his lips. Unfortunately, that was about to disappear.

"I think... Captain Tus has Dad on ice."

His face froze, as if he himself had just been locked in the fridge.

240

"What? How?"

"The walrus tail that had been flashing in my head for weeks now since I time traveled."

"What are you talking about?"

"Jet, I told you about this already." I shifted my weight and turned to face him more directly so he could see the seriousness in my face. "What if... the reason that it keeps flashing in my head is because it's related to finding Dad? And, when I saw Dad back in time..."

"Wait, you saw Dad?"

"Yes, I did. He was at Luigi's Pizza Parlor, and he had his phone out and I saw *that logo* on it briefly. It was just a quick glance that I took but I'm so sure that was it. Now it all makes sense!" I started shaking, and Jet pursed his lips while wrinkling his forehead, deep in thought. A slight redness colored his cheeks, and that's when I knew my brother believed me. Or at least, he believed the possibility that I was right and took me seriously enough to consider it. "I bet those distress signals were from Dad!" The color drained from my face as the words fell out of my mouth, and Jet remained stoic, allowing the silence to wash over him calmly while the storm raged on our insides.

He got up from the living room couch and tugged me over to the front hallway, further away from Mom's office on this far-from-typical Thursday evening.

"Vera, if this is true... we gotta tell Mom. Maybe she'll know what to do. Maybe she can help."

I shook my head, even though my reasoning baffled even me at this point. "Not until we're absolutely sure. Can you do some investigating? Do you still have access to the databases you saw when you were working for them?"

"No, but I bet I can hack my way back in."

"Okay, so do that. Find out everything you can about what they're doing. Now you have nothing to lose, since you already quit anyway. Right?"

Jet nodded slowly, but his face was still pinched with fear of the unknown - or maybe he was more afraid of what he was about to find out. "Right. Yeah. Okay. And Vera? Stay calm. We don't know anything for sure yet."

I sighed sharply as my nerves pinched with worry and frustration. Suddenly the dim lighting of the foyer was an eerie sort of darkness, only allowing me to make out Jet's taller frame and half-brushed shoulder-length hair. He patted my shoulder, giving me a gentle squeeze, and then disappeared up the stairs to his room where his newly-purchased average-guy laptop was perched on his recently emptied desk to replace the bigger monitor he had destroyed. The dim light moved and swayed around him as he ascended the steps, and I found myself too shaken to stand there, so I trudged to my own room and went to sleep early. My shaken psyche had thought it better to put me to sleep than to allow my thoughts to run free while awake.

Per usual, I slept fitfully. I tossed and turned, imagining my dad held as prisoner in various different configurations. First he was in a dank jail cell like I'd seen in movies, then it was a high-tech prison with sterile-white bars. I'd try to reach out to him, but he'd fade away while his mouth hung open in a pitiful scream. Various versions of this continued until my chirpy alarm clock brought me back to my complicated reality. That's when I realized that my dad really might still be out there somewhere, and we were going to do whatever it took to find him.

Despite the level of stress my body was experiencing, I had the sudden urge to just go to class like always, probably just to preserve some level of normalcy in all this. When I passed by Jet's room, his door was open for once, and I saw him hunched over his laptop, hard at work. I wondered if he had been at it all night, and if he had, what he might be finding in the depths of the dark web Captain Tus had woven. So I grabbed my backpack, said 'good morning' to Mom, and munched on a bagel as I made my way to my car.

Walking into class was pleasant because the weather was pretty nice, and I happened to see Willow and Zander on my way.

Unfortunately though, there was still a storm brewing in my mind.

"Hey Vera!" Zander waved me over and Willow gave me a hug. He smiled at me pleasantly, but I could sense the sympathy pooling just behind his irises.

"Hey guys." Then I turned to Zander and shrugged. "So, I guess Willow told you, huh."

He nodded and pulled me into a bear hug. The musky scent of his Gucci cologne was comforting in that moment, while Willow patted my shoulder and gave me a hug too.

"How are you feeling?" She smiled at me pleasantly, but her expression read more like an ASPCA puppy shelter commercial than an empathetic friend.

"I'm... hanging in there. Just been thinking about my dad a lot lately."

Zander smirked for a split second, probably thinking of some dirty joke to make about the clunkiness of my sudden topic change, but then must have thought better of it as the mischief dissolved out of his face, leaving only a sullen sort of compassion in its wake.

"That must be really tough, not having him around." Willow was an only child, so she understood feeling close to her parents.

"It really has been." I found myself wondering how much I should say here, but thinking of how ridiculously sci-fi and fake cryogenic suspension sounded, I figured I'd just keep it to myself until I had some real answers.

"Well, I mean it *is* Friday, after all. We should hang out tonight! If you're free." Zander's suggestion was sweet, but I couldn't decide how much social interaction I could really handle. I shifted my gaze to the bright blue, cloudless sky and inhaled the light scent of the flowers in the planter to my left.

"Yeah! What do you say, another round of drinks at Blue Pelican?" Willow flipped her beach waves over her shoulder as the tiny bells on her light scarf jingled in the warm morning breeze.

243

"No!" Zander and I responded in unison. Willow's face dropped, but then she smiled slightly and shrugged her shoulders.

"Well uh, okay. What do you want to do then?"

I sighed. "Maybe a game night at my house? I can invite Alex too." That last bit tumbled out of my mouth before I could stop it, and it was probably largely out of compulsion - but it felt right as my momentary lapse settled into my reality.

"Sure, that'd be cool." Zander nodded, and Willow smiled.

"Whatever you want, girlie. We're here for you."

I couldn't tell if she meant they were here for me about Gavin or about missing my dad, but then I decided it didn't really matter. They were my friends, and they cared about me. What more could I ask for?

"Thanks guys. I'll see you at my house around five-ish? And bring food."

"Sure thing. See you then!" Willow gave me a hug, and Zander waved as they headed off to the math class I knew they had together.

Before I knew it, I had grabbed my phone out of the little zippered pocket on the front of my bag and texted Alex the same details. He responded back almost immediately with a thumbs-up emoji and the smile that I felt my face create completely on its own left me a little blindsided, but happy.

I walked into class, and Professor Amelia smiled at me. She was one of the younger teachers, and encouraged everyone to call her by her first name, which I always liked. Usually seen wearing Doc Martens and trendy skirts, I bet we would've been friends if I was just six or seven years older. Her journalism class was easily my favorite this semester, and I would sorely miss it when I graduated.

After my favorite class was spent writing my piece about the upcoming Los Angeles music festivals, I was in a much better mood and shockingly able to separate my mind from the images and thoughts that had been plaguing me for weeks now.

I drove back home in complete silence. I wanted to listen to the radio, but something about my headspace seemed to demand

244

silence. Without much else to think about, I started wondering if Jet would really be able to finally find out what happened to our dad after all these years. Neither of us had any clue if he was even still alive, but I hoped that he was more than anything. Even if he wasn't, I was determined to seek justice for him. My dad was a good person and an even better father, and since Edgar reappeared on the scene, I could feel all my old wounds reopening over and over again. Edgar's presence in our lives was a catalyst for change, even if I hadn't decided if that change would be good or bad.

When I got back into the house, Jet was still hard at work in his room. I put my bag down and walked downstairs to get ready for my friends to come over. Then I figured I should probably let Mom know about that as well.

"Hey, Mom?"

She was in the kitchen refilling her coffee, likely to remedy her typical mid-afternoon slump. "Yes?"

"I uh, invited Willow, Zander, and Alex over for a game night. I guess I should have asked you - hope that's okay."

"That's fine, Vera. Thanks for letting me know. I'll just be holed up in my office anyway making the final adjustments for the spring issue. Just as long as the noise level stays at a dull roar." She winked at me, sipped her coffee, and then tilted her head. "I didn't know you were hanging out with Alex again. It's been a long time since you would play together as kids. When did that happen?" She winked at me, as if she assumed something was up when it most certainly was not.

"Oh um, recently I guess. Yeah, it is nice. Casual, you know. He met Zander and Willow recently so now we just all hang out together."

"Well I think that's great!"

"We're friends, Mom."

"I know."

I wasn't convinced by the way she smirked at me and smiled whenever either of us said his name, but that would be a discussion for another day.

"You doing okay, Sweetie? You seem… upset."

Mom always seemed to have such an uncanny ability to sense when something just wasn't right. I don't know if it was the way my arms were crossed, or if my face gave me away somehow, but that's when I crumbled. I started crying, and Mom immediately put her coffee down and ran around the peninsula countertop to wrap her arms around me. Little kisses on my forehead just seemed to make me cry even more. In between the snot pooling in my sinuses and tears tracing lines down my face, I let my mom just hold me until I could get coherent words out. For a fleeting second, I almost told her everything, but thought better of it because it was so unbelievable, and worrying her for no reason - or giving her false hope - certainly wouldn't help anyone.

"I just, miss Dad so much."

"I know Sweetie, we all do."

She hugged me even tighter, and then eased herself onto the barstool next to me while I just stared down at the swirled pattern on the granite countertop.

"Sorry to interrupt you, I know you're probably busy." I sniffled as some stray mucus dripped from my nose, and I awkwardly wiped it on the edge of my sleeve.

Mom shook her head and handed me a tissue. "I'm never too busy for my kids. You know that." Squeezing my hand though, I did catch her sneaking a peek at her watch. I hate to admit that it hurt me a little to see that, but I understood. She had a very well paid, but demanding job. "I do have a conference call in about five minutes with one of the other staff writers. Will you be okay if I go take that? I can reschedule, whatever. You just let me know." Patting my hand with each syllable, I knew she meant it. But no way in hell would I sabotage my mom's hard work.

"No - yeah I'll be fine." Wiping away my tears with the back of my hand, I smiled slightly as if to prove that I was doing okay despite my sudden blowup. "Go ahead, I gotta do some homework anyway before my friends get here."

"Okay, good. Thanks Vera. And after the call, we can talk more. Or just cry - you know I'm always down for a good cry." Her

246

face grew a bit redder, and I could see the beginnings of tears pooling at the corners of her eyes.

"I know, thanks."

She gently touched my shoulder, and then padded back to her office in her lavender-quilted Kate Spade knock-off slippers. I sat by myself for a few minutes, trying to piece myself back together enough so I didn't totally bum out my friends. At least, no more than I already had.

Then I ventured down to our basement to dig out some of my favorite board games. A quick glance at my phone told me it was about quarter of five, so my friends would likely be showing up very soon. Grabbing Monopoly, Twister, Pictionary, and Scrabble, I balanced the stack carefully and put them on the living room coffee table. That's when I noticed the various crumbs and food wrappers left on the couch by my brother's latest Netflix binge-watching session, so I cleaned up that stuff too. My mind began drifting toward what he might be finding upstairs about Dad, but I didn't want to start crying again so I just took some deep breaths and popped open a can of sparkling water. I didn't feel particularly hospitable at the moment, but I remembered that the distraction would be good for me. Nope, scratch that - any distraction was probably the only thing that would keep me stable. With every day that passed, I could see why Edgar had thrown around the term "insanity" in the same breath as time travel.

The bright ringing of the doorbell shook me out of those more depressing thoughts, and I jumped up to open it. Alex met my gaze with a smile, and held out a batch of his mom's freshly made chocolate chip cookies. I recognized their scent immediately - the barely-melted chunks brought me right back to my childhood.

"Your mom made these? Ugh it's been way too long. Come on in, and bring those cookies." I closed the door behind him, and he eased himself onto the couch like he'd been living here for years - and in many ways, he basically had.

"Yeah, she insisted on it. Hope there's enough."

"Are you kidding? This container is huge." I smiled at him, and then placed the massive cookie tin onto the kitchen table for later. "Willow and Zander should be here any minute."

"Cool." Alex shifted his weight on the couch, and I sat across from him on the floor in front of the board-game laden coffee table.

"So uh, how're classes going?"

"They're fine. Just typical."

"Cool."

We sat in silence for a few minutes until he broke it in probably the most awkward way possible.

"So uh, I don't want things to be... tense between us. Is there any way we can avoid that?"

I could tell he was having trouble making eye contact with me, but I couldn't judge him too harshly because I was doing pretty much the same thing.

"Things aren't tense." I shrugged, hoping speaking it into existence would be enough to manifest it.

"Vera, it *is* totally tense. I'm not sure which one of us started it but the small talk pretty much tipped me off."

"Well uh, yeah. I guess so. I don't know." My voice trailed off, and I felt myself mumbling.

"I didn't mean for things to be awkward. I guess just... being alone with you after, well, you know. I'm just awkward in general, it's nothing personal I swear."

"I know." He moved off of the couch to sit next to me on the floor. I could feel the heat of his body from our close proximity, and his musky cologne filled the air around us. "So what are we playing first?"

"I brought a bunch of games up from the basement, take your pick."

Alex reached for the Scrabble as the doorbell rung, announcing Willow and Zander's arrival.

"Hey Vera!" Willow breezed through the door, pushing past me to grab the Twister game before I could hide it. Zander nodded at me behind the precarious pile of pizza boxes and soda cans he balanced on his arms.

"How's it going?"

"I'm doing okay, come on in, and let me carry something before it falls." I grabbed the pack of soda and headed to the fridge to keep them cold. "Thanks for bringing food! I'm starving." Placing the pizza on the kitchen table, I washed my hands and grabbed some plates and cups from the cupboard. I tried to paint on a believable smile for my friends, but I mostly just went through the motions. We still weren't sure what was going on with my dad, and the recent clues we found were equal parts hopeful and terrifying.

We ate a very casual dinner of artisan pizza and homemade cookies, and then made our way back to the living room for board games. Just as I was about to pop open the Scrabble box, Jet ran down the stairs in a terrified huff. His face was pale white, and his eyes seemed to be popping out of his head. I felt my own face mirror his expression, and my friends just stared at us both. He didn't say much, but his words were chilling.

"They have him. We need to go. *Now.*"

Thirty-Five: Game Night in Vegas

"What? Who has who? Is this something about your dad who's missing?" Willow jumped up from where she sat on the floor, and Zander and Alex followed slowly, their faces scrunched into question marks.

"He's not anymore. We know where he is. He's being held in Vegas in some kind of storage facility. And we're gonna get him home." I grabbed my purse from the chair I hung it on earlier, and fished my keys out of my bag after recounting what Jet had just revealed to me. The air condensed as an enlightened fog settled over the room. We were smarter now, but in danger. The uncertainty of what was about to happen hit hard, and pulled us toward the storm brewing outside these walls. My lungs constricted as I tiptoed on the edge of hyperventilating.

"Well then, we're coming with you guys." Zander nodded his head as he spoke, stating it as a fully confident fact.

"What? You really don't need to, we got it." Jet shoved his laptop into his case and zippered it tight. "But we have to go now."

"Doesn't matter. It can't hurt to have backup. We're coming with you." Willow crossed her arms and stood next to Zander.

"Me too. I'm not letting you guys do this alone." Alex stood next to me, with his arm around my shoulder. I felt comforted by his willingness to help, but Jet didn't seem so thrilled with the idea. His face was white with terror still, but that also meant he was too paralyzed with fear to challenge it any further. He glanced for a moment towards Mom's office, but she was clearly in the middle of a conference call.

"Don't worry about her, I don't think she'll be too mad we left without telling her. Once we bring Dad home with us, I think she'll let it go." I paused, and turned to my friends. "You guys are nuts! Why would you want to come with us to Vegas in the middle of the night? This is going to be dangerous. It's crazy scary. I don't even want to have to go. But Jet can't go alone and our dad needs rescuing - so we have to do this for him. Why would you want to risk your lives like this?" My whole body shook, wondering which of us had suddenly gone insane.

"The better question would be to ask 'why wouldn't we?'" Alex patted my shoulder, and Willow and Zander nodded. "I remembered your dad from when we were kids, and I always thought he was pretty cool. If I can do something to help bring him back when we were so sure he was gone, you better believe I'm going to do that."

"Yeah, I mean up until today, everyone believed he was gone. If there's hope for him, and for your family, we gotta help out." Willow chimed in, and Zander agreed. We all marched toward the front door, even though terror was written on each of our faces and tattooed into our skin. All of us had shaking limbs and short breaths as we made our way outside.

Jet eventually complied, but even as we exited through our front door, I saw him glancing back in Mom's direction a couple more times. This day couldn't have come soon enough, and yet, on the cusp of finding our dad, I felt like my life was about to shatter into a million pieces. Funny how just when things were seemingly about to come back together, the new normal shattered all over again, and the sense of loss was inversely experienced, but the change hurt all the same. What I wanted most now was stability, and just when I began to find it, everything unraveled again like a loosely knitted sweater. Now I was laid bare at the mercy of the people and situations I found myself tangled up in.

"I'll drive!" Willow grabbed my arm and tugged me toward the door. "We'll all fit in my car."

"The scion? Doesn't it break down every ten feet?" Jet rolled his eyes, but I noticed his shoulders shivering from something more powerfully cold than just the slight evening breeze.

"Not since I had it worked over in the shop last week. It's fine, I swear!"

"Oooh you had it *worked over*, eh?" Zander winked at her and poked her side.

"Zander! This is *not* the time for dirty jokes! Ugh." She elbowed his side eliciting a small yelp from her boyfriend, and then unlocked her car door as we piled in. Jet sat in the back furiously typing away on his phone, while his laptop sat at attention on his lap. We peeled out of the driveway as Willow's tires made a loud screech on the asphalt.

"Where we headed, boss?"

Jet kept typing on his phone, but told her where to go. "I tracked the online activity to a warehouse in downtown Vegas. It's about four hours away."

"Four hours? Wow. Well, okay. Hope no one has to pee, it's gonna be a long drive."

I sighed, and pressed my face against the window as my finger traced and erased patterns on Willow's gray fabric seats. About twenty minutes into the ride, I decided to ask Jet what he had been doing so intently on his phone - and that quickly proved to be a mistake. Or maybe a very lucky break, depending on how you looked at it.

He hesitated to answer, and then swallowed hard, avoiding eye contact. "Vera, I told her everything. It was time."

My stomach flew into my throat, and it wasn't just from Willow's erratic driving. "You mean Mom? What exactly did you tell her?"

"Everything." He sighed, and continued to avoid meeting my gaze.

"No, no. Jet. How, how could you!" The words seethed as I spoke them, sparking venom on my tongue. The other passengers in the car grew silent.

"She's our mother, Vera! She needed to know." His voice grew in volume to punctuate his point and his perspectives, but all it did was serve to infuriate me even more. I could feel the hairs standing on end on the back of my neck, and my face grew rosy red as the capillaries below my skin heated up.

I opened my mouth to speak, but then Jet's phone started to ring. It was our mom, and she was hysterically yelling on the phone. I could hear from where I sat in the opposite window seat from him.

I tried to tune it out and distract myself with the humming of the engine and the street noise, but my efforts were fruitless.

"Mom, do whatever you think is necessary. I'm sorry we kept it from you for so long. We're going to do whatever it takes to get him home. No, don't call the cops yet, we have to investigate the situation first. I used to work for this company, remember? Just trust me. We're going to assess the situation and then do what needs to be done. Yeah, I'll handle it. Okay. Yeah. Bye."

I struggled to steady my breathing as I tried to figure out what Jet had done - and what I could do to undo it.

"I'm glad you told her not to call the cops, we don't know what we're even getting into yet. Probably better off carrying out some surveillance on our own first." I deadpanned my response because I had no idea how to process it any other way.

Jet still avoided my gaze. "Yeah, at least you and I agree on that."

"Jet? Is there something else you're strategically not telling me? Jet? This is not the time to be holding back."

He sighed, and then busied himself with tracking the location of the warehouse on his laptop. "Well, I didn't *just* tell Mom we were heading out to get Dad."

"Jet! What. Did. You. Tell. Her?" I crossed my arms, and flicked him hard on the side of his head.

"What the hell Vera!"

"Tell me, right now, or so help me there's more where that came from!"

Zander chuckled to himself as Willow rolled her eyes. "Zander what exactly is so funny about any of this?"

"That's what she said." He laughed infectiously all alone at his own joke.

"Oh, real mature. Just great." Willow was not at all amused - she just kept her eyes on the road ahead and mumbled some expletives under her breath.

"I'm serious Jet, tell me right freaking now." I let the words crawl out of my mouth, loud and clear.

"I told her about Edgar and how he abducted you and forced you to time travel."

"But he didn't force me! Jet, you could not be more wrong!" *I'm gonna kill him. I'm gonna literally kill my brother.*

"Doesn't matter, the authorities should know what he did to you."

"But-"

"No 'buts' Vera. This is just how it is. I'm your big brother, and I have to protect you. This has gone on for way too long."

I couldn't help myself. I screamed at Willow to take us to Edgar's house, while I tried my hardest to kick my brother's ass from the unfortunate locale of the small enclosed car space. My punches did little more than irritate him though, and he just kept typing away on his laptop while I tried to get his attention by hitting his arm over and over again with Alex awkwardly between us.

The car went silent for a few solitary moments, and then exploded in a cacophonous frenzy.

"Woah, time travel? What the hell, Vera?" Willow turned to look at me for a second, much to Zander's dismay.

"Eyes on the road Will! Can't save her dad if we're all dead!" Zander sat back in his seat, relieved that Willow had turned her vision back to the road even if her mind was running miles ahead elsewhere.

"Okay, but time-travel? That's impossible."

"Well actually, I've heard it might not be." Zander met her surprised retort with some long drawn-out scientific explanation, which I didn't mind missing because I was still mid-slap fight with my brother behind them while Alex's face was just zoned in on us and our sibling drama. Embarrassment was currently the least of my worries.

"Vera, stop." Jet's words hit me harder than they ever had before, and the scalding look he had in his eyes told me this was a matter he would not bend on. I rationalized to myself that the most he could do was tell Mom - he couldn't stop me from getting to Edgar's house before the cops did.

254

"Willow, detour to Edgar's house. *Now.*" I mumbled the words as I exhaled, trying to calm myself even though I was pretty much freaking out at this point.

"On it. Just give me the address."

I did that, and then sat in silence in the back seat. Alex patted my knee and offered a reassuring smile, while Jet just closed his laptop and stared out the opposite window. The car was silent aside from Willow's pop music playlist ironically pouring over the speakers while we were all experiencing varying degrees of a bad mood. I half expected Alex to say something, but what can you say when you're en route to rescue your friend's dad from a sketchy warehouse in downtown Vegas after hearing that time travel was a thing?

As soon as we pulled up to Edgar's house, I was relieved to see that there were no cops there yet, but I had a sneaking suspicion that they would be very, very soon. Practically tuck-and-rolling out of the scion, I ran to his front door and rang the doorbell a million times. Edgar appeared only seconds later, but it felt like it took maybe half an hour.

"What in the world is the panic, my dear? You had this old bachelor almost dropping his deep-dish pizza." He stood in front of me, with a plate in his hand and an irritated scowl on his face.

"They're after you, you gotta come with us now!" I found myself struggling to convey the information with the limited air I could get into my lungs while hyperventilating. Leaning awkwardly on the doorway, I pleaded with my eyes for him to follow me.

"Who's after me? What's going on?" I turned around as I started to hear the high-pitched screams of sirens growing in the distance. The whir of their repetitive noise was terrifying - like an angel of death, they had one target in mind, and they would not leave without him. That is, unless we left with him first.

"The cops! I can hear them coming, get in the car!"

He shrugged, put his pizza down, and shut his front door. I pulled him forcefully to Willow's car, but he wouldn't move as quickly as I would have liked him to. He sat down where I was sitting, and I double-buckled on Alex's lap (which would have been totally romantic if this wasn't turning into a life-and-death car chase). Willow peeled out of there, thankfully driving in the opposite direction of the wailing sirens.

"As fun and exciting as this is, who here is going to explain to me why my niece just showed up at my house demanding I pile into this car with her and her friends? I take it this is not a spontaneous night out."

Jet avoided Edgar's gaze, while the rest of us stared right at him - well, all of us except for Willow, since she was driving and if she turned back again, Zander would probably turn her head toward the road for her.

"I dunno, something about time travel? I'm pretty lost here myself, actually." Zander looked like he had seen a ghost - his face was pale and his wide eyes showed how unglued he had become.

Edgar tilted his head, and then looked at me on Alex's lap. "What's he talking about, Vera? You told them?" His face too showed signs of terror, ironically mirroring Zander's.

"I did, okay? Well, just today. Sort of. It's a long story." I nervously wrung my hands in my lap, feeling my nerves and blood vessels constrict under the stress and pressure of everything happening both inside and outside of Willow's car.

"We found our Dad, Edgar. It's my company - the company I used to work for. They have him and I figured Mom should know what you did to Vera." Jet's words were articulate and calculated, out-of-place over the perky teenage pop music that played over the speakers. Luckily, Zander had the good sense to turn it off during this conversation.

"I didn't do anything to Vera! I merely helped her realize her purpose and direction with a path that she was already headed down on her own." Edgar pointed a curt finger toward Jet.

"But you sacked her in the middle of the park!" Jet's eyes pierced Edgar's, but my uncle remained strong and sure under the scrutiny.

Edgar shrugged. "I didn't have many other options then. I needed to get her to talk to me, that's all. I didn't mean to scare her

256

or worry you, but I had no choice. Then she came back to me, completely *voluntarily*, to hear more about my device. And that's when *she* decided, completely without coercion, to try it out. That's all." His voice rose and fell as he spoke, but Jet's face just fell. Actually, it seemed to crash down harshly to Earth - especially once he realized how epically he had screwed up.

Staring down at his lap, Jet sighed. "Well uh, yeah. I guess, that sort of makes sense. I'm still upset you abducted her that way, but it probably wasn't worth calling the cops on you."

"I'll say!" Edgar chimed in, crossing his arms across his chest.

Jet took out his phone. "Maybe I could call Mom and tell her to stand down?"

I shook my head. "I think it's too late now, Jet. I heard the sirens, they were already almost at Edgar's house." Then I turned my head, and saw the police cars slowly gaining on us at the horizon line. I couldn't make out the vehicles so much as the flashing lights, and then the incessant whine of their sirens reentered my ears. "And now they're following us! Willow, you gotta lose them."

"How the hell am I supposed to do that?" She glared at me in the rearview mirror, her auburn curls bouncing in rhythm with the car speeding over a bumpy stretch of road.

"Just pretend it's a racing game or something! It *was* supposed to be game night, after all." Alex chimed in with a suggestion that was only partly stupid, but Willow shrugged and then took a sharp right turn off the highway.

"All right, hold on tight then - this toad is about to find a secret shortcut to Vegas." I grabbed onto Zander's seat in front of me while the car swerved onto another road and I found Alex's arm around my midsection. If I wasn't significantly fearing for my life, I would have melted right then and there. I smiled, but then I noticed him shift my weight a little and re-position me on his lap, causing me to hate my very bony butt for existing.

257

Once we got off the highway, Willow took a few more erratic turns only slightly over the speed limit to get the cops off our tail. Eventually the navigation app on Zander's smartphone recalculated and we found another route to the downtown Vegas warehouse where Jet had said our dad might be held.

"So now that we're out of the woods for now, how about you start talking, Vera." She met my gaze briefly by glancing up at her rearview mirror. "I am so out of the loop here and yet, I'm the one driving your sorry asses around. We've still got some time to kill, so icing me out probably won't work too well."

Zander nodded. "Yeah what's this, something about time travel?"

I swallowed, and looked at Jet and Edgar sitting next to Alex and me. "Well uh, it's real. I've experienced it."

"Yeah, and I remember it." I craned my neck as far as I could to see Alex's face behind me.

"You do? Like really?"

He nodded. "Yeah I thought I told you about this recently - like how I have memories of being visited by an older version of you."

I shrugged. "Yeah, right, you did say that. I just, can't believe it stayed with you after all these years."

"It's not everyday that kind of thing happens, you know." Alex shrugged, and I could feel his arm brace me protectively as Willow took another erratic sharp turn.

"Willow, they're not chasing us anymore, you can probably chill out for now." Zander patted her shoulder but she glared at him.

"That's just how I drive!"

"Oh. Right." His face turned beet red, and then he looked out the passenger window at the darkening evening sky. He probably felt bad for saying that, but I swear I saw Willow smirk into the rearview mirror, and I was convinced they'd be in it for the long haul.

The long drive continued pretty uneventfully after that. We didn't see any more cops on the way, and I marveled at how easily we shook them off our tail - how many actual criminals have escaped punishment this way? I shifted my weight a few times, feeling bad for Alex's sore legs at this point, but he didn't seem to mind. He just kept his hands on my waist, even though Willow was back on the highway and hadn't taken any spastic turns in a while. Edgar must have noticed this and winked at me a few times, but I didn't want to entertain any more fantasies - there were far more important things to occupy my mind with. Like the way the warmth of his hands seemed to soak through my thin tee-shirt and hoodie, drawing sparks around my midsection.

After an agonizingly boring few hours of conversation trying to convince Zander and Willow that time travel was very real, we turned off the glittery main drag and started heading to a large warehouse that appeared in the darkening distance. It looked typical enough - so typical, in fact, that I asked Jet if we had the right place.

"Yeah, best I can tell, this is it." He swallowed a lump in his throat and opened his laptop again, just in case. "Yep, this is definitely it."

"So uh, what's the procedure for breaking into a sketchy warehouse to break out someone held prisoner? I'm guessing I don't just park in front. And there's probably no drive-through." Willow tilted her head and smirked, probably using humor to mask the fear in her eyes. Who could blame her? This whole thing was pretty unbelievable, and until we actually got inside and saw any incriminating evidence of our hunch, this whole thing very well might feel like some sort of twisted prank.

"Yeah good intuition, Will." I patted her on the shoulder. "But seriously Jet, what do we do?"

"I dunno, park in the back."

"Is that really going to be any better? Look, why don't I have my cousin loan me his cloaking device from the CIA?" Zander grabbed his smartphone from the center console and started scrolling through his contacts.

"I don't think this is the best time for your rich boy sci-fi jokes, Zan." Willow grabbed his phone from him and slipped it in her own pocket while keeping one hand expertly on the steering wheel.

"Well I wasn't kidding, but okay." He sighed and looked out the window while Alex, Jet, and Edgar exchanged shocked glances as I just smiled and nodded. Zander never liked to flaunt his family connections or wealth, but Willow and I knew that he had plenty.

"There's no time to get it here anyway Zander. Thanks anyway, though."

"Well okay, I'll just pretend that whole conversation wasn't completely bonkers and I'll ask - what's the plan then?" Alex's mid-range voice reverberated through my chest as I had quickly formed a habit of leaning on him. I sat up to attention as I spotted a great way to hide Willow's garishly painted vehicle.

"Bushes! We're going to park it in the bushes!"

"Voluntarily?" Willow put the car in park and turned around to look at me directly. "But it'll scratch!"

"Come on Will, this is an old junker anyway. I promise I'll give you my Porsche after this if you want."

No matter how generous it was, Willow wouldn't be satisfied by such an extravagant offer. Instead, she glared at Zander until he made a counter-offer that was more her speed.

"Well, it makes no sense but I'll pay to have any scratches repainted on your *beloved* purple scion. Happy now?"

She put the car back in drive. "Very." Careening it into the nearby underbrush, she sufficiently hid the bright violet paint. "How's that?"

"Great, except that now we can't get out." Jet tried his door, and nothing happened.

"That's because you gotta unlock it, dumbass." I rolled my eyes as he blushed, and undid the pop-up door lock.

"If I wasn't saving my energy to rescue Dad right now, I would totally kick your butt for that." Jet forced the door open against the underbrush.

"I'll take a raincheck." I eased myself off of Alex's lap, and followed Jet out the path he had blazed through the overgrown twigs

260

and bushes. Alex followed after me, a bit visibly sore from supporting my weight for hours based on his slight limp from limited blood circulation as his legs woke up. Good thing I was skinny, I guess. Zander and Willow made their way out of the car and toward the general direction of the building, but Edgar hesitated to move much farther than the car door.

"So uh, do you kids want me to come along, or wait here? I'm not sure what you'll be walking into, and although I probably should be there to protect you, I'm just... not sure how."

"Well you can't just stay out here like a sitting duck! What if the cops show up again?" Willow clicked her key fob to lock her car and then tossed it into her small fringe-covered cross-body purse.

"That's a good point. I can't believe I'm saying this after what I've done to you, Edgar, but I guess you should stick with us. And don't worry about protecting us. I know Jiu-Jitsu, and Zander's probably got some kind of solid-gold pocket knife, right?"

Zander rolled his eyes. "Well actually silver is a more durable metal for weaponry, but yeah - I've got one."

"See? So it'll be fine. And you guys took some kind of anti-D-bag self-defense chick class like six months ago right?" Jet turned to Willow and I, hoping we'd be able to apply what we've learned.

"Well sure, but it's hard to say how much of that we'd be able to -"

"Perfect! Edgar, we'll be fine."

"What about me?" Alex jumped into the conversation, hoping to be assigned some sort of direction in this borderline-crazy mission.

"Well I dunno, what *about* you?"

Alex backed down, a bit embarrassed by Jet's unwillingness to ascribe some kind of skill to him. He rubbed the back of his neck and stared at the loose gravel under our feet. "I guess I'll just have to use my fists."

"Sure yeah, whatever. So if I consult the map on my phone, we'll see what the best access point is." Jet scrolled around on his phone for a few agonizing minutes, until an interactive map popped up.

"I'm guessing that's not a feature for tourists." Willow tapped her acrylic nails on her front teeth, and flicked her long hair over her shoulder in the slightly chilly night air.

"Oddly enough, it looks like our best bet is going straight in through the front entrance. We need to make our way to holding room 'E12'." Jet's voice broke at the mention of the room number. "It seems that Dad is in there. Vera, we really might find him today - but we gotta play our cards right." He paused, waiting to figure out what to say next. With his face reacting to the chilled air and the water welling in his eyes, he did something I wouldn't typically expect him to - he hugged me.

Then he whispered in my ear: "Dad is going to be *so proud* of you. And we're going to see him very soon. Be tough, and be brave, okay sis?" He backed away from the hug and patted me on the shoulder.

Looking to the rest of the group, Jet began to smile nervously, and cleared his throat while wiping away some stray tears. "Okay so, I have a reasonable idea of where they may be holding him - that's really all I know. It's holding room E12, based on the messages he managed to send me online. I still have no idea how. We also don't know *how* they are holding him captive. Vera and I assumed it could be cryogenic suspension, but we won't know for sure until we get in there."

"Charlie sent you messages?" Edgar's question hung in the air, and Jet shrugged.

"Nothing is guaranteed, but if my hunch is right, yeah, it was our dad. It was a series of code that I had to put through the system to analyze into alpha-numeric codes. Those codes ended up being what I could best describe as distress signals." Jet scratched the back of his neck as his cool-guy facade started to significantly waver.

"Thanks again guys, for coming along. This probably wasn't how you expected tonight to go." I smiled bravely at my friends and my uncle, even though I was pretty terrified about what

262

we were about to walk straight into. I could feel my lungs constricting my oxygen intake, as well as my hands and neck tensing up. Suddenly my senses seemed heightened, like walking in there was a shock to my system. Even just the sheer anticipation of the unknown was paralyzing.

"Nope, but I think it might be better." Alex draped his arm around me, pulling me into a hug. "I haven't been a very good friend to you lately, and the way I see it, maybe helping you get your dad back could make up for a lot of the time when we weren't talking."

"Alex, don't worry about it." I hugged him back. "That's old news."

Alex shrugged, and drew me in a bit closer. "I'm just glad to help any way I can."

"Yeah and we're happy to be here too." Willow nodded at me, and Zander smirked at me with raised eyebrows, and nodded slyly at Alex's arm around my shoulder. I rolled my eyes in response to him, and Zander just smiled at me and shook his head.

"I wish there was more I could do for you kids." Edgar rubbed the back of his neck and looked up at the building looming over us in the darkness as we made our way over to the front entrance. Sparse fluorescent lighting lit the way in the darkness emphasized by the starless night.

"You've already done more than the average uncle would be able to." Jet patted him on the back. "I'm sorry for how I jumped to conclusions - even though things were a little weird for a while, I guess I shouldn't've reacted that way."

Edgar shrugged, but I saw the creases near his eyes crinkle in the moonlight. "I don't blame you one bit. You're a bit like Charlie in that way - a real firecracker." He patted Jet's shoulder, and as we arrived at the entrance, I'm pretty sure my heart split in half and dropped into pieces at my ankles.

Thirty-Six: Infiltrating the Tricked-Out Lab

Our little group made our way to the cold metal entrance of the facility. I marveled at how oddly routine it seemed - definitely not the kind of place you'd expect to be holding your dad captive for the past nine or so years. The avid reader in me fought the urge to compare it to the sorts of places I had read about in science fiction novels. Aside from being pitch-black and almost ten at night, it all seemed pretty routine and typical.

The main entrance consisted of two double doors that slid open as we got closer, not so unlike a hospital entrance or any other reputable public place. Our footsteps echoed over the stone flooring, and I noticed everyone's breaths hitch in their throats - we still had no idea what we were walking into, and the tasteful lobby with trendy potted plants flanking the sides of contemporary leather couches definitely threw me for a loop. Willow nervously shifted in her moccasins while Zander patted the pocket of his corduroys, probably making sure he had his pocket-knife on him. Alex walked close to my side - whether to offer or receive protection from the unknown, I wasn't sure. Jet walked ahead of us with Edgar, scoping out the place.

There were three different hallways. One appeared to lead to restrooms and offices, another with an unmarked door or two, and the third with some rather innocuous-looking plaques and wall art. *Did we just stumble into an actual business? This is definitely not what I expected at all.*

Willow sniffed the air. "What is this, a granite factory? My mom dragged me to places like this all the time when we had the kitchen re-done."

"Nah, I doubt it. This is probably just a well-thought out disguise." Jet shoved his hands into his pockets, and looked around. Edgar separated from the group momentarily to get a closer look at the front desk. He thumbed through some pamphlets about technology, and Jet walked a bit behind him to get a look at the wall behind it.

"Hey guys, there's a bell." Zander pointed at the oddly-familiar brass object on the corner, and shrugged. "Should I ring it?"

Alex made eye contact with me and shrugged. "It's up to you, Vera. What are your thoughts?"

"How would I know? We're sneaking in, not looking for assistance."

Jet nodded. "Sure, that's true, but consider this - what if, maybe we need a diversion? We could pretend to need help, and then some of us could head to the lab and find Dad."

His word choice caught me off-guard. "You, you think it's a lab?"

My brother shrugged, his shoulder-length sandy-blonde hair creating a stark contrast over his black long-sleeved tee shirt. "I just assumed it would be, since I'm pretty sure he's not in a typical jail cell. The coding I deciphered seemed to imply some sort of high-tech trap."

"So what does that mean? How are we going to get him out?" Edgar jumped into the conversation, and I marveled at the way in a wild situation like this, even our uncle was at a loss. In the face of adversity, it seemed normal generational roles like leadership and protection were blown to smithereens. Instead, whoever had the most direction and confidence stepped up to lead the mission. And at the moment, that seemed to be Jet.

"I just pulled up the map of the building, and it seems that the room we need to get into is accessed by one of those hallways." He paused to zoom in on the map he managed to access on his smartphone. "Yep, okay. It's that middle hallway that would lead us in that general direction."

"Lead you where, exactly?"

We all turned to the front desk as an attendant appeared. Her light-brown hair was straightened pristinely, accompanied by a tasteful pearl necklace and an aqua-blue blouse. "Welcome to Captain Tus Nevada Headquarters. How can I help you?"

265

Something about her was unsettlingly familiar to me, but I couldn't put my finger on it. Alex seemed to notice it too because his face mirrored my curious look. Then I caught a brief glance at her laminated nametag, and it hit me.

"Sue? You work here?"

One of the lackies from middle school blinked her eyes once, twice, and then once more as recognition filled her face.

"Uh, yeah? Why wouldn't I? Wait, you're, uh, Lynn, right? And wait…" She paused, taking in Alex's face as well. "Oh man, Alex? It's been way too long!" She waltzed right around the front desk, clearly excited to see us. For what reason though, I still had no idea. This warm temperament was certainly not present years ago, and it only made me more suspicious as to what her angle might be. Willow, Edgar, and Jet turned to witness what became a fairly awkward interaction.

"Well, I actually go by my first name now, Vera. But yeah, it's me." I cleared my throat, hoping that someone who came with me would take the lead here, because seeing her threw me for quite a loop. I wasn't prepared to actually know one of the people we'd have to outsmart. Some might consider that an advantage, but for me, I saw it as a need to literally revisit some old demons. And one of them had just appeared to me in a pencil skirt with obvious hair extensions.

"This is so cool, oh em gee. What can I do for you?" I marveled at the way she reverted back to her middle-school self. *Maybe I could use that to my advantage somehow.* Unfortunately though, nothing came to mind as I pulled an absolute blank.

"Well uh, we're here… looking for… something."

"New software?" She reached around my shoulders to give me a very awkward hug. I cringed, and felt my whole body stiffen but she didn't seem to notice or even care. Then I caught a glimpse at the sparkling rock on her finger.

"Sort of. Hey uh, so you got married?"

Her face lit up at the mention of her beau, and nodded excitedly. "Yeah! It'll be almost three years in November. He's the love of my life." She sang that last part with lust in her eyes like she was talking about Ross Lynch or something.

I nodded politely, but wondered why anyone would get married at eighteen if they didn't *have to*. The idea nauseated me. Or maybe part of me was a little jealous - the truth was hard to pinpoint and even harder to admit.

"Well uh, congrats!" Alex piped in, and nodded politely at Sue.

"Thanks so much Alex!" She smiled at him, and walked back around to her desk. Her face glowed with pride, and her superiority complex was on full blast. "So software, huh? I guess it must be a last-minute thing, since you're here pretty late. I can schedule an appointment with a technician tomorrow if you want? Although it'll have to be over Skype since more of our experts are overseas." She typed away on a nearby monitor, and I shivered as I realized how closely the information she spouted matched that of Jet's experiences with the company and all the contacts in Japan he often collaborated with.

"Sure uh, I guess that'd be fine." Jet stepped forward, and pretended to scroll down some info on his smartphone. He slyly motioned to me with his eyes to try and sneak past Sue somehow to get to the hallways. I nodded quickly and dragged Alex with me. I wasn't sure what the others would be doing, but we all had our cellphones on us, so I figured I could always reach out to them over text if needed.

We still had no idea what we were walking into, but as Sue chatted happily with Jet, Edgar followed Alex and I down one of the hallways. It was fairly easy to deduce which one we needed - the one for the restrooms was obviously not it, and neither was the one with the cutesy employee-of-the-month paraphernalia covering the walls. So we chose the middle hallway with the foreboding-looking doors. I chanced a quick peek behind us, and noticed Sue totally talking off Jet's ears, completely oblivious to our disappearance. Since Jet worked with this company until recently, I trusted his ability to B.S. things as long as necessary.

267

Zander and Willow stood with him casually, but their faces showed some fear as we separated. Unfortunately though, we didn't have that much of a choice - if everyone except Jet walked away from her, Sue would probably notice something was up. We'd have to catch up with them later.

I tried to open the door, and to my surprise, it opened up to another long hallway, with many more doors. There was still some employee-related paraphernalia on the walls, so I kept wondering if we were in the right place. Alex and Edgar filed in quietly behind me.

"Okay, so now what?"

"Jet said something about room E12 right? So... we just gotta find that."

"Yeah, like it's gonna be that easy." I threw my long hair over my shoulder and nervously tapped an indiscernible rhythm on my thigh.

"Well what else do we have to go on?" I felt my cellphone vibrate in my pocket, and it was a text from Jet with the map of the building he grabbed from the Internet. Grateful for his foresight, I opened it up and guessed our location relative to whatever "E12" might be. Unfortunately, there was no "E12" marked on the map, but there was a large clump of storage rooms, so I decided to lead the group in that general direction. Hopefully the others would catch up soon. Looking around our immediate surroundings, it was a little unclear which door to take, so I started walking along, reading the different signs on each door. What once seemed oddly normal about this building had already started to fade away as I realized that this place had more doors than the building appeared to have from the outside.

"Text from Jet?"

I nodded at Alex's query. "Yup. Gotta head towards the storage facilities."

"Where are those?" I handed him my phone with the digital map on it, and Edgar peeked over his shoulder.

"I assume one of these doors will lead that way. I just have no clue which one - start looking." I pointed on the map where I

268

thought our approximate location was, and then Alex and Edgar started looking. I turned on my heel to explore the other end of the hallway and nearly crashed into someone.

"Hey, watch where you're going!"

A somewhat irritated voice hit my ears, and I found myself face-to-face with another previous classmate. "Wyatt?"

"Who's asking?" He grabbed a mop off of his janitorial cart and started cleaning the floor, nearly tripping me in the process.

"Vera."

He blinked, not recognizing my name.

"I mean, Lynn. You would've known me as Lynn." I crossed my arms, clearly irritated and confused. Alex walked over to stand next to me, his hand on my shoulder as a form of silent support.

"Oh right! Uh, what are you doing here?" Wyatt paused to meet Alex's gaze. "I know you too, right?"

Alex nodded. "Yeah, but it's been a while."

"It certainly has." Wyatt had gotten a little taller, but he'd also put on a fair amount of weight. Surprising, even though he'd never been particularly skinny. His breath reeked of what I could only assume was salami or some other low-grade deli meat, and he continued mopping amidst our conversation. "So yeah, can I help you with something? It's after-hours, but since the Internet never sleeps, I guess we don't either." He shrugged, and I noticed some pretty obvious pit-stains on his beige jumpsuit. I couldn't help but enjoy the fact that he used to be one of the bullies, and now he had a pretty lackluster night job. Talk about getting your "just desserts" - still kind of odd that both he and Sue were employed by the same company and both worked at this particular location. Maybe they applied together? As mean as they were to me, I understood that they were pretty good friends to each other.

I looked at Edgar, hoping he'd think of something to say. He caught my subtle cue and jumped right in.

"We have some business with the storage rooms, could you point us in that general direction?"

269

My uncle was so bold. I both respected that and slightly feared what might happen because of it.

"Sure, we got storage rooms. They're that way." Wyatt jammed his thumb in a general direction, which seemed to imply a door to my left.

"This one?" Alex walked over to it, pointing. Wyatt nodded, and continued mopping.

There's no way it's gonna be that easy to get into. I held my breath as Alex tried the door handle - unsurprisingly, it didn't budge.

"You'll need a key card for that, it's private. Employees only." Wyatt kept mopping as he said that, rhythmically dipping into a plastic tub of murky pale blue floor cleaning solution that smelled like bleach and desperation.

"Okay, well uh, we work here too."

I looked at Alex, wishing he would've waited to strategize a little more before banking on Wyatt's blatant stupidity to allow us access to where we were heading.

"No you don't."

"Says who?" Alex crossed his arms.

"Says me." Wyatt kept mopping the floor, not even bothering to look up from the blue puddle of cleaning solution.

I shrugged, trying to think of another plan of attack. Edgar looked at me, and silently pointed to what appeared to be an access card reader next to the door we needed to open. *Maybe Wyatt had one of those.* Then I saw a lanyard hanging out of his pocket, and I decided to get a little creative.

"Hey Wyatt, I think you missed a spot." I pointed to the floor where he had just mopped.

"What? I just got that spot. It's fine."

"No like, look. Look real closely." I bent over an imaginary blemish on the floor, and luckily for me, he followed suit. As he did, Alex grabbed the lanyard from Wyatt's side pocket. If Wyatt noticed, he didn't react.

"That's not going to work."

270

All three of us turned around to look back at the bully-turned-janitor, who looked up only to dash our hopes. "Huh? Alex, try it anyway."

Alex did as Edgar suggested, but to our dismay, the card reader lit up in red and beeped sadly to prove that Wyatt was right.

"Yeah. I don't have access to everything, because I'm just a janitor." He swiped the key card from Alex's outstretched hand and shoved it back in his pocket, taking care to tuck in the lanyard this time. "I probably should ask what you're doing here, but lucky for you, I don't care." His words dripped with apathy, and his eyes had dark bags under them that further illustrated his exhaustion.

Wyatt had become a hollow shell of himself, clearly disillusioned with life and his lackluster job. The part of me that took comfort in this reality now was starting to feel a bit sorry for him. I searched for something to say, but he started shuffling away to another hallway before I had the chance, with a half-assed river of blue cleaning solution left in his wake.

"So uh, we went to school with him too, Uncle Edgar." I nodded in the direction Wyatt had left, and Alex nodded.

"That's an interesting coincidence."

"It sure is, since we knew Sue from middle school too." Alex raised one of his bushy eyebrows and opened his mouth to say something, but then must have thought better of it. I was about to ask him more about it, and then the rest of our group burst into the hallway.

"Hey, so Sue went to use the restroom, and we managed to get away from her desk." Jet marched over to me with Zander and Willow close behind. "What's next?"

"Well, we just saw Wyatt - apparently he's the night janitor here."

"Another old classmate? Huh." Jet scratched his chin, and then looked around the hall. "Anyway, where to now?"

"We looked at the map you sent Vera, we think the storage rooms are through that door." Alex pointed and Edgar nodded.

"We tried to use Wyatt's key card, but it didn't work. And I think this is the only door that will lead where we need to go." I shrugged, frustrated but grateful for more time to collect my thoughts and prepare myself mentally to handle whatever state we found my dad in. I had a pretty good hunch it wasn't going to be easy seeing him laid up however they had him.

"We just gotta think, there's gotta be another way." Willow chewed on her fingernails, and Zander started to pace around in small circles. Then his gaze landed on a section of the wall behind Edgar, and I could see a light bulb practically materialize over his head.

"There's a vent system here, and we could climb in right over here. As long as no one here is claustrophobic, I could use my pocketknife to unscrew the grate. Thoughts?"

"Fine by me." I looked around at the rest of the group, and Edgar and Jet nodded. Alex shrugged and stared at the floor while Willow shook her head excitedly.

"Tight spaces, nah. That's so not my thing."

"Come on Will, I'll be right there with you. You trust me, right?"

"I trust *you*, I just don't trust myself to not freak out." Willow leaned against the nearest wall and tried to steady her breathing with a dainty hand resting on her lacy blouse. "I don't have a choice, do I?"

"Not unless you want to stay in the lobby by yourself." I shrugged. I wouldn't want to make Willow uncomfortable, but for her safety, she'd be better off sticking with us. And we were all going.

"Look, I'm not thrilled about it either, but I'm gonna suck it up. You can too." Alex smiled at Willow, and even though they had only met recently, she seemed to perk up a little at the encouragement. Most boyfriends might've been petty and jealous about someone else being sweet to their girl, but Zander was more mature than that and just held her tighter. That is, when he wasn't making dirty jokes left and right.

"Yeah, listen to Alex - you don't wanna be left here by yourself. We don't know what's going to happen. Okay? Okay. Here, maybe we can figure out how long the stretch of ventilation is that we have to climb through."

"Maybe I can figure that out from a different map." Jet took out his phone again, and some more hacking yielded a map of the building's ventilation system. "Their fire wall is *so* lame - that took me like, three minutes to break through. Anyway, if we're here, um, I'd say we have about a hundred feet to climb through. As a rough estimate." Jet replaced his phone into his pocket as Zander kneeled down to start removing the screws from the vent.

"Okay, okay. That's not so bad, Will. We got this." I turned to Jet. "We'll be fine, right? The air vent can hold our weight?"

He shrugged when Willow wasn't looking. "We're gonna have to wing it." I swallowed my fear and just nodded. We were hours from home and I wasn't about to let logistics like locked doors and air vents get in our way. "Maybe we'll crawl in groups to minimize that risk." I nodded, grateful that we would be able to adapt enough to make this work.

"Okay, we're ready to go." Zander moved aside, and put his pocketknife back into his pocket. Then Jet jumped into full leader-mode.

"Vera, I just texted you the map of the ventilation. I traced our route in purple - follow that one. Zander should go first, and you should start climbing after he gets maybe ten feet away from you." Then he turned to the rest of the group. "Try to space yourselves out accordingly so we don't max out the weight distribution."

"Weight distribution?" Willow started shaking and heavily sobbing. Zander pulled her close and kissed her forehead.

"Shhh, it's okay Will. I'll be right there with you, okay? I'm going to go first, and then you'll follow me." Zander's phone vibrated with the map that I texted him.

"You'll want to use the flashlight functions on your phone. It's gonna be dark in there."

"Jet, you are not helping!" I tilted my head toward Willow who was turning into a puddle in Zander's arms.

"Oh uh, sorry kid. It'll be okay." Jet patted her awkwardly on the shoulder and then resumed giving out orders. My brother had become a fearless leader before my eyes - I was proud of him, but also a little worried that his confidence might land us in trouble.

"Willow, if you really need to stay by yourself…"

"No, she can't." Zander piped in, and glared at me. "If she's with me, she'll be safe. I'll worry if she stays behind. She's going to be fine." He whispered something comforting in her ear, and she managed to stop crying long enough to wipe away most of her tears.

"Okay. Let's go."

Thirty-Seven: Venting My Feelings

"How much longer is it? My knees hurt."

I grunted at Willow's complaints ahead of me, but at least she wasn't worried about the confined, dark space anymore. Light from our cellphones helped guide our way toward what we hoped was holding room E12 - that's where Jet suggested our dad might be.

"I dunno. Hey Jet, you think we're getting close?" The cold surface of the stainless steel pricked my palms as my warmth breath filled the air surrounding my face in the shadowy darkness.

"Guys, shut up - we don't know who might hear us. And I dunno, ask Zander - he's leading."

Jet's mumbled expletives hit my ears as he trudged along on his hands and knees maybe ten feet behind me. My body was starting to ache from the hard surface challenging the strength of my joints, and although I don't consider myself to be claustrophobic, my brain was starting to feel stifled by the inability to stand up and stretch. I heard Alex sigh and shuffle along behind me, probably wondering what possessed him to go along with this craziness. Honestly, I kept expecting him to back out at any time, but he never did.

"Zander!" Willow whisper-yelled past me and Alex, hoping to get Zander's attention. He must have pretty good hearing, or maybe her voice echoed over the acoustics of the air vent, because he heard her.

"Yeah, getting there. Hang in there, babe."

"Guys, shut the eff up, seriously!" Jet used a particularly ugly word that I didn't care to repeat, and I just kept on moving, turning another corner after I saw Willow do the same thing ahead of me. I marveled at the way the vents seemed to be able to hold our weight so well - but then I tried to take my mind off of that in case I jinxed our good fortune. The dry, recycled air tasted stale as it hit my nostrils, and I wondered how much mold and other carcinogens we might be breathing.

Our uncle crawled fairly quietly in front of Jet, who pulled up the rear. But he never complained, perhaps just happy to be there with us and no longer a pariah like he was until recently.

A slight scratching noise ahead of us suggested that maybe Zander had made it to the other side. The other vent opening grunted and moaned under the pressure of his dislodging it, and then it sighed and clattered to the floor of what I assumed was the hallway. "We're in, guys. Let's go." I heard him clamber out into the hallway, and we all followed suit. I was feeling pretty relieved until I heard Willow start to panic again.

"Where's the floor? If I break a leg someone's gonna get it."

"It's right here babe, just a little six-foot drop to this table, and then the floor. Here, I'll help you down." Zander begged her to keep moving, and once I rounded the final corner, I saw what she was worried about - the vent we navigated to wasn't a smooth connection to a hallway like the one we had entered from. Instead, we were exiting a ceiling vent into the middle of a room.

"Uh, okay." She eased herself into the vent exit as the metal groaned under her shifting weight, and then she must have let go as Zander groaned under her weight and eased her down to the table he was standing on.

"You did it, babe! Okay, who's next?"

I poked my head out of the vent next, and gladly accepted Zander's assistance getting down to land safely onto the stainless steel table below me. Hopping down to the floor from the there, I took in my immediate surroundings, wondering what kind of room we had found ourselves in. All around me was what appeared to be a pristine white lab, with stainless steel tables, chairs, and cabinets. I shuddered to think what might be found behind those closed doors, and I crossed my arms around my chest as if to prepare for impact.

Then Alex jumped down onto the table behind me and I practically jumped out of my skin.

"Sorry, I'm not the most graceful, I guess."

I shrugged. "I'm just on-edge, is all. This place gives me the creeps, and every corner I turn, I just keep thinking…"

"You'll see your dad?" Alex eased himself down to the floor next to me, and touched my shoulder as I saw Edgar make his way out of the vent in the corner of my eye.

"Yeah, I guess. Which you'd think would be a happy thing, but if he's stuck here or something… I'm just scared of what we might find."

Alex opened his mouth to speak, but a door slammed shut directly behind him, and everyone froze. Jet's butt was halfway out of the ceiling vent, but he paused at the unfamiliar sound.

"Scared? What could you *possibly* be scared of?"

Everyone turned to the back of the room, where a petite, skinny woman with a tanned complexion appeared in a white lab coat, holding a tray of vials carrying who-knows-what. She sauntered over to our rag-tag group, tapping her manicured neon talons onto the stainless-steel surfaces.

Her face struck me as oddly familiar once again - just like Sue's and Wyatt's faces did. And then she smiled at me, as if she knew me too. Heck, she probably did. When she smiled, I was so sure I figured it out - it was Chloe who stood in front of me, one of Summer's lackies from almost ten years ago.

"Oh come on, you're not happy to see me, Lynn? Well, I'll try not to be too offended, I guess." She stripped off her lab coat and laid it casually on a nearby chair. "I guess we're going casual, so no need for me to wear that thing."

"Why do you all work here? What even is this place? Why the *hell* would you even need a lab in a software facility?" Alex moved in front of me protectively, while Jet finally edged his way out of the ceiling vent, mumbling more expletives the whole way down. As soon as he caught wind of who we were talking to, he rolled his eyes and stood in front of me, next to Alex. Edgar followed suit, but seemed to feel slightly more out-of-place by the way his eyes shifted to the area of floor directly in front of him.

277

"Shit, another one? What, your middle school have some kind of partnership with the company or something?" Jet crossed his arms and stared down Chloe as best he could. She just flicked her braids off her shoulder and glared at him. I marveled at the way her appearance had only slightly changed since middle school - she still wore the same nails, hairstyle, and knee-high black Converse - which was extra weird as an adult.

"No, we just had the good sense to buddy up and get jobs together. We made a good team, after all." Chloe's smile oozed venom, and her eyes seemed to glaze over with a Medusa-like viscosity - with the potential to turn us to stone at any moment. "But what I wanna know is, what are you doing here? Not that it isn't just great to see you - as long as you're not gonna snitch on me or something."

"For what? You got something to hide?" I pushed through my friend and my brother, and tried to stare her down with an equal and opposite intensity. Just once, I'd love to see one of these bullies squirm because of *me*.

"Of course not, Lynn."

"I go by Vera now, actually."

"How nice for you - I still don't care though."

Jet tilted his head and whispered in my ear. *"You want me to just pummel her now and ask questions later?"*

The thought made me smile, but I think Chloe heard him because she narrowed her eyes, wrinkled her nose, and growled.

"Well uh, we should just get going then. Lots to do, you know." I started to make my way to the nearest door, but Chloe planted one of her talons on my wrist.

"Oh really? Like what? Fill me in, why not?" She rested her other hand under her chin, like we were at some kind of demented slumber party and I promised to give her the juicy details of my first kiss.

"Well, to put it in words that you'd best understand - 'none ya business'." I shook my hand out of her grasp and tried not to show weakness at the red scratches her sharp nails left on my skin.

278

"Fine. Then I guess I'll just use this phone right here and ask my boss what you're doing here." She grabbed a receiver off of the wall and started dialing, and since I was absolutely out of options at that point, I didn't even bother to stop the metal chair that hit her square in the back of the head - effectively knocking her out. She collapsed in a heap onto the floor, her braids laying on the tiled floor. Her odd black-and-white footwear made me think of *The Wizard of Oz* after Dorothy's house crushed the witch.

"You were out of options, okay? Had to protect my niece. Now come on!" Edgar nudged me forward, and tried to open the door to exit the lab we found ourselves in, but the handle didn't budge. Jet nodded at him in approval, and even though it was kind of extreme, it was nice to see them forming an alliance from a place of common ground.

"Grab Chloe's keycard, I bet that'll work!" Alex awkwardly found the lanyard dangling from her hip, narrowly avoiding her hand that twitched slightly. He ran to the card reader next to the door. "Open sesame! Now, where to next?"

Jet and I both opened our phones again to check the map - and it looked like there was a large group of holding rooms just off the hallway we were about to enter. Breezing through the open doorway afforded by Chloe's keycard, I noticed how this hallway appeared very similarly to the first one, except this one had a series of small screens littering the walls. It felt less like a hallway, and more like a control room - minus the panels and buttons.

"What's all this?" Zander pointed at one of the screens, which showed a complicated pattern of blackness contrasted by red, oranges, and yellows.

"No idea. Heat signatures, maybe? But it's shaped like... a person." My breath lodged in my throat for what I assumed wouldn't be the last time that day.

"There's... so many." Willow walked a bit further down the wall, her fingers tracing the outside edges of the screens.

"Jet, what if one of those is Dad?" I started crying, and my brother pulled me close. Our uncle patted me awkwardly on the shoulder, but I knew he cared about everything we had going on too.

"Wouldn't be surprised if one of them is. But that just means we're getting very, very close." Suddenly, the fluorescent lights seemed to bore down on my tired shoulders, and I felt my resolve start to crumble. Even with my friends and family by my side, I was downright terrified. Heck, I bet they were too. But at the moment, it was getting pretty hard to even keep going.

"We should get moving, kiddo." Edgar nodded at me and smiled encouragingly at my blotchy-face and tear-stained cheeks.

"It's gonna be okay, we're all here together." Zander's voice made me turn my head, and Willow nodded and then gave me a tight hug.

"Yeah, we're gonna get him out of here. And maybe we'll even kick some ass along the way."

"I can help a little with that." Alex shrugged. "I'm no expert but I'm here and I'm not *that* scrawny anymore."

I sniffled back some of the mucus forming in my sinuses and nodded. "Yeah, I know."

Alex blushed as I smirked, my eyes shifting briefly over his broadened shoulders.

"Okay, let's go. Sorry, I just - I guess it's been kind of a lot." I shook myself out of my hormonal daze and refocused on our mission.

"No kidding, sis. But it's gonna be okay soon. I think Dad might be in that... storage room over there."

"You still think he's frozen?" The question fell out of my mouth like a deathly incantation, leaving my bones chilled in anticipation of the answer.

"Based on those heat sensors, nah. If he's in there, he's fully thawed."

I punched my brother in the shoulder, and he smiled even though I could sense he was terrified too.

"Can we open that door?"

Alex patted his pocket to check that Chloe's key card was still in there. "Try this again, maybe it's a master key."

Jet accepted the lanyard from him, and took a deep breath before opening the big, heavy door in front of us. To my relief and terror, the sensor lit up green, and the door hissed open. The air inside the room was hazy, like an eerie fog had descended on everything even though we were indoors.

I found myself leading the way, even though I had no idea where I was heading or what I would find in there. What I saw next, though, was probably the most terrifying thing of all.

Thirty-Eight: Meet My Least Favorite Season

Stark overhead lights beat down on our heads as we slowly entered the cavernous warehouse. A cold breeze caused the lights to sway and undulate, casting moving shadows on the concrete floor. My breath caught in my throat as my muscles constricted, preparing me for the terror of the unknown.

Our footsteps slowed as we took on our immediate surroundings. I wondered if the others were as terrified as I was. By the way Willow nervously squeezed my hand, paired with Jet hesitating to stand in front of the group where Edgar led the way, I'd say that was a safe bet. Alex and Zander hung a few paces behind with their wide eyes ingesting the uncomfortable vibe of the room.

A faint buzzing was just barely audible over our suddenly extra-loud heartbeats, and I felt my pulse quicken as the air grew colder and my skin moistened with a nervous sweat. As we moved further and further into the empty room, some kind of vertical structures started to come into view. They looked a bit like glass tubes, each attached by a complex wiring system to the implied ceiling which was obscured by the low-hanging lights and the harsh fluorescent lighting they created.

"What, uh, what are those things?" My words tumbled out of my mouth in a whisper, as Jet turned to face me.

"Not sure. They seem like some kind of containment system." He scratched the back of his head, placing his hands on the stainless-steel side of one, even though we still couldn't see inside.

"For what?" Willow asked, a bit louder than I felt was really necessary.

"People, most likely." Jet's words were as matter-of-fact as if Willow was asking about the color of the sky or if Santa Claus was real.

"For what?" Her follow-up question made him purse his lips and clench his eyebrows together.

"Well isn't that just the million-dollar question."

"This feels like some kind of elaborate horror attraction. Or maybe like an escape room." Zander mused as he walked around one of the structures. "Hey, there's a scanner here. Someone give me the key card from that weird lab chick."

Alex handed it to him, but his hand shook. "Do you really think that's a good idea?"

"We don't have much to go on. I'd say, find out everything we can. It's lucky we have that key card." Edgar piped in unexpectedly, and nodded his approval. "Go on, kiddo. We've got nothing to lose."

Alex raised his hand to the scanner, but backed away before it made contact. "Wait! What if it opens up whatever's in there? Do we... are we prepared for that?"

"Nope. But we have no choice. What if my dad's in there?" I crossed my arms to make my point, but I quickly realized how rude and insensitive that may have looked. Fear did weird things to people, and frustration was even worse. I loved Alex, but his inclination toward paralyzing fear was inhibiting our mission - albeit, a borderline insane mission, but a mission all the same.

"Oh just let me do it." Zander snatched the key card from Alex, and Alex stepped back, happy to be away from the action. Then Zander gingerly held the keycard underneath the scanner on the side of the tube, and I could swear my heart completely dropped to my knees as soon as the light turned green.

The fogged-over tube clarified to reveal the shape of a woman's body completely wired into the cell, with wires above her head attached to various areas of her scalp. Her face seemed peaceful, but her body jerked at odd intervals while her eyes remained closed.

"What the f-" Jet let a certain four-letter word out of his mouth, and I'm ashamed to say I did the same, just less audibly. Willow actually fainted at the sight of her, whoever she was, but luckily Zander caught her before she hit the floor. Alex covered his eyes, and crouched onto the floor in an almost fetal-position while

Edgar stroked his chin and stared through the now-clear glass casing.

"And *that* is why I didn't want to scan the keycard. That's some nightmarish shit right there." His words were high-pitched sing-song at a loss for what to do or say next.

"We have to get her out! Who is she? That's not my dad. What do we do?" My legs started pacing me around in small circles, while Zander managed to get Willow to wake up. I suppose I should've been more worried about her fainting, but my mind was processing too much at the moment to care.

"Do we break the glass?" Alex walked slowly around the case, looking for an access point.

"We gotta find Dad. We'll come back for her." Jet started pulling me in another direction as the others followed us, deeper into the forest of glass tubes-turned-prison cells.

"*Then* we break the glass?" Zander found his overpriced pocket knife, ready to do some damage.

"Geez guys, cool it with the demolition. We don't actually know if doing that could kill them or not." Willow rubbed her head as she started to remember where we were and gently eased Zander's knife hand back into his pocket.

"Well we don't have any better ideas!"

I sighed as Alex started to show more irritation with the whole thing, but who could blame him? This whole mission was bizarre and there are only so many ways to react to crazy.

"We gotta find my dad. Leave the others, get him out, and report this whole god-forsaken place to the cops as soon as we leave. Deal?" Jet reached his hand out in a mock handshake, but Zander actually relaxed his shoulders slightly and shook it.

"Okay, if that's what we gotta do that's what we'll do."

"So uh, you think these are alphabetized, or what?" Edgar's question filled the air, but all I could feel was the invisible buzzing in the room but also in my head. Like an invisible wire trapping me here, I felt connected to this place and this time. The eeriness of the uncanny environment made my adrenaline surge and relax, over and over again. Fatigued by the repetition and terrified of the result, I followed Jet but let my eyes wander.

"Names. We need to find his name." Jet took charge of the mission from this point onward, which was a good thing because I was becoming borderline useless at this point.

"But I thought you said he was in holding room E12? We haven't found that yet." I crossed my arms, and wondered if there was a chance he was mistaken.

"Based on the digital map, it appears this is the only holding room. It's pretty massive though." Jet tapped around on his phone, and then nodded his head again. "Alex, start scanning more of the tubes."

"But if this is the only holding room, then where is he?" Another chill traveled up and down my spine as I wished I had dressed a bit warmer than just the thin hoodie I wore over my band tee.

"Maybe 'E12' isn't a holding room. Maybe it's... a tube." Willow shrugged her shoulders. "Just a stab in the dark."

Jet nodded. "Possibly. Yeah, uh, maybe. Let's look at this one, for example." He pointed at a fogged-over tube just behind him. "Look for numerical digits paired with a letter somewhere on here."

Edgar crouched down to look at the small screen on the lower end of the container after Alex activated it with the key card. "This one says 'D15'."

"Okay, okay. So maybe it *is* alphabetical!" I ran to the tube next to him, cringing at the glance I got at the dissipating fog as the person inside was revealed. This entire room felt like something out of a nightmare - like we had been trapped in an alien ship with human subjects on board. We were lucky enough to not be trapped ourselves, but I had a sinking suspicion it was only a matter of time until we got caught.

"Zander, give me the keycard."

He happily obliged, probably happy to get the offending object out of his hands. "All yours. That thing creeps me out."

I started scanning, and noticed that the tube next to the previous one was digitally imprinted with an E1. "Guys! I think each letter goes up to fifteen. This is 'E1'." I gulped, the next words sticking to the roof of my mouth, whether it was because of the worry, or because of the impending excitement.

"So he's close?" Edgar touched my shoulder, and worry pinched his tanned face, making his crows-feet appear slightly more prominent.

"Seems like it." I swallowed my fear, and hugged Jet. In this moment, I felt obligated to be close to my brother - someone who hasn't always understood me, but always cared about me.

"We're gonna see Dad again, Jet. He's probably right here."

Willow, Zander, and Alex, stood around in a circle, probably unsure of what to do next. Then Edgar visually counted eleven more tubs down the row, and walked briskly over to the tube that he knew was holding his younger brother captive inside.

"Vera, scan this one." Edgar's voice was no longer that of the smug eccentric engineer I had time traveled for. Now, he was an uncle and brother terrified of what he was about to see. In this moment of anticipation, having come all this way, our goal was finally directly in front of us.

With a shaking hand, I raised Chloe's keycard to the scanner, and held my breath as the fog disappeared, revealing the undeniably recognizable face and body of my dad.

"Dad, Dad! Can you hear me?" I banged on the glass, even though I wasn't sure why. We already agreed that breaking it might be a bad idea.

"Jet, that's Dad. He's alive! He's, he's alive right? Jet, what do we do?" My voice squeaked out of my throat.

My brother was silent, frozen in disbelief. His calloused hand reached up to the glass as tears formed in his eyes. Edgar just stared at the ground. I started to full-on panic. Being so close to my dad who was basically dead for almost a decade, a flood of emotions came over me and I was grateful to my friends who reached out to me to support my body, weakened by terror and relief swirling through my brain at an alarming rate. My adrenaline spiked, and breathing became harder as my words became shorter.

"Cryo? Jet, is… Dad… frozen?"

Jet's face became as poised as stone, and he examined what he could from the large transparent surface of the tube. "It doesn't appear to be cryogenics, but I'm not sure. Although we did see the heat sensors earlier. Can't rule it out though." Then my father's body twitched as if to answer us, much like the first woman we saw with the key card activation. Could he sense we were here?

My friends, uncle, brother, and I just stared and stared at the tube, periodically re-scanning the keycard to keep the fog from obscuring his face again. Willow was surprisingly calm, but clung tightly to Zander while the rest of us thought hard about a solution. That's why none of us heard the footsteps.

"Of course they're not frozen! We're not animals, you know."

We all turned around at the same time, and my eyes met the gaze of a woman not too much taller than myself. She strode toward our group with a clipboard in one hand, and some kind of a long weapon strapped to her waist. Her hair was dark black and cropped harshly above a pair of extremely unnatural-looking eyebrows - that's probably why it took me the better part of a minute to recognize her.

"Summer? Is that you?"

She tilted her head, and I noticed the unsettling way the fluorescent lighting caught her double nose rings and her septum piercing all at once, forming a mustache of light under her nostrils.

"Well well, I suppose we meet again, don't we… Lynn?" Her lips curled into a gleeful smile as I found myself stepping to the front of our crowd, tears still tracing tracks down my face.

"You want me to deck her?" Alex whispered next to me, but I shook my head.

"Let me talk to her first."

He nodded, and backed away, absent-mindedly leaning on my dad's capsule while I approached her royal bitchiness in the flesh.

"It's actually Vera now, but whatever." I crossed my arms, searching for the right words. None came, so I settled for my next impulse instead. My voice wavered but I went for it anyway. "Why did you capture my dad and keep him here for almost ten years?"

Summer tilted her head, and then shifted her gaze to her overdone manicure. "Excuse me? *I* didn't do anything. I merely work for Captain Tus, managing new conquests in the digital realm and conducting new strategies for improved efficacy."

"That's total bullshit and you know it!" Alex yelled at her with a start as Edgar pulled him back momentarily.

"Those sure are fighting words, aren't they Alex? My my, you may want to watch that in the presence of such ground-breaking research. This is hallowed ground, you know." She tilted her head to the other side and strolled toward us, relishing in each step. Her sensible bell-bottom trousers sashayed with her sultry steps across the room as her gaze landed on Jet. "Well well, you sure grew up nice, didn't you Jefferson?"

He shrugged away from her as she stepped uncomfortably close to him, but Jet's body remained as rigid as a stone column while her fingertips grazed his chest. "I'm giving you about five seconds to back away from me before things get ugly." His words seethed fire but her ego was flame retardant.

"You? Ugly? Never." She smirked at him, squeezed his bicep, and moved toward the front of our group.

"Can I deck her now?" Alex whispered in my ear not as quietly as he could have, so Summer heard and snarled at him. I shook my head, and stepped slightly closer to my old middle school bully. Even I surprised myself at the grace I was showing the girl who made my life a living hell for a good chunk of my childhood. I was intrigued by the oddity of her essence and didn't want to jinx anything until we figured out how to free my dad.

288

"Geez, another one from your school?" Willow shook her head in disbelief. "They must have had some insane health benefits or something."

"Yeah, that's just weird man." Zander nodded his head along with his girlfriend's commentary, while I tried to process what I was seeing. Then, for the sake of my dad, I decided I had to level with Summer, because the only thing separating me and my dad was a thick layer of tempered glass, and as soon as we determined that it was safe to shatter it, we were going to literally break him out of there.

"Wait a second, did you say *your* dad is in here?" Summer's eyes widened with a sparkle of what I could only assume was an excitement only paralleled by her childhood obsession with Nick Jonas.

"Yeah, he's in this capsule behind me!" I pointed to the glass as I handed the keycard to Alex, who re-scanned it again to temporarily part the frost. My whole body shook as I uttered the words that I hoped would set my dad free. As my patience started to wane, I hoped we could get in and out of here before things got bad - but of course, that wasn't guaranteed. "Look, Summer - I'll give you the benefit of the doubt. I assume... that you didn't know about this. If you can just tell us how to get him out, we'll get out of your hair."

"But what about the others?" Edgar whispered in my ear, and I shooed him away just long enough to hear what Summer had to say.

"Well, I didn't know *your* dad specifically was here. Isn't this quite a treat!" She threw her head back for a moment, and I could swear she started cackling, even holding her heaving chest. "We just pulled a random sample of the healthy population for the experiment - I had no idea we would select anyone we might know! That is so *rich*."

"Okay, so uh, you knew about the others though?" I waved my shaky hand to the rest of the holding room, wondering how she could live with herself knowing that all these innocent people were

289

imprisoned. I sucked in my breath, trying to steady my pulse - but it didn't work. My friends and family around me were in varying states of discomfort - some more fearful, while others like Jet and Edgar were about ready to crack some skulls.

"The others? Yeah, I knew. After all, I'm the one who developed this system."

Thirty-Nine: The One Where I Throw Hands

"You *what?*"

I could physically feel my muscles constricting as my pulse quickened, only restricted by the curiosity brewing in my brain. Summer couldn't answer my questions if she was out cold - and if we fought her, she definitely would be.

Summer sighed and rolled her eyes at me - ironically one of the "offenses" they tried to bust *me* about in middle school. "Yeah, it's a digitized world made as a simulated reality - we needed to monitor how human psychology would evolve in a trapped environment that was almost real, but not quite. It appears very much like the real world, and every single subject is monitored from a control room upstairs. The test subjects were captured and held in stasis long before I thought up the virtual reality idea a few years ago during my internship, but my boss loved the idea. And then this all began."

"Summer, I just ran diagnostics on segment 62, we have a slight digital breach in quadrant 17."

My clenching fists and snarl were only interrupted by another person walking into the room, and only upon seeing her pale face framed by an extremely unflattering light brunette ponytail did I realize that Captain Tus was not only the hotspot for all my old bullies, but also for my number-one frenemy: Hazel.

"Okay, go handle that and report back to me. But before you do, look what the cat dragged in..." Summer motioned over to Alex and me with a flourish, clearly relishing in our captive pain since she knew we wouldn't leave without at least trying to rescue our dad.

"Alex? Lynn? Well it's been a while, hasn't it?"

And that's when I snapped. "Hazel, literally, I only have one thing to say to you. If you really are responsible for all this, that is?"

"Oh? And what would that be?"

I shook my head and shrugged my shoulders, pretending to give up, even though that was pretty much the opposite of what I was going to do. "Go. To. Hell."

"I appreciate the suggestion, but I'll pass. I don't do too well in humidity. Besides, that's not a super nice thing to say to someone who was a friend of yours." She smoothed an invisible stray hair that must have escaped from her militant ponytail that was probably cutting off circulation to her brain at this point. "Besides, we've got lots of research to finish! There have already been numerous breakthroughs…"

"That's really effed up! What the *hell* is wrong with you?" My words seethed, and Willow held me back, but only by my elbow and only for a few seconds. "And by the way, I stopped being friends with you the moment you started pulling off petty shit with Summer's horde of obnoxious jerks. Now you're one of them, and that makes me hate *you* the most of all."

Summer stepped forward, and draped her arm around Hazel's blouse-clad shoulder. "Now Lynn…" She drew out my middle name, even though I mentioned that I go by Vera now, as she rolled right over my accusation of Hazel. "A questioning mind for scientific discovery is never something to be ashamed of. Then again, look who I'm talking to? You can't relate, you've never been all that good at science or math…"

That's when I stepped forward, and allowed my right fist to connect with Summer's nose - a defining *crack.*

She recoiled from the hit, and met my intense glare with an animal-like rage in her eyes as blood began dripping from her nose. Her ridiculously fake drawn-on eyebrows scrunched into a giant mutant-caterpillar as my throat started to close with the realization of what I might've been able to pull off.

In the corner of my eyes, I could see Willow backing away from the fight as her boyfriend tried to intervene. Zander tried to kick out Summer's legs to knock her off balance, but he just kinda fell instead. Uncle Edgar caught him as Willow screamed from a nearby corner of the room and ran to help.

Jet tried to shield me from Summer's attack but I shoved him away. A swift knee to her gut made her gag. Then I elbowed her hard in the ribs and she fell to the ground. My breathing intensified as a sly smile spread over my face. *Finally. This. This is what they always deserved.* Hazel stood next to Summer, helping her up. She was horrified, but then threw a punch at Jet. He caught it inches from his own face and then kicked her down to the cement floor.

Alex moved behind me, guarding my six. "I got your back, Vera." He breathed through hyperventilating, and then decked Hazel. She fell on her butt again but sprang up, dragging him down with her. They started rolling on the ground in a mess of arms and legs as I fended off Summer best I could, swinging my heavy purse at her face. Then I heard someone cackling with pure, unadulterated joy. And it was me.

While I was distracted, Summer came at me with a taser attached to a selfie stick. I wasn't fast enough to prevent her attack but thankfully, Jet was. He grabbed her wrist and twisted it hard, rendering Summer vulnerable as her weapon of choice slid across the floor to Alex's feet. He pinned Hazel down just long enough to get her to stop fighting him, and a quick punch to her throat made her gag, allowing Alex to get away.

Alex bent down to pick up the device and started laughing. "What the hell even is this? A *selfie* stick? With mustache duct tape? What are you, thirteen? You know, because imprisoning humans against their will in a coma-like state is totally Instagram-able. In fact, maybe I'll just do this..." He took out his own phone to grab a snapshot of the gory scene unfolding, probably more as a joke than anything else, but Hazel didn't find it so funny. Instead, she clicked a button on a tiny remote from her pocket.

Suddenly, a stainless-steel cage dropped from the cavernous ceiling with Alex, Willow, Zander, and Edgar trapped inside.

"You wanna play games, huh? Okay, you can play." Summer walked around the cage, grinning as blood continued to flow from her nostrils and color the pristine white of her teeth a

293

sickening dark raspberry. Willow screamed like a banshee and hid behind Zander, who had moved into full-on protective mode. Edgar was alert but calm with his hands in fists but left at his sides, but Alex was pissed, treating Hazel and Summer to some choice words and vulgar hand gestures.

"In exactly three minutes and twenty-eight seconds, your friends here are going to be joining the digital world we've constructed. There are electrode pulses in the metallic frame of the cage that will activate their brainwaves wirelessly, and they'll be staying here just like the rest of them." A timer-like clock appeared above the cage with red numbers swiftly ticking down, and I found myself questioning if this was actually real life, or a cheesy low-budget science fiction movie. Unfortunately it was very real, even if the fantasy world my dad was stuck in was not.

"Vera! Help!" Willow's screams were panicked, while Alex and Edgar seemed more calculated. Zander seemed resigned to his fate, his head hanging from his neck without much resolve to fight. I had nothing to say, my voice stuck in my throat like a vat of thick molasses.

"You wouldn't dare!" Jet stood in front of me, blocking me from the perceived danger. "Our dad is in here, and we are going to free him. Then we're all going to leave this god-forsaken place." His upper lip flared, and I froze, only flinching when something slid across the floor to my foot. I turned, and saw that Zander had slid his pocket-knife to me through the cage. I swiped it up before the fluorescent light caught the glint of the precious metal. Alex slid the selfie-stick-turned-lightning-stick to Jet, who stashed it in his pocket for safe-keeping. The bullies both went to grab it from him but were too late, bumping heads with each other instead.

"Yeah that would be nice. Pity it won't happen." Hazel shrugged while she rubbed her head, and then laid into Jet with a punch to the gut which he quickly recovered from and countered with a swift kick to her ankles. I turned to try to disable the timer on the cage but Summer grabbed my wrist and punched me in the jaw, hard. I kneed her in the gut as pain exploded in my face, and tried for her remote. She deftly swatted my hand away though, and then pinned it behind my back. I cringed as I felt her bloody nose drip on my left shoulder and her coffee scented breath attacked my senses.

"You won't make it out of here alive, so why even try?" Her words seethed as each syllable seemed to bring her an almost sensual kind of pleasure as she tightened her grip on me.

"Bold of you to assume I'll be the one going out in a body bag." I growled at her in response, and then bashed my head into her forehead. She screamed and let go of me, giving me just enough time to run to get behind Jet who had managed to knock the pathetic and unattractive Hazel onto her butt and pin her down. Summer came after me and grabbed my fists. I managed to flick Zander's pocketknife open and I slit the back of her hand with it.

She screamed as blood gushed out and then Hazel came to her aid, giving Jet just enough time to shove her to the ground again and pin her down. Meanwhile, I caught a quick glance at the timer on my friends and uncle, and started to panic as it had ticked down to one minute and ten seconds until their brains were taken over by the game. I didn't see a way to save them or a way to get my dad out of there.

These weren't just bullies, they were psychos. I wasn't trained to handle psychos. My dad was here, but he was at their mercy, even more then we were. I wanted to help him, and I was so sure we could - until now. My lungs burned as the adrenaline rushing to my limbs made me feel weak, despite the punches and attacks I managed to dodge and deflect. How much longer could I keep this up? Could I save my friends in the process?

A pair of hands reached around my neck, and I could feel the room darkening around me, but I knew with a sickening sort of dread that it was actually just the lack of oxygen to my brain. Her hands were sticky and wet from the warm blood oozing out of the gash I had slashed. Just when I thought I would succumb to the attack, Jet knocked Summer in the head with Hazel's clipboard.

"Get off my sister, bitch!"

"You know, you really shouldn't hit girls!" Hazel jumped back to her feet and tried to kick him where it would hurt, but Jet expertly deflected it and managed to tie her hands together with a stray piece of electrical cording that was on the floor.

"Maybe, but you also really shouldn't force people into a coma." Jet shrugged and then tied her to a nearby support pole.

"Ooh kinky…" She smirked at him, her pale skin reflecting the artificial light, and I shuddered at her blatantly cringe-y deviation from the stodgy denim-skirt wearing good-girl persona that she previously held to an annoyingly fake degree.

Summer decked me from behind as I tried to catch my breath after almost being choked. I fell to my knees and cried out in pain. Jet came to my aid but Summer zapped him with another taser, this one apparently without the aid of an attached selfie stick. He dropped to the ground, and then she walked over to where Hazel was tied up. In a second of pure, unadulterated rage, I managed to throw the pocket knife at her, and even though it wouldn't be a lethal hit by any means, the blade did hit the back of her neck, causing her to pause just long enough for Jet to recover and pin her arms behind her. He's stronger than I am, so he actually managed to tie her to the support pole with her own arms, bent at an odd angle and tangled up in the same long electrical cord that held Hazel.

"You may have caught us, bastard - but not for long. My bracelets are linked to my nervous system, and they're going to melt this cord in about thirty seconds. So you have until then to set your friends free. Oh wait - it looks like you're already too late…" An evil grin spread across her lips as she motioned with her chin over to the cage. The timer had expired, and now my friends and uncle were collapsed on the floor, their brainwaves taken over by the technology. "They're in the game now, care to join?" Her eyes sparkled in anticipation, like a truly power-hungry psycho.

I snarled at Summer, as I noticed her bracelets somehow melting the cording with rhythmic sparks pulsing to the invisible beat of the stark overhead lighting. Jet had run away from the fight, using the last few moments that the two bullies were still tied up. I had no idea what he was doing, but suddenly, the entire massive room darkened, until all I could see was the sparking of Summer's bracelets.

296

"Jet! Where are you?" The question exploded from my mouth in a desperate scream, until I felt hands around my waist, and I threw a punch, assuming Summer or Hazel had gotten free. But instead, it was Jet - and he threw me over his shoulder, running out of the room under the cover of darkness. He closed the door behind us and started running to the front of the building.

"We can't just leave them in there! Dad is still stuck in there!" My lungs burned from exhaustion.

"We need to get to the control panel upstairs. There's no other way to break everyone free. Run, now!" He put me back down and we paused for a second once we were conceivably far enough away to buy us a few moments of time to catch our breaths. "I killed the power strip in the holding room so we could get away. Unfortunately, the machines appear to have an internal power system, as the digital world is still up and running."

I nodded, unable to offer anything else helpful.

"Please tell me you still have the keycard?" I panicked for a second, until I patted my pocket and found the laminated plastic still in it.

"Yeah, got it!"

"We don't have much time."

I felt tears streaming down my face as the emotional turmoil of seeing my dad again started to hit me. Although Jet seemed to be a bit more well adjusted than I was, I noticed his face was red and his eyes were glassy. I followed him up a few flights of stairs after he checked the digital map again, and I pushed my lungs to their limit. I felt an uncomfortable stickiness of congealed blood form on my face and shoulder, and I shuddered to think that I had no real idea if it was my blood or someone else's.

"We're gonna get them out, right?"

"I damn hope so, kid. But even if we don't, you better believe we're gonna raise one hell of a scene."

I smiled sadly at that, and then cringed as we nearly ran right into an orderly in the hallway, who I surprisingly didn't recognize from middle school. He opened his mouth to say something, but Jet just punched his lights out without hesitation, and that was that. We kept running, and after scanning the key card, we got into the control room. It was a massive room of lights and levers, none of which we knew how to use.

"How do we, what do we do now?" I felt tears pricking at the corners of my eyes, as my tired muscles and adrenaline started to succumb to exhaustion.

"We gotta kill the power settings on the digital game."

"And break the pods? You don't think that'll hurt people?"

"Do you have a better idea, Vera? Because I don't." Jet ran right over to a large control panel, but he didn't get too far, because another door flew open to reveal a very bloody, and enraged Summer flanked by a frazzled Hazel.

"Miss us much?" They walked slowly into the room, calculating their steps through exhaustion.

"Like a butt rash." I backed away from them both, too tired to physically fight them again. Jet got to them and knocked them both out cold with a rusty metal folding chair. First Summer, and then Hazel. Their bodies hit the floor and crumbled like defunct robots on a bed of lies.

"You - you got them!"

He was breathing hard, but nodded. "Now we hack into the system. Luckily, I used to do this professionally for this very company. I'm gonna find out how the victims are wired in, and if I can extract them out of it without any damage to their nervous systems."

"Everyone? You mean all..." I glanced at a screen near the ceiling, which displayed a fairly large number, which I could only assume was the amount of humans trapped in the game.

"Yeah, everyone. It's for the best, and I wouldn't know how to isolate tubes anyway."

I took the liberty of sitting in a nearby chair to let my heart rate slow down, and found myself thoroughly enjoying the sight of my bullies laying on the floor in a heap. A long line of saliva dripped from Hazel's lips and to the linoleum floor while her head hung at an odd angle bent over Summer's hip. Blood from

298

Summer's lacerated hand and bruised face and body added bright shades of red to their artful defeat.

I shuddered, wondering if there was a chance my newfound pleasure in inflicting pain meant that I could've already become as psychotic as them.

Forty: My Brother, the Flirt

I stood over Jet as he frantically typed away and pressed a bunch of buttons. To the untrained eye, it would look like he was trying anything and just hoping for the best, but I knew there was a method to the madness. At least, I really hoped there was.

Summer and Hazel were still piled in a heap on the floor. Summer's face was almost completely covered in blood, as was her hand. Hazel appeared to have been largely without any visible injuries, but like me, she now wore a good amount of Summer's blood. They were still breathing, but pretty blacked out. I didn't actually want to kill them, but to rescue my friends and family, I did need them to be out of the picture - at least temporarily.

"They still out?" Jet's voice carried over the beeping and clicking of his work, but his face remained tuned into his task.

"Yeah."

"Good. Make sure they stay that way."

I nodded, and then shouted an affirmative at him since he was facing in the other direction. "Should I call the police?"

"I don't think so. We gotta get them out on our own, and I'm the only one who can do it. Well, besides your middle school shit eaters. If you called them now, it'd be months until we could get the victims out since the crime scene will have to be investigated."

"If you say so." I cringed at the irony that Jet finally understood the importance of keeping things under wraps. I was glad the cops didn't arrest Uncle Edgar, but there was no telling what could happen if we got out of here.

I saw Hazel's left foot stir slightly, so I gave her another good whack to the head with the folding chair just in case. She'll have a pretty bad migraine tomorrow - and it won't be from her tight ponytail for once - but she'll be fine.

"Any luck over there?" I was equal parts curious, but also in desperate need of a distraction from the guilt and satisfaction warring for dominance in my mind.

"I'm almost past the digital world's fire wall. Once I log everyone out, I'll start the wake up process in the tubes. That's much safer than just taking an ax to the glass. Don't wanna fry any brains."

"And the cage?"

"Already lifted off of them about four feet from the ground. Once they're awake, I assume they'll be okay but we can check on them soon."

I looked out the massive observatory window at the dark warehouse full of glowing tubes and human forms being imprisoned inside. The pale blue glow afforded by the emergency lighting cast a ghastly pallor onto the prisoners. A sea of humans illuminated in the pale light made them seem more like fish suspended in bubbles - a haunting image that sent chills down my space. My eyes scanned the cavernous space outside the observation window. I couldn't see my friends from the window as there weren't any lights near them, but I knew they were lying on the floor maybe a hundred paces from the entrance where we left them. I *hated* leaving them. I felt guilty and selfish.

"Vera there was nothing else you could have done." Jet sighed and kept typing away.

"Did I say that out loud? Oh, well okay." I shrugged, and then walked over to where Jet was sitting. "I know, it's still hard though." That's where I waited for the next few hours, thinking about what we were doing and the uncomfortable way I had suddenly become so comfortable with fist-fights and violence.

"Almost there now, take a look out the observation window."

I gasped as one by one, the emergency lighting inside each tube changed from a pale blue to a bright lime green. Slowly, the screen in front of Jet glowed with a progress bar, slowly filling with a red digital line.

"You really logged them out?"

Jet nodded, and spoke in almost a whisper. "Dad's going to wake up any minute now."

"Well, not just Dad… all of them, right?"

"All eight-hundred of them, yeah."

No words could properly express how I felt in that moment. I just ran over to my brother and hugged him tightly. He was still sitting in the leather rolling chair, but he stood up to hug me back.

"Ready to head back downstairs?"

I swallowed as tears began to form behind my eyes and in my throat again. "We're gonna see Dad now?"

"I think so." Jet smiled at me sadly, and then led me back to the door we came in.

"So we just leave them here?" I motioned to Summer and Hazel, who were still out cold.

"Unless you have a better idea."

I paused, and then it came to me. "Yeah, I really think I might." Pointing to a nearby rolling cart, Jet loaded them onto it, and then we pushed my limp bullies out the door, into an elevator, and back down to the holding room.

Scanning the keycard again let us right into the massive room that seemed to stretch endlessly in all directions. True to what Jet had suggested, the dark room was awakening with resurrected life. The capsules had begun to open, and the people inside were opening their blurry eyes to take in their surroundings. A few probably even tried to walk right out, but fell onto the concrete floor.

"Jet, what's happening? Are they paralyzed?"

"No, but I bet their muscles are atrophied. They'll need help. More than we can give. Vera, call the police. And request all the ambulances they can dispatch. We have eight-hundred people who need our help."

I swallowed while I did as he requested. Neither of us could find Dad yet, as navigating the room in the dark was tough even with the emergency lights activated. I ended the call, and nearly jumped out of my skin as someone grabbed my hand. Hazel and Summer were still out cold, lying on the rolling cart, so it couldn't have been them. I slowly turned, and found myself face-to-face with Alex.

302

"Well, that was quite a trip."

"Alex! Are you okay? Where are the others?"

He hugged me tightly. "They're running this way, I was the first one to wake up and find you. That game is, well, really *not* a game. I couldn't find you right away. Why's it so dark in here?"

Jet piped in. "We had to kill the power so we could get away from these two goons." He pointed to my bullies, and then swiftly caught a woman from hitting the floor while exiting a tube nearby.

"Hey, hang in there. You're probably atrophied, but you'll be okay. Help is on the way."

She looked at him with terrified bright green eyes, as her long red hair nearly swept the floor. She was stunningly beautiful, and Jet noticed immediately. The screen on the tube she escaped from said her name was Alyssa Desjardin. She didn't speak, and I wasn't sure if it was because she had been detained for so long, but her eyes were wide and her breathing ragged. He just held her, with his hand gently supporting her head and neck, letting her feet rest on the floor.

"Those ambulances are on the way, right Vera?" There was an urgency in Jet's voice now as he stroked Alyssa's long hair off of her glistening forehead, and I wondered if he suddenly had an ulterior motive for wanting the medical help to arrive quickly.

"They said five minutes. Where do you think Dad is?"

"Oh shit you're right! Uh, he's in E12 right? This one was… M9. We gotta walk that way." He pointed to my left, and Alex followed.

"But before we do?" I motioned to Alyssa's open capsule. "What do you say we shove these guys in there? Not activated, of course. Just a way to freak them out a little and detain them in case they wake up."

"Woah, you really grew a dark streak since I last saw you." Alex smirked, and then helped me lift our old bullies into the empty tube. They both fit, but just barely. Then we closed the door around them. There was plenty of ventilation in there due to the many holes

303

bored into the tempered glass, so they wouldn't suffocate or anything - but I giggled at the way their faces smushed against the glass. Then I grabbed a piece of printer paper I took from the observation room upstairs and wrote "I'm with stupid" on it. Immature to stick on the tube, I know. But it seemed apropos to have some kind of middle-school level revenge since I wasn't allowed any when I was a kid. Sometimes I wondered if one solid punch to the nose would have ended the conflict all those years ago.

"Ha, nice one." Alex fist-bumped me, and then the others caught up with us. Edgar trailed behind Willow and Zander, holding his head and blinking erratically.

"Well well kid, that was wild. Crazier than time travel, I might even say." Edgar shook off the haze and hugged me tight.

Willow clutched tightly to Zander, spooked out of her mind. "That was so real. You're sure it was totally fake?"

Zander sighed, and patted her on the shoulder. "For the fifth time, Will, it was fake because this whole entire warehouse was full of people sucked into the same game. Hence the whole reason why we're even here."

"Well how do we even know this is real?" She waved around the dark room, full of the prisoners waking up and falling to the floor. I didn't have a ton of time to rescue Willow from an existential crisis, so I just patted her on the back instead.

"I guess you'll just have to suspend your disbelief." I shrugged.

"Or talk to my cousin who's a quantum physicist if you want…"

Everyone in our little group collectively rolled their eyes at Zander.

"What? It's an option!"

We walked a bit further dodging awake but immobile bodies on the floor with Alyssa on the rolling cart, lovingly pushed by Jet. He kept checking to make sure she was properly balanced every few feet, which was both adorable and a little weird. He just met this chick - scratch that, she wasn't able to speak yet so really, he just sort of claimed her. I figured that as long as he let the

304

paramedics take care of her as soon as they arrived, it was okay if he wanted to make sure she was okay until then. Willow screamed a few different times, but Zander shushed her with a quick kiss. The zombie-like people were definitely creepy, but they were still people and they needed help. And somewhere in this massive room, our dad was one of them.

Sirens could be heard from outside, and I was glad to hear that they were getting close. It was getting tiresome explaining the situation to the people over and over again. Their eyes always held a mix of either relief or terror. Some were even extremely angry - the level of their awareness was impressive, given that they were held in stasis against their will for years.

I heard a scuffle from the hallway, and then the doors to the dark room burst open. Paramedics rushed in with the police, and I ran to meet them. Jet ran with me, and told my friends to keep an eye on Alyssa.

"Officer, this is a crime scene. We came to rescue our dad who was imprisoned in stasis for almost a decade - but it turns out, there were hundreds of others abducted as well." Jet shifted his weight from foot to foot, but his gaze stayed locked on the officer.

"Excuse me? You mean to say this has been a mass abduction?" The police chief planted her hands on her hips, and tilted her head to the side while a hoard of EMT's rushed in with equipment and rolling beds. More police filed in behind them, and started collecting data and clues. The entire room was suddenly filled with chaotic energy, but I was encouraged by the presence of the good guys to get everything sorted out.

Police ran around shining flashlights everywhere while teams of paramedics ran to the victims. I could've even sworn there was a helicopter or two approaching in the distance. Their whirring lights in the night sky shone through the windowed rafters of the holding room.

"Yes, and the victims appear to be suffering from muscle atrophy." I motioned toward the room.

"Okay, we'll take care of them. One more question though?" The police chief looked me up and down. "Why are you covered in blood? Do *you* need medical attention?" She placed a hand on my shoulder kindly as another officer asked Jet some more questions.

"No - well, I don't think so."

"What do you mean you don't *think* so?"

"Well, there was a bit of a scuffle with the criminals, I had to defend myself until my brother was able to hack into the system to free everyone."

"You know where the criminals are?"

I nodded as she pulled out a notepad. "This way. We had to detain them into a capsule in case they came to, because they're violent."

The officer walked with me, along with a few others, and I told them everything I knew. Then I managed to pull my little childish note off of the capsule holding Summer and Hazel in it so the police didn't think I was an obnoxious kid.

"This whole company is guilty of criminal activity, but these two have been heading up this particular branch of it." The police nodded and thanked me, and I left them to gather clues and incarcerate the bullies if they saw fit.

Jet caught up with us, with Alyssa in tow. The poor girl was still sitting on the rolling cart, unable to support her weight very well, but probably grateful for the makeshift seatbelt Jet had fashioned out of his sweatshirt. He turned to one of the hundreds of EMT's. "Can you help her? She's one of the victims, and her name is Alyssa Desjardin." He gently cupped her chin in his hand. "Beautiful, isn't she?" And then his eyes moistened and he wiped his face on his shirt.

"We'll take good care of your girlfriend. She's going to need a lot of physical therapy to regain her musculature, but she appears to be reasonably healthy given the incredible circumstances." The EMT nodded at him, and then lifted Alyssa onto a stretcher, her long red hair trailing off the side of it. Jet shamelessly handed one of the paramedics a sticky note. "Give her

this when she's able to take it? I'd like her to call me sometime."
The emergency worker tilted his head, but then nodded and quickly
wheeled her away.

"Jet! Snap out of it! You are shameless!" I clapped my
hands in front of his face, and then he seemed to wake from a
trance.

"Right, right! Okay. Yeah, where's Dad?"

And then, as we walked to my dad's capsule, we were
shocked to discover it was empty. But Dad wasn't far. Our gaze
shifted down to see him on the floor, flat on his face, unable to
move - just like hundreds of others.

"Dad? Dad!" I ran to him, and Jet managed to gently move
him onto his back. Brown eyes that I never thought I would gaze
into again this side of eternity were wide open, and staring back at
me, wide and shining. He couldn't speak or move very much, but he
was every bit the dad I remembered. My chest and lungs were
reacting to the pounding in my head with the shock of actually
finding him - and then I crumbled into a heap at his side. I was
crying, inhaling my dad's familiar scent, and feeling the warmth of
his hand trying desperately to hold mine.

"We found you, Dad. We really *found* you."

The words kept repeating out of my mouth like I was a
record player with the needle stuck in the groove. Jet knelt down,
with tears and mucus streaming out of his eyes and nose. He wasn't
typically a crier, but we were both completely overcome by actually
being able to track down our dad.

"Dad, don't speak. We have to get you to a hospital. I saw
your distress signals, and we came to get you. I just, I wish we came
sooner. I should have known - I worked for this company. But that
was before I realized what they were really doing." His words were
obstructed by the bile rising in his throat, and his voice wavered
with the pain of uncontrolled anger and regret.

I ran my hand gently over his forehead, brushing off the
wires stuck to his face with my fingertips. The sticky green adhesive
came off on my hands, but I couldn't care less. This was my dad -

he was here, and he was going to be my dad again - instead of just a person we mentioned off-hand in the kinds of hushed tones one might use to show respect to the dead.

Uncle Edgar was pretty speechless throughout this ordeal. He took one look at our dad - his younger brother, and started openly sobbing like I never would have expected from him. Crouching on the floor, he rested his shaggy head in his hands. My uncle, the eccentric scientist, was just as affected by this as we were. We were all family after all - and today, we recovered one of our own.

Jet and I just sat with him while Willow found an EMT to check my dad's vitals and load him onto a gurney to head to the nearest hospital. The emergency response woman was incredibly kind to all of us, even personally reassuring me that he was going to be okay since I was blubbering like an absolute baby. Jet's emotions cleared up just long enough to tell her everything we knew about his health, and then gave her our contact info so that we could be notified as soon as he was stabilized.

Zander gave me a hug while I cried, and Alex awkwardly patted me on the back. Neither of them said much about it - but who could blame them? There's no expected reaction to your friend recovering their dad from a psychotic programming company.

After maybe another thirty minutes of telling the police everything else we knew about what happened to the victims, one of them took some witness notes from us to file a report - and told us we were free to go. On the way out though, I had to stop myself from gleefully laughing at the sight of a very beat-up and bruised Summer and Hazel being dragged out in handcuffs. Summer shook her fist at me, and yelled some inappropriate slurs at me while I just laughed in her face and flipped her off. Hazel was pissed too, but seemed much more resigned to her fate. They had woken up out of their knocked-out stupor and were now fully awake to witness themselves being thrown in jail - for a very, very long time.

As I watched them being dragged away, I felt a gleeful smile creep over my lips, and once again, I was haunted by the very real risk of becoming just like them. If the social scene was a vacuum of cruelty, and they had just been taken out of it - would I be the one to replace them?

Epilogue: I Make Peace With Second Chances

Ten Months Later...

"So we're thinking maybe a Fall wedding could be nice. I'm just obsessed with those kinds of red-brown-mauve color palettes - plus I could order those cute little votive candle things for the center pieces. Don't you think that'd be cute, Zander?"

My recently engaged best friends from college sat across from me on the couch while Alex clicked through the channels on the TV trying to find something the four of us could watch for movie night.

"Yeah totally! I think that'd be really fun. You're kind of like a woodland pixie, so you gotta play into those vibes."

Willow clapped her hands excitedly, the neon glow of the TV glinting off of her almost comically-large engagement ring in the darkened living room. Zander had spared no expense for her, and it was flashier than I would think she'd like, but she loved it - and him - endlessly. "Perfect! Ugh I love everything about this. And you are going to look so incredible in that plum purple maid-of-honor dress I picked out for you." She got up off the couch to give me a quick, tight hug and then sat back down with her fiancé.

After he popped the question while we still wore our gowns at graduation, their very long engagement had begun because Willow wouldn't rest until every detail was picture-perfect. And since it obviously meant so much to her, Zander was happy to wait as long as it took to make her happy. At least, that's what he said, but I could tell my friend was getting a bit antsy every time his fiancée pushed off their wedding date just a *little* bit more, every time swearing it would be the last.

"Yes! Most definitely! See Zander? It's gonna be all worth it, I just know it!" Willow cuddled up next to him excitedly while Alex kept flipping channels.

He shrugged, and then wrapped his arm around her, planting a quick kiss on her forehead. "Okay, just keep in mind that if you still want Ed Sheeran to be the wedding singer, you'll have to pick a date before his tour schedule is announced."

Yup, Zander was fully prepared to get Willow's favorite pop singer to be in attendance. He had family in high places, and they weren't above pulling some strings to make things happen. The farm that Willow managed full-time would be the perfect autumnal backdrop to their special day.

"Yeah yeah, I know." She drawled out the words, and then cuddled up next to him.

"Hey guys, how's this one look?" Alex pointed the TV remote at the screen, which was lit up by some kind of science fiction thriller. I shrugged, since I knew it's not like we'd be watching a rom-com or anything.

"Works for me!" I sunk back into the cozy armchair, and then Alex hit play. Zander and Willow were too busy staring into each other's eyes to have an opinion, I guess.

"Hey who wants popcorn?" My dad hobbled into the room on crutches, but managed to grab the big bowl of popcorn from the kitchen table. I got up to take it from him before it spilled - and it's a good thing, because that bowl was filled to the brim with fluffy, buttery goodness.

"Thanks Dad." I beamed at him, and then Zander grabbed the bowl from me, clearly distracted from Willow at the sight of the salty snack.

"Anytime, Punk." He smiled at me, ruffled my hair, and then made his way back to the kitchen table a few paces away. Mom came up behind him, surprising him momentarily with a kiss on the back of his neck. He smiled up at her as he sat down in the wooden kitchen chair, and tapped away on his new smartphone. Crazy to think he wasn't around for so long that the handheld gadget had advanced more than he was familiar with. It would be a while before he could get back to his construction work, but the intense physical therapy his doctor prescribed had already helped him regain a lot of his muscle function. Now he could walk with crutches, or sometimes use a wheelchair if he got too tired.

I'll never forget the moment we told Mom that we found him. On the way home from Vegas the night everything hit the fan, I called her myself, and she actually dropped her cellphone. First she yelled at me through her sleep-coated throat, saying that if there was even a tiny chance that I was pulling her leg, I'd be grounded for life. I had to calmly reassure her that I wasn't, and that she could meet us at the hospital and we would be there around maybe four in the morning, according to the navigation app on Zander's phone. She was half-asleep when I called, but she beat us to the hospital.

By the time we got to Dad's room, her tear-stained face was pinched into an emotional frown, swaying slowly with her body pressed against Dad's limp frame. He was awake, but extremely weak. Even so, I could've sworn I saw a tiny smile pull at his mouth. His eyes still sparkled as big and bright as they did when we rescued him - but in the arms of my mom, they seemed to outdo the stars. She sat with him for hours, only getting up to stretch occasionally. And at those rare times, she would hug Jet and I strongly enough to practically liquefy our insides.

Willow and Zander offered to drive Edgar home, which was fine because Mom had taken her car to the hospital, so we could tag along with her when we were ready to go. Even though I was still somewhat covered in congealed blood from various fist-fights and more tired than I thought was physically possible, I refused to leave Dad's side. Jet agreed too, so we just spent that first night as a reunited family in that tiny hospital room. One of the nurses brought in a cot which Jet collapsed on, while Mom cuddled with Dad, and I claimed the armchair by the window. Edgar returned early the next morning with donuts and coffee for those of us who could eat solid food, while Dad was given nutrients through an IV. Slowly, we started discussing a game plan for Dad's lengthy recovery, and even though it was overwhelming at first, it gave us hope for a new tomorrow where we didn't have to pretend we were okay living without him.

In the months that followed, my family's relationship with Edgar also improved rapidly. My mom had a long talk with him, and apologized profusely for calling the cops on him. After everything turned out so well, she agreed to keep everything about the time traveling under wraps in favor of keeping the CIA off his tail. Turns out she never mentioned the time machine to the authorities, because she didn't even believe it herself. She also called the police to explain she was mistaken about her previous distress call. I was honestly surprised she offered to be so cool about it all, but I think she would've have agreed to just about anything after we brought Dad back to her. Now I realized I totally should have capitalized on this more than I did by asking to upgrade my car or something. Oh well.

My grandparents were thrilled to have my dad - their youngest son - back in their lives as well. Similarly to Mom, the unique circumstances inspired them to give Edgar a reprieve on their past grudges. My grandmother almost fainted the first time she saw my dad after almost a decade of believing he was gone for good, but Grandpa kept her calm as everyone got used to having Dad around again. It's an extraordinarily uncanny feeling - having someone return from the dead like this. I was even surprised how quickly things became routine again.

"Aw come on Alex, we've seen this one before." Willow whined while stuffing her face with popcorn and pulling out her phone.

"But it's a classic! Besides, it's not like we have any other ideas."

The room went silent aside from the movie still playing, mostly because we couldn't think of anything else to say. Plus, Zander had already fallen asleep like he did just about every time we tried to watch a movie together. It didn't even matter what it was - just something about the lights being turned off and sitting on the couch knocked him out.

As for Captain Tus, the entire United States government got involved in its swift take-down. The president released extensive statements, apologies, and promises to prevent something so terrible from ever happening again. All employees associated with the company were given lie-detector tests to determine who was involved in the nefarious aspects of the situation, and those deemed innocent were let go, while those guilty were sentenced to time locked up - depending on the depth and intensity of their involvement. The media covered it as well, and if I closed my eyes, I could still see and hear the whipping of the helicopter propellers in the wind as various news channels sent their reporters to comment on the state of things.

Funny enough, I actually reported on it for my senior journalism final thesis, and thanks to my professor, it got some notice from some of the more prestigious networks. Then the literal, most crazy thing ever happened: people from the Ellen DeGeneres show called our entire family, wanting to schedule an appearance on her show. I'm still shocked it even happened, but last August we actually sat on a plush couch across from one of my personal heroes. It was Mom, Dad, Jet, Edgar, and I who got to chat with Ellen, and I couldn't believe how cool and funny she actually was in real life. Ellen even fangirled about how she got to talk with the "sensational Bartlet family, who defied the odds and heroically saved hundreds of people."

After that incredible day, I sent a thank you-note to the producers for having us on the show, and as a last-ditch effort at getting my dream job, I mentioned I'm looking for work in media. To my surprise, they called me back with info about an internship opportunity that I might like. After I reattached my jaw that fell on the floor, I took the job at the studio and have been, quite literally, living my best life since then.

Although things have really turned around for me, there is one area of my life that has remained pretty stagnant. Yup, nothing happening with boys right now. I thought that would really bother me - and for a while, pining away for Alex really did - but I quickly found myself being far too distracted to care. Alex had come back into my life, and it's funny how despite drifting apart for years, we were back in each other's lives like nothing had really changed at

314

all. If anything, we were even stronger now than we ever were before. We had just been through time travel, a spontaneous kiss at the club - not to mention our alleged first kiss that I never even experienced thanks to a glitch in my current reality compared to the previous one. I would also never forget that time we went full-on hand-to-hand combat against our old middle school bullies, practically fighting to the death.

I never could figure out how much of that was fueled by extreme anger for me, or maybe just revenge. A lot of it probably could've been avoided if I was allowed to react normally as a kid and not just take what the bullies threw at me with a smile and curtsy. One good clock to the noggin might've just done the trick - but hey, better late than never, right? I'm not proud of how things ended up, but it was still pretty satisfying. Oddly enough, I felt pretty well-adjusted to life at this point. After all that happened, I don't think I'll be letting the bullies take up any more space in my subconscious. I think they've just been evicted from living under my skin - for good this time.

For me at least, memory was always this odd amorphous entity that seemed to disappear just out of reach whenever I tried to connect the dots or make sense of the craziness that was my life. I wanted to believe that everything happened (or didn't happen) for a reason, but my analytic mind was still very much getting used to that harsh reality. For all I knew, it could be years before I fully comprehended or processed the crazy stuff that happened this past year. Whenever I had time to actually sit and think about the fact that I traveled through time, I still get a little bit spooked. I can only imagine what Edgar must have felt about it the first time he figured out that time travel was actually possible. Must've been quite the head rush.

"See, I told you it was a classic!" Alex elbowed me in the ribs as I clicked off the TV after the movie he chose.

"Yeah, I mean I've seen it a few times but I forgot how hilarious that ending was." He brought his glass of water to the sink while Willow tried to wake up Zander.

"Thanks for the movie night, Vera. You free tomorrow to help me pick out the cake?" Willow grabbed her bag off the couch while Zander rubbed the sleep out of his eyes.

"Yeah, I'm leaving the studio at four. Can I meet you at the bakery then?"

"Sounds good, see you tomorrow! Come on Zander, I'll drive you home."

Zander gave me a quick hug, and then followed Willow out our front door. Alex lingered in the foyer for a second. The whole house was silent, because my parents had already gone to sleep and Jet had an early job interview tomorrow for a company he triple-checked wasn't hiding any nefarious plots under its pristine surface.

My brother suffered from a lot of guilt after what happened. My whole family told him over and over again that he had no way of possibly knowing about what Captain Tus was brewing under the surface, but he still hated ever having been a part of it in the first place. One good thing that came out of this, however, was his relationship with Alyssa.

She was one of the other victims taken in by the company, and aside from having missed about eleven years of her life due to being held in stasis, the girl was incredibly well-adjusted to her new reality. He kept in touch with her after breaking her fall from her capsule, visited her in the hospital while she recovered, and genuinely enjoyed her company. Due to her missed years, she had the emotional age of a young teenager despite being physically twenty-seven years old, but Jet was more than willing to help her progress. Like my dad, she too needed extensive physical therapy, but Jet was positively enamored with her - and she seemed to really like him too. In between his interviews and job searches, he would visit her at the hospital, and then later, her house - which was coincidentally only about twenty minutes from our home.

As for my uncle, he has since told me that he's seriously considering destroying the machine. Although in this isolated instance, it was an incredible gift for our family, he didn't believe that such a capability should exist much longer in this world. You can never really know what hands it could fall into, and even though

316

we were smart about it, not everyone would be. I wanted to tell him to keep it, to just keep it hidden, but I really think he's going to dismantle it. And honestly, a small part of me would be kind of relieved if he did.

I think a large reason why humans are so good at adapting to life, is because they have no choice. If there was an alternate cosmic re-do option, would humanity become weaker as a result? And that's best case scenario - worst case would be some kind of crazy psychopathic dictator ruling the world across time and space, forever. Time is both a safeguard and a healthy limitation. We need it to give us context for our reality and a reason to get up every morning and give everything our best shot. There should be no second chances at living life. Believe it or not, I still believe that - even though I was lucky enough to have one.

My bullies were behind bars now for very significant crimes, and I tried to remind myself that they deserved it. Whatever I did was merely seeking out justice for sick, twisted people whose shadows had haunted me far too long. But at the edges of my mind, I could still feel the darkness creeping in. I was terrified by the pleasure I felt by seeing them suffer – it was unsettling, and although legally permissible, the purity of my own heart was definitely at risk. I wasn't guilty, but with becoming an adult, my personality had become more nuanced and complex with the previously hidden areas of myself coming to light. And in a strange way, I also felt a new sort of freedom that allowed me to finally move on. Memories of their childhood stupidity wouldn't disturb the perception I held of myself any longer. And I'd say that was pretty damn fantastic character development.

"Vera?"

I paused, not sure what to expect. "Yeah?"

Alex pulled me into a tight hug, and I quickly wrapped my arms around him, doing my best not to audibly inhale his cologne – because even after all we'd been thorough, that'd come off as super weird.

"I hope you know that even though we're not... together... I just." He paused, taking a deep breath to steady his mind. "I want you to know that I still really care about you. I probably always will, actually." He planted a quick kiss on my forehead - a gesture that was clearly more protective than sensual. I still shivered under his touch, and a big, stupid smile took over the bottom half of my face against his shoulder.

"I know."

Post-Epilogue: Future

"Heave it onto the wagon, dumbass. We don't have all day."

"I know, I know. It's just... heavy."

"He'll be back soon and I'm pretty sure he'll notice *this* missing."

"Oh, this giant hunk of psychedelic metal? Yeah I'd say so."

"Grab the other side, I can't lift this myself!"

"This is *so* below my pay grade but FINE."

"Got it? And... good. She's gonna be thrilled."

Author's Note

This story was easily the most difficult thing I've ever written. That's largely based on the fact that I really was bullied as a kid all throughout elementary and middle school. As a recent college graduate who has since found truly wonderful friends, it's easy to feel a bit silly for even entertaining a plot like this. But I felt that in order to fully lay it to rest, I needed to. As one of my biggest influences John Green so aptly puts it, "pain demands to be felt".

To properly address these latent feelings, I had to dig up some pretty old wounds and memories that I would rather forget. And a lot of the specifics were repressed – so I couldn't even access them at all. But I'm convinced it was absolutely worth it because in the end, I brought a story to life that I know would have made me feel better when I was suffering. The odd thing about bullying, especially in school, is that nothing really gets done about it unless two very specific things fall into place:

#1 Those in authority actually have concrete evidence of what's been happening.

#2 Those authority figures are able to properly navigate consequences and healing for those that need it.

In my case, neither of those things lined up, which is why my bullies were chronic instigators that severely damaged me emotionally over an extended period of almost nine years. They were manipulative, vindictive, and just plain mean. I'm sure they're probably not as awful anymore (I hope), but I don't plan on any rendezvous to find out.

It was only in more recent years that I finally started to heal and grow once I realized some things that probably were obvious but not nearly emphasized enough.

#1: None of what happened to me was my fault.

#2: The bullies weren't my enemies so much as the authority system, which was a toxic breeding ground for exclusivity and petty deceit.

I hope that whoever reads this story has the chance to reflect on their past struggles and find healing similarly to the way that I did. Or if you're currently at the business end of bullying, I sincerely hope that this story changes your perspective. Maybe like me, you can find liberation in taking the emphasis off of yourself, and realizing that there may be nothing you can do about those in authority over you at school, but you can determine not to let the bullies get inside your head.

Of course, that is much easier said than done, but it's all about mindset. Granted, there are different levels of bullying, and I count myself very fortunate to have escaped without any physical attacks – but if that's happening to you, tell any adult you can. They can help you feel safe and defend you.

But if you're like me, and you don't have tangible proof of the bullying because it's largely invisible mind games and angry words whispered behind mouths concealed by grimy fingers, it can be a lot harder to get the help you need. Really, it just takes one adult to hear you out – and once they do, things will get better. Maybe the bullies won't be punished, but you'll get the support you need. Keep talking about it, telling your story to anyone who will listen. And above all, never, ever, give up.

As a recent college graduate, I actually have found some truly wonderful friends in more recent years. I have at least a few from high school that I am very close to, and a few from college as well. And thanks to social media, I've even forged very significant long-distance friendships with other authors my age (Joel, Syreeta, and Ife – you guys enrich my life more than I can ever properly say).

Point in case? Your friends are out there – all you have to do is be calm and patient enough to let them come to you in due time. Everything truly does happen for a reason, and even though being bullied was a really unpleasant thing I had to carry for years, I know that God used it to make me a stronger person with nerves of steel and even thicker skin.

Hang in there, because it really will get better. If you were looking for a sign, this is it: you are so loved, you have worth, and you will *get* through this. And I'm happy to say that through the course of writing this book, my old bullies no longer haunt me. They've been vanquished through the power of creativity. This is how I've healed, and you will find your way too.

Angelina Singer graduated Magna Cum Laude from Stonehill College in 2019, where she studied English, Music, and of course, Creative Writing.

In her spare time she enjoys crocheting (with a portfolio of work available for purchase on Instagram @asinger320), as well as mentoring younger music students at a local music store, where she has been studying guitar for over a decade. She views her writing as a way to simultaneously escape from and embrace reality. Follow her on Facebook @AngelinaSingerAuthor and Instagram @angelinasingerauthor for exciting updates, exclusive content, and giveaways.

The Upperworld Series

Book 1: The Sorting Room
Book 2: The Fall of Zephyr
Book 3: The Rise of Onyx

From *The Sorting Room* -

"Who decides where we are born and who we love?"

Luna is an immortal entity in the Upperworld learning how to assign human souls to the body and life they're intended for. Onyx is her mentor and guide there, teaching her everything she needs to know about assigning souls and dispatching them to Earth. Everything goes well until Luna's friend makes a major mistake and Luna is sent to Earth after covering for her.

In her absence, an unbelievable secret is revealed that changes everything she thought she knew about how the world works. Will Luna survive long enough on Earth to fix things? Or will she succumb to the pressures and pitfalls of living life as a human girl before the entire system unravels?

Available NOW on Amazon, Kindle, and Audible! Please leave reviews if you enjoy the stories (or not – I don't judge!).

Angelina Singer's Debut Novel

Just Like a Pill

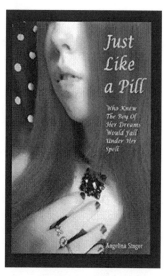

When Scarlett gets a sinus infection the week before Homecoming, she never knew that she would be plunged deep into a tangled mess involving the hunky guitar player, Maxx, who goes to her school. She quickly develops a mysterious side effect that appears to cause Maxx to be instantly attracted to her. With her health-freak fashionista friend Izzy by her side, Scarlett searches desperately to find answers about the sketchy "antibiotics" that she took to combat her symptoms. The time clock is set to one week, and between dodging the fiendish escapades of the high school "it-girl" who dates Maxx, as well as the feeble advances of nerdy Greg, Scarlett has to figure out what's real and what's not before anyone she cares about gets hurt.

Follow Angelina Singer on social media!

Instagram: @angelinasingerauthor
Facebook: @AngelinaSingerAuthor
Twitter: @asinger320
Blog: https://angelinasingerauthor.wordpress.com